The Pale Huntress,

The Road

By. B.D. Weddell

This is for James, for Gebeine

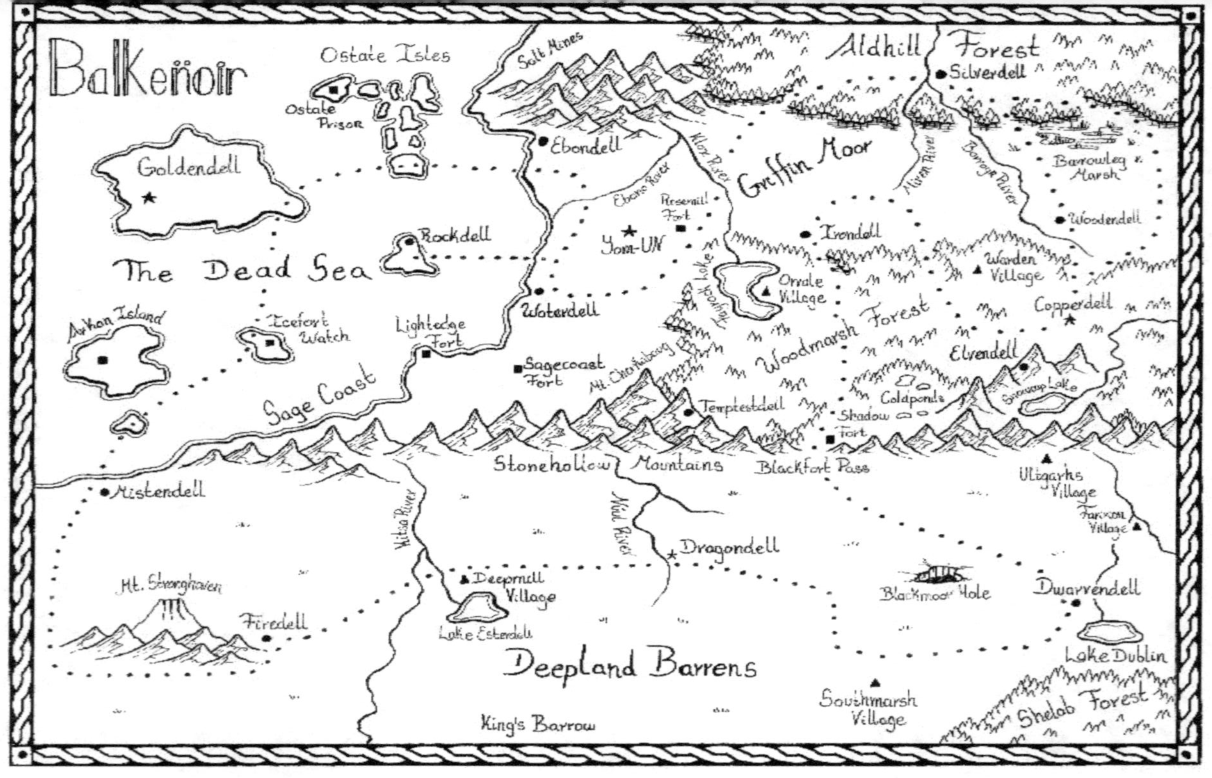

Balkenoir
Ostate Isles
Ostate Prison
Salt Mines
Aldhill Forest
Silverdell
Ebondell
Klor River
Griffin Moor
Aliven River
Bowrie River
Barrowley v. Marsh
Goldendell
Ebono River
Reservell Fort
Yom-UN
Woodendell
Rockdell
The Dead Sea
Irondell
Warden Village
Ayrkan Island
Icefort Watch
Lightedge Fort
Waterdell
Fayrock Lake
Orvale Village
Woodmarsh Forest
Copperdell
Sagecoast Fort
Mt. Chorkleberg
Elvendell
Coldponds
Sunswamp Lake
Sage Coast
Temptestdell
Shadow Fort
Stonehollow Mountains
Blackfort Pass
Uligarhs Village
Mistendell
Mell River
Dragondell
Farixon Village
Mt. Stronghaven
Deepmill Village
Blackmoor Hole
Dwarvendell
Firedell
Lake Estendell
Deepland Barrens
Lake Dublin
Southmarsh Village
Shelob Forest
King's Barrow

Table of Contents

Once upon a time, deep in the cold and harsh Stonehollow Mountains of Balkeñoir, lies a small village deep in the forested peaks, overlooking the vast realm. A village belonging to no tribe but their own, as many of their brethren had fallen to the outsiders.

For centuries, the people who have lived there hunted throughout the peaks, battled vicious tigers, bears, and even more dangerous Wendigo spirits, all the while the world changed far below. Even when the country of Noyii came to conquer and to settle, only to become Balkeñoir, the village remained. After the Vampire Wars the village remained. No one knows of it's existence, save for who they called The Shadowman who lived in a castle on the bank of what was now called Stonehollow Pass.

All through this time, the village remained, forgotten by their Nisthgúlian brothers who have long since moved south to the empire's reservation and still unknown to the world. They continued their traditions, and still paid homage to their gods both old and new. As the world passed on by, the village if seen by any outsider, would have been considered to have been frozen in time. Untouched by the influence of machine or medicine, the land was pure, natural just as the gods have made it. Even the great lake that the village thrived on. The goddess of the lake was once good to them, providing great fish for the ancestors of those who live there today. But when the god of the sun passed on and gave way to the cruelty of the Unending Winter, the village, slowly but surely, began to fade away. Their numbers were dwindling as well as their faith as they sacrificed again and again in order to somehow please the gods, and bring back the sun.

And on this particular cold and stormy evening, a young woman was about to be sacrificed to the goddess of Snowcap

Lake. This woman, unbeknownst to anyone in the village but especially the world, would change it all forever, long after the village whose name has been forgotten, passes on into the void of lost memory.

But for now, the Stone of Dullahan weighed heavily on her shoulders.

It was her sin, her burden; this was her stone. The massive heap had been carved by her own two hands out of the mountains, and she had brought it herself down to the village. She then slept dreamlessly, her mind seeming to already accept her fate and seeing that there was no point in dreaming any longer. She was only twenty-two; having birthed one child and was about to doom the second which would be her last. And now, now she was walking down the road with the entire village following close by with candles in their hands; the flames illuminating their faces with ghostly flickers. All of them were warm in their cloaks of furs, while she was covered with nothing but the sacrificial tattoos all over her body. Markings and symbols which would become extinct never to be decipherable again. She bore the weight, as the crowd walked beside her in eerie silence. Aside from the snow that fell like feathers around her, the only sound was the crunching of boots over snow, and the occasional grunt of discomfort and pain.

Her feet hurt terribly and practically burned with frostbite. The cold wind snaked around her naked torso, and her tears froze upon her cheeks. She wanted to scream, but she had no voice. They had cut out her tongue, to prevent her from speaking out. Her pregnant belly ached beneath her as she hunched over it in order to carry the weight of the boulder on her shoulders. The villagers, all holding candles led the way until they finally stood before the legendary Snowcap Lake. The vast lake stretched out across the horizon, with mist hovering just above it like a lover too terrified to touch it. The full moon shone bright and silver in the sky, and the rainbow lights swirled and shifted like a serpent across the sky, giving the mountains a ghostly beauty. Beyond the great pond, the forest continued to stretch out and beyond them, the peaks that hid the lake from the rest of the world. If one were to climb those peaks, they would see all of Balkeñoir to the Dead Sea to the west.

But all she saw, was the lake; glassy, and undisturbed- for now.

The crowd stopped as soon as soon as she stood just before the glassy waters, already feeling its chilling presence. All at once the gravity of what was happening finally sank into the boulder she was carrying and began to weigh her down even more, causing the child growing in her womb to writhe as if sensing what was to come.

This was wrong, she wasn't supposed to be next. It wasn't her turn- it couldn't be! She lowered her head, and started to cry as the crowd around her began to chant a chilling prayer to whatever god asked them to begin such a horrible thing. The language they spoke in soon to fade away, just as she would.

She wanted to scream at them; she wanted to scream and cry to tell them that killing her like all the others wouldn't bring the cursed sun back. This was all just a thirst of the whole village- a thirst to watch the life of another get snuffed out like the candles they were holding. She herself liked it- in fact, she *enjoyed* watching the others before her drown right before her eyes. The first one had been her favorite. The way she struggled to get her head up despite the stone she carried weighing her down to the bottom of the lake. She had such pale skin, and she walked right into the water like a ghost only to try and escape like a struggling fish.

Desperation had led them to do this. Desperation had made her volunteer to do this. Oh, how she wished she could take it all back.

Just who had they, the village, who had they all been praying to this whole time?

"Walk," the Chief said with a stamp of his staff. Momentarily she either couldn't or simply refused, which earned her a slap on her rear, sending her forward as if she were cattle. She walked, closing her eyes and praying that out of all who had attempted to sacrifice themselves in order to bring back the sun, that she would be the one to survive. That her child would be the one.

As soon as the waters touched her toes, she howled like a banshee towards the unforgiving moon. The water crept up her leg as she walked, and then swallowed her lower body. Ice felt like it was shooting up into her body, and as she dipped deeper beneath the water, only her head remained above.

It was then at last when she saw something walking across the water towards her. Everyone else saw it too, and many fell to their faces in reverence. As the figure drew near, she realized that the person wasn't walking on the water, not literally. In fact, with each step they took upon the rippling surface of the lake, it froze instantaneously like a platform, allowing the man for it was no doubt a man, to walk across the lake and approach her.

Her foot then tripped over something concealed in the water, and she fell forward. The boulder came loose from her shoulders and came down hard and mercilessly. Her leg was smashed underneath and with a bubbly scream she reached out towards the surface that was just barely out of reach in her desperate attempt to suck in air rather than the icy water that bounced in her lungs like glass. The cold water numbed all feeling in her limbs. Just past the glittery surface, she watched as the candlelight on the shore suddenly went out as everyone blew out their flames; leaving only the Rainbow Lights to illuminate the figure now standing directly over her, staring down with eyes blacker than death.

She reached for the Star above so that he might pull her out of the water, but still, she was trapped. So she just stayed there, tethered to the rock she carved out with her own

two hands, and under the watchful eye of the one who chose
her and her distressed unborn, drowned.

Di

The Huntress stood in the small village of Wardan deep in the Woodmarsh forest.

The village was mainly brought up by foresters, who escaped into the woods in order to have their freedoms from the local cities like Irondell or Elvendell which were not far from where they were; which were also their primary source of trade. There was Woodendell further to the east, but the city had been abandoned over a century ago and had at some point after become the unconcluded kingdom of the witches, who were all but gone at this point in time, those who remained still scattered across all of Lunokean. Today, the city remained abandoned, and no doubt full of dreadful beasts.

With the mountains to the south and Winter seeming to never end, the entire village was covered in snow. With the snow, brought darkness, and the darkness brought horrible beasts that the village had managed to ward off ever since it's founding. No troll, ogre, wendigo, nor any of the woodland spirits could frighten a Wardan villager away.

That is, until a more ancient evil had come to the village at last.

The Huntress who was brought in had arrived in Wardan just this afternoon, having being invited into the Chief's house for tea and details as to what was happening. The scrawny scarecrow of a man shook in his seat as he had beheld the dark and menacing beauty of the Huntress before him; as well as all the warriors who were even more afraid of her. After being asked if she was indeed a Huntress from the Black Hand, the Huntress after revealing the tattoo on her hand, was then invited into the man's home. The tale was finally finished when the sun had sunken into the Dead Sea to the west, and the darkness of night had fallen upon the realm of Balkeñoir.

Now the Huntress stood still and quiet in the village square, while the villagers waited inside their shacks and shops, watching her from the gaps of their shutters quivering with fear. Livestock and dogs were locked into their barns, with some dedicated warriors lying in wait with them. Though the wind howled and made her black cloak billow around her like a pair of large black wings, she stood still and quiet, her right hand wielding a sinister sword with a jagged edge with a sharp and widely serrated edge, and the pommel depicting that of a snarling wolf. It was a strange blade, but it was one that served her well since she had it forged for the first time.

She breathed in deeply, taking in every scent the village had to offer. The sweat of fear from those hiding in their homes constructed of thick logs slathered in tar, the stench of livestock cowering in their pens. Her ears turned and almost twitched at every sound that came from beyond the village, the chittering of a rat, the deep hoot of an owl, even the whispers of a nearby Sprite no doubt having taken notice of the Huntress whose eyes were closed as her other senses took in everything.

Then she caught the stench of long-hibernated fur, the stench of something ancient, and her eyes flashed open bright and purple, two lavender lanterns within the confines of a face worthy of the goddesses of the Stars.

It was coming.

She eyed the forest line to her right, where a field of potatoes were caged within a thick fence. Beyond it stood the tall, dark pine of the rest of Woodmarsh. From within, she could make out a pair of eyes that glowed bright like her own, but yellow like a pair of regular lanterns. It shifted, it's bulk momentarily visible in the cover of darkness. No ordinary human being would have been able to see it, just the eyes.

But Angela Dragos was no ordinary human, and she watched as the creature whom the village chief and others had described, emerged from the thicket.

It was a massive and reptilian beast, a dinosaur from an ancient timeline. It had the bulk of a bear, but it had thick leathery skin that was coated with red fur all the way to the hands and feet, which were scaled and bearing great black claws, making it look like it was wearing the fur as a great coat. The monster's hunched shoulders bared more fur, but across it's flank as a deep wound that had scarred over, and Angela could see that the flesh beneath was scaled as well. The monster's head was crowned with a thick mane of even darker red fur, and it's pointed snake-like face bared large fangs and it's scales reflected against whatever light passed over it as it crossed the potato field and made it's way towards Angela, unafraid, unchallenged.

"A Crota," the Huntress sighed as she tilted her sword, catching the moonlight in its silver edge. The glare illuminated across the creature's broad chest, its glowing eyes narrowing to show it's displeasure. It knew what the sword was made of, it was ancient but it was certainly not stupid.

And deep within it's broad chest, the Crota huffed out some breaths of air that sounded like chuckles. Of course it would sound like though, for Angela knew the sound of a Crota's laughter when she heard it. As ancient as their line was, she was surprised that one had escaped it's subterranean home deep underground and came to the surface. There hadn't been a Crota in all of Balkeñoir since before even the Nisthgúlians had inhabited this continent.

"Poor creature of the night," the Huntress said though there was no pity in her voice. "Your time of terror upon this village must come to an end. I do not know why you've lingered this far, but you will never feast upon human flesh ever again."

She then got into a stance, her slender legs stretching far apart to achieve perfect balance. The Crota stood up on it's hind legs, bringing up it's full height as it bucked up to accept her challenge. It towered over her by a good meter or two, but that did not intimidate the Huntress in the slightest. There was very little that she feared in the world.

Seeming to sense this, the Crota roared loudly, its claws digging into the snow as it snorted and shook its head, it's forked tongue tasting the air for the fear that it had come to recognize and finding none. Outraged now, the Crota bellowed it's challenge again and dropped to all fours and charged at the Huntress, kicking up snow and lunging with black claws capable of rendering a human being into two.

It happened fast- *too* fast to be seen clearly by the normal eye. The villagers inside their homes couldn't even see what happened the Huntress moved too fast against the beast. They would only comprehend the aftermath, which was nothing short of incredible.

She had ducked beneath one of the creature's massive arms and slashed at the armpit, spilling blood like a waterfall all over her and drenching the snow around her. The beast had howled, and then brought its head down ready to rip her to shreds with fangs of ivory. But with a free hand, she had grabbed one of the thick fangs and pulled down hard enough to cause the Crota to become hunched over like a bull about to be tamed. Then with another swing of her sword, the blade sunk deep halfway into the creature's neck.

The Crota screamed an unworldly cry, but try as it might to move its head the muscles that were severed refused to pull it up so it instead it bucked and forced the Dhampir to let go. It retreated albeit halfheartedly for the wound in it's armpit was still bleeding profusely. Still, it lunged again, ready to grab at her with its massive claws. Angela rolled to the side and slashed at the creature's flank, spilling more blood and forcing it to come at her again. She got within it's reach however and struck at the creature's neck again. The squeal of silver against bone sounded shrilly in the air but the monster was still kicking. She grabbed a whole lock of the Crota's mane, holding it still and with a bellow of rage it reached for her as she danced back, still keeping a firm grip on the coarse hair. She slashed at the hands, forcing them back and severing several scaly fingers in the process. As soon as the *hand* of the beast struck the ground, the Huntress leapt up and brought all her weight down into the ground; ripping the neck muscles that remained on the creature, and with it's spine revealed to the pale moonlight, she swung upwards and the head was completely removed from the massive body that collapsed into the snow at her feet. She held the head out whose face was frozen in a despicable grimace of immense pain and surprise. The Crota looked like a snake coming out of the furry carcass of it's prey. She dropped the head into the snow and let it bleed out. As if this was a sign, the villagers slowly came out, the Chief included who stared in awe as the Huntress flicked the gore off her sword and sheathed it over her shoulder.

"The job is done," she declared.

"Wow…" one villager said from afar. "Did you see…?"

Murmurs of questions as to how the Huntress could do such a thing. Many brave men had tried to fight off the beast, but all had been dragged into the forest and no doubt devoured. And this woman, who had only met the creature just today, had managed to slay it, it's head now in the hands of the villagers who would no doubt mount it in honor of her.

The Chief bowed his head and offered a shaky hand towards her, the fist holding a sack of coins. "It's all there, feel free to count it." He stammered his words, and wouldn't stop shaking as she curled her white fingers with black nails around the sack of copper and silver. "Th-thank you, for slaying of that beast."

The Huntress said nothing, taking a short peek into the sack. Seeing that the amount offered for the job was all there, she hooked it to her belt that held all her various weapons and tools. "Crota's are usually lonesome creatures. There shouldn't be any more of them, and you shouldn't be troubled by such a thing again."

The Chief, though still nervous, bowed again. "Again, I thank you. The Black Hand, they really do honor their contracts."

"We do our best," Angela said with a turn and starting to go. "I wouldn't report this to any city however. You'll be in trouble if someone finds out you made contact with us."

"You won't stay in town?" the Chief asked.

"No," she answered over her shoulder. "That isn't a good idea."

"It's late though!" a warrior called out.

"You're all covered in blood too; you'll attract a bear or tiger or something worse!"

"Yes, why would you want to leave?" the Chief asked.

Because you are afraid of me, the Huntress thought.

Instead of answering outright, she went to her horse which was tethered to the station just outside the Chief's house. Although she hadn't said it out loud, it was clear on everyone's face. Some of them still couldn't believe that the Crota was dead, let alone someone like Angela doing such with such inhuman speed and ferocity.

"I have no reason to linger about here," said Angela and with a click of the spurs on her boots, the horse nickered and started to trot for the exit leading out of the village.

"Wait!" one villager said stepping forward while holding her child in her arms, who cowered into her shoulder. "At least tell us your name!"

The Huntress didn't answer, and just kept on riding until she was out of the village and into the forest. She didn't turn to look until she no longer smelled the scent of the Crota or the village where it had come from. With a sigh, the Huntress reached down and stroked the neck of her horse. Midnight nickered as if asking a question, and perhaps he was.

"There is no point in telling my name," she told the beast as if trying to justify her reasoning's. There really was no point however; none at all. The job was complete, and it was time to head back to Shadowfort Castle. The less people knew about her, the easier it was. After all, she was a Huntress, her job was to hunt, and nothing more.

Well, that, and she was also not meant to converse with the humans too much. They all feared her, and for good reason too.

She was a Dhampir.

After a week's long ride and after stopping for one extra day at the foot of the Thousand Steps, the Huntress and her horse made the climb and eventually made it to Shadowfort Castle that overlooked the entire realm of Balkeñoir.

The massive monolith stood black in contrast to the gray clouds, with the sigil of a black hand waving on one of the towers. She placed her horse into the stalls and after staying behind to feed it from her own hand, she started for the castle grounds while the other horses nickered nervously around her. Her own horse was never nervous, whether it was because he was so used to the Huntress or there was some unknown bond between the two. Whatever the case may be, Midnight watched his rider disappear into the castle, and only then did he begin to settle down and become warm after the long journey.

The Huntress herself entered the castle, seeing that just between the two spiral staircases just before the doors leading to the main hall, stood a familiar figure speaking to one of the cursed armor sets that guarded the door. The spirit that he was speaking to was talking about extra precautions in the case of wolves or bears, but the armor stopped and pointed towards the Huntress which caused the man in white to turn. Dr. Oskar Jecklyn smiled warmly at the Huntress, adjusting his glasses slightly as she neared them.

"Ahh, Angela, you've returned," he stated. "I assume the cursed beast attacking Wardan was no problem?"

"Hardly," Angela said tugging back her hood and revealing her long hair that shone as white as snow being struck by the rays of the brightest sun. It had taken a while for all of the black gunk she had in her hair to become fully washed out, but now it was clean with all of it's Noyiian beauty.

Jecklyn smiled, unsurprised. "I don't suppose you had a chance to use my charm, did you?"

The Huntress answered by reaching into her belt and pulling out an antler charm that had been dipped in the blood of a demon and decorated with copper wire and beads. "There was no need."

Jecklyn pouted but accepted the charm. "It wasn't a Wendigo?"

"No. It was a Crota. This would have been useless against it; Only Nisthgúlian relics could have affected such a beast."

"A Crota... damn," Jecklyn said, disappointed. "Oh well. Maybe I'll have someone else use it. A pity. The spiritual seems unfit for science. Or perhaps it's the other way around."

"Do not be ashamed," said Angela. "I have no doubts that it would have worked on the beast it was intended for. You can't account for everything, Oskar."

"At least *you* remember my name," Dr. Jecklyn said smiling brightly. He grew somber almost just as instantaneously. "If you were planning to visit The Master, I advise you leave him be, for now. He is praying."

Angela looked at the doctor. "Velinar? Praying?" Ever since the supposed Star of Death, Velinar was cursed to walk the world forever, it was strange for Angela to think of the deity in a boy's body to be *praying*. It was usually often the other way around; when someone needed a contract done by the Black Hand.

"Everyone needs someone to look up to," Jecklyn shrugged. "Even the Stars themselves. There has been... a death."

Angela tilted her head, silently asking for more.

Jecklyn said in a low voice, "Luca Harker, has fallen."

Luca Harker, partner of Vladimir Kane, the most dangerous Werewolf Hunter in the Black Hand, dead? The man was a terrifying force to reckon with, and despite having hated Angela for what she was, she herself respected the man of his talents. To hear that he was gone...

"Was it his own beasts?" she asked.

"No, no Werewolves," Jecklyn said dreading having to answer. "The Ravens got to him. Three of them, all pounced on him the moment he felled the Werewolf in question he had been dispatched to. Velinar seems to think they had been waiting."

Angela felt a fire flare up in her heart. The Thunder of Ravens, the Emperors elite soldiers, and supreme Hunters of Balkeñoir being the cause of it…

"That… doesn't surprise me," she told the doctor.

Six weeks ago, Angela herself had a run-in with one of the Ravens, who happened to have been holding an entire city hostage while searching for an Immortal. During which at the same time teaching the late Count Andrei black magic of the demon lord, Kawfka. The group was a deadly and dangerous force, and the fact that they were so close to the Empire now made it even more dangerous to walk the realms- especially if you were inhuman, or even a regular Hunter it seems.

"Velinar will speak later tonight about it," said Jecklyn. "Right now, it is just you, Jacob, Vladimir and Sabina tonight. The others are still hunting- though I believe that Matei is coming home as well tonight. I've sent a message to all the ones still out there, telling them to exercise extreme caution and to return immediately."

"Where was this?" asked Angela. "The attack on Luca, I mean."

"It happened in Ebondell. He was hunting a werewolf deep in the mountains when the Ravens jumped him."

"Close to Goldendell and the bulk of the Empire." Angela shook her head. "Despicable."

"I agree. From what I can understand, Velinar is planning to have everyone now work in pairs or groups regardless of what kind of contract it is. Looks like you'll be working with your fellow Hunters a lot more now." He said this with a knowing smile.

But there was only one Hunter that Angela even felt close to hunt with, and even he was still a dangerous risk, as well as an immature child. Still, there was no one else in the world Angela trusted more as of now, he had earned that much at least, whatever length that may be.

"How is Jacob, anyway?"

"Completely healed just a few days ago. We took off the splint and his side has healed beautifully." Jecklyn emphasized this with a chef's kiss on his fingertips. "He's back in action- in fact, he is training out in the courtyard right now."

"So soon?"

"We humans are not as fragile as you may think," said Jecklyn with good humor.

Angela relented a small smile. "I guess I shouldn't be surprised. That is good that he is moving a lot more now."

After what happened back in Irondell, Angela was nervous leaving the young man here to heal alone. The man had been invaluable in the Hunt, but it nearly cost him his life. But more than that even...

Angela looked around, breathing in deeply to ensure that no one was around to hear her ask in a low whisper that not even the suits of armor could hear, "And his neck?"

Jecklyn shook his head. "The mark is still there. I'm sorry, Angela. But it seems that not even alchemy can close the wounds. I've tried everything but it is as you had feared: They aren't healing, not entirely. But no one knows you have bitten him, so for now you both are safe."

Angela supposed that was a good thing, but it still didn't erase the fact of what she had done- what he had allowed her to do in order to break the illusions of the Immortal, Count Horla and save them both. It was her action that caused him to be marked by her forever, but it was also because of him that the two of them were even alive. It was a debt that she could never truly repay.

But that only created more complications, more than Jacob truly realized.

"I'm going to my room, then," Angela said turning towards the staircase leading to the east wing. "I'll come down later when Velinar calls for the meeting."

"You are not going to go see him?" Jecklyn asked to the Huntress' back. "Jacob, I mean?"

"There is no need. I'm sure I'll see him tonight."

In all honesty, Angela didn't want to see the Hunter just yet. She was still wary of him, but not as much as before. There was still so much about the cursed Hunter that she didn't know about, nor him about her. Despite she agreeing that the two were at the very least friends, she was still weary of getting to close to the man. Especially considering the boundaries he had overstepped during their time together. If Velinar indeed planned on the Black Hand working in pairs, there was no one else in the castle Angela would rather work with, for better or for worse.

But she could worry about Jacob and their partnership later. Right now, she just wanted to bathe, read, and be with Sebastian, her feline companion.

Meanwhile, Jacob Tepes, Hunter, Witcher, and a cursed man squinted across the field and loosed one of his arrows. He was shirtless and his new scar gleamed white and red in the setting sun beyond the mountains. The cold hardened his body, making his strong physique all the more prominent. His favorite bow twanged as he released the string, and his arrow soared straight and true right into the head of the practice dummy, splitting the last arrow down the middle. Though he only had one eye open since the other was covered by his eyepatch, Jacob was still a formidable archer, even if archers really weren't a thing anymore.

He then slung the bow around his shoulder and reaching for his belt, he pulled his revolver and walking sideways, he shot the six bullets within at the six bottles he placed at eye-level on posts. Each and every bottle shattered into shards of brown and tan. He then rolled back and then pivoting, he pulled one of his daggers and drove it into the armpit of the dummy right behind him, proceeding to bring his knee up into the 'belly' and gut the figurative man with the ferocity and precision of a mountain cat gutting a rabbit. When he stopped, he stepped back and allowed himself to breathe the cold and clean air of the mountains.

It was good to be back in action.

"Not bad, not bad, although I really wish you would practice more with a rifle and maybe even a sword."

He turned to see Dr. Jecklyn coming out of the castle with a cigar in his mouth. The man took a drag before approaching the Hunter and offering it to him. Jacob took one drag, and then returned it to the doctor.

"How do you smoke those things?" asked Jacob, coughing up some smoke.

"What?" asked Jecklyn, only slightly offended. "This is good stuff, imported from Ukusvit; Ukusvitian tobacco. Can't be touched by the Nisthgúlian crop."

"Ship it back," Jacob pleaded. "Ship it all back."

Jecklyn shrugged, chuckling as he took another drag. "How are you feeling?"

"Much better. I feel like a million crowns."

"And look the part too," Jecklyn said whilst releasing another puff of smoke into the air. "Although you'll give yourself hyperthermia next if you aren't careful."

"All right, Mother dearest," Jacob said chuckling. He started for the posts so he could clean up the shattered remains of the bottles he had shot. Jecklyn walked with him, eyeing the rune and wings tattoos on Jacob's back. As he stooped to pick them up he asked, "So, what brings you out here on this cold evening?"

"I'd thought I'd come by and let you know that the Dhampir has returned."

Jacob looked at the man genuinely pleased, the remaining shards forgotten. "Angela's back?" When the good doctor nodded, Jacob went to retrieve his undershirt. "Thank you for letting me know, I'll go see her."

Jecklyn smiled knowingly, saying, "I'm sure she would love that."

"Not like she'll admit it," Jacob agreed as he slipped on his shirt.

Jecklyn laughed and he watched Jacob as the Hunter grabbed his gear and made for the castle. Jecklyn remained outside, cleaning up the rest of Jacob's mess while watching the sun set well beyond the mountains, casting brilliant colors of orange and purple across the skies and made the snow shine like a blanket of diamonds, the clouds the peak stuck up from appearing like a stormy sea. It was absolutely breathtaking.

But the winds carried an unnerving sense; like death crawling through the shadows of darkness. Jecklyn shuddered at the sensation, as he looked up at the sky, wondering why he was feeling such dread now. Was this fear for the future? He supposed that was good. He had almost forgotten what it felt like.

If only I was a few years younger...

As Dr. Oskar Jecklyn was feeling the goose walking across his grave, Matei Coventon hissed a low curse beneath his scarf as he willed his horse to begin their climb up the Thousand Steps back to home. The horse, not looking forward to the trip any more than his burden was, neighed in distaste as it started up the slippery stone steps.

"Too damn cold..."

He had been on a long hunt for a potential witch lingering about near Mistendell, only to discover that it was really a group of necromancers from Noyii. What they were doing in Balkeñoir had been anyone's guess, but Matei along with the Mistendell Watchmen, had been able to storm their hideout in the caves near the Mistendell cliffside. Unfortunately none of the cultists remained alive for long, for many had taken blades to their own throats the moment the Watchmen and Matei stormed the caverns. Gracefully, they had been able to uncover carts of dead bodies that had been stolen from the cemeteries and were all returned to be traced and documented before being reburied.

His job complete and after weeks of traveling, Matei was finally going to be home soon. It was so much colder near the mountains than it was by the sea, and Matei Coventon just about had enough of all the snowy blizzards. His horse, having enough as well, once again neighed to show its displeasure. Matei stroke the beast's neck, praising him for his hard work and promising warm hay and dried apples brought in from the same country the cultists had come from. It still made him wonder why illegal aliens had come to Balkeñoir in the first place, and what they were planning to do with all those bodies.

As they made their climb Matei turned his eyes to the north, where he saw the land of Balkeñoir stretch beneath the clouds as far as his eyes could see. He had seen much of the world ever since becoming a Hunter, and after being trapped in his town for many years, he had finally found true freedom. With Sabina by his side, it made the freedom even more wonderful than all the gold in the country. Every time he climbed these steps, passing by the massive statue of St. Peter who stood by the stairs with a knee down and his sword pointing towards the rest of the way up, Matei felt more proud of himself than he ever would have as a scholar at the Marathium College. As soon as he had a chance, he had once fled for these stairs, took shelter beneath the giant saint of stone, and made the climb up to Shadowfort Castle and swore his life to Velinar and his Black Hand.

He wouldn't have traded that decision for anything else in the world, and as he passed by that same statue again, he dipped his head in a silent salute to the old saint and Hunter.

"There he is," he said to his horse who appeared like he could have cared less about who the human of stone was when he had one sitting on him right this moment while *he* made the climb.

With a chuckle, Matei willed the beast to stop and he slid off the horse's back, taking ahold of the reins and taking lead for the rest of the climb. They were just now rounding the bend past the statue, when something caught the Hunter's eye and made him stop. Two things at the feet of St. Peter, huddled under what looked like a massive blanket from the snowy winds that continued to blow like a hurricane around them. Two heads peeked out and one of the suddenly shot up as it recognized that Matei was there. As a reaction, the Hunter placed a hand on his revolver as the figure stepped out of the statue and started for him.

It was a young boy, having to be just stepping out of boyhood by the looks of him. Red hair, a Nisthgúlian to be sure. He had broad shoulders beneath a tunic of brown, and his coat flapped around him loosely; Matei figured he might have stolen the coat. A sword hung at his side, as well as a small musket pistol opposite of the blade. The boy stopped within ten feet of the Hunter, and behind him, another figure, smaller, a young girl, peeked to watch.

"You are a Hunter, aren't you?" the boy called out, his voice nearly carried out of the mountains by the wind.

Matei narrowed his eyes to protect them from the snow pelting his face. "Who's asking?" he demanded.

"Are you with the Black Hand?" the boy asked instead resting a hand on his hip, mere centimeters away from his sword.

Matei answered as the boy had. "As I said before: who is asking?"

"No one- an employer."

Matei's eyes narrowed. "You both are a long way from home, son. What business do you have with the Black Hand?"

"Protection- and a proposition!"

"Protection?"

"Please, will you take us to Shadowfort? My sister, we both need your help."

This troubled Matei greatly. What could two children out here in the god-forsaken mountains want with the Black Hand? And protection, from *what* exactly? He pitied them, seeing them trying desperately to stay warm just as he had many years ago. Difference was, he made the climb himself in order to sell himself to the Black Hand. These kids... they came to *hire* them.

"Please," the boy implored. "The Black Hand is our only hope. They're going to kill us."

"Slow down," Matei said pulling his horse towards them but keeping a hand at his hip, ready to draw if the need arose. "*Who* is after you two?"

What the boy said, chilled Matei worse than the blizzard blowing around them ever could. "A Raven, and The Empire."

"What?" Matei demanded. He looked back behind himself, as if trying to see if he was being followed. He hadn't spotted any movement on the road, at least nowhere near the mountains.

"We lost them in the storm," said the boy. "But they are sure to come after us at first light."

Matei turned his eyes back to the boy. "You're leading them right to us!" He went for his revolver, and took aim at the child.

"Wait!" the boy exclaimed and he suddenly dropped to his knees, and practically slammed his very face into the ground. "Please! I need to speak to your master! My sister and I just need refuge from the storm and then we'll move on up the mountain."

"Why would I want to help a couple of runaways from the Empire?" Matei demanded. "And where do you plan to go? There is nothing beyond those peaks aside from Shadowfort Castle."

"We have to get to Snowcap Lake!"

The name sounded familiar, but Matei couldn't recall where he had heard it from. His momentary pause had been confused by the boy for consideration, for he kept talking.

"Please, take us to your master. At least let him hear us out!"

Matei thought about just ending this conversation here and now, and leave the two to the Empire who would more than likely track them down at first light- if they don't freeze to death first.

But he was torn by the looks of how desperate the two were. The little girl didn't make an attempt to move forward, but she was now standing with her hood falling off her head. She was bald, and her eyes were completely blue as a sapphire gleaming against sunlight, the little pupils barely visible and making her stare inhuman, primal. Seeing those eyes sent shivers down Matei's spine. They didn't look like Dearg eyes, but still. What business did they have at Snowcap Lake, whatever and wherever that was.

And what did the Empire want with them?

With a sigh, Matei made up his mind, and declared his decision.

Words alone can never fully express the immense relief of one finally escaping the bitter cold where temperatures range from -20 to a cruelly comedic 0° Fahrenheit, to starting a warm fire before plunging into a hot bath of bubbles and salts.

    Now as Angela stepped out of her elegant bathroom wearing her underclothes, her white hair put up in a fluffy towel, she entered the little hallway where her workshop sat. She paused to look up at the map that hung right above her desk which was still cluttered with notebooks and papers. Akira's journal, which she had obtained back in Irondell still sat where she left it, a debunked playing card marking where she had left off reading. She had forgotten to mark Wardan on her map and taking a pen full of red ink, she circled the little village nestled in Woodmarsh Forest and crossed it out, hyphenating with this red ink with the word, 'Crota.' This was marked as well as Firedell, Lake Dublin, Barrowleg Marsh, Yom-University, and a spot near the edge of Aldhill Forest to the east of the Salt Mines. These spots were the locations where known Immortals might had gone into hiding, but out of all these places, only two of them had been correct, and Angela had slain them both.

    Realizing that she had also forgotten Count Horla, she marked his place of death on the marker for Irondell. This task complete, she sat the pen down and admired her map once again. Although she was officially finished with Hunting for the evening, she felt herself often browsing this map and her notes every so often, constantly checking up on the history of the Immortal Nobility and taking note of any rumors she would hear during her travels. No doubt either later tonight or tomorrow she would come back and reflect on what she had on the remaining Pudidrac Court.

    But for now, it was time to rest.

As she padded across the room to her bookshelf, Sebastian, her black cat followed close by, purring and mewing at his master as after a short pause she selected a new book to start and sat into her chair by the shelf to read. After a brief consideration she got up and went to one of the pantries she had in her workshop. On the top shelf above some dried ingredients and jars of liquids she often used for potions and remedies, was a wine shelving unit. She scanned the many branded corks and eventually selected a Goldendell Ridge 1910 Merlot, one of her favorites despite the place of origin. She uncorked the bottle and after pouring herself a glass she returned to the chair and began to finally read with incredible speed. Her eyes taking in everything faster than any human could and she was soon lost in the warmth coming from her fire and the world she was delving into. She tucked her feet beneath her and allowed Sebastian to rest in her lap. Hearing him purr and reading a book, to her, this was paradise. This was what Angela longed for after a long hunt. If she had her way, she would lock herself away in the Great Library of the Chronicler and read for all eternity. What a wonder it would be, to separate herself from the world and live in the world of fantasy and fiction and not have to worry with what was real.

As she read she reached delicately towards her stand where her wine sat. She brought it to her lips and sipped as she continued to read still, breathing in the aroma of sour grapes as she tasted the wine. 1910, a good year. Before she knew it she was emptied, and she poured herself a second glass with the same hand. She did not fear for getting drunk, for she had discovered that it took a lot for her Dhampiric brain to become intoxicated. Also, only wine seemed capable of intoxicating her as beer and liquor was practically unaffecting. The last time she could remember being drunk was in 1994. She had been with-

Angela paused in reading, her ears twitching as they caught the sound of footsteps approaching her door. They paused, she sat and listened. Sebastian, sensing the presence as

well, looked towards the door with emerald eyes. Hoping against hope, Angela sighed as a knocking began upon her door. She looked at the door and sniffed. Sweat, and the unfamiliar scent of something feral; dormant but still dangerous. But she knew that sweat well. She had to put up with the stench throughout her time in Irondell.

"Angela?" the familiar voice called out from behind the door.

With a sigh, Angela sat Sebastian down on the floor and retrieved her robe from her chair. After making sure she was decent enough to answer the door, she opened it up to reveal Jacob, the newest Hunter of the Black Hand, smiling and looking better than he had since the two of them had left Irondell.

"Excuse me, ma'am," the Hunter said with a teasing smile. "You wouldn't happen to have seen a dangerous Huntress prowling about, have you? You couldn't have missed her, white hair, wearing all black, sapphire broach, as gorgeous as-"

"You're so stupid," said Angela helplessly.

"Oh, come on," Jacob said laughing. "I was just getting to the good part." He smiled warmly at her now. "Welcome home."

"Thank you." After a moment's consideration Angela then added, "I suppose it is good to see you as well."

Jacob chuckled. "You 'suppose.' Funny. I'm glad you're back. Your hunt went well then?"

"I wouldn't be back if it hadn't."

"Great point. How come you didn't come to see me?"

"I was told you were busy."

"It never stopped you before."

"I was tired," Angela tried to drop hint after hint for the young Hunter, but he just wasn't getting it. That, or he didn't care.

"Oh, I see. Well, I'm sorry if I was bothering you, I just wanted-

"There's no need," said Angela. "Perhaps it was inconsiderate of me not to drop by again. I was glad to hear that you were up and about."

Jacob smiled more easily now. "Yeah. Been up for about a week, trying to get back into shape. I've been antsy the last few days in my bunk."

"You are unhurt then?"

"Never better."

Angela looked him up and down and asked, "Jecklyn approves then?"

Jacob's smiled turned charismatic like a magic trick. "Worried about me after all?"

Angela rolled her eyes. "You are impossible."

With a laugh, Jacob's blue eye lingered down towards Angela's feet, where Sebastian had slipped around and stared at the Hunter with piercing eyes. Jacob stooped down and stroked the cat's back, giving Sebastian the attention he was obviously desiring. Angela watched how gentle Jacob was with her pet.

"Well, like I said," said Jacob without looking back up at Angela. "I just wanted to stop by and tell you I'm glad you're back. I didn't mean to intrude."

"Thank you. And... you didn't, really. I guess I am not used to people checking in on me when I return from a hunt."

Jacob looked up at her. "Guess you'll have to get used to it."

Angela looked at Jacob coolly. "I suppose..."

"You glad to be home?"

For the love of Yohnah and all things holy... she thought and then said, "Yes. Just me, and a really good book."

Jacob's mouth made an 'o' shape and he nodded as he stood back up. "Well, I'll be taking on more contracts soon. Maybe you and I will get to work together again."

"We'll see," said Angela.

Though she would be glad to work with Jacob again, there were still many things that irritated her about the Hunter.

Jacob was still young and naïve to the world of monsters, despite having being raised by one who turned his body into a test subject for her various spells and experiments. One of them was what Jacob hid behind his eyepatch, the other being under the glove he always kept on his right hand- the same hand that he had used to cast a spell on her before going off thinking he could deal with an Immortal on his own. Though Angela had forgiven the Hunter of his mistakes back in Irondell, she was still bitter about it, and made sure he understood that if he ever used his black magic on her again, she would cut that hand clean off and rid him the temptation of ever using the one thing he hated ever again.

That, and there was also the bite...

And...

Still, if what Jecklyn had said was true, then if it was working with Jacob or one of the other Hunters, she would much rather be with him.

The young Hunter then shuffled a foot, obviously having more to say. "I'm sorry, I'm sure you'd rather be reading right now. But, I am glad you are back, Angela. I missed you."

Though touching, Angela was still not used to someone saying they actually missed her. With her being the spawn of a Vampire and a human, she didn't get along with the other Hunters in the Black Hand. Though she worked really closely with Velinar and Oskar, the two men had other business to deal with beside her, and the maids and spirits that took care of the castle were always busy. Only Jacob seemed to be the only normal human to really care for her and she in turn, though she would never admit it to him, cared about him as well.

"I... missed you as well," Angela said at last.

Jacob's face lit up with that confident and yet also irritating smile of his. "Um, now that you're back, if you aren't busy later, would you like to join me for dinner?"

"In the hall?" she asked.

"Where else?"

"This again?" Jacob suddenly spoke out, now, standing up and pointing a finger at Vladimir. "I went hunting with her and nothing happened. I trust Angela just as I trust any of you here. I will speak for her behalf."

Angela just wished the man would just shut up.

"Of course, you would," Vladimir said turning an evil glare at Jacob. "I bet you two got really comfortable together. What? Has she made you her pet, Tepes?"

"Watch it, Vlad," Jacob warned.

Before either of the men could say anything else, Jecklyn cleared his throat and said, "If there was something to be concerned about when it comes to Angela, I'm sure if not me, Velinar would have informed us."

"Thank you, my *rational* friend," Velinar said with a tinge of spite towards the men who settled back into their seats ashamed.

"That was really stupid of you," Angela whispered to Jacob.

"No, it wasn't," Jacob said crossing his arms. "He's an asshole and you need to stand up for yourself."

Angela suppressed the urge to growl at him.

"Vampires," grumbled Vladimir. "You can never trust them, no matter what. Especially a half-breed bitch like her."

"Mind your tongue," Matei said in a low and impatient voice. "You're just wasting your breath."

Vladimir turned on Matei. "Listen, you-"

"Vladimir," Velinar said with a growling voice that seemed to drop down upon the great hall like a massive and cold shadow. "This is *not* open for discussion. Your job is to obey my commands, according to contract. You all *will* travel with these two into the mountains, and you *will* ensure they reach Snowcap Lake. Most importantly, you will work together on this, regardless of what you feel about your peers."

Angela was watching Velinar as he spoke. She had speculated that he had been testing her when he threatened her guildship during the Irondell contract. This was not just a matter of ensuring the contract was complete out of necessity. He was trying to make sure all the Hunters had each other's backs.

"Sir," Sabina said speaking out for the first time. "May I please ask, what is so important about this lake?"

"As I said before," Morgan said speaking with the permission of Velinar. "That is not important for you to know. I just have to get my little sister there, and soon."

Velinar cleared his throat and said in a soft voice that hardly carried throughout the room, "They deserve to know, you know."

Morgan shook his head defiantly. "It's supposed to be a secret. Besides, I doubt they would believe me."

Angela eyed the little girl again, those bright and glowing blue eyes seeming to glow brighter as she too stared at the Dhampir. As much as she too wanted to know about the secrets the two children were keeping, Angela knew her place. She was a Hunteress, bound by an oath with Velinar and the Black Hand. Wherever she was sent, she must go. That was the way of the Hunt, that was the point of her existence.

"Very well," Velinar said with a sense of amusement towards the boy. "I will leave the details for you to tell. As for the rest of you, you will all leave at first light."

"Morgan, Charlotte, you both follow me, please," said Jecklyn.

The two children thanked everyone in the room, and followed the doctor out of the Great Hall. As they passed by Angela and Jacob's table, little Charlotte turned her eyes once again upon the Dhampir, and for a moment it seemed as if they had suddenly flashed brighter. In her eyes, Angela thought she saw a woman with the same eyes, almost the same face, and garbing gauntlets that had long curved talons of iron across her fingers with little flames dancing in her palms. The vision quickly vanished as the little girl disappeared behind closing doors, leaving the Hunters alone with Velinar and the other servants.

"Sir," Vladimir said rubbing his eyes. "I will follow your orders. But I will speak my mind one last time: this is foolish."

"And I shall respectfully remind *you*, that I have made my command," Velinar said politely but also sternly. "Put your petty rivalry aside. You are both Hunters, and you should act as such."

"Very well," Vladimir said grumpily whilst up and bowing stiffly. "As you wish, I shall work alongside the monster." And saying his piece, Vladimir stormed out, without another word or glance at anyone. The other Hunters were now whispering amongst themselves and Jacob was looking back at Angela concerned.

Monster.

Angela glared at Jacob as if he were the one who said it. Instead of looking away, he held her gaze. "He's full of shit, Angela. Don't listen to him."

"Don't talk to me about him," said Angela getting up. She looked towards Velinar and then turned away and started out of the grand hall.

Jacob followed, walking alongside her. When she told him to go away, he didn't.

"What are you thinking?" he asked.

"What do you think? Just leave me alone, Jacob. I want some time to think about what we are getting ourselves into."

"Hate to say it, but it sure doesn't feel like we have a choice."

They were now in the entrance hall, the spiraled staircases right above them. Angela paused at the foot of her respective stairwell and looked back at Jacob.

"Yes, I suppose not," she agreed.

"What do you make of it?" Jacob then asked. "Of the kids, I mean."

"I believe Velinar already explained it."

"What do *you* think?" Jacob asked again, not accepting her runaround answer.

Angela sniffed. As much as she just wanted to be alone, she felt herself planted, feeling the need to answer just so that Jacob knew that she wasn't angry with him. Annoyed, maybe, but not angry.

"I think it is strange. Those children... there is something strange about them. I am also curious as to why the Raven and the Empire wants two Nishgúlian children so badly."

"Hey, just because they have red hair- or at least *one* of them," Jacob admitted. "How can you tell they are Nishgúlian?"

"Why else would they know of a secret cave in the mountains that even we never heard about? They obviously know something of importance up there that we don't, and the Empire seems desperate enough to chase them into the mountains. I think Velinar knows more than he is letting on."

"But we are Hunters, not escorts," Jacob looked away in thought, that childish look he had before long gone. He was serious now, a Hunter on a mission and conversing with his partners. Angela thought he had matured a bit since Irondell.

"Also, I understand the whole pair-thing, but why a whole group? Even without Matei and the other two, that's four Hunters working together. Doesn't that seem like a bit much to you?"

Instead of stating what Angela had been thinking about earlier she said, "It is because the Stonehollow Mountains is a place where Man was never meant to dwell. It is like the deeper woods of Aldhill and the unknown wilderness to the east. If there really is a village up there, then it has to be a source of something important. I don't think Velinar thinks a pair is incapable, but where Man doesn't belong is where we may be most challenged."

Jacob was watching her closely now. "Do you know anything about Snowcap Lake?"

"Rumors, mostly," said Angela. "Nothing concrete. If Morgan and Charlotte are unwilling to tell us, we can only hope that we figure that out when we reach it."

"But you have no other idea at all as to what we will find?"

"Angela," Velinar's voice called out through a nearby suit of armor which trembled with the deity's words. "Come back here for a moment."

"I'll explain later," Angela said turning back to the grand hall. "Go."

Jacob didn't bother to follow her, and instead went straight to the men's dormitory as the other Hunters started to come out of the hall. He didn't stick around to talk with anyone which was probably for the best. After Vladimir's comment, if people saw that Jacob was wearing a scarf a lot more often, they may grow suspicious. They couldn't keep what had happened a secret forever and Angela knew that, but they could at least buy themselves some time. Velinar was counting on them for that much at least.

Angela stopped before the deity who still remained in the same spot and bowed her head. "My Lord."

"You disagree with my decision," was all he said, coolly, but also indifferent and uncaring whether she disagreed or not.

"Yes," Angela answered. "Concerning the legends these mountains have, and the fact that *children* wish to venture out to find the mystical lake, makes it even more dangerous. Some would even say foolish."

"Hmm," Velinar hummed thoughtfully. "Well, it is a good thing that I am no fool. Between you and Jacob, and Vladimir and Sabina, you'll make it out okay."

"I don't doubt it," said Angela. "But can't you send Adriana and Nicolae with them?"

"I *could*," Velinar admitted. "But I need them to help fortify our defenses here in case we are indeed attacked. Also, I have a special request for Adriana to track down and bring back

Bram. I don't doubt that you could do it, but I want you to be there in the mountains. Besides, it will do you some good to be with the other Hunters."

"Then can't we replace Jacob at least? He just got better and…"

She faltered, as Velinar was now watching her with a peculiar look in his black eyes. A small smile tugged at the ends of his mouth.

"You should give him some credit," said Velinar. "He is strong for someone his age. Besides, I think we both know he won't let you go without him, not on this contract."

Refusing to be baited into a conversation she didn't want to have, Angela said instead, "This all just seems too risky. Do you really trust those kids?"

"I do," Velinar said. "I sensed no misdeeds in the boy, only desperation. And the girl… she is definitely more than meets the eye. But you already know that, don't you?"

Angela swallowed before answering. Hoping and praying that she was wrong. "Is she an Immortal?"

Velinar shook his head. "She has bizarre eyes, yes. But she is not a Vampire, that much is for certain. She is mortal, but she is not entirely human either. I can sense a power within her, but I didn't pry. Whatever their reasons are for going to Snowcap Lake is none of our concern. Yet."

"What do you mean by that, Master?"

Velinar shook his head. "Just a hunch and nothing more. But, the power I sense coming from her… I have reason to believe that she might be an Ice Walker."

Angela felt as if a cold wind had just blown into the hall. She had heard of Ice Walkers before. Human beings harnessing the power of ice and snow and were even considered among many cultures around Lunokean as the children of gods.

Well, one 'god' in particular.

Feeling as now she had a better lead to do some research before they left for their contract, Angela switched back to her previous concerns. "I still think at least Jacob should stay."

Velinar eyed her closely and then said, "If you really want that then I will leave you to it. You can see if someone will take his place, but I doubt he will let you do it. I will not do that business for you."

Liking the idea of talking to someone about replacing Jacob did not sound fun to Angela. But if that meant making sure that Jacob had a little more time to recover…

"Make sure you get those kids to the Lake," Velinar continued. "Speak of my hunch about Charlotte being an Ice Walker to no one. The last thing we need is Charlotte being asked questions even she may not know herself."

"Do you think that is why they are going to the lake?" asked Angela. "Because of what she may be?"

Velinar looked to the ceiling and then said in a soft voice, "We will speak no more of this."

"Very well. Your word is my command, My Lord." Angela bowed stiffly.

"Thank you, Angela." Velinar nodded with a genuine smile on his face. "Oh, and… keep an eye on Vladimir. The loss of Luca has impacted him *tremendously*. I do not think he would do anything rash while on your journey, but I can sense his hatred towards you. This job will be frustrating for him as well, and I hope that you can make sure nothing befalls him- or any of you."

"Let me guess: another chance to earn my respect?" Angela ventured her guess.

"Well, that. And I don't want to have to pray on behalf of any more lost souls."

Angela nodded, understanding dreadfully. "I won't let you down, Master."

Velinar nodded. "Go, eat and rest. You leave at first light, and I have the night to pray." He refused to say anymore, even as Angela stalked out of the Great Hall and headed for her room. She had a lot to look up and very little time to do it.

It would be a long job, for all of them.

An Ice Walker... how interesting.

Jacob left his room with the intent of finding Angela. Given that they would be leaving in the morning and needed their evening to rest up and prepare for their Hunt, he decided he would stop at the kitchens and bring her something to eat; just so that she would know that he had been looking forward to dinner, but understood if she wanted to be alone before they got to work.

Vladimir was waiting for him in the men's hall, leaning against the wall with his arms crossed. He flashed a filthy look in Jacob's direction as the young Hunter transcended towards the stairs. Seeing this and out of spite, Jacob flashed a cocky smile to the Werewolf Hunter.

"Last time someone gave me a dirty look like that," he said slowing his pace as he approached Vladimir. "She told me to quit staring."

"Cut the shit," Vladimir said in a low voice, unamused. He pushed himself off the wall and stood in Jacob's way, blocking him.

Jacob, though his smile remained, stood dangerously close to the man, doing his best to make his own presence suffocate the hallway. "What? No hello?"

"This is no joking matter," Vladimir said pushing off against the wall to meet Jacob eye-to-eye.

"All right," said Jacob keeping his expression neutral now which was not difficult. "So what sort of matter is it then?"

"You already know."

"Clarify, please. Pretend I don't."

The corner of Vladimir's mouth twitched. Whether it was out of legitimate amusement or out of anger was impossible to tell. "Why would you defend that... *her*?"

"Because she is just as much a Hunter and you and I," Jacob answered with no hesitation. "And also because she won't speak up for herself."

"So you speak for her. How noble of you."

"What is your problem?" demanded Jacob. "She obviously keeps to herself, so why does it matter to you if she is Hunting with you guys. Velinar trusts her, shouldn't that be enough?"

"Yohnah trusts humanity a lot, doesn't make it valid," said Vladimir. "It doesn't matter if Velinar trusts her or not. I don't, and while I'll follow my orders, that does not make Angela my equal, nor will it ever."

"Why?" asked Jacob, feeling his temper flaring but keeping a hold on it. "What did she ever do to you?"

"That's none of your business," growled Vladimir, his temper likewise flaring. "And besides the 'why' wouldn't matter even if there was. She's not one of us."

"She's just as human as you and I."

"She's just as human as a savage bear," argued Vladimir, smiling now as if exasperated. "By the Stars, Jacob, she's *still* a Vampire. I don't know what happened between you and her in Irondell, but I warned you once and I'm trying to warn you again: stay *away* from her. I can tell you fancy her, but that is like playing with fire."

"That has nothing to do with-"

"Don't lie to me. I see how you look at her."

Jacob glared at Vladimir, neither confirming or denying anything. He let the veteran Hunter have his say.

"You've taken a likeness to that... that, Dhampir. She's already got you in her clutches. That is how her kind works. She works on you, gets you to drop your defenses, and when she has her chance, she'll suck you dry at the neck. It is her nature; it is what she is."

"Angela is *not* like that," Jacob insisted in a low and threatening voice. "She saved me, more than once back in Irondell, and I did the same to her. I wouldn't be here still if it weren't for her. I trust her, as much as I trust any Hunter in the Black Hand."

"Then you're a fool," grumbled Vladimir, in a way that sounded eerily similar to how Angela had said it long ago.

"Seriously," said Jacob. "What has she done to you? If nothing, then you are hating her for nothing."

"I don't need a reason," Vladimir crossed his arms again. "She is a monster. That's all the reason I need."

"She is not a monster."

"Says you."

"You don't even know her."

"I don't need to."

Jacob's smile that he managed to keep on, quickly vanished. "You know nothing about her."

"And you do? I bet she told you a lot, hasn't she? Or maybe she hasn't. Maybe she just whispered sweet *nothings* in your ear. Maybe... maybe she *seduced* you." Vladimir then flashed a smile of his own which was cruel and uncharismatic. "I understand *that* much, Jacob. I get it, I really do. I'm a man too. A body like that, I'm sure it was hard to resist-"

Jacob grabbed ahold of the man's shirt and slammed him into the side wall. He then felt a sharp prick under his chin as Vladimir pulled a dagger and pressed it against it. Both Hunters glared at one another, neither willing to back down or let their own smiles falter.

"You trying to pick a fight, Vlad?" Jacob said his voice low and dangerously calm. He had no intention of fighting, not in the castle anyway. But he was willing to put the Hunter in his place should he try anything. He wouldn't even have time to run the dagger the rest of the way with where Jacob's hand now was, as he had placed his hand right against Vladimir's chest to hold him against the wall. It would be over before Vladimir even knew it.

"I just want to be sure what side you're on," Vlad said.

"There shouldn't be any sides other than The Black Hand's," answered Jacob.

"Good. Then are you with us, or them?"

He didn't need to explain to Jacob what he meant. Us or them. Humans, or monsters. As far as he was concerned, Angela was no better than a savage beast from the woods. Now he wanted to know if Jacob was on the side of humanity, or on the side of a vampiric being.

"What I saw in Irondell," Jacob said to give his answer. "I saw men do horrible things to other men. Families and friends left at the mercy of the Vampires. They were willing to do terrible things, even sacrifice many to save a few or commit terrible acts of sin. Those men, they were *worse* than monsters. You ask if I am on the human's side or with the monsters? Well, I'll give you my answer when I am sure who the *real* monsters are."

He released Vlad, and the Hunter in turn removed the dagger from his throat. Both men stared at each other, unblinking.

"Everything I do now is for the good of the realm."

"And I understand that," Vlad said keeping his voice just as level. "You don't seem like the kind of man who would do otherwise. But I want you to be absolutely sure of who you defend and who you protect. Because whether you like it or not, we are Hunters, we hunt beasts. I don't give a damn what happened in Irondell for that Dhampir to earn your trust. Just make sure you know who to really trust, when she turns and ends up at your throat."

As if to emphasize his point, the Werewolf Hunter tapped his dagger against the scarf still around Jacob's neck. He kept his eyes locked on Jacob's however as he said, "Just be careful, *mate*. I don't want to have to put you down if you turn."

And with that, Vladimir turned to the nearest door, and disappeared behind it with a hollow slam, leaving Jacob alone with his thoughts.

He meant what he said, to Vladimir and to Angela both. He would not betray either of them, not for the entire world. He was a member of the Black Hand, and he had the backs of all who bore the Black Hand of Velinar, regardless of who or what they were.

But he wondered just what would happen during this job they would be doing first thing tomorrow. He wondered this as he made his way down to the kitchens in order to grab himself and Angela some dinner.

With the food on a platter covered by a glass dome, Jacob made his way to the women's dormitory and knocked on Angela's door. A moment later, Angela answered, wearing her night attire and looking tired. She looked-

No, more like *glared* at Jacob for a moment before looking to the food.

Jacob cleared his throat, wondering what had that look been about. "Just wanted to make sure you had something if you wanted it," he said. "Since we obviously need to rest up for tomorrow."

"You shouldn't have," said Angela, pulling the door shut a little more. "I usually don't eat this late anyway…"

"Oh, should I take it back down?" asked Jacob. "I didn't mean to oppose if-"

"No, it's fine. Place it on the floor, I'll grab it when you leave."

This confused Jacob. She was clearly decent and had no qualms about eating with him before, why was she all of a sudden reluctant to just take the food from him? He felt foolish bringing with him both of their meals on the same platter.

"Um, you sure?" he asked. "My dinner is here too, but I guess I can just take it out. If you want to just take yours too I can-"

"I'd rather not open this door," said Angela in a chilled voice. "You really shouldn't have come unannounced, especially *twice*. I appreciate the gesture but now's not a good time."

"I… I understand," said Jacob. "It's late, you're probably busy. But can't you just-"

"I said *no*. I'm not letting you see me right now," said Angela scornfully. She got a grip on herself however, leaving Jacob staring dumbfoundedly at her.

"Um… did I do something wrong?"

"What do you think?" Angela muttered not looking at him.

"Well, can you tell me what I did so that I can try to fix it?"

Angela still didn't meet his eyes. "It's complicated."

"What is?"

She shook her head. "It doesn't matter. Again, I appreciate you bringing me food, but you shouldn't have without telling me."

Jacob nodded. He supposed he could have spoken to one of the armor sets downstairs to pass a message along to Angela, but he had never done it before and had always been reluctant to do so.

"I'm sorry," he said. "I assumed you would want to dine with me, and I really shouldn't have. I'm barging in on you, aren't I?"

"Yes, you are."

Jacob felt a twinge of pain in his chest. "That's kinda harsh…"

"Jacob, I don't want you invading my privacy without calling. You…" Angela looked away again and said, "You already invaded my privacy enough."

An audible *click* sounded in Jacob's head, and he felt a poisonous strain spread across his chest like a growing spotfire. He realized what Angela was telling him at last and he felt just a little scorned by it. He had done what Zoser said just so that he could save her. Shouldn't that have meant for something?

But then he thought about how she probably felt today, having been exposed as she had been to Jacob. And although he could still picture that time clearly in his head and was only slightly ashamed of it, realizing this made him feel sick as he considered how embarrassed she must have felt not just that day, but whenever she herself remembered it. Quickly, he removed the lid from the platter and sat it on the floor, removing his own plate before replacing the lid, stuttering apologies and feeling hot in the face.

"But Angela," he said as he stood upright, his plate in hand. "I really didn't have a choice that day. I did that to save you."

"I understand that," said Angela, now looking at Jacob cautiously, not as she had before but more wearily now, like a wounded animal. "But that doesn't mean I'm comfortable with you seeing me outside of uniform. It was… bad enough earlier."

Jacob almost said that he felt comfortable with her seeing him outside of uniform but he pulled the words back before they could leave his stupid mouth. That was *definitely* not the right thing to say. There was after all some things that didn't mean the same when mentioned towards the opposite sex- as well as species perhaps.

"Still," he said. "I understand you're… not comfortable with me, but… I swear on my life I didn't do anything to you."

"How would I know?" Angela demanded coolly.

"Why would I? I'm not that kind of guy, Angela. I did what Zoser said because he promised it would save you."

"And it did. I'm not saying you did the wrong thing, Jacob. You saved my life, and I am grateful to you. But that doesn't make it *right*."

"How can it not be right when it wasn't wrong?" asked Jacob, feeling defensive now.

Angela sighed impatiently. "Jacob, you *saw* me."

"Zoser did too."

"That doesn't make him right either. Also, he isn't here."

"You're not making any sense."

"Then I'll make it easy for you," Angela said with her eyes glowing dangerously at him. "As grateful as I for you saving my life, you still saw me *naked*, Jacob. And no matter the right or wrong I can never forgive you for that. I don't trust you."

Jacob couldn't help but huff out a contempt bark of a laugh. "I thought we were okay, you and I."

"And we are. As long as you don't ever invade my privacy again."

"Angela, I really didn't have a choice. I even argued against it at first, honest!"

"How do I know that?"

Jacob shrugged his shoulders. "I guess you don't know for certain. Probably never will. But I would hope that you at least trust me when I say I'm telling the truth."

Angela shook her head. "I'm sorry, Jacob, but I can't. Whether your actions were noble or not, you are still a man, and a very young one at that. I know what men your age think about when it comes to women."

Jacob felt the heat rise further in his cheeks, embarrassment mingling with frustration like ingredients in a boiling pot. "I didn't… I didn't look at you that way, Angela."

Again, she asked, "How do I know for certain, Jacob? Tell me that, and I will trust you."

But Jacob couldn't tell her how she could know for certain. Like it or not, she was weary enough of all people in general, but evidently was more weary of men. He should have connected with her need to not be touched without permission, why she was always so careful to not be seen. Of course she would be embarrassed by being seen nude and of course she would find it hard to trust Jacob afterward. And that question that seemed so important to her as well: How do I know? She couldn't, and it was clear that she didn't trust what she didn't know for certain, and never would.

"I… I can't make you know for certain," Jacob admitted.

Angela nodded as if he had passed a test like a child in class. "Exactly. Just… just go to your room, or something. I will see you in the morning."

"Okay."

"Jacob?"

He paused mid-turn and looked back. "What is it?"

"Thank you for the food. I mean it."

"I'm sure," said Jacob, and he left her there, feeling the strain leave his chest but leave it's unbearable ache. He didn't look back but he knew that Angela was watching him, no doubt waiting for him to leave her sight before grabbing the food like a goblin under the cover of night. As he reached the base of the stairwell, he paused and sat down on the last step, placing his plate of food to the side and rubbing at his eyes with the heels of his hands. His appetite had suddenly left as if embarrassed to be around him.

And while Jacob remained there, reflecting on how he had felt and how Angela was feeling since that day in Irondell, the Dhampir had slipped out of the room and taken the plate of food. She ate it in silence, not tasting the food and offering small scraps to Sebastian who sat beside her by the fire, enjoying his feast.

She stared blankly into the flames, unsure of what exactly she was feeling as she did so, and growing evermore frustrated when she couldn't comprehend it still. All the while she unconsciously was gripping the flaps of her nightgown tightly against her chest with her free hand, as if afraid they would come undone and someone would see.

That night, Sabina slept with Matei.

The Hunter was tired from his latest hunt, but he accepted Sabina with open arms, and after a quiet dinner of ham and bread, they both bathed together and were now curled into one another in Matei's bed. Their clothes were strewn across the floor, and Matei's armor sat at the chair by his desk; where his workshop rested. He had the option for a bigger room, but he had always been comfortable in a small space and ever since Sabina joined the Black Hand, his small room had felt more fulfilling than ever. She had wished he had gotten a bigger bed at least, but tonight it didn't matter. She would enjoy his warmth against her body, feeling the rise and fall of his chest against her back as he hugged her closer, pulling her deeper into the curve of his body.

"Have you been practicing?" Sabina asked kissing the Hunter's calloused fingers.

"Only with you," said Matei. "The women in Mistendell make poor company."

"Good to know."

Yohnah above, how much she loved this man.

This was how it normally went for the two of them. One would be off on a job, they would come back and be together, and then the other would go. But that was okay. They were both making money, delivering justice to a world of darkness and cruelty, and in the end they always had each other. They had both joined the Black Hand seeking their fortune as well as a place of belonging. And now they had found it; within one another.

Sabina felt Matei shift slightly, and his goatee brushed against her neck as her nuzzled her, whispering in her ear that caused her back to erupt with gooseflesh. "How are you feeling about tomorrow?"

"I feel like it is going to be cold," she answered simply, trying to keep her voice level without succumbing too early to his teasing. "I'd rather be here with you, where it is warm."

"And I'd rather be with you. I don't like the thought of you going into the mountains, even for a job."

"I'll be fine," Sabina turned her body so that she could face her man. The concern on his face made her grateful that this was her man, and no one else in the entire world had a claim of him. "I'll have Vladimir and that guy, Jacob with me. Angela too. We'll all be fine."

"I'm not worried about the *boys*," Matei said softly. "I trust Jacob, and he proved himself beautifully on that Irondell job. Vladimir, I have no doubt in my mind. But those children... they make me nervous. Not to mention, you will be traveling with Angela."

"I already said that I would be fine."

"You know why I'm nervous then."

Sabina looked at Matei for a brief moment before saying, "She isn't *too* bad. She brought Jacob back, which I certainly didn't expect but was glad to see. I have no doubt that she would look after us as she did with him."

"I suppose..."

They laid together in silence, relishing in their comfort and enjoying the silence they shared together. His Matei's mind was restless, and would no doubt remain as so until Sabina returned. She held him close and allowed herself to be held just as, and she tried to express her love and promise to him through their touch.

"I want you to be careful still," Matei said at last. "She might have saved Jacob and made sure he came back, but we still don't know what she did to him. She is still a Vampire. Don't tell me you didn't notice how he is always wearing his hood up or at least a scarf, even indoors?"

In truth, Sabina *had* noticed. She noticed when the two Hunters first came back. She didn't ask about it at first, since they had just got back from making the climb in the coldness down the mountain. But ever since then, Jacob always stayed outside and despite training without a shirt sometimes, he always wore a scarf, even indoors until he locked himself in his chambers. It was strange, but at the same time it had been weeks. If she had bitten him, he should have been converted long ago. But then again, she was a Dhampir, only half a Vampire. Maybe it took longer, Sabina didn't really know.

But like all the Hunters, they all noticed that Velinar showed no alarm, even Angela, so they haven't said anything. But the fear of the unknown, whether Jacob was infected or not still resided, and the thought of asking and being wrong felt all the more humiliating.

"He trusted her," Sabina said. "Velinar, I mean. Maybe it's about time we trust his own judgement. After all, she brought Jacob back, and that is all we know. If she did do something, would she really make sure he got back?"

"I don't know," Matei admitted, his eyes lingering to the side and away from her.

Sabina gently placed her fingers upon his chin and turned him to face her again. She then scooted further up, and kissed him on the lips. "I love it when you worry. *Don't* worry though, I'll be back before you know it. Besides, I know how to deal with Vampires. I'll be okay."

Matei smiled slowly, relenting to her persistence. He hugged her close and kissed her head and they remained together all throughout the night well into morning. The few times Sabina awoke in the night, she would watch as Matei slept deeply and soundly, before falling back to sleep herself, the same thought always returning to her again and again.

I love you, Matei.

By the time morning was just peeking across the horizon of the world of Lunokean, both Sabina and Matei were loudly woken up again by the suit of armor by their fireplace. The suit was shrieking like a banshee and Sabina, who never liked the spirits in the first place, sat up in her bed and growled at the inanimate object and the soul that resided within while Matei groggily began to awake.

"This had better be good," she hissed.

"Emergency on castle grounds!" The armor pipped up. "Enemy soldiers approaching- it's the Empire!"

Matei swore as he slipped out of bed, Sabina following suit. In no time at all both had slipped into their armor and raced out of her room armed with their weapons. They ran into the other male Hunters who didn't bother giving them a snide look as they all converged towards the main castle doors donning minimal armor but were ready for a fight to defend their invaded home.

They stepped out into the blinding morning which shone across the freshly fallen snow like a glistening sea. As the members of the Black Hand's eyes adjusted, all could hear the clanging of armor as the first responding suits of armor who had left their posts to intercept the invaders did battle with an enemy that was just starting to break through the tree line; deeper than the wards that protected Shadowfort should have allowed them entry.

Above them all, squatting, perched like a hawk before a battlefield, Jacob overlooked the fight going on in the field just before Shadowfort Castle. His feet were bare which made it easier to grip the tiles hidden beneath the numbing snow. He had his quiver of arrows slung across his bare back, and with his bow in hand, he eyed his enemies and prepared to pick them off as they emerged from the trees and continued to clash with the suits of armor.

There was a whole group of them, at least thirty strong. All of them garbing the black and golden armor of the Empire and the Capital of Goldendell. The sigil of the falcon gleamed in red on their breastplates, and the last soldier in the rear followed in the siege while carrying a flag bearing the same symbol of dominance. All the soldiers wielded rifles but they had swords at their sides, and Jacob knew that they were trained to use them, and he was glad he was not down there. He saw many chinks in the armor even from this distance on the parapet. While the chinks provided the invaded soldiers optimum mobility, it also made them easy targets for a Hunter who was a practiced sharpshooter.

Near the stables, some of the Hunters who had finally adjusted to the bright morning sunlight had taken cover behind the stables and were engaged in a firefight with the soldiers, picking off those who managed to break through the line of armor before they could reach the castle itself. He spotted Vladimir in particular downing soldier after soldier with his revolvers, and Livia had slipped around the tree line and had begun shooting at the soldiers from their right, causing many to collapse to the ground and stain the snow crimson.

With a deep and slow breath, Jacob reached over his shoulder and grabbed ahold of a single arrow. He picked his target, a large soldier who had broken the line from his group, and was now taking aim at Matei who stood on the stall rooftops shooting his own gun. Quick as a flash, Jacob nocked the arrow and pulled it all the way back to his ear and loosed it just as the feather brushed his shoulder. He watched as the arrow sailed right between the chest plate and face mask of the soldier, plunging into his neck and letting loose a spurt of blood into the snow. None of his brothers stopped to help him as they continued to overpower the empty suits of armor and converge on the stalls. Many had dropped to the ground and were shooting at the Hunters prone. Jacob who was able to reach them from his perch, shot them as well.

Again and again he loosed an arrow, and each and every single time Jacob watched as soldier after soldier fell; their armor useless against his aim. He watched one man stumble as a bullet struck his armor, not stopping it but at least slowing the impact as it struck him in the chest which he clutched as if having a heart attack. Jacob made sure to quickly put the man out of his misery and loose an arrow right into the visor of his helmet. Still the group charged in unrelenting as they neared the other Hunters who stood their ground at the castle, and Jacob watched as he saw a flash of silver rushing past the group and towards the soldiers.

He and the others watched as Angela garbed in her leather armor alone, unleashed hell upon the soldiers of the Empire.

Quick as a rabbit, she leapt aside as some soldiers fired upon her. She was right on top of them in a moment's notice and their heads went flying with a single swipe of her sword. She then lunged forward and after sliding her sword right through another man, armor and all, she leapt up and kicked another in the chest, sending him flying nearly across the clearing and right into a tree, leaving a gory smear across the trunk. The man was still alive but Livia got in and stabbed the man twice in the throat with her dagger for good measure.

Angela then grabbed ahold of the soldier she had stabbed and used him as a shield as more soldiers took fire upon her. Sliding her own blade out of the dying man, she then hurled him with her inhuman strength, knocking all of the soldiers back with hardly any effort. At the collapse of this group, some of the Hunters broke from the stall and pushed forward, meeting the remaining soldiers and firing at them time and time again. Those who didn't shoot intercepted soldiers with swords and easily dispatched them with their own training and experience.

Those who stood before the Dhampir drew their swords stammering and scared for their lives as they looked into the eyes of Angela Dragos, which glowed bright and purple without mercy or the thought of. Behind her, the other Hunters continued to move in closer, shooting at the men who foolishly dropped their weapons and tried to flee. Jacob continued to provide covering-fire from the rooftop, as Angela danced and lunged with deadly accuracy; making anyone unlucky enough to stand in her way a blur of silver and blood. She stabbed through the chest of one more soldier and leaping up and wrapping her legs around the head of another, she twisted and broke the man's neck before tossing him aside into the snow and throwing the other towards the edge of the mountain, watching him tumble down to the valley below. One more man, the flag-bearer, took up a fallen soldier's gun and took aim at the Dhampir. She probably would have dodged it, probable would have dispatched the guy in no time at all. But before the man could even pull the trigger, the arrow that Jacob loosed stuck right into his eye. The boy whom he could not age, stumbled slightly, and fell dead into the snow.

Angela turned to look up at Jacob, her face and armor coated in blood spatter. She waved her sword over her head, and then proceeded to flick the gore right off the blade. Jacob waved back at her, glad that she and the others were unharmed.

The dead laid all around the Hunters, who checked the bodies to make sure they were actually dead. As they did so, they all took numerous glances at Angela, probable trying to relay what they had just witnessed. Have any of them seen such ferocity before, or was this their first time? Either way, the entire group of soldiers that had been chasing the children had been completely devastated, dead and torn to ribbons by the Black Hand. Angela sheathed her sword and proceeded to pick up and drape one of the soldiers over her shoulder, piling on a second and third with inhuman strength. As she carried her burden over to a clearing where the Hunters would proceed to burn the soldiers, she wiped the blood off her face, making sure not to have any of it touch her lips as she did so.

As Jacob finally joined the others to drag the dead over to their pyre, Velinar watched the Hunters drag the dead over to the side and build them all up into a great pile away from the castle. At his side was Dr. Jecklyn, who was still observing all the bloodied snow from the fight. To his left, the children stood staring amazed at the many dead that would soon turn to ash once the Hunters were finished.

"They killed them all…" Charlotte whispered. She hardly ever spoke a word, and it still amazed Velinar in particular how quiet her voice was. He likewise did not fail to notice the greater chill in the air as she had spoken.

"They're all dead…" Morgan chirped as his voice cracked.

"Yes, our Hunters are quite resilient," Jecklyn agreed.

"That woman," Charlotte said pointing out Angela who released the last of her burden onto the pile of dead. "How could she move so fast?"

"Yeah," said Morgan. "Who is she?"

"She's one of our finest Huntresses," said Jecklyn. "A force to be reckoned with, indeed."

Velinar looked at the girl, and saw how her black and blue eyes seemed to sparkle as she looked at the Huntress. She admired Angela. The thought of it made Velinar smile.

Now the dead were completely piled up, and Matei was just returning from the castle with a keg of oil. He proceeded to douse the bodies while the rest of the Hunters excluding Angela, began to slowly return to the castle itself. By the time they had disappeared from the four's sight, Matei had already lit the match which began to taste the flesh of the dead before erupting into a devouring inferno.

"They are content," Velinar mused, speaking of the Hunters who had returned.

"Content?" Morgan asked.

"He means our Hunters," said Jecklyn. "They didn't see any sign of any survivors hiding out in the woods. Livia, who we saw near the trees would have picked up on stragglers. Means we don't have anyone to concern ourselves with anymore."

"But what if the Empire sends more troops?" asked Morgan.

"They would have to find their way through the woods after climbing the Thousand Steps. By then, our wards will be checked and reinforced. Isn't that right, Master?"

Velinar nodded. "Yes. This invasion is truly a disturbing one. I would not doubt it if they had a magician or a spiritualist among them to find their way here."

"This could mean trouble in the future though," Jecklyn pointed out. "We don't know if the Emperor would want to have a search party sent because these men won't ever return. Also, about the Raven these two mentioned, I did not see one among the dead."

"Could your Hunters have made a mistake?" asked Morgan.

"Perhaps," Velinar admitted. "Still, once I have our wards reinforced, it will take more for an intruder to find our sanctuary. I have been comfortable within our nest, and it's high time we take greater precautions."

"That still doesn't answer what has become of the Raven," said Jecklyn as the smoke from the burning pyre rose over the parapet and further into the sky, leaving a black stain across the clear blue like an ink blotch.

Velinar turned his eyes over to the pyre itself where Matei was starting to leave, leaving Angela alone. She stood looking across the horizon of trees and rocks below the stretch along the mountain.

"Wherever they are," he said when Angela finally turned away from the burning and started for the castle. "It doesn't seem like even she can find them."

"What is she?" Charlotte then asked. "That Huntress... she isn't human, is she?"

Morgan looked at Velinar, who looked at the girl, and then looked back to Angela who was just disappearing from view. "No, child, she isn't."

"What is she then?" demanded Morgan. "Is she like you?"

Velinar chuckled, and Jecklyn smiled with amusement. "Believe me when I say, son," said the good doctor. "That there are very little people like Velinar in the world right now. Fewer than the kind that Angela Dragos is a part of."

"Then what is she?" asked Charlotte.

Velinar was curious as to why the little girl showed so much interest in that Huntress in particular. "That, my friend, is a Dhampir."

"What's that?" Morgan asked.

"You'll have to ask her when you have time," said Jecklyn.

"Jecklyn, have the servants prepare their horses," said Velinar. "I will speak to them immediately. It's time to move."

The good doctor bowed his head and hurried off to carry out his orders. Velinar, meanwhile, escorted the children back into the warmth of the castle where they proceeded together down to the main hall like three children about to meet for lunch. There, most of the Hunters were already waiting to discuss what had happened and after Velinar gave his announcement to the main hall's armor to get the others to come, he waited near the end at his usual spot until all Hunters were present. All were tired, some covered in blood from the battle but all were unhurt, thank the Stars.

"Good work, all of you," he then told them. "I am sure that this was a terrible wake up call. But you all responded quickly, and efficiently. I am proud of you all."

"Thank you, Master," the Black Hand all said in unison.

"But our job is not done yet," Velinar said. "I will have to double-check our wards and those who will be going to Snowcap Lake will need to leave immediately."

"Master," called Livia. "How did the soldiers break through our barriers?"

"We will find out and deal with it," said Velinar. "In the meantime, we have other concerns. Angela, did you sense anyone else out there?"

"Nothing but wolves and whispers in the wind," the Dhampir replied to which everyone shuddered at the sound of her voice, apart from Jacob who merely listened. "However, I didn't see the Raven mentioned among the dead."

"Neither have I," Sabina said looking back at Velinar. "Do you think it's possible that they fled?"

"I doubt it," Morgan answered immediately. "The Raven chased us practically across the whole country. She didn't stop then, and I don't think she would stop now."

"Maybe we should just stay here at the castle," Vladimir suggested. "Wait them out, have them come to us. Then we can all take them all out within the safety of our barricade."

"We *can't* wait them out," Morgan said impatiently. "We're running out of time, we have to get to Snowcap Lake, and soon."

"I'm starting to get a little irritated by the likes of you," Matei spoke up in almost a growl. "You want to get there 'now, now, now' when you refuse to say anything about *why* you are in a hurry. And with the Empire itself at our doorstep, you don't have a lot of ground to stand on here, boy."

Morgan pouted while doing his best to glare angrily at the Hunter. Velinar had to give the boy credit for trying so hard. How hard it must be, having to be in charge of a little sister out in the wilderness while the Empire is chasing after them.

"Tell me," he then said to Morgan loud enough for his Hunters to hear. "At least tell us, *why* the Empire is after you both."

Morgan hesitated. Charlotte looked uncomfortable.

"If you tell us that much," said Vladimir calmly. "We won't bother you anymore with the reason why you wish to get to Snowcap Lake. We won't even complain."

Velinar returned his attention back to Morgan and nodded to the boy. "Go ahead, son."

"It's so creepy," Morgan shuddered. "Being called that by someone who doesn't look older than me..."

The boy looked at the deity, and then he looked at the Hunters waiting patiently. He then turned to his sister, who appeared to be trying her very best to hide in her hood and cloak. She said nothing; gave no indication of whether he should or not. But eventually, Morgan sighed, and relented at least why they were being chased.

"They want her," he said gesturing to Charlotte. "The Raven, not the Empire. Those soldiers, they are just hired hands. We found out while escaping them in Temptestdell. We were heading to Snowcap Lake, with a traveler who once served in the Empire. But then that Raven came and killed him in the house we were staying at. Charlotte and I fled, but that woman, that Raven, she chased after us. For weeks, she has been chasing us with her gang of soldiers. It didn't matter where we went or who we turned to. They would always appear, and those who tried to help us either wound up dead, or sold us out. To ensure my sister's survival, we fled and came looking for you guys. We don't know who else to trust to get us to the Lake. We don't know why the Raven is after us, but I won't let her catch us. I won't let her take Charlotte."

The little girl nodded, to confirm her brother's story. It didn't seem to be enough for the Hunters whoever, who glanced at the children with doubt.

Jacob surprised everyone by walking up to the three adolescents and dropping down to one knee to meet the two children at eye-level. The very idea of approaching Velinar in particular was unusual and often dangerous, but the deity didn't seem bothered as Jacob addressed Charlotte kindly.

"Honey, you sure you have no idea why the Raven wants you? None at all?"

Charlotte shook her head quickly. The lie was blatant, and obvious to all. But Velinar didn't want to press the matter any further.

"Jacob," he said turning to his Hunters. "Step down."

When Jacob had done as he had been told, Velinar continued. "Everyone, aside from Matei, go and prepare for your journey. Come back out here as soon as you are able. Matei, when Jecklyn is done I want you to work with him in fortifying our defenses. He will explain what we have to do here."

"Yes, Master," the Hunter said still scorned that he was not going as well, but understood his place and his necessity here at the castle.

"And you two," Velinar said turning to the children as the Hunters began to disperse. I'll leave you in the care of my Hunters then."

"We are to leave then, Master?" asked Angela, voicing the Black Hand's next orders.

Velinar nodded. "Immediately."

The Fallen Star had spoken.

After feeding Sebastian and taking the necessary measures to ensure he was taken care of in her absence, Angela came out of her room in full armor, her gear in her satchel or holstered. She locked her door and pulled up her hood as she made her way downstairs.

Jacob was the only one ready downstairs near the front entrance. His bow was strapped and tucked beneath his cloak, and at his side was a small sword that he never carried before. His arms were crossed revealing his gauntlets that held hidden daggers and by the look on his face he seemed to be upset. When he spotted her however, he smiled.

"Heck of a way to start the morning, eh?"

"What is it?" Angela asked as she approached him.

"What do you mean?"

"What's troubling you?" Momentarily, Angela worried that he was upset with her, given their discussion last night and for a brief moment, she felt guilty. But she knew that it was because she was more modest and wearing full armor and could therefore not be intimidated by him.

Intimidated by him… Even thinking it, Angela thought it inconceivable.

"I just don't like this," Jacob said, no longer trying to hide behind his smile again. "Those kids are hiding something, I can feel it."

"It doesn't matter if they are or not," Angela told him as she turned and leaned back against one of the stone pillars with her arms crossed.

"What if this only gets us into more trouble?" asked Jacob. "This attack on the castle is no doubt the first of many."

"Velinar will strengthen the barricades and will take the precautions necessary to defend Shadowfort," said Angela. "Don't worry, it will still be standing when we return."

"That's not what I'm worried about. I'm worried if we'll return."

"We will. We have our orders, and we know our job. We escort them through the mountains and drop them off at their desired location. Do not worry, Jacob."

"Nothing is that simple," Jacob argued. "A particular Huntress taught me that."

Angela felt her mouth twitch at that. "We'll be fine. With four Hunters, we'll be fine if any beasts or environmental problems arise. I also highly doubt they will send us off without packing our horses."

"It ain't just the beasts I'm worried about, it's also the Hunters themselves."

"You don't trust your companions?"

"Do you?"

"That's not the question."

"No, but it's something I considered." Jacob turned to face her. "Are you going to be alright? I know you and the others don't get along."

"It doesn't matter," Angela said. "As long as we just stick to our jobs and out of each other's business, we should be fine."

"You don't sound so sure."

"Don't worry about me, Jacob. I don't need you to look out for me."

"I don't doubt it. Doesn't mean I can't-"

"Well, try not to worry, please." She was starting to grow frustrated and just wanted him to shut up.

Jacob raised his hands up. "All right, all right, sheesh."

Angela looked at him. "We will be fine, Jacob. I will be fine too. Do us both a favor and just worry about yourself."

"There it is," Jacob muttered with a knowing smile. "Getting all distant and setting rules before we even begin."

"Don't push me, Jacob."

"It's my job."

"No, it isn't."

Jacob looked at her and asked, "Is this about last night?"

"We are not talking about that right now."

"What if *I* want to?"

Angela growled in her throat and glared at Jacob who only smiled cockily at her.

"Growling at me isn't going to change my mind."

"Knock it off."

But Jacob had no intention of doing so. "Angela, I understand where you're coming from, but think about where *I'm* coming from."

"Jacob-"

"For crying out loud," he continued. "I only did what I could to save you. You act like everything is okay, check on me every time you get back, and now all of a sudden you're giving me the cold shoulder. Had I done something wrong lately?"

"No. But you *did* do something wrong, Jacob, and I can't just let that go. I'm not just giving you the cold shoulder, I-"

"Then what *are* you doing?" Jacob demanded.

Angela's temper flared like a combusting log on a fire. "Right now, I am resisting the urge to smash your head in," she growled. "If you have *any* respect for me, Jacob, you will stop this right now."

Jacob glared back at Angela, his frustration and anger visible within the conflict of his expressions. He had been clenching his fists, but then they slackened and they opened with his palms flat against his thighs.

"I *do* respect you," he told her. "But I guess it's clear that the feeling isn't mutual."

"That is not true."

"Sure as hell feels like it is," he argued further. "I didn't have a choice, Angela. You act like I wanted to see you… you know." A tinge of red had started to appear on Jacob's cheeks, but he pressed on. "But I didn't. My one and only concern was keeping you alive, and in my mind, if it really bothered you that much before, why decide to just now tell me? Why come back every hunt and check on me and even consider having dinner with me if you were only going to hold that night against me?"

"I'm not holding anything against you, Jacob." Angela raised her hand to stop Jacob from saying anything else. "I hear someone coming. We are not going to speak about this any longer. I do respect you, Jacob, even when you act like I'm not grateful for you saving my life. But that doesn't change the fact that you are a young boy who doesn't respect another's privacy, *especially* when she is uncomfortable with that."

Jacob stared slack-jawed at the Dhampir who stared back with a defiant expression that clearly said, 'explain yourself all you want, it will make very little difference to me.'

"Do not bring this up again," Angela warned him as she pushed herself off from the pillar and started for the door. "In fact, it is probably best that we don't speak to one another at all during this trip if that is how you are going to 'respect me.'"

Jacob laughed. "Finally, something we agree on."

But even as they both stepped out into the cold and started down the walkway towards the stables where Vladimir was already waiting, both regretted the last things they said to one another. Nevertheless they worked to check their mounts and Angela in particular watched as the children arrived with Sabina at last, and they too began to prepare for the journey ahead.

As all of this was happening, hidden among the trees far beyond the border of the wards that had given away the positions of the soldiers before, *she* watched the Black Hand mount their horses in front of the ancient castle.

The two children were there, including that Ice Walker who had evaded her for the longest time. The Raven, smiling a sharpened smile of delight, curled her fingers around her sword. They were so close, and yet so far away. After sending the soldiers in to test the Hunters of the Black Hand, the Raven had managed to get all the data she needed. Those men and women, they were dangerous- especially that one with the white hair. As long as they were in their protective circle which had driven many of her men suicidal by rushing into battle, Shadowfort was untouchable.

She looked behind her where her elite soldiers stood waiting, bitter and cold from the hours of travel up the mountain. Those who had war dogs looked upon their mongrels with pity as they shivered from the cold. They all wore similar armor to that of their fallen brethren, but they also now donned the sigil of the Thunder of Ravens on their shoulders, indicating their eternal service to the Ravens behind their leader Emperor Ion. The good leader of the realm had no idea that she as on this mission however- and he didn't need to know. This was a personal mission for the Head Raven, and Sorina Narcisa had her instructions on capturing those children and bringing them back to the Covenant. Her head was covered by her hood, and face by the traditional beaked mask of tin, hiding her smile as she returned to her suffering soldiers.

"We move in on them at sundown," she told them. "We will catch them in the night when they rest."

"Should we send a courier down the mountain?" suggested one of the soldiers, no doubt wanting an excuse to escape the harsh coldness of the mountain.

"No, we thirteen are all that is left. Your comrades have served their purpose, and now it is time to serve yours. We need all of us in order to take on the Hunters- though I *am* curious as to what secrets they have in that castle..."

Sorina had thought of storming the castle again, but thought better of it. If the Black Hand was as dangerous as everyone said they were; including the rumor about a Death god lingering about inside, she thought it better to leave it be. She had enough dealings with Death through the powers of Oblivion itself- courtesy of her god, Kawfka.

"So we are to follow them, My Lady?" another soldier asked.

"Soon. Rest and eat, we will pick up their trail later in the evening. When they stop to rest, that is when we strike. Remember: I want the girl alive. As for the others…" Sorina smiled at the thought of bathing her sword in the blood of Hunters from the Black Hand. "We'll make sure the wolves have something to eat tonight."

When the horses were mounted, the Hunters of The Black Hand started down the pathway leading past the castle towards the mountains beyond. They rode single-file with the children in the very middle while Angela and Sabina took the front and the men took up the rear- under Vladimir's 'orders.'

"I want you up front where I can see you," he told Angela in particular, who could care less where she was as long as she could see the world around her. So, she led on.

As the group began their ascent into the mountains, the sun rose up high above the world, glaring down upon the miles of snow and making it appear like the blanketed trees were on fire it was so bright. Sabina who rode just ahead of Morgan, glanced numerous times at Angela, probably noticing that despite the sun-glare hitting her skin, the Dhampir was unfazed by the light of the world. It appeared to be true that Dhampir's aren't affected by sunlight, not that Sabina would have known for certain until today.

An hour into their ride as the trees became more and more scarce, the group soon came across a small cave that appeared to be hand-carved into the side of the rockface. According to Morgan who was doing most of the guiding as they rode, the road that they were taking went through the tunnel and through a supposed valley that cut across the spine of the mountains like a groove through sand.

"The valley is on the other side," he explained. "We make it through there, then we will be able to see the ancient road leading to Snowcap Lake."

"Ain't nothing here but snow," said Jacob. "I see no signs of there ever being a road here."

"It's all buried," Morgan told him and the rest of the group. "When we go through the cave, you'll see that it is man-made."

"He's right," Angela said looking down the length of the cave. To mortal eyes, there was nothing but darkness beyond the mouth. But with her own eyes, Angela could see right down the tunnel, almost clear to the other side where light was barely getting through. The walls were smooth and unblemished. "The walls looked carved, not formed."

"Strange…" Sabina mumbled under her scarf. Her horse started to turn away but she managed to bring it back to face the cave. All of their horses had begun to grow nervous by the unfamiliar terrain. "Vladimir, what do you think?"

"Is there anything we need to worry about in there?" Vladimir asked, looking at Angela.

"No. Aside from a few foxes cuddling near what looks like an old carriage, I see no other animals inside."

"A carriage?" asked Jacob. "Up here?"

"Lead on, *Dhampir*," Vladimir spat the last word out as if the very name was bile, ignoring Jacob's question and giving no one the opportunity to answer.

Without making a single comment, Angela started forward. Morgan and Jacob on the other hand lit torches, to help light their way as they entered the cave and walked through it, hearing the whistling of the wind as it passed the lips of either side of the tunnel.

As they traveled down the length of the cave it became more and more obvious that what Morgan had said was true. The cave walls were perfectly carved like a cylinder and upon the walls themselves looked to be carvings of numerous pictures and messages in the Nisthgúlian language; the memories and thoughts of those who had carved this tunnel right through the peaks of the Stonehollow Range. True to her word as well, there was a broken-down carriage laying in ruins near the side of the wall, the skid marks and shattered remains of wheels indicating that the driver might have crashed. For what reason the Hunters didn't know, not even the foxes who poked their heads out of the carriage doors to look at the glowing red flowers that Jacob and Morgan carried to light their way.

"Look at that," Jacob said pointing in particular to a carving depicting stick-figures wielding what appeared to be spears as they cornered a large beast that Angela recognized immediately.

"That is the Crota," Sabina answered Jacob. "A beast who hides underground and rarely comes to the surface. It is one of the ancient beasts that used to plague Balkeñoir alone, back when the Nisthgúlians ruled the continent. Most were driven back underground long ago."

"Wow," Jacob said. "How many legends are in these mountains? How many curses?"

"No one knows for certain," Vladimir said. "But as you could have probably guessed it, it doesn't look like anybody has been down this tunnel aside from animals in a long time." He turned to Charlotte and her brother who rode in front of her. "Have you two been through here before?"

"Once," was all Morgan would say. Charlotte remained silent, petting her horse as she rode quietly along with the group.

"You're not making this easy on us," Sabina said looking back at the boy.

"I don't care," Morgan suddenly snapped but then caught himself. He took a deep breath to calm himself before saying, "Just... leave me alone, please. Both of us. We need to keep going."

Angela stole a quick peek at the boy, as well as his sister. Despite Morgan's wish to be left alone, she asked, "You say 'once', because you left, right?"

When Morgan looked at her, she clarified.

"You left Snowcap Lake once, and now you are returning. Am I right?"

Morgan glared furiously at her. "What's it to you?"

"Nothing. Just an observation."

"Mind your own business."

"Hey," Vladimir warned him. "Last I checked, we're helping *you* out. So I'd show some respect if I were you. Though I can't really blame you for the likes of *her*." He flipped a thumb over at Angela. "But keep up the attitude, and we'll tie you both to a tree and leave you to the wolves."

"And return to your Master empty-handed?" Morgan said glaring back at Vladimir this time. "Heh, yeah right. I'd like to see you try."

"Morgan..." Charlotte said nervously.

"That's enough," Sabina spoke up irritated by the chatter. "From *both* of you."

Vladimir said nothing, neither did Morgan. At this point the end of the tunnel was drawing near, and after a short period, the group emerged back into the sunlight, and beheld the valley beyond the cracks of the mountains and the unseen world within.

The mountains stretched for what looked like miles like a carved out boat with jagged teeth ready to take a bite out of the sky, the peaks blocking the rest of Balkeñoir from the forested valley. Black pine stood tall and stretched up the mountainsides until there was nothing but rock. The trees themselves seemed to stretch like the tallest buildings in the major cities, some had trunks wide enough for ten people to hold hands around them. Some minor cliffs reached out from the cracks of the mountainsides, making it appear that the mountain itself was about to swallow the forest and all within. Somewhere in the distance, an elk bugled.

"Wow," Sabina said as everyone rode out of the tunnels. "This was all hidden inside the mountain?"

"And we never noticed," Angela agreed, likewise admiring the vast beauty of the deep forest.

"How far is it to the other side?" Vladimir asked Morgan. "Unless that lake of yours is down there somewhere?"

"It's a three-day ride straight from here," the boy answered. "But the place is swarming with trolls and other beasts that we had trouble with the last time we had come through. This is part of the reason why I wanted to hire you Hunters."

Angela was just considering that very thing as the other Hunters looked at one another. This was possibly one of the very few wildernesses in all of Balkeñoir. While much smaller in scale than that of Woodmarsh and even the unexplored and uninhabited north of the Aldhill forest, this was just as desolate it seemed from human occupants. Even the deserts of the Nisthgúlian Reservation and even that of the Deepland Barrens which had human settlements were considered part of the only true wild lands left. With barely any human traffic coming through here, it was likely that even the most ancient of beasts still stalked these trees, even beasts more ancient than the Crota or even the Immortal Vampire.

"Let's make camp," Jacob suggested. "I'd rather give ourselves some time before we go down into the forest down below. We'll have a better vantage point as well."

Looking down from the cliff they now stood upon, the bottom of the valley looked like a good hundred-foot drop. Nothing for Angela by herself, but there was no point in risking Midnight's life, nor the rest of the horses. Trailing her eyes to her left, Angela spotted a game trail carved along the rock almost hidden in the snow. It zig-zagged down the side of the cliff down to the bottom, where a stone path seemed to have been laid out. The dry snow appeared to have been blown off by whatever wind managed to slip through the jaws of the mountain peaks up above. Looking back up, Angela figured that it was high-noon. They had been riding for a good couple of hours now, and there was still a very long ride ahead of them.

"Shouldn't we camp closer to the treeline?" asked Sabina.

"That's not a bad idea," Jacob said, although he had meant them to camp up on the cliff where they could see everything coming their way.

"Let's head down there before the sun gets too low," Vladimir barked. "Let's go!"

They rode on.

When the group got to the bottom of the game trail and finally down into the alley, they only had to ride a few meters before they stood before the forest that filled the cavernous-like mountain. Being so far down and with the crevice's blocking the strong winds, the air seemed be frozen both in movement and temperature. The horses trotted in place on the man-made street which upon closer inspection past brushes of deep snow, seemed to be made of well-placed stones of the same shape and size. Within the forest, white powder speckled the road itself but most of the snow appeared to have been caught in the boughs of the great trees to which the Hunters were looking upon with unease and great distrust.

For contained the trunks of the trees, as if carved by some artist beyond human capacity, were the many strained and twisted faces of human beings.

There looked to be over a hundred just in the few trees that they could see thus far. Men, women, and even some children, all appeared to be trying to push their way through the bark, the wood stretching over their skeletal features as they all seemed to cry out in silent screams. Many were contorted and twisted, their images blending with one another like color bleeding across a painting. Some even had hand-shaped limps trying to break through, their hollow eyes seeming to stare right at those who had approached their forest. Every single face, the hundreds they could see and no doubt the thousands within the rest of the forest, all mutely screaming while desperately trying to break through, but they remained frozen and mute, unable to escape their little prisons.

What made this distorted scene even worse, was that there was nothing the group could hear in the forest; no birds, no snap of a twig, nothing. It was as if they had just stepped into a strange dimension with no sound, and no warmth. Just those thousands of hollow eyes and screaming faces, staring right at them.

"My god..." Jacob whispered, being the first to break their silence and allow the group to finally catch their breath. The only ones seeming unfazed by the sight was Angela, as well as the two children, who looked upon the trees with only minor curiosity.

"What..." Sabina said. "What is this? What are they?"

"This is one of the secrets hidden within the Stonehollow Mountains," Morgan gulped.

"Why are..." Vladimir shook his head, unable to word the dreadful question.

"They are the faces of a lost civilization," Angela answered. "Probably those who lived here long before the land was conquered and made into the Balkeñoir we know of today. They are now part of the forest, for what reason we will never know."

But she said this while looking across the limbs of the trees. There was only one thing in her memory capable of doing such a thing; to merge those willing and unwilling to leave the forest into the very organism that made up this valley. If such a thing was here...

To the rest, what she said was completely believable. It was worse for Jacob, whose ties with ancient thaumaturgy brought back memories and sensations of a time he rarely tried to reflect on. He could almost feel those eyes staring down at him, and almost hear the screams of many people in whatever wind whistled in the crevice far above their heads. The still coldness around him made his flesh erupt in goosebumps, and he could sense his horse's own fear as it shook his head, trying to tell his master not to go in. He calmed Starlight with a gentle hand, his eye still on the nearest tree that looked to be reaching out to him.

Little Morgan, turned to look at the Dhampir. "How would you know that?"

"I can hear them," Angela said almost sadly. "They are crying, crying to escape. They must have been here for centuries. I doubt they had much of a choice in becoming part of all of this."

Vladimir cleared his throat. "We should get moving." He shuddered as he took another look at the forest. "I don't like it, but I'm assuming this is the only way?"

"As long as we stay on the path, we'll be fine," Morgan said, though he did not sound so sure himself. Even he stared at the mouth of the forest like it was the mouth of a great and terrible beast, ready to swallow them up and devour them.

Angela clicked her tongue, and her horse moved forward without any struggle, unlike the rest of the riders who practically had to fight their mounts in order to get them to move. Jacob had less trouble, having calmed Starlight enough so that his horse felt confident enough to move forward. Both Morgan and Charlotte had no trouble at all, and eventually Sabina and Vladimir followed. Soon they were all swallowed by the forest, the darkness of the trees above making the cold air feel like ice in their eyes, and the feeling of being watched ever more terrible.

Jacob could not shake the feeling that invisible hands were reaching out, and trying to grab him as he rode just behind Angela with Charlotte to his left, Vladimir on the other side. The Werewolf Hunter practically squirmed in his seat at the discomfort as thousands upon thousands of eyes stared at them with hollow screams. Still, the Hunter did his best to ride steadily, his eyes always on the lookout and his ears listening for any sound. There wouldn't be any bandits, not in these mountains. But there would be creatures; and as Morgan had said, trolls lived in these woods. All rode on, all listened carefully and kept their heads on swivels.

At some point, the little girl, Charlotte, encouraged her horse to move faster, so that she was right behind Morgan and keeping up with Angela who kept her head raised and watching the lower boughs of the overhanging tree limbs. No one appeared to have noticed, until the little girl started to speak.

"Ex-excuse me?"

Angela turned her head and her purple eyes fell upon the girl. Charlotte shuddered as she stared back with those glowing blue eyes like orbs of condensed ice. "Um… the man, with the scythe, he says that… you're a Dhampir?"

Jacob watched as Angela merely stared at the girl. When she turned her eyes forward and in a low and quiet voice but loud enough for Jacob to catch, said, "Yes."

Charlotte now looked at Angela with curious interest rather than fear. She was still nervous, there was no doubt about that. But she seemed to relax a little, hearing the Dhampir's voice. "Um… what is a Dhampir? I have never heard of one before."

Before Angela could even attempt to answer, Vladimir pounced like a tiger lying in wait, and bringing his horse to a faster trot, caught up with everyone and gave his own response.

"You don't want to bother with asking her," he told Charlotte. "One of her parents was a Vampire."

Charlotte now looked at Angela with a slight glint of fear, and she looked Angela up and down as if trying to see more clearly. "A… Vampire?"

"Yes," Vladimir said quickly. "I wouldn't get too close to her if I were you, girl. There might be some human in her, but Dhampir's are very dangerous creatures. They can turn on anyone at any time."

There was a slight hint of a dare in those words, and Jacob felt his fists clench tightly on the reins at this. As upset as he was at Angela, Vladimir had no goddamn right talking about her like this.

"Just do yourself a favor, girl," Vladimir said again. "And stay clear of her. She might be docile now, but I don't want you to sleep too close and wake up with her nibbling on your neck."

Docile? Such a word threw Jacob into a rage, and turning to Vladimir, he snapped in a low but dangerous tone. "That's enough, Vlad."

Vladimir glared at him, his horse slowing only slightly. The damage was done, and Charlotte had fallen back just a little further behind, same as Morgan. The Dhampir meanwhile seemed to refuse to let Vladimir's words sting her, but Jacob could tell that that just wasn't the case.

"Charlotte," Morgan then said willing his horse to create a little more distance between him and Angela and closer to Sabina. "Get back- *now*."

That was all it took, and the little girl willed her horse to stop entirely and turn away with her brother, sticking between Vladimir and Jacob. She looked at Vladimir, who nodded in approval. She then looked at Jacob, those crystal eyes full of curiosity. As if she was trying to ask, 'why'?

Deciding to end this now, Jacob flashed her a dashing smile. "What Uncle Vlad said, is a little... overexaggerated." He felt Vladimir's eyes on him, but Jacob ignored the Hunter, keeping his focus solely on Charlotte. The young girl tilted her head in question, and while her brother was now eyeing Jacob distrustfully, he had both of their attention nonetheless.

"You see, what he said *is* true. Dhampir's *are* dangerous, but they're no more dangerous than us humans can be. They are simply difficult to understand. Again, just like humans. They are unpredictable, and have their temptations just like you and I when it comes to things we want or need. Yes, there is Vampire blood in her. You can see it just by looking at her. You've felt it too, didn't you?"

Charlotte nodded, slowly, carefully.

Jacob continued. "But, just like humans, Angela cares about her comrades. She is loyal to the Black Hand, and the missions she is sent on. Her job now, is to get you and your brother to Snowcap Lake, right?"

Another nod.

"Then you got nothing to worry about. Because Angela will make sure you get there; take my word for it. She's not going to let anything happen to you two, or to any of us."

Charlotte stared at Jacob for a long while, but then, eventually, a small smile tugged at her lips. She looked at the Dhampir, who no doubt had heard the conversation, and then she looked back at Jacob. "She is safe then?"

"Of course, she is."

"Jacob..." Vladimir warned. Sabina only looked uncomfortable.

Jacob glared at him. "Let's be adults here, Vlad."

"The fuck's that-"

"No. We got a job to do, don't go scaring the kids from someone you know nothing about."

Vladimir said nothing, but his eyes told Jacob exactly what he was thinking. *Like you know her?*

Charlotte pursed her lips, and then one of her hands released the reins she had been clutching tightly. She then reached out towards Jacob, holding out a pinky. The gesture was innocent; an innocent gesture from a small child wanting reassurance, no matter how silly that assurance came from. She didn't even have to repeat her question. Jacob obliged willingly, and hooked his own around hers. The two shook on it, and relief seemed to spread like water across Charlotte's face.

"Okay," she said.

Jacob nodded as he pulled his hand back. "Good." Charlotte looked forward, and Jacob looked over her hooded head towards Vladimir.

Oblivion itself had no fury like the fire in the Werewolf Hunter's eyes. Disgust, anger, and humiliation seemed to bulge out of the single vein throbbing in Vladimir's forehead. The very cold and controlled expression he gave Jacob could not have sent an even clearer message. *How dare you?*

Jacob merely shrugged, and brought his eyes forward. Sabina still said nothing, didn't even look back at him. Morgan, still not that far away, remained just as silent.

Lastly, though Angela had not moved or even reacted to his words, he knew the Dhampir had heard him too. That was just as good, if not just as important as the others hearing it. Whether Angela herself appreciated it or not, Jacob figured he would never know, not anytime soon given the circumstances between them presently. Probably even if they hadn't fought earlier, she'd never admit it or tell him in the first place.

But he was glad to have at least made it easier for Charlotte to feel more at ease around her. Whether the others felt the same or not was irrelevant. They had a job to do and taking time to start some petty drama wasn't going to help.

Still, he couldn't shake the possible feeling that he had just made an enemy, among the Black Hand.

The sun set far too soon and only pale orange light stretched across the sky beyond the crevice, shrouding the valley and all within it in darkness. The group decided to camp out right by a small clearing somewhere deep in the woods; a meadow where no doubt many great elk or moose laid to rest.

There was great boulder nearby as if it had been placed here on purpose or perhaps fell out of the sky, where they could sleep with something to their backs without the fear of being snuck up on. The only disadvantage being that if the hunter that decided to prey upon the group and it was a powerful creature, there would be nowhere to run. But no one in the group was afraid. All of them were more dangerous than anything they had come across; they were trained for it. Still, they all agreed to sleep in shifts when it was time to retire.

The group had already begun gather dead branches for spot-fires as well as a regular cooking fire when Angela suddenly started to leave the campsite.

"Hey!" Vladimir called out to her. "Where are you going, Dhampir?"

The Dhampir stopped, before turning a cold and purple eye to the leader of the group. "I'm going hunting." She said simply.

"For what?" Vladimir demanded. The tone of his voice made it clear just what the first thing that came to mind was.

"The children need to eat, and so do all of you," was Angela's response. "I'll go and find some food."

"I'll go with you." Jacob said dropping his armful of wood onto the ground and starting towards her. Before Vladimir could tell the young Hunter to stay, the Dhampir beat him to it.

"No. I'll hunt alone. It'll be faster. Be useful here, and help with the fires and sleeping rolls."

And with that, Angela started off again, her cold and dark demeanor seeming to melt and blend into the shadows beyond the screaming forest without a single sound; even the spurs on her boots didn't so much as jingle with her steps. Before anyone knew it, she was gone.

Like a bloody ghost…

Vladimir turned an eye to Jacob, who started digging a hole with a vent for one of the spot-fires. Morgan had come to his side and offered more wood, and the young Hunter accepted it graciously. That damn smile of his flashed in Vladimir's sight again.

Bloody bastard…

Taking out a flat piece of rock, Vladimir began to dig his own pit. They needed a couple of fires around the site, as well as one big pit to keep warm at. The small spot-fires would make it easier to spot any creature coming in and give the group time to react appropriately. Every order Vladimir gave, even Jacob obeyed without even such a bat of the eye. But that damn smile of his lingered, mocking the Werewolf Hunter it seemed.

"He knew what he was doing…" Vladimir growled in his throat as he began to make a teepee of twigs in the fire pit. He reached for his tinderbox when he realized he had forgotten it. He cursed. He had brought his cigarettes but not his tinderbox. He soon came aware that someone was standing nearby, and he looked up to see Sabina holding out a box in one hand while holding onto more pieces of wood in the other.

"Here," she said, shaking her head and allowing her golden hair to hang loosely around her shoulders.

Vladimir took the tinderbox gracefully. "Thanks." He muttered as he got to work getting a flame going. When he was done, he used the same match to light a cigarette. He needed it.

"Anytime." The Huntress started to go to her own little pit.

"Sabina," Vlaidmir called without looking up. As expected, the young Huntress backtracked and sat on her haunches, looking at Vladimir with an impatient expression. "I want your help on something tonight."

"What is it?" Sabina asked smirking at the Hunter. "You looking for a little fun? I'd have to ask Matei first."

"Hilarious," said Vladimir.

"C'mon, what is it?"

Vladimir took a quick glance at Jacob who was far enough away so that he wouldn't hear. With Charlotte helping him with starting his own fire and Morgan off to get more wood, this was a good time to talk without anyone eavesdropping. It was possible that Angela was close enough still to overhear, but it was a chance he was willing to take.

He scooted closer to Sabina, and whispered to her. "I want you to check Jacob's neck when you take watch tonight."

Sabina looked at Vladimir with narrowed eyes, thinking. "Why?"

"He's been wearing that scarf…"

"In case you haven't noticed, it's *winter*, Vlad. Winter normally means it is cold out."

"It's *been* winter, but that isn't the point," Vladimir hissed. "He even wears it inside the castle."

"So?"

"He never wore a scarf during his training, and now all of a sudden after he gets back from that Irondell job, he's wearing that scarf. Not only that, but he defended her, and he is now taunting me about it."

"You *were* a little harsh…" Sabina muttered.

Vladimir looked at her. "Are you on her side now, Sabina?"

"I thought we were all on the same side."

"Not that Dhampir. It will be a cold day in Oblivion when I ever trust that mongrel."

Sabina didn't like that word. 'Mongrel.' It was almost as bad as the word 'bitch' in her opinion.

"Do you think she bit him or something?" asked Sabina.

"That's *exactly* what I am thinking."

"Don't you think Velinar would have been concerned if he thought Jacob was?"

Vladimir looked at Sabina. "He can't be right about everything; he sure doesn't *tell* us everything."

"We don't have to know *everything*," Sabina argued. "I really don't think it's anything to worry about. I don't like her any more than you, but I don't think it's worth getting riled up about."

Velinar looked riled all right. "Need I remind you just what she is capable of? What her kind makes *her* capable of?"

"I know what she could do," Sabina said. "But… she brought Jacob back. Isn't that proof enough that she is on our side?"

"To feed on him little by little, no doubt," Vladimir took another glance at Jacob, and then turned back to Sabina. "I'm telling you: it is too strange and too much of a coincidence. I want you to just take a peek and let me know."

"What if you're wrong?" Sabina demanded. "What if you're wrong, and your hatred of Vampires is just blinding you to just who Angela is? What if Jacob is telling the truth?"

"What if, I am *right*?" Vladimir challenged. This rendered Sabina into silence and he nodded. "If I'm right, then we'll have to do something. You being a Vampire Hunter, you know what this would mean for Jacob. It's been weeks, but that means nothing, especially since we don't know the absolute effects of a bite from a Dhampir. So, we can only hope that that means Jacob is alright. But we have to find out soon, so that we know whether or not we need to save him."

"Just what are you planning to do?" Sabina asked nervously curious. Even if he was right, Angela was a Dhampir. She had to be powerful; more powerful than any of them. And Velinar, he trusted Angela. There was no way the Angel of Death would not find out if there was foul play.

Vladimir simply smiled. "We are in the woods, in a remote mountain where a dangerous road lies for us all. Accidents could happen."

"Accidents?" Sabina said trying to gulp down the thought of what would happen.

"Find out tonight during your shift, and then we'll see." Vladimir said.

"Why don't you do it yourself?"

"Because I told you to." Vladimir's smile vanished instantly, threateningly. "I can only imagine that Jacob won't sleep while I'm on first watch. So I'm relying on you when he lets his guard down. He isn't thinking straight if he's under Angela's spell, and I don't want him hurt. I'm counting on you, Sabina. Don't let me down... don't let Jacob down either."

Sabina wanted to argue. She wanted to say that the plan was too risky, that many things could go wrong. Not only that, but if they were wrong, then they were not only invading Jacob's privacy, but proving that they simply didn't trust Angela. And though Sabina herself didn't trust the Dhampir all that much still, what Jacob had told her upon returning from Irondell made her think twice. That maybe Angela was more than just a half-breed Huntress and actually cared about her comrades- just as he had said while riding earlier.

But then again, a small part of her was curious, and she wanted to find out the truth, sooner than later. And if they were wrong, then they were wrong. But if they were right...

"Alright," Sabina said with a sigh. "I'll take care of it."

Vladimir smiled, that hungry look that an alchemist might have upon the discovery of a new element that he had worked his entire life to finally uncover. "Excellent."

And that was the end of that.

By the time all the fires were made and the bedrolls were spread, the Dhampir had returned carrying two bundles of rabbits tied at the hind legs. Wordlessly, she handed them all to Sabina who began to skin and stick them. There were eight in total, plenty for seconds if need be. Vladimir stared at Angela, confused. The Huntress had not taken a bow, nor did Vladimir hear a gunshot. In a forest this quiet in such a tightly closed valley, there was just no way that he wouldn't be able to hear it.

Angela took a seat on her bedroll that Jacob had Morgan roll out. She unsheathed her sword and began to use a sharpening stone on it. As she did so, she was inspecting some of the nearby trees.

"Welcome back," said Jacob when he realized she had returned.

Angela grunted in response.

Vladimir looked at Sabina, who had finished butchering one rabbit. She looked confused and as she inspected the second rabbit, she looked up at Vladimir and turned the plump doe over to expose its neck.

"Heh," he chuckled bemusedly, staring at the bloodied fur. "Of course." He looked over at Angela who little Charlotte was now sitting beside. The little girl said nothing as she watched the Dhampir with those inhuman eyes of hers. In the firelight, those blue eyes seemed to glow like a cat's. If Angela noticed, she gave no indication.

"Hey, Dhampir." When she looked, Vladimir asked, "Do we need to clean the wounds?"

"No." Angela replied going back to her weapon. "All of them are bled out already, just so you know."

"I noticed," Sabina said. "Thanks."

The thought of eating something that had been drained by a Dhampir appalled Vladimir, and he spat on the ground. Nevertheless, he told Sabina to go ahead and start cooking them.

"Make sure mine is cooked to hell. I want all germs killed."

"Whatever you say," the Huntress said starting for the large fire in the middle of the campsite.

Vladimir turned back to watch Charlotte watch Angela. *Jacob... the fool has made the girl too comfortable with the Dhampir.*

From where he sat before the fire, Vladimir kept a hand on one of his guns, just in case.

He heard something slice through the air and he turned to see Jacob near one of the spot fires swinging his sword. Morgan sat watching, poking the flames with a stick. The Hunter practiced some stances as well as thrusts. The sight was simply... embarrassing.

"Jacob," he called over. "Spread your feet out more and keep your knees bent. Your balance is off."

Jacob spread his feet out to the point where he comically looked like he was about to take a shit.

"For the love of Yohnah..." Vladimir growled getting up. He drew his sword and approached the young Hunter who stood immediately at attention. "Come here."

As the two faced one another, Vladimir could feel the eyes of all the others on him. He hated this kind of attention, but he couldn't stand to just sit and watch Jacob make a fool of himself. The man might be a master at the bow, but a fool when it came to the sword.

"Who taught you how to use a sword?"

Jacob pursed his lips as he swung his sword around in his hand. "The Bell-Ringers only taught me how to shoot. The master I've had afterwards knew how to use a bow and knife. I never got proper training on a sword."

"You're a Hunter," Vladimir reminded him. "You should know how to use any weapon- regardless of what you are best at. I might be a good gunner, but I need to know how to use a sword where bullets or bolts are useless. Same applies to you. You can't just stay perched on some rooftop all the time."

Jacob looked at Vladimir, not with distaste but with respect. Like a student to the master. He kept his face set and stern as he mimicked Vladimir's stance, his feet spread out just enough and his knees bent to allow him perfect balance and good spring when he attacks.

Maybe the guy can learn something after all.

"Step forward, and lunge."

When the Hunter did so, Vladimir struck at the tip of Jacob's weapon, knocking the weapon aside and pointing the sword towards the Hunter who would have impaled himself if he hadn't stopped in time.

"I'm going to lunge at you. If someone does this, strike at the tip. I will then back away, and come at you again. I want you to keep knocking me aside; swing from both sides. Little by little, I will come at you faster and take different swings at you. Every time I want you to adapt and use your footwork and reflexes to keep me from whacking you. Every time I hit you, I want you to retaliate and try again because I will not slow down. You can take swings at me as well, but if you cut me, I will be mad."

Of course he had no intention of letting Jacob actually hit him. He would deflect the attacks as much as he could, because Jacob wasn't quite there yet. But then again, he didn't want to get injured by his own comrade this early in the game. *And besides,* he thought as he and Jacob stepped closer to one another. *He might get worn out and I might have a chance to remove that scarf without all the drama.*

But Angela was there, and she was watching. Is it worth the risk? Vladimir thought about it as he struck at Jacob, who successfully deflected the first blow-

Only to get whacked in the arm with the flat of Vladimir's blade when the Hunter attacked again.

"Try again," Vladimir told Jacob and the two started again, this time without giving one another even a chance to recover.

And Jacob, flashed a confident smile as he began to get the hang of moving his sword on instinct rather than educated deduction. "I'll get this," he said. It wasn't wishful thinking, but a promise.

Vladimir allowed the smile to escape on his lips. "Good." He said and struck out again.

By the time Jacob finally sat down dinner was ready, but his arms legs and even on the side of his head was throbbing and would no doubt be covered in bruises come morning. Vladimir said nothing as he sheathed his weapon and sat beside Sabina, who passed him his blackened rabbit. The rest of the food was passed around, while Jacob merely laid on his sleeping roll dreading the morning.

Still, it was fun to spar with Vladimir and get a little practice. Though he had no doubt that the Werewolf Hunter had plenty of fun beating on him because of what he did earlier that day concerning Angela. A small price to pay, but it hurt.

He noticed that Morgan was staring at him, and the boy was stifling laughter as he held his rabbit in his hands by the sticks that it had been roasted on.

"Shut up," was all Jacob had to say as Morgan couldn't hold it in any longer and began to chortle loudly.

"That *was* rather embarrassing," Angela said now laying on her back and staring up at the night sky through the jaw-like crevice high above them. She appeared to finally relax. Her hood remained up but her body was stretched out and despite the cold she didn't shiver nor did she move any closer to the fire.

"That means little coming from you," Jacob grinned. "You're faster than any human I've ever met when it comes to the sword."

"I know what a human is capable of still. And you got a long way to go."

Morgan laughed again.

"Yeah?" asked Jacob. "At least I'm a better shot than you."

"I highly doubt that," she replied in a bored tone that only made Morgan laugh more.

"Don't worry," Vladimir said between bites. "You'll get better."

"I hope," Jacob said honestly. He sat up and accepted his piece of rabbit before scooting closer to the fire to eat. Angela remained laying on the ground close to her own spot fire while everyone else ate close to the main cooking fire. At some point, he leaned back and cleared his throat to get her attention.

"Don't you want to join us?"

"No thanks," she said closing her eyes.

"But-"

"Don't bother," Vladimir said. "I don't want her anywhere near me eating."

"Vlad..." Sabina said behind her rabbit but she didn't make an attempt to say any more. Even Morgan and Charlotte ate their rabbit ravenously, having no interest in getting involved with the adults.

Frowning, Jacob stood and started for Angela. "Fine. Enjoy the meal she brought you," he said over his shoulder and he could practically feel Vladimir's eyes in particular stabbing him in the back like daggers.

He half-expected her to tell him to go away. But he was allowed to approach and when he reached her, she opened a single eye and watched him.

"Want some company?"

"I think you already know the answer to that."

"So, no?"

Angela stared at him, an obvious question. What do you think?

Flashing a smile, Jacob took a seat beside her but gave Angela enough space for her to be comfortable. He could feel the eyes of the other Hunters on him, but he didn't care. He waited for a moment then dared to look again. Angela had closed her eyes again, possibly because she realized that Jacob was not going to leave her alone.

But then again, she wasn't telling him to piss off either.

"Thanks again, for the food, I mean," he said.

"It was no trouble."

"Do you want any?"

"No thank you."

Jacob nodded, took a bite out of the greaseless meat. He swallowed and then asked, "So, how long are you going to keep up with this act?"

"What do you mean?"

"With them. With Vladimir."

"Oh. That is what you meant."

Jacob frowned, knowing what she must be thinking about but not about to bring that up. He stuck to his guns. "I don't see why you put up with it. The Huntress I knew back in Irondell wouldn't take this kind of shit."

"The Huntress you knew back in Irondell was dealing with a *rookie*, not a professional Hunter."

"That shouldn't matter," Jacob said and added in a lower tone, "I bet you're a better Hunter than he ever will be."

"Thanks, but that doesn't matter. If I hurt them, you, or any of the members of the Black Hand, then I am to be sent away. That is one of the rules in the guild, remember?"

"Worked out real well when we got back, didn't it? Besides, he's the one starting it."

"And I'm not allowed to end it," Angela said her eyes finally opening up and staring at him. "Besides, it won't do us any good anyway. I don't care if they hate me. All that matters is that we finish up this job. I appreciate it, but you don't need to look out for me, Jacob. I don't want you to."

Jacob stared at Angela, his one eye never wavering before her bright and purple ones. He wasn't happy with her answer, but he doubt that he would be able to change her mind. "That doesn't make it right. But... I'll leave it be I guess."

"Thank you." Her eyes closed again.

"On a different note," said Jacob after a few more bites of rabbit. "Since you didn't send me away, I'm guessing you aren't mad at me?"

"I wasn't mad at you."

"Could've fooled me."

Angela's eyes opened again and stared at him questioningly.

"C'mon," he said. "You know what I'm talking about. You were thinking about it when I first came over too."

Angela's eyes darkened. "I'm not mad at you, Jacob."

"Then you won't be giving me the cold shoulder anymore?"

"That depends on your behavior."

Jacob lowered his rabbit into his lap, not taking his eyes off of Angela. "What can I do then? It's obvious what I did is still bothering you badly and maybe I was inconsiderate of how you would feel after. I never said I was the smartest in the world."

"Indeed."

Jacob snuffed out a puff of air in amusement. "So what can I *do* then? Is there a way I can apologize… better? Better than just an 'I'm sorry?'"

Angela's eyes shifted back towards the stars, considering. "I don't know."

Jacob nodded. He was frustrated still, didn't quite understand how he had made her feel so hostile when everything had felt all right. But at the same time, he valued her friendship almost as much as his partnership with her as guildmates. They had both saved each other, and he didn't want to lose that.

"Well, is this okay then?" he asked. "Me coming over to see you?"

"It's not," said Angela. "But… it's not… *not* okay."

Hearing her say that surprised Jacob. "Why did you say it that way?"

She looked at him. "What way?"

"You sound so unsure. You never sounded so unsure before, not even in Irondell."

Angela shook her head. "Forget it. Don't worry about it."

Jacob smiled. "So is it okay, or not not-okay?"

"Whatever."

Jacob's grin broadened. "Well, if you need space or decide I 'invaded' your space or whatever, tell me, and I'll try not to take it so personal."

"Thank you. As... as you shouldn't."

"But you gotta do something for me as well."

Angela looked at him. "And what might that be?"

"Try to speak up for yourself at least," said Jacob. "When it comes to the others, don't let them talk down to you that way."

"That isn't any of your-"

"Actually, it *is* my concern," Jacob interjected. "I can't sit idly forever. Just saying."

Angela shut her eyes. "Whatever."

"You do care, I can see it in your eyes even if you say you don't."

"That's enough."

"It's okay if you lie to me, just don't lie to yourself."

A growl emitted from the Dhampir, warning Jacob to tread carefully. He only stared back.

"You know I'm right," he told her. "You don't have to just take what they say."

"You have three seconds to get away from me," she growled.

"All right, all right," said Jacob and he stood and stretched, taking his sweet time. "Just try, okay? Sleep well."

Angela said nothing as he walked away. But her eyes never left him either.

"You're wasting your time," Vladimir said as Jacob joined the others. He had taken out his pack of cigarettes and had lit one using the flame of the fire. He breathed in deeply, putting his boots up against the boundary of the pit.

Jacob glared at the man. "What do you have against her? Really?"

"She's a Dhampir. I don't need a reason."

"She got you food, and that's how you thank her?"

Sabina threw a bone into the fire, sending up embers that danced through the air like fireflies. She said solemnly, "Even if we said anything, she wouldn't come."

"Not that we want her to anyway," Vladimir added.

"You too, Sabina?" Jacob asked the Huntress.

Sabina tucked a bang behind her ear before she answered. "Look, that's just the way things are. Her kind and our kind, we don't belong around one another. She has the blood of a Vampire in her. There has never been one who could get too close to a human without the lust for blood."

"What about me when she and I went to hunt in Irondell?" Jacob demanded.

Vladimir bit into his rabbit again and Sabina's mouth twitched. "A fluke," she decided.

"A fluke." Jacob laughed out loud. "You call the hole in my belly a 'fluke'?" he demanded loudly.

"Who knows her real reasons for saving you." Vladimir said with a mouthful of meat.

"She isn't like that," Jacob insisted. "She isn't the monster you all make her out to be. She's a person too, just like the rest of us. She is just as human as you or I."

"Don't give me that shit," Sabina suddenly snapped. She turned her gaze back to Jacob who was shocked to see that her eyes appeared hollow and cold towards the Hunter. Even Vladimir was surprised.

"Don't *ever* say that anyone with Vampire blood in them is our equal. Humans and Vampires go as well together as oil and water. We are complete opposites. They are our *enemies*, they prey upon humans. I'm glad Angela saved you, really, I am. Because of that I trust her just a little bit. But none of that- *nothing* she will ever do will excuse the fact that she is a Vampire as well as a human."

Suddenly everyone fell silent. The only sound came from the crackling fire, and the occasional hoot of an owl somewhere in the forest of screaming souls. Morgan and Charlotte watched the interaction between the Hunters with big and curious eyes. They felt awkward and out of place, unsure of what to say or do. Vladimir merely watched as well, seeing how both Jacob and Sabina seemed to stare one another down. Her sudden outburst appeared to have startled him, just as much as it had startled Jacob- maybe even more.

"Do you think she chose that?" Jacob eventually asked, his voice just a little above a whisper. When Sabina just continued to stare, he pushed on. "Do you think she *chose* to be a Dhampir? What her parents did? None of us are to blame for what our heritage is. We don't get to choose what happens to us."

"Don't try that," Sabina said shaking her head, her voice just a whisper. "If you only saw the things we've all seen in the Black Hand, then you would understand. The Vampires are our mortal enemies, been that way since the day of Creation. And Angela, being a Dhampir, is no different. Someday, she *will* bear her fangs. That is the fate of all who have Vampire blood in them."

"If there is such a high risk, why does Velinar allow her to be a Huntress?" Jacob challenged. "Why put you all as well as her clients at risk? Hell, why does she risk her life for humans who offer her no more kindness than the Vampires do? She's hated by their kind as well, not just humans."

"Probably for good reason," Vladimir said. "But then again, Velinar always has his own reasons and he keeps a lot of them to himself. You're right, Jacob. It isn't fair. It wasn't her fault that her parents did what they did and conceived her. But that doesn't erase the fact that she was *born*. It would have been a lot better for mankind, but especially herself if she hadn't been. As long as she exists, she is a danger to humankind everywhere. Sabina, being a Vampire Hunter, she's seen many people killed by Vampires. You've seen Irondell, what they are capable of. The only good Vampire is a dead one. That should have been Angela's fate long ago, but for some reason that we don't know, Velinar took pity on her. We probably never will. But the moment someone demands the Black Hand that she is gone, then I won't hesitate. No one will. She should have never been born. That is cruel, but that is just the way it is."

"The way it is, huh?" Jacob nodded, trying his very best to keep the words from spewing out which his heart demanded he say. "Just like she told the Immortal who took over that city, that Vampires are to be eliminated so that the world of Man may continue. But is that her talking? Her will or a greater nature? Or is it what you guys say?"

With that, he stood and bowed his head to Sabina. "Thank you for making dinner." He started off, but then stopped. "I don't know what happened, and frankly, I don't give a shit. But you can't blame Angela for something that someone else did. Especially when she's done nothing to you."

Vladimir spoke up before Jacob could walk off and get to bed. "No Vampires are Dhampirs. But all Dhampirs are still Vampires. Remember that, when her fangs finally gleam over your throat- if they haven't yet already."

The threat ringing in Jacob's ears as well as the comical irony of the matter, the Hunter went off to bed without another word to the others. He apologized to the children, but that was it. He was soon in his bedroll, and zipped it all the way up to get what sleep he could before his watch began later in the evening.

He was unaware this time, that Angela had been listening the whole time. Silently, staring in the darkness beyond the forest that felt as deep as her own heart.

Sol

No Vampires are Dhampirs, but all Dhampirs are Vampires.

How bitter and cruel the truth could be. It *was* indeed the cold and hard truth. And those words that Angela said to Count Horla, was just like that; the truth. Vampires were to be sent back to Oblivion in order for the world of Man to thrive. Man was the greatest creation of Yohnah and Vampires were mere visitors of a dark and cold past; a challenge really created by Kawfka himself, who despises his own creation for their betrayal.

And Angela, whether she liked it or not, was the offspring of such darkness. There was no greater truth than that. Someday, just as Vladimir said and what she said to Jacob not too long ago, her time would come. The Vampire Line would most likely end with her. The reason she never fought the other Hunters, the reason she put up with their words, was because they were right, and it wouldn't matter later down the road. Maybe not tomorrow, or even decades or centuries later, but one day, those words wouldn't matter. When Immortals become no more than legend, there would be someone sent out for Angela and any other Dhampir who may still exist.

Because Angela really didn't belong, and it didn't matter the injustice of it was. Even if she continued to live for centuries longer, everything about today would no longer matter. No one in the world would remember The Black Hand when other monsters along with the Immortals faded to legend. Even Jacob, who would be dead long before she would die, would one day no longer exist and wind up forgotten. The world would move on, generations will forget the past. Even if she lived to be a thousand, she would continue to be alone because no one would be able to understand how cruel time could be. It would only become worse; the isolation of today was nothing compared to the centuries to come.

That was her curse, among many due to her bloodline. Until someone is finally sent after her when there are no more beasts to slay, no more nightmares to send to Oblivion, she would only persevere alone; a relic of the past. She fully intended to make the most of the time she had, and have her revenge on those who have wronged her worse than the Black Hand ever could, as well as annihilate the Vampire race so that no one would ever suffer as she did again. But in the end, she too would disappear; someday, she would die and fade away from the world's memory like a forgotten shadow. A bad memory, either buried forever, or forced to endure for a long time. Immortality does one very little good when you are left behind in the world and destined to be put down and forgotten.

That was just the way things were.

Sabina's eyes lingered at Angela, who same as everyone fell silent as sleep eventually took her as well. She had stayed awake through Vladimir's shift, and just a little of Sabina's. The Huntress watched, until the slight rise and fall in the Dhampir's body slowed and grew heavy. Having watching her, hearing the rhythm of her breathing along with the crackling of the fire, Sabina just knew that Angela was asleep.

Just like Jacob, who had finally passed out when Vladimir went to bed. Sabina looked over to the Werewolf Hunter, who only had his head and a single hand sticking out of his bedroll; the plan no doubt still on his mind, even in sleep.

Sabina turned back to Jacob, watching the man sleep as shadows flickered across his face from the firelight. The conflicting battle raged in her chest, threatening to tear her apart unless she picked a side. But now that the time has come, Sabina wondered if she *should* do it.

On one hand, she would have gladly torn off the scarf without a second thought just to find out if it is true or not. She would rejoice in silence if that wasn't the case, and dread the morning when she informed Vladimir. Her hatred of Vampires and what they could do to humans fueled the fire of her final decision. If Angela had indeed bitten Jacob, then he was Marked by her, and if she had enough Vampire blood in her, she could bend the man to her will; making him a prisoner within his own body.

But at the same time, Sabina couldn't see Angela doing that. The Huntress risked her life to save Jacob. Yes, that could be just because she didn't want to lose her prey, but that couldn't mean anything. If she really did save him because she cared, then that would change everything. No Vampire Sabina ever encountered would risk tooth and nail in order to save a human- tasteful or otherwise. She believed that there might be *some* overexaggerating instances directed towards the Dhampir, but it was like what Vladimir said; she was still a Vampire as much as a human. Though her conflicting feelings continued to tear at her guts and shift them around in her body, Sabina knew that she had as much of a duty to protect her fellow Hunters from any supernatural threats- both foreign, and domestic.

And so making her decision, she stood from the log she was sitting on, and began to cross over to where Jacob laid asleep.

The snow around the fires had melted, revealing soft and mossy dirt which made it easier for Sabina to sneak over without making a sound. She kept her eyes on Angela, ready for any movement the Dhampir might make. Having heightened senses, she was worried that Angela would hear her moving, even if she moved as silent as a wraith across the shadows. Still, even as Sabina crept and crouched close to the sleeping Hunter, the she-demon didn't stir. She remained still- almost too still like a statue.

Sabina's eyes turned slowly to Jacob, who slept soundly, his mouth slightly open to reveal those all-too-perfect teeth. Seeing him all peaceful and asleep like this without the smartass attitude made Jacob seem so much younger- cute like a young boy. All too often he would appear confident, the act he used to not only comfort himself but others around him. But now he was relaxed, knowing that he was safe among his brethren. His whole body remained tucked into his bedroll, with only his head sticking out.

His neck, covered by that thin scarf, was loosened to allow him to breathe.

There was no guarantee that if he was bit however, that he was bitten on the neck. Sabina knew that although the neck was the desired place for Immortals and even their Disciples to bite and gain access to the most blood, she had seen people bitten in other areas as well. Wrists, calf's, anywhere where the blood flowed the most. If Jacob was bitten and there were no marks on his neck, there was the possibility that he would be bitten somewhere else.

However, Sabina would never think of this or even mention this to Vladimir. She just didn't think it was possible that Angela would go for anywhere else other than the neck. The scarf, the way Jacob always defends her, there was just too many coincidences if this was indeed the case. As Sabina reached slowly for the scarf, despite hoping that she was wrong, she also wondered what would happen if Vladimir was right. If he was, what would they do?

Accidents could happen.

The thought of killing Angela, a fellow member of the Black Hand, made Sabina nearly quiver before she touched the scarf. One, Angela was a Dhampir. Though she might have the attributes of a Vampire, there was no telling what exactly she was capable of. And what about Jacob, and the brats? What would they do? What was Vladimir's plan around that? And what about Jacob himself? Would a vaccine work on Angela's toxin like a Vampire's? There were just too many questions; too many circumstances to risk this. But still, Sabina hoped and prayed she was wrong, as she began to peel away the scarf to expose the Hunter's throat.

But something stopped her. Not a sound, nor a smell, but a feeling, stopped her. She felt as if something was watching her, and for a moment, just for a moment, Sabina thought she felt someone tug at her hair. She turned around fast towards the Dhampir, but it wasn't Angela who had alerted her, but rather who was on top of her.

It was a sprite, and the little creature was staring at Sabina with huge eyes as blue as Jacob's own if not brighter with no iris that the Huntress could see. Its naked little body shimmered in colors of green and blue, and its hair was as black as the Huntress' cloak. Without disturbing the Dhampir, the little creature merely pointed at Sabina, and then to her left. When Sabina looked to where the fairy was pointing, she almost cried out loud for another pair of eyes were on her. These were blue as well, but the entire eye was blue with small pupils that stared at her both accusingly as well as fearfully. The little girl said nothing, as she looked Sabina up and down, afraid of what to say next.

"Something is coming..." Charlotte whispered as the very fairy that had been on Angela buzzed past her and disappeared into the night like a firefly seeking sanctuary.

Sabina swallowed hard as she stood straight up. "What is?" she said trying to keep her voice even. Even as she said it, she thought she heard one of the nearby trees groaning as if resisting a strong wind.

Angela suddenly sat bolt upright. Her lavender eyes glowed brightly and she breathed in deeply. Her eyes lingered towards the surrounding trees.

"Something's here."

Sabina acted immediately, shaking Jacob awake and calling for Vladimir. Charlotte was shaking her brother awake, and Morgan groaned irritably at his sister.

"What? What?" demanded Vladimir. "What is it?"

Another groan from a tree closer to her, and Sabina looked and at the last second, she thought she saw something.

She almost didn't believe it, but the image flashed in her mind again and again. Because one of the faces that were molded into the bark of the tree had been looking at her.

Whatever it was, it had *dissolved* back into the tree.

"Get away from the trees," Angela told the others who were all on their feet and drawing their weapons. Vladimir wielded his knife and revolver, Jacob his bow. Sabina and Angela both drew their respective swords and Sabina went as far as to tell the children to stay near the fire, away from the trees.

Angela eyed the trunks of the trees, ready for everything. She closed her eyes and focused her energy on building up a vision through them. When she felt she had caught hold of it, she snapped her eyes open and a flash like a camera illuminated the forest in front of her, revealing to her the near future.

She whirled around fast, drawing her revolver and taking aim towards Vladimir. He saw it and started to retaliate, turning his own gun towards her.

"Get down!" she snarled and Vladimir heard something crackling behind him. He ducked just as Angela fired the gun which was deafening in the otherwise quiet. As he struck the ground something shrieked behind him and he rolled over onto his back and took aim at what had been creeping up behind him. He only saw it in the flashes coming from his own revolver, but it was enough to give him the terrors nonetheless.

The thing that had sprouted from the tree was humanoid, brown and murky like the bark it was coming from, and in small parts were green stains of moss. It had been creeping up behind Vladimir, reaching out with limbs that wriggled and creaked about as if they were tentacles and not part of the tree itself. Bullet holes erupted across its chest and face, and splintered wood peppered the snow as it pulled back into the tree and melted away before popping back out again on the opposite side and colliding into another tree which accepted it like a stone to water.

"What the fuck!?" Vladimir cursed as he scrambled to his feet, rapidly discharging the empty casings of his gun and reloading them from a pouch attached to his belt.

"What is that thing?" Jacob demanded, turning his bow to a third tree which the creature leapt into.

Angela stuck her hand into one of the firepits and pulled out a piece of wood. The blackened end stained and burned her hand but she hadn't noticed. She eyed where the creature, whatever it was, had gone. When it leapt back out, quick as a flash she hurled the burning wood at it, striking it in the belly and causing it to screech as it tumbled into the snow. It leapt up again and jumped into another tree, this time retaliating towards Angela.

Spiny limbs shot out of the trunk of the tree like spikes towards her. Angela twisted about, narrowly missing the majority and only getting cut across the bicep by one. She swung her sword upward and severed them all, sending them scattering across the forest floor while the stumped spines shot back inside their host. Once it did, the creature came out and began to rush across the forest floor like a chimp before diving into another tree, this one closest to Sabina who had fired her rifle into the tree's bulk. The creature in turn caused the higher limbs to reach down like knobby fingers and seize the Huntress by the arm. It hoisted her up and she drew her knife and began hacking away at the limb. Before she got too high however, Angela had leapt up and with both hands cleaved the limb off the tree like a lumberjack prepping to drop it. She landed against a nearby tree like a salamander and turned just in time to see the creature escaping the last tree and lunging towards her, claws outstretched and its mossy mouth peeled back in a snarl.

Angela rolled away and swung at the creature, slicing it in two and causing it to tumble into the snow. She had severed it from the left shoulder to the right hip, and it's lower body and left arm wriggled and shriveled in the snow as if it were drying out in the sun. The monster had begun to crawl away but Jacob had fired an arrow and it came down at an arc, spearing the creature through the neck and pinning it to the ground. It had just gotten itself free from the ground when Vladimir put six more rounds into the creature, stepping on it and putting the last one between its eyes, destroying the head completely.

Angela was on the ground now, helping Sabina to her feet who grunted in appreciation. Both women and Jacob joined Vladimir who was still standing over the creature, who like its lower half had begun to shrivel and blacken.

"Is it dead?" asked Sabina.

"Seems that way," said Vladimir nudging the shrunken husk.

"What the hell was that anyway?" demanded Jacob.

"I don't know," said Vladimir and surprised even himself when he turned to Angela.

Angela shook her head. She then snapped it upright as she breathed in the air. "We aren't done yet."

"What?" demanded Vladimir. "More of them?"

"No… something else. Something lured by the noise we made."

Angela kept her eyes focused on the direction the smell was coming from. A moment later she recognized the stench immediately and released a low hiss. She had only encountered one of these lumbering beasts once, but she could never forget the smell. The smell of sweat, almost that of a pig's. The smell of something wallowing in its own filth, as well as the stench of rotten meat stuck between teeth. It grew worse as it got closer and closer. The other Hunters were now on their feet with their weapons drawn, and Morgan and Charlotte were huddled close together with their backs against the boulder. Morgan had his own sword out, though by the smell of the boy, he didn't want to fight. He was afraid, as he should be. Jacob and Vladimir lingered off to the side, Jacob's bow and Vlad's revolvers out to provide cover-fire for Sabina and Angela who stood ready. Though the other Hunters couldn't see the creature yet, Angela's eyes pierced through the darkness and sized the ogre up before the others could see.

It lumbered near, huffing and puffing through a large nose that spilled slimy mucus of green. Huge hulking muscle roped beneath thick skin of dirtied pink, all standing at least twenty feet high despite having to stoop low enough to cross beneath the thick branches of the trees. The creature wore a loincloth over its groin, and the rope that acted as a belt bore the skulls of many creatures; animal as well as human. It's pig-like eyes peered through the darkness as its massive nose sniffed the air, catching the scent of the Hunters who hid among their fires. In one of its massive hands it held a massive club that looked to be merely a large bone with vines and weeds wrapped around the handle. When it stepped into the light, its ugly feet sunk into the snow and shook the ground beneath it. It looked over the group of Hunters, sizing them up and determining the risks in its tiny brain. This would first be a battle of wits, to see whether or not the humanoid beast would deem it worth it to attack, or wander off into the woods again.

"Jacob," Vladimir hissed. "Put an arrow in its eye."

"Don't," Angela warned the Hunter which earned her a glare from Vladimir. He looked back at the beast who licked his purple lips and revealed a set of stone-like teeth in its massive mouth.

If they attacked, the ogre would simply retaliate. Besides, a shot through the eye wouldn't kill the lumbering beast. There was no brain within that thick head. The brain, was in the chest, next to the heart somewhere in that massive body of muscle. The beast eyes every single Hunter, its rancid breath visible in the cold air.

"What do we do?" Jacob then asked. "Dance with it?"

"No, Angela is right," Sabina said curling her fingers around her sword. "You'll just piss him off. A headshot won't kill it."

"What?" Vladimir demanded. Obviously, he had never encountered an ogre before. But Sabina has, and it relieved Angela slightly at the mention of that.

"It will still have control of its body if we shoot it." Angela said. "Keep back near the kids. We have to find the brain, only then can we kill it. Otherwise, it will just keep coming at us."

"But why isn't it attacking now?" Jacob asked keeping his bow drawn with an arrow aimed right for the beast who continued to just sway slightly, as if it was indecisive about what to do.

"It's trying to decide whether to attack or not," Sabina said. "For the sake of the rest of our evening, I hope it decides to piss off."

Unfortunately, but not surprisingly to Angela, the creature roared loudly at the Hunters; its challenge heavily guttural and the smell of rotting meat pelted Angela like a storm. The creature then charged forward, its massive legs quaking the earth beneath its feet as it raised its club towards Angela in particular and swung down with all its might.

Fast as a serpent, the Dhampir had already rolled out of harm's way and closed in fast on the hulking creature. Her movement so swift that the other Hunters could not see when exactly she had severed the ogre's club-hand. All they saw was her dodging, the club striking, and the severed hand still holding onto the makeshift handle as blue blood dripped from the stump.

"Reeeaaaarrgh!" the ogre screamed out as it backed up fast while clutching a hand over the bleeding stump. The blue blood soaked into the snow as the creature glared angrily at the Dhampir. It's focus was quickly diminished however, when two arrows suddenly sprouted from its eye sockets, blinding it and making it unable to see the bullet holes that then rippled along its massive chest; courtesy of Vladimir. Jacob retreated back towards the children as the ogre began to swing a massive arm blindly around him as Sabina rushed in, and ducking beneath one of the swings she slashed at the tendon just behind the ogre's right ankle, and the beast fell to one knee with a groan. It then turned its ugly head towards the Vampire Huntress and went to smash her with its last fist. Sabina managed to step aside but her ankle slipped over a stray root, and she fell before the beast. The ogre, sensing its prey's fall, lifted its fist again to smash her.

"Sabina!" Vladimir cried out unleashing another spray of bullets in an attempt to stop the ogre but the beast was determined and its fist came down-

And smashed right into the ground for Angela had lunged for Sabina and pulled her out of harm's way before she could get crushed. The ogre roared in frustration and reached out for the two Hunters but it reared back as another arrow shot up its nose.

Seizing her chance, Angela rushed towards the beast and leapt up into the air and began to come down towards the ogre's head. The beast somehow sensed her presence and began to swing its one arm over its head in an attempt to swat at the Dhampir as if she were a fly. However, with a flash of Angela's eyes she saw the near future, and kept straight towards her target. She saw Sabina slash at the ogre's belly and the beast stopped its flailing about in a desperate attempt to grab for her; leaving its chest unprotected as Angela stabbed down with inhuman strength and dragged her sword from the collar of the groin. Muscle was severed and bones were sliced like twigs and the entire chest cavity opened up as Angela leapt back to avoid the bluish spray coming from the screaming ogre. Its intestines slithered out of its torn front like wet eels and Angela caught sight of the heart peeking through the ribcage.

"Jacob!" she shouted and the Hunter heeded the Dhampir's calling and in one shot of his bow, an arrow shot right into the heart of the creature, sending forth another spray of blue blood all over the place. With its body and the ground before it slathered in gore, the blind ogre made an attempt to grab at Angela and Sabina, who kept clear back as Vladimir reloaded for another shot.

"Save your bullets." Sabina told him. "It won't kill him; he ain't even dying now."

"But the heart!" Jacob exclaimed behind them.

But Angela had ignored him as she slashed at the other hand of the ogre, severing it completely and leaving the now armless beast defenseless- save for the stony teeth that lashed out wildly as the ogre caught wind of the Dhampir. She however ran her unique sword up through the bottom of the ogre's jaw with enough force to send the blade shooting up through the top of the mouth and out the top of the head, pinning its mouth shut as she got right in and dug her hands into the two flaps of the opened chest. Then with one mighty tug, she ripped the chest opened more, revealing the rest of the ogre within. The beast gurgled and coughed and more blood spilled, drenching Angela as she retrieved her sword and in one last thrust, pierced the brain that resided in the top of the cavity just above the heart. With the brain destroyed, the body of the ogre immediately began to shut down, and the bloodied beast fell back with one last moan, dead.

Angela turned around, her body spattered in blue blood to see the Hunters simply gaping at her, unsure of what to do or say. With a flick of her wrist, her sword was cleaned and she stuck it into the snow while she proceeded to wipe the gore off her armor and clock to the best of her abilities.

"Everyone all right?" she asked.

"All good," said Jacob who was grinning like a child.

"We're good," called Morgan.

"Sabina?"

"I'm all right. Ankle's fine."

"Good work, everyone," said Vladimir to the group. "You as well, Angela."

Angela said nothing, only taking a rag from her saddlebag and wiping at the grime and gore on her face. Meanwhile Jacob helped Vladimir attach the body of the ogre to two horses and they worked to drag the body away to avoid attracting any more predators. They returned about an hour later. By then the children had already been coaxed back into their sleeping rolls and Sabina was fast asleep.

She told Vladimir and Jacob to go to sleep, that she would keep watch now. After refusing Jacob's proposal to take over, both men retired for the evening, leaving Angela alone with her thoughts and the stink of the ogre's blood.

Most of her thoughts, aside from keeping alert for any other predator, was of Sabina.

She didn't bother Jacob for the rest of the night, which both relieve Angela but also worried her to the point of dreading the morning rather than looking forward to getting rid of the horrible stench of ogre blood.

She wondered if Sabina had really seen anything, or if the Sprite had been lying when he had whispered in the Dhampir's ear.

She watched them through the eyes of the owl that sat perched on a nearby tree just above the mangled corpse of the ogre. Even from this distance, the bird could see them all, hear them all, and through the bird, Carmilla Darkholme spied upon the two groups that had entered her forest.

Being nearly five hundred years old, the witch had lived to see many generations of Hunters, and she was pleased to see such a dedicated group of them bringing the little Ice Walker back home. She had seen her and her brother leave many years ago, and now they have returned. The thought of seeing them again made Carmilla's spine tingle. She stretched out her left hand, where her dagger-fingered gauntlet was able to scratch at her crystal ball, creating a high-pitch squeal throughout her workshop. The light from the crystal ball made her leather bracelets full of beads and shells glisten in the eerie light. Her bright green eyes wavered between the faces of every Hunter, and smiling with blackened teeth when she looked at the men.

"Such strong-looking warriors, agents of death…" she whispered to herself, tightening the red cloak around her shoulders as the runes and ancient writings carved in her skin began to emit incredible chilliness throughout her body.

Isolation, high in the Stonehollow Mountains made Carmilla feel lonely and desire the company of men. She loved it when travelers came to her valley. She loved it when it was men. Men made great company- as well as delicious meals. Carmilla didn't mind the taste of a woman's flesh, but men had more firm meat, juicier, and held the delectable amount of salt and sweat that Carmilla desired. The men would be hers, as well as the Ice Walker. She had foolishly let the child escape when their mother took them out of the mountains, and she didn't want to lose her chance again. The other villagers had paid dearly for their hiding of her, but she wouldn't escape this time. Both she, the boy, and the two men would be hers.

The women on the other hand, she would allow her children to take. That one with the white hair... she wondered about that one.

"Lithus, Mithus, come in here," she called to them.

Silent as shadows, she waited and then she heard them right above her head, dangling like the little bats they were from the ceiling's rafters. Looking up, she saw their eyes. Two pairs of silver, glaring down at her like predators watching prey. They *were* predators, hiding in the shadows, just as she was.

"Yes, Mother?" both children said in chilling unison.

"We have some visitors nearing our home," she told them. "They all look like such pleasant company. Shall we go see them tomorrow morning?"

"Can we?" Mithus chirped.

"It *would* be a lot of fun," Lithus admitted.

"Yes, it would," Carmilla agreed. "We leave at first light. I am tired, and need to sleep. Besides, why bother crossing over to the other side, when they are more than capable of coming to us?"

The only reason that group was here because of those kids; who were no doubt trying to return home on the other side of the valley. To get there, they would have to pass by Carmilla's home. The witch believed that the best things in life comes to those who wait. And to an immortal being like her, time meant nothing.

"Wonderful idea, Mother," Mithus hissed.

"Brilliant," agreed Lithus.

"Yes," Carmilla grinned with her blackened smile. "I am."

She gazed into the crystal ball again. The owl had taken flight, further back into the woods where it perched upon another branch, overlooking a second camp, this one with a few more people than the Hunters; all of them appearing like soldiers of Balkeñoir.

Carmilla watched as her two children melted back into the shadows, leaving their mother be for the night.

Sorina lifted up her head at the sound of some beast bellowing somewhere within the creepy forest of many faces. Her crew had settled in for the night, deciding to pick up where the trail led early in the morning. The roar of the beast carried and echoed for what felt like minutes before it finally fell silent. She sat perched on her rock, waiting, listening. When the beast no longer screamed, she assumed that it either caught its prey, or died a tragic death of survival. In the world, that was how it was. Kill or be killed, eat or be eaten. That was the world Sorina had lived in her whole life, long before becoming a Raven.

She turned her attention back to her crew, who sat huddled around a small fire swapping stories of war and women. Such simple-minded men. The Empire really just wanted killing machines, nothing more and nothing less. Even the few starving dogs at their heels would no doubt turn on one another for a chance of a fallen scrap of meat. If the men could entertain themselves with such silly stories regarding their pride, then they deserved to serve their master until their blood quenched the thirst of the crows.

Not her, however. She was a Raven, a soldier of darkness. She didn't particularly believe in the Kawfka superstition that the Head Raven demanded they worshiped in order to gain insight against the world of monsters. The saying kept as that if you understood true darkness, you could battle the darkness of the world. That made no sense to Sorina, nevertheless she attended the prayers and watched the sacrifices in order to obtain Black Magic and use it against their enemies. Sorina would never touch the stuff, but she had one rune on a little trinket she always kept close to her person should she come close to meeting Death himself.

She reached into her satchel and pulled out her silver pocket watch. The lid had the carving of a lion holding up a bright star, its mane flowing like fire. The two hands inside the watch were of iron, the tips shaped like barbed-tipped arrows. It was a gift from her grandmother before she left to join the army as a soldier. The watch had long-since stopped, but Sorina always carried it around with her, for luck. Even though a Raven was not allowed to carry excess baggage, she managed to smuggle it on her person, even when she was in the castle back at Goldendell.

Finding the Ice Walker would not only bring her glory when she returned to the Thunder of Ravens, but also make her own grandmother who raised her from birth to womanhood exceedingly proud. She was killed by a Werewolf, the very first beast Sorina had killed upon signing her life away to the Ravens and their heathen god of darkness. She remembered being bathed in the beast's blood, watching its chopped-up corpse slowly turn back into the human it once was. Seeing the man, naked and cut up into ribbons, only proved to Sorina that even humans can become monsters. And in a kill or be killed world, sometimes becoming a monster was all the options one would have. But not for Sorina. Not on her mission to eliminate the world of monsters completely- including the last Ice Walker in existence.

Time was running short. Though she was still a child, the Ice Walker would grow. Just like a troll or even a Shadow Leopard, it would grow into a terrible beast. A beast willing to shed innocent blood in order to live its haunted life. She would cover the mountain in another halo of snow, in order to punish those who have chased her mother out of the mountains in order to appease their own gods. Though she only wanted to return home, soon the Ice in her blood would call to her primal instincts, and she would begin her terrible path of destruction. Winter would last longer if she was allowed to live. And the snow around her, would fall crimson with blood.

"Madam Narcisa."

Sorina turned her head to the young soldier who had come up to her while she handled her pocket watch deep in thought. How long had the lad been standing there, she wondered.

What was his name again? Jacob? No... J- Judas! Yes, that's right. "What is it?" she demanded, pocketing her watch while keeping her steel gray eyes on the young soldier, who shuffled a foot in the snow under her piercing gaze.

"Why don't you join us?" the young soldier suggested. "It's warmer by the fire."

"I'm fine over here."

"I'm sure. But... being alone in the cold isn't a place for a lad-"

Sorina gave a soldier a look that stopped any more words for passing through his rotten teeth. Judas wilted under her gaze, as he should.

"I am not a 'lady,'" she said in a low voice. "And I am also not one of your comrades. So do not try to be friendly with me. As far as I'm concerned, we are simply business partners. I am the leader, and you are the subordinate."

She looked up at the men who were noticing the commotion. "Just like the rest of you," she told them. "Your friends, they died to find out whether or not the children are with the Black Hand, and our job now is to find them again. Now we know how they work, and we will slay them all and leave their bodies for the wolves. Then we will return to Goldendell with the Ice Walker as promised. As long as you lot do your job and keep your noses out of my business, then you will all return home to hot meals and beds warmed by your loved ones. Understand?"

"Yes, Ma'am."

Though there was no hesitation in the men's voices, she could tell they were still uneasy. Good. It wasn't their place to be comfortable around her. She was a Raven, an agent to the

Empire when they are merely soldiers made to carry out the will of their Lords and Ladies.

'Lady', pah! Sorina turned to Judas and sent him away. "Now go with your own lot, if you know what is good for you."

Judas gulped, bowed, and the pivoted almost all in one movement. The pathetic way he scrambled back to his buddies made Sorina's skin crawl.

Neither him, nor the rest of his group would make it out of these mountains alive. She had already decided this.

It was their fate, as pawns in the game.

The very next morning the Hunters drank coffee and ate the last of their meat scrapes. When the fire was snuffed out and the bones buried, they packed up and retrieved their hitched horses and rode as the sun rose in the sky, burning with it the very light of the Morning Star.

Morgan led the way beside Vladimir, leading the group to where he said some springs were located. The air was bitter and frosty, but the group stayed warm under their cloaks. Sabina in particular kept her hood up and tight around her head, trapping the heat on her cheeks before frost could coat them. Jacob tucked his jaw under his scarf, while Angela who had taken up the rear sat still and unfazed by the bitter cold.

The sun shone through the jaws of the mountain, setting all the snow on the trees ablaze in beautiful golden light, the meridian something only Kawn could behold. It made for a more enduring scene, despite the many faces still etched within the trunks still moaning at the Hunters. Charlotte had said nothing all day, not to Sabina, or anyone else. This both gladdened Sabina, for she hated small-talk while riding. But it also concerned her, for it was Charlotte who saw her standing over Jacob last night along with that sprite.

Not wanting to think about that, Sabina quickly snapped her attention forward, hoping not to draw any more attention to herself for the rest of the ride to the springs Morgan mentioned. It would be good, for Angela mostly, for she was still covered in the blue blood of the ogre. Thankfully, the gore didn't attract any more beasts for the night, but as they rode, Sabina was sure she heard wolves howling somewhere within the valley.

When they had finally come across the hot springs, it was no surprise to Morgan that some deer was eating grass near the warm waters, who immediately bolted at the sight of the Hunters. The springs themselves were concealed by thick juniper bushes and were fed underground. It made sense given the location of the mountains themselves and how they were made many centuries ago; perhaps one or even many of these high peaks in the range of Stonehollow were actually dormant volcanoes. As of now, the only volcano active on the Balkeñoirian continent was the one near Firedell. There was a possibility of others in the northern country, where the Empire hadn't dared to cross given the height and dangers of the Aldhill Forest.

Presently, at the springs, everyone decided to stop and wash. The children were okay Angela would need to at least rinse the ogre blood off her armor. The Dhampir surprisingly asked Sabina to join her; to keep watch and make sure none of the men got any ideas. Vladimir was appalled to the very thought, but Jacob looked away almost immediately. Sabina took a mental note on this as she agreed and joined Angela behind the bushes while the boys fed and watered the horses. Soon they would wash their faces in the warm waters of a nearby spring uncovered by the juniper, all the while Sabina kept a lookout while Angela washed her clothes.

Angela sat on her heels along the bank of the smallest pool. Her clothing under her armor had not been stained by the blood of the ogre, but it had saturated into her leather armor and cloak. The cloak had been easy to scrub out and she hung it above the pool to dry as she worked on the leather. Not all the blood would come out and she would have to scrap the armor, but it would still hold for the duration of this contract. When she was done the Dhampir held her breath and stuck her head into the spring, looking comical in Sabina's opinion before coming back up and squeezing the water from her hair which was tinged blue with the blood. She would do this a few more times until her hair while not being clean would no longer look like she had been doused in blue paint.

During this time, Sabina would steal glances at the Dhampir. Notice her strong figure, notice her side profile, and what little was left to the imagination when it came to what was under her clothes. She had no doubt that any man or woman would find the Dhampir attractive, and Sabina knew that if Angela had not been tamed, she would no doubt use that advantage to capture her prey.

Tamed, she thought bitterly. *As if she were a wild dog.*

If one were to ask Sabina what she thought of Angela before she had left for Irondell with Jacob, Sabina would have said that she was really just that; a tamed beast fit to do the bidding of the Fallen Star. But after Irondell, after seeing how Angela came and went between contracts to check on Jacob, how the two had been close, Sabina didn't think of it as some sort of possession as most vampiric beings were capable of. She knew what men were like when they were bewitched by a Vampire, and Jacob didn't have that look on him. Because of this, she had been hesitant to assist in Vladimir, but it did not stop her for her prejudice was still strong against Angela. Regardless of how she currently felt about Angela as a person, it didn't dismiss the fact that she wasn't human, not entirely.

Then why does she care for herself like one? she thought as Angela strained the last bit of blood out of her hair. *Also, why is she nervous about Jacob or Vladimir peeking in on her? It's not like she's taking a bath.*

"Thank you," Angela suddenly said, her voice breaking through the steam created by the pool that now swallowed her.

"For what?" Sabina said trying to get her head back on straight.

"For keeping watch," the Dhampir replied closing her eyes, really letting the steam take her away it seemed. "I appreciate it. I don't like it when people- primarily men watch me."

"I, uh... I think that is actually quite common for women."

"Not all."

"Yeah, I suppose that's true."

"Still, thanks."

"Of course," Sabina's eyes softened upon Angela's face. Despite not being human, Angela acted just like any other person. Her eyes hardened however, when Angela yawned, displaying two elongated canines that gleamed in the sunlight.

Deciding to set that sudden internal outrage aside for the moment, Sabina decided to ask something that was on her mind, particularly what she had noted before entering the springs with Angela.

"May I ask you something?"

"You may," Angela said as she inspected her drying armor. She had already slipped on her bracers and was now working on fitting the torso pieces across her back and shoulders.

"Did, er… something happen between you and Jacob? I mean, when you said you didn't want any men watching, he kinda…"

Angela opened her eyes and stared directly at Sabina. For a second, the Huntress felt as if cold hands had suddenly seized her throat, preventing her from saying anything more.

"No," Angela said sternly and almost too suddenly. "Nothing happened."

"R-right." Sabina raised a hand in apology. "I didn't mean any disrespect."

"Understood." Angela went back to work strapping on her armor.

Sabina peeled her gaze away, and settled her eyes on the pile of weapons near the drying cloak. Her gun, crossbow and sword laid apart from her belt, and having removed the sword from its scabbard to wash it as well, Angela had left it gleaming in the sunlight. The strange hand-and-a-half weapon appeared heavy, despite having sharpened teeth along the edge opposite of the sharpened side of the sword. The pommel with the décor of a snarling wolf, seemed to growl at Sabina as she stared.

"That sword," Sabina said wanting to break the silence that had settled between her and the Dhampir. "Where was it made?"

Angela's nose twitched, as the Huntress tried to remember. "A blacksmith down in Mistendell. I was doing a job back when I first became a Huntress, and part of reward was that weapon. It once belonged to an Immortal, who had passed the sword along to the blacksmith when she left the village and disappeared into the Deepland Barrens forever."

"Why did the Immortal give her weapon to a regular blacksmith? A human?" Sabina wondered aloud.

"The man said he didn't know," Angela said. "But on my way out, he noticed that my sword was rusted and on the verge of shattering. So he offered that sword there, after conducting repairs to the silver metal and re-forge it into the type of blade I wanted."

"That was nice of him," Sabina wondered how that conversation must have gone. She had a feeling there was more to the story, but by the look on Angela's face as she began to quickly gather her things, Sabina decided to ask something else.

"What is the sword's name?"

To name a weapon was to have a bond with it. You could have many swords, guns and bows, but if you had one sword to serve you for as long as you served the realm, then you had to name it. It was practically an unspoken tradition. If you took it from a fallen enemy, you had the choice to either change the name or keep it for the sake of its original owner. Sabina's own sword was named Cezanne, the name of freedom; representing her own freedom from the world she longed to escape. It had been a gift, from Matei. She had heard every name given to a weapon, from every woman's name to mere lines of poetry. She was curious as to what the Dhampir named her own weapon.

Angela was silent, only breathing it seemed for a long while. When she did speak her sword's name, her tone was hollow, as if the name itself brought back terrible memories.

"Its name is Riçana."

She then proceeded to fasten her belt and scabbard onto her person. She holstered her guns and her sword, and then took the still-damp cloak off the juniper bough and hooked it around her throat.

The task done, Angela pulled up her hood and told Sabina that she was good to go and the two ventured back out to join the men and children who had not moved from their spot. After making sure their horses were watered, they started down the road again, Sabina stealing numerous glances again and again at the Dhampir as they rode.

As she did, her eye would sometimes catch Vladimir staring back at her. The Werewolf Hunter always gave her a peculiar look with a raised eyebrow. His question obvious and driving dread into Sabina's heart. She shook her head however, telling him that she didn't see anything. She didn't have a chance.

No, Angela had said when Sabina had inquired about if something had happened between her and Jacob personally. *Nothing happened.*

She had been defensive, there was no doubt about that. But why did it sound to Sabina that Angela had been answering more than just her own question?

She was thinking too much on it, that was all.

When a Vampire claimed a person, when they didn't allow that person to transform into a Dearg or Disciple, eight out of ten times it is for a fresh supply of food. Some Immortals especially would keep people prisoner for months, slowly draining them of their life until they became nothing more than bloodless corpses, doomed to reawaken as what is called a Baptized Immortal. The other two times is because they love the person; the enhanced emotion and pride of an Immortal succumbing to the tenderness one would share with a lover. Neither Jacob looked as if he was being drained over the course of time of healing after the events of Irondell, nor did Angela seem to care for him in an emotional way. There was no deceit that Sabina could detect and even that aside, Jacob was as healthy as a horse. Sure, one could argue that as a Dhampir, perhaps Angela didn't need to feed as often as an Immortal or a Dearg.

But Sabina didn't quite believe that. Or she couldn't bring herself to believe that, anyway.

That in it of itself, made it difficult for Sabina to want to carry on with Vladimir's request and assist in exposing whatever secrets the Dhampir had. She highly doubted that she would find anything, but even if she did, Sabina couldn't help but think, 'so what?'

This confliction made her physically ill, and she needed time to think as they continued to ride through the harrowing forest.

La

The group eventually came across what looked to be an abandoned cabin resting beneath a tall birch tree. The roof had caved in and the snow had filled it in. The picket fence was rotted out and even smashed in some areas like the windows of the cabin; even the door was hanging on its hinges.

The most unsettling part however, was an overhead sign that stood where the walkway had once been. Two large poles of wood held up a weather-stained sign That was warped and the letters faded and illegible. But the Hunters weren't paying attention to whatever message of the past the sign said, but what instead *hung* from the sign. For dangling just beneath it, was a rope tied into a gallows loop. The rope itself was frayed and looked to be on the verge of falling apart. The fact that it hung there, sent a clear message: keep out.

"Shit…" Jacob groaned his eye staring at the loop. All the Hunters agreed, and decided that it was best to keep going.

Before they could keep going however, Angela suddenly stopped her horse, forcing Jacob to nearly bump into her from behind. Sabina slowed down her horse as did everyone else, who stared at the Dhampir who was now looking around swiftly, her purple eyes glowing bright as she did so.

"What is it?" Vladimir demanded clearly annoyed that they had stopped so suddenly. "Why are we stopping?"

Angela turned her head to the left, to the right. She turned all the way around, her eyes burning through the forest it seemed, as if she was looking- no, more like listening for something.

Vladimir willed his horse to move towards the Dhampir, and upon moving alongside her, he grabbed ahold of her shoulder. "What is it?"

Jacob blanched. "Don't-"

But it was too late. Quick as a flash, too fast for even Sabina to register in the moment, Angela whirled around and upon grabbing Vladimir by the hood, the Dhampir hurled the Hunter right off his horse. He fell into the snow opposite of his own horse who neighed at the sudden loss of weight on its back. With his head in the snow and ass in the air, Vladimir grumbled in the snow while everyone merely stared at Angela, who was snarling at the Hunter.

"Don't ever touch me again," Angela hissed as Vladimir pulled his head up out of the snow.

He glared at the Huntress as he pulled himself to his feet, his hand on one of his pistols. "You bitch," he sneered. "Who the hell do you-"

"Woah, woah!" Jacob said, spurring his horse forward and causing Vladimir's to move while at the same time getting between the man in question and Angela. "Vladimir, easy."

Vladimir glared at Jacob. "No. That mongrel threw me off!"

Sabina said, "Take it easy, I'm sure-"

"I don't want to be touched," Angela said, having spurred forward so that she could see Vladimir clearly. Her eyes were hard, her expression stonier. "Ever."

Vladimir started for her. "Listen you, I can do whatever-"

Jacob made his horse trot back, blocking him again. The two men stared at one another, Jacob staring down and Vladimir up. The children looked uncomfortable, and Sabina was just dawning on what was going on.

"Back off," said Jacob.

"Jacob, get out of the way."

"No."

Vladimir looked back at Sabina, as if asking if she believed what was going on here. Then he turned back to Jacob and started to say something when Sabina spoke up.

"Vladimir, Angela didn't mean to hurt you."

He stared at her, dumbfounded. "'Didn't mean to?' That *thing* nearly broke my goddamn neck!"

With Vladimir's outrage directed at Sabina, Jacob turned to look back at Angela who appeared to calm down now. "You okay?"

"Move."

Jacob spurred his horse forward, clearing the way between Angela and Vladimir. When Vladimir saw that his path was cleared he glowered at Angela.

"I'm sorry," she told him. "But please, don't touch me again."

Vladimir looked between her and Jacob and then sneered. "Whatever. That goes double for you."

"Fine."

"Angela," said Sabina trying to change the subject and get moving again. "What was it you heard?"

"There's something out there," Angela said looking past them all towards the direction they came from. "Something has been following us, keeping their distance. I thought I smelled something... different. Listen. It's too quiet."

"The whole bloody forest is quiet," Vladimir hissed. "That means nothing. Are you sure you're not just smelling one of us? None of us got the pleasure of-"

"Quiet," Jacob said removing his bow from behind his back. "I just saw something move out there."

Angela immediately snapped her eyes towards the direction Jacob was looking. She reached up and placed a hand around the hilt of her sword, watching and listening again. This time, Vladimir didn't question as he turned towards the forest that continued to silently moan at its visitors, both of his hands on his revolvers as all Hunters stood frozen, listening, and waiting.

Sabina felt her heart begin to slam in her chest. If another ogre or a pack of trolls came after them, they would be in trouble. She looked beyond the trunks of face-riddled trees, looking for anything that looked like it didn't belong.

And then, she saw it. The flash of a muzzle, followed by the crack of a rifle, and Jacob flying off his horse as more gunshots erupted from the depths of the forest they had left behind.

"Get down!" Vladimir shouted as he rolled off his horse and struck the ground. Everyone did the same, even Morgan and Charlotte who took cover behind a nearby log as all the Hunters took cover and commanded their horses to flee. Midnight was wounded in the right flank as he thundered through the trees that had begun to splinter as more shots sailed over the Black Hands heads.

Angela was crawling prone across the snowy road and taking cover behind a tree just as where she had been peppered with shots sending up little plumes of powder and dirt. She unsheathed her sword and drew her pistol. She was looking across the road towards Jacob and Sabina who had drawn their own weaponry, Jacob looking as if he were in the wrong timeline altogether when ready with his bow as opposed to Sabina's rifle. Sabina took aim around the tree they were taking cover behind and fired off a shot. Jacob locked eyes with Angela and the Dhampir nodded and he returned the response, his face set and his mind ready.

Angela stood, still keeping her back against the tree and she closed her eyes. When she opened them again, Jacob as well as Vladimir who had been watching Angela rise, saw that her eyes had brightened considerably. She stepped out from behind the tree and into the road, and with one swing, sliced an incoming projectile in half from behind. She had spun about and caught the bullet which screamed as lead was split by silver, and the two pieces fell somewhere past her lost in the confusion. She was staring in the direction the group had previously been traveling and now Jacob and Vladimir were looking and they could see more muzzle flashes hidden among the trees.

It was an ambush. "Behind us!" Vladimir shouted as he fired his revolver into the trees and rolling away as more shots came from either direction. Men were moving in on them, realizing they had the Hunters closed in and they just had to push in and crush their enemies.

"Goldendell!" Sabina called out as Angela twisted and turned away as she was shot at again. She had raised her pistol and fired, and likewise the Hunters returned fire towards their adversaries while the children kept under cover, Morgan in particular clutching his pistol tightly with both hands, ready to fight should he be forced to act.

Jacob nocked an arrow and loosed it down the road the group had come up from. He heard a yelp and a man stumbled out from behind one of the trees with an arrow in his neck. He choked and blood spilled until he dropped to his knees. Sure enough, on the man's leather armor was the golden eagle sigil of the Empire. Jacob pulled his head back as someone poked out from behind a tree and shot at him, the place where his head had been splintering with bark fragments. He nocked another and loosed it, smiling as it sunk right through the man's right eye.

Vladimir sprinted towards the cabin's picket fencing and dove for it as he was shot at from the left. Drawing his second revolver, he fired twice at the closest soldier who jerked and twisted as his rifle rose up and fired blindly into the sky. He dropped like a sack of laundry and his buddies were inching out of the woodwork. Vladimir was in the midst of reloading when one soldier was shot, collapsing against a nearby tree and leaving a gory smear. He didn't know who took the shot and didn't care. By then his speed-loaders were ejected and stocked into his revolvers and he was firing again, the smoke from his guns as well as the others clogging the otherwise clean air of the forest with the stench of cordite.

He swore when he heard the sound of barking dogs and he saw Jacob taking aim and shooting one of the soldier's war dogs with an arrow. One got close and he was forced to draw his pistol and shoot it. The schäferhund staggered for a bit but the second shot went through it's left eye and it collapsed to the ground twitching and bleeding. Jacob almost got shot during this endeavor but the rookie despite his time off since Irondell was quick and responsive; definitely not a rookie anymore.

While Vladimir was thinking this, he heard a distinct wet sound coming in close from behind. He had been stalked by werewolves and dealt with wild dogs and wolves to know what that sound was. He turned around fast and the schäferhund had already lunged, bearing it's strong teeth. Vladimir dropped his pistol closest to the dog and balled his fist and held it out as if expecting a fist bump. The jaws of the dog closed over his hand which sunk deep into the flesh and he swore as the dog jerked and twisted it's head. He shoved his fist further into the dog's mouth and down it's throat, locking it's jaws open and preventing it from biting again. He had to step down on the dog's hind leg to pin it and force it to stop thrashing. He shoved the barrel of his revolver against the dog's head and shot it. Brain matter erupted from the opposite side and with the dog dead the jaws were still locked on tight and he had to pry the dog off before he could properly fight again. He cringed with every shot taken with his right hand as his knuckles and wrist continued to bleed profusely.

Sabina rushed for the nearest tree and took cover just as bark splintered past her, a hole now present in one of the faces sticking out of the wood. Being so close to these cursed trees made Sabina's skin crawl, but it was better than getting herself shot. Clutching her rifle tightly, she took a peek out and immediately aimed down the length of the barrel and fired two shots at a group of men coming in from the side. The ones on the road were being taken care of by Vlad and Jacob, who fired bullet after bullet and arrow after arrow to keep the men from advancing on them too much. She saw Angela taking cover behind another tree, her sword still out as she reloaded her revolver. The Dhampir looked at Sabina and made a gesture towards the men, telling her to provide cover while she moved in. Sabina nodded, and then following Angela's fingers indicating the countdown, she emerged from cover on zero and fired at the men who were now drawing closer so that Angela could charge in.

The Dhampir rushed in like a wolf among sheep. She leapt off one of the trees and fired her revolver, hitting the eye of one of the soldiers she vaulted over before stabbing down into another. The third screamed and tried to shoot at Angela but the Dhampir lunged forward, slipping beneath the line of fire and in one quick slash from groin to right shoulder, she cleaved the man entirely in half, armor and all. Sabina watched in horror as the two halves staggered and hopped almost comically before collapsing into the snow, staining the haunted forest in red. Angela lunged through these halves and ran her sword through the fourth, her serrated blade sawing through flesh and bone as she wrenched it free and became clotted with gore as the man collapsed dying and clutching at his ruined middle.

Another soldier emerged from the wood with a rifle aimed at Angela, and Sabina took aim and fired her own. The man's head erupted like a splintering pot full of cherry syrup and the gore sprayed across the faces of a nearby tree which all seemed to scream in protest. Quickly reloading her rifle, Sabina turned to see more men moving in from down the road towards Jacob and Vladimir. The two men had split up, both shooting at the soldiers from different areas to add to the confusion. Vladimir bounded behind the decrepit cabin, firing his two revolvers again and again and falling men in mists of crimson. One soldier emerged from one of the trees shouting while swinging a sword at the Werewolf Hunter who ducked and then shot the man right beneath the jaw. The top of the soldier's head blew off like a beaker in a laboratory.

Sabina turned, seeing more men moving in rifles raised. She had not heard them coming and was twisting and falling back into the snow. Before she struck the ground however, a blur of motion brushed past the three soldiers and their heads flew from their necks as Angela landed close by. All collapsed with their heads expressing surprise as their blood became soaked into the snow.

Sabina landed on her back and spotting another head poking out from behind another tree she took aim and fired with little preparation. The man jerked back as a surge of blood arced through the air. Angela was upon her now, taking Sabina's hand and hauling her to her feet. Then she turned and charged at two others who had come in from the left and took cover behind some rocks. There was one more soldier coming up from behind and Sabina took cover behind yet another multifaceted tree- there seemed to be no limit to them, firing blindly and forcing the two soldiers to take cover again. The moment they peeked around their trees she shot them, using her last two shots to bring the final man down. She had just begun to reload her rifle so she could help the others when she felt something prick against the side of her neck. She froze upon the touch of a blade, and the sight of a tin beak peeked from her peripheral vision.

"Don't move," the Raven hissed in her ear. It was feminine, and dead serious. Sabina dropped her weapon, and allowed her captor to lead her out into the open where Angela had just gutted another soldier. The Dhampir turned to Sabina covered in blood that wasn't her own, and her expression didn't change as the Raven led her out, the dagger pressed firmly against her neck and her other hand pushing Sabina from behind.

"You're making a mistake," Sabina warned the Raven with her hands raised.

Ignoring her, the Raven acknowledged the Huntress now in front of her. "You there, Dhampir, drop your weapon."

"Sabina!" Vladimir's voice shouted somewhere in the forest, almost drowned out by the constant gunfire as he and Jacob continued to do battle.

Angela never took her eyes off of Sabina's captor. She studied the brown eyes piercing her from behind the tin mask. Trying her best to buy some time at least, Angela dropped her sword as well as her revolver. Now she was weaponless, but she still had her throwing knives on her boots or the blunderbuss still hooked at her belt.

"Smart woman," Raven hissed although she did not relax her body nor her blade still pressed against Sabina's throat. "*If* you can even be called that."

Angela contemplated her options, annoyed that her prediction hadn't included this.

The Raven still had Sabina by the throat, the dagger drawing blood across her jugular. Vladimir and Jacob were still holding off the remaining soldiers, their guns and Jacob's bow sounding somewhere distant. She heard the groan of a door being opened and then immediately being closed, and she determined that Morgan and Charlotte had taken refuge inside the deserted cabin away from the firefight. Good. At least they were safe. Jacob might be injured, but between him and Vladimir, they'd be able to hold off the soldiers still coming in. They'd be okay.

But Sabina… she was the primary concern, and the way the Raven held her tightly, her eyes now hidden by her hood and beaked tin mask, and her feathered cloak ruffling as she shifted her arm, drawing more blood from the Vampire Huntress' throat. Without her sword, Angela would have to resort to speed and accuracy, should the Raven go through with her threat.

"Tell your monster to back away," the Raven snarled into Sabina's ear.

Sabina said nothing at first, only stared back at Angela, her eyes hard and unrelenting. Angela didn't move either. When the Raven gave her command again, Sabina said, "Tell her yourself."

"Don't fuck with me," the Raven demanded. "Tell your monster to back down- *Now*."

Angela regarded the woman with cold eyes. "Release her."

The Raven sneered. "You, back off, *now*."

"If you hurt her," Angela said in a low voice. "You won't make it off this mountain alive."

The Raven chuckled. A nervous chuckle, Angela could tell even if she couldn't smell the woman's fear. "You think I'm afraid of you, Dhampir?"

"If you aren't afraid, then release her," Angela hissed. "Then we will see how brave you really are, Raven."

"Like what you did to poor little Virgil?" the Raven said which caught Angela off guard at the mention of the dead Raven. Now the Raven sounded brave alright, brave and now conceited.

"Yeah, I know who you are. You're the biggest news back at Goldendell; didn't you know? Every Raven in Balkeñoir knows what happened to Irondell, we all know about you, Dhampir."

"Then you know what I'm capable of."

"Yes, and I know that the moment that I let your master go or slit her throat, you'll just attack me like a savage dog. But... you're clearly capable of reason."

Angela said nothing, much to Sabina's surprise despite her predicament.

"So, I'll make you a deal," the Raven continued. "I don't need the Black Hand. I'm not here for any of you. Let me back off and take the children; they are of no use or concern of yours. I'll take them and leave your master behind the moment I mount my horse. You can take the rest of your buddies and kill off the rest of my men- if you can."

"You goddamned coward..." Sabina hissed despite the dagger never moving any further from her neck. "You'd sacrifice your own men?"

"They're not *my* men," the Raven chuckled. "I serve the Ravens, not the Empire. Though we might have a contract, they are nothing but sniveling lumps of meat in my eyes. All that matters is that I get those children back where they belong. Now, what say you, Dhampir? Do we have an accord? I'll just keep my hands on her until I have the brats, and then we'll all be done."

"As I said," Angela said now taking a daring step towards the Raven and Sabina. The Raven trembled but otherwise did not step back. "You kill her, and you'll join her in the afterworld; wherever that may be for the likes of you devil-worshippers."

"S-Stay back!" the Raven said grabbing Sabina all the tighter, trying it seemed to melt into Sabina's back. "I'm warning you, Dhampir!"

"*I'd* rather not die at all," Sabina grinned clicking the heels of her boots together, and Angela was surprised to see a small knife shoot out from the back of the heel before Sabina brought her leg back and up like a horse about to kick. The knife plunged into the groin of the Raven, and the woman cried out in surprise and pain as Sabina wrenched her foot free upon her release as the Raven doubled over, blood oozing from her clutched hand which cupped the area between her legs. Sabina then spun about and round-house kicked at the woman's in the head. The Raven was quick though despite her immediate danger, and she rolled away drawing her revolver and shooting at Sabina who dove for the ground. In the same instance, Angela lunged, scooping up her sword and drawing her blunderbuss in the process. Upon firing it, the Raven spun away as one of the heads on the trunk exploded into splinters, but Angela was already upon her, swinging her sword ready to cleave the Raven in two.

Clang!

For the first time in many years, Angela was utterly surprised at what beheld her. Despite the bleeding from her groin and how fast the Dhampir had come upon her, the Raven had been able to draw her sword and not only block the attack, but *hold* it as well. The two held each other at sword's length, their arms trembling against each other's strength. Despite keeping a straight face, Angela stared at the Raven's mask in complete shock.

"He-he," the Raven chuckled with some effort. "You almost got me there…"

The Raven twitched and she spun away and deflected Angela's sword aside just as Sabina had drawn another revolver and shot at her. The Raven leapt back and sidestepped away from every bullet until Sabina had used up all of her shots. The Raven tensed her legs, ready to lunge for her but Angela stepped in her way, her feet planted between Sabina and the strange Raven in front of her. She caught the Raven's blade in the teeth of her own and bending her arm and twisting in, she punched at the Raven, causing the woman to stumble back but appear unharmed- another rare phenomenon in Angela's experience when the woman's chest didn't appear caved in.

"Get the kids," Angela told Sabina who was getting up behind her. "Get them away from here, *now*."

By the lack of movement behind her, Angela determined that Sabina wanted to argue, and hesitated running. But eventually, she heard the sound of snow getting crushed underfoot as the Huntress rushed towards the cabin. As long as Vlad and Jacob could hold the remaining soldiers and their dogs back, Angela herself could focus on the Raven who now held a hand over her bleeding crotch.

"Bitch got me good," she hissed. "Just a scratch though, you know what I mean?" She removed her hand, appearing not to be too wounded by it.

"What are you?" Angela demanded, uninterested in her wellbeing.

The Raven chuckled, and brought her sword up to point it at the Dhampir. "Wouldn't you like to know?"

Angela tossed her blunderbuss aside, placing both hands on her own sword. Trying her best to sniff out whatever creature this Raven was, she decided to try to gain whatever information she could before attacking or being attacked. Bide her time, estimate what she was dealing with.

"What do you want with the kids?"

The Raven chuckled. "I don't care about the boy, but I want the girl."

"Why do the Ravens want her?"

"Who gives a shit?" the Raven charged forward, sword swinging and rushing towards the Huntress.

Angela angled her sword so that the teeth in her blade would catch the sword and hold it there. Then spinning and causing the Raven's arm to slacken, Angela planted a heavy kick into the woman's chest, sending her flying right into a nearby tree with a sickening but satisfying *crack*. Such a blow should have shattered her ribs; crushed her entrails or even ruptured her spine. But the Raven rolled back into a standing position, seeming unfazed by the kick. Not only that, but she stopped bleeding entirely.

A regenerator? Angela wondered as she kicked the Raven's sword aside; it had fallen from the Raven's grasp when she had been kicked.

"Heh, is that all you got?" demanded the Raven. "This is the monster of the Black Hand? *This* is what bested Virgil?"

Reaching within the confines of her feathered cloak, the agent of the Empire removed two more short swords which she spun in her hands dramatically. The mark of Yohnah had been branded on the flat of each blade, as the Raven took a stance while crossing the two swords into an 'x'. The sight of the swords, puzzled Angela, considering the god the Ravens are known to worship.

"I'm taking those kids," said the Raven. "You will not stop me, I can see that now."

"Turn back, now," said Angela. "And you may live."

"No. No, you she-demon, I *won't* turn back. That child, do you even understand what she is? Do you realize just *what* you are escorting into these accursed peaks?"

"I know exactly what she is," Angela said. "I'm more curious to know what exactly the Empire wants with her."

"Like I said, 'who gives a shit'? I have my own agenda: she needs to die as does everyone who sees her on this mountain."

"If you want her so bad," Angela said getting into a stance. "Then go, get her. But consider that your final warning. Because I'll make sure you never make it to the cabin alive."

The Raven chuckled and then shifted her elbow. Angela watched as a glass vial of yellow liquid slipped out of her sleeve and crash onto a nearby rock. A pungent odor then struck Angela's nose and she hissed at the scent.

"You're mad," she said, her nose wrinkled and her fangs bared.

The Raven shrugged before charging in at the Dhampir. "We'll just have to wait and see, won't we!?"

And the two clashed with a thunder of swords as Angela heard the distant bellowing of trolls somewhere in the valley of damned trees.

Jacob had been startled by a soldier who managed to get in close to him. The man's rifle had a bayonet attached to it and would have run Jacob through if the Hunter hadn't been quick enough. He slipped past the deadly blade and got a dagger out of his belt in the same motion, plunging it into the man's neck. He twisted the blade, ripping open the wound and causing a thick rope of blood to spray his front as he let the man stumble to the ground choking to death.

Sabina had taken up a position within the doorway of the cabin while Vladimir provided cover. He was still bleeding from the dog bite but was otherwise all right as Sabina slipped inside the cabin. As she did so, another soldier came out from around the corner behind Vladimir. Jacob made quick work of him with an arrow that went right through the temple.

Despite being shot in the shoulder, Jacob was still able to pull his string all the way back, and the pain no longer bothered him as he saw that there were only a few soldiers left.

He would bind the wound best he could when this was all over; he didn't want to have to use his Mark on this trip, not after using it too many times back in Irondell.

A loud roar then echoed throughout the valley, followed by a couple more joining the first. Everyone ceased firing to listen to the sound. The sound then stopped, and the forest seemed to have frozen, save for the clashing of swords somewhere in the background.

Jacob then felt the ground tremble beneath him. A light pulsation that gradually grew and quickened in rhythm. He looked over to Vladimir who seemed to have notice as well, his sword dripping with blood as the bodies around him remained still as the forest continued to rumble with the strange sounds. As the sound got louder, Jacob realized that the thumping, were footsteps of a great many- many that were large and rushing straight for them.

"Take cover!" one of the soldiers shouted just as something crashed right through a cluster of trees and with a mighty hand that was thick and calloused, struck the soldier and sent him flying through the air, his armor falling apart from the blow. The creature which now stood among the panicking soldiers was massive, just about as a young Nephil, with massive shoulders covered in thick white fur, and a large snout that stuck out past its primate face. In its hand it held a rusty battle axe and with it the beast sliced two men in half just as two more trolls emerged from the thicket, all carrying makeshift clubs and rope for netting.

"Get the halflings!" the berserker bellowed with a maw of jagged teeth. Immediately, his two brethren joined in on the fight, wielding their makeshift weaponry. Jacob watched in awe as the one with the club smashed it down upon a soldier, reducing him into a gory smear across the ground.

"The smell's thataway!" the troll the growled pointing his bloody club towards Angela and the Raven who appeared to be putting up a fight.

"Let's get these morsels first!" the berserker growled running one guy down who managed to get only one shot into the troll who dropped his terrible axe and seized him in both large hands. The man screamed until the troll opened it's gigantic maw and chomped down hard on the man's head.

"Get out of there!" Vladimir shouted to Sabina who was coming out with the children. "All of you, go! Run!"

Jacob didn't need to be told twice as he took off running towards Sabina, helping her snatch up Charlotte as Morgan ran alongside them. Vladimir kept close behind, reloading his weapons as the trolls decimated the remaining soldiers. There was little hope for the remaining men and dogs; it was a massacre. Men screamed and dogs whined as they were smashed underfoot, picked up and violently pulled apart like maple candy. One man was screaming for help as he was lifted up by one leg and brought crashing down on his head as if he were a landed fish. The berserker who led the trolls then turned its ugly head towards the fleeing Hunters, his terrible grin salivating a disgusting pink at the thought of human meat.

As they ran, Jacob looked towards Angela, seeing that she was still having trouble against the Raven. The two moved way too quickly to keep track of who was really winning, and even then he could see that the Raven maneuvered with such grace and speed as the Dhampir, which worried him, as he believed there was no one as fast as her- no one who was human, at least.

"Keep going," he told Sabina and he crouched down and nocked an arrow. A normal archer and perhaps most riflemen may not be confident given the distance, but not Jacob.

He took aim at the two, trying to see a pattern in their movements; where their feet would go. The Raven was taking most of the offensive against Angela, whereas Angela only attacked when she saw even the smallest of an opening. Even then it wasn't enough for the Raven was just too fast and too skilled with her two swords to slip up. He watched as the Raven swung at Angela with one sword and began to lunge forward with the other. Jacob's eye then caught where her foot was just about to land and he released his arrow, just as Vladimir grabbed him and told him to keep running.

He watched as his arrow went right through the left knee of the Raven, and a terrible cry escaped her lips before she began to crumble right before Angela. The Dhampir planted a heavy kick into the woman's chest, sending her flying back and smacking right into a nearby tree, close to one of the trolls who happened to notice her fall. Without looking back, Angela took off running in the same direction as the rest of the group, catching up swiftly and with minimal effort.

They managed to find three of the horses and after hoisting Charlotte up, Jacob took a seat behind her as Sabina helped Morgan onto the one she grabbed. Vladimir waited for Angela, but the Dhampir shook her head.

"Just go," she told them. "I'll keep up."

Without arguing, Vladimir mounted his horse and after spurring the beast forward, everyone took off riding down the road once again, with Angela keeping up with the horse with her long and powerful legs. It amazed Jacob, just how fast the Dhampir could run; especially compared to that of a galloping horse.

"Behind us!" Morgan shouted pointing past Sabina.

Jacob turned and sure enough two of the trolls were chasing after them. Even with their large hulking bodies, they tore across the landscape as they chased after the group, snarling and calling out to them to slow down.

"We just wanna show you something!" one barked stupidly.

"Yeah, something cool!" barked the other.

Vladimir and Sabina were already shooting at the trolls, who growled and barked as bullets bit into their skin. One eventually did fall, when a bullet pierced through its massive black eye, killing him instantly. Still, the last one didn't slow down in pace, neither letting his dead comrade slow him down or allow the rest of their prey to get away.

Jacob began to wonder what more they could do, when Charlotte began to tug on the front of his armor. He looked at the girl, who nodded toward Angela with those inhuman piercing blue eyes.

"The snow," she said to Jacob. "Let me touch the snow."

Jacob was about to ask why when he saw Angela immediately snap her attention towards the young girl. She looked back behind them, and then looked towards Jacob and Charlotte.

"Come to me!" she then said while reaching out to Charlotte.

Jacob hoisted the girl up and tossed her to the Dhampir. Sabina shouted out at him but he knew that Angela had her. Upon catching the girl, Angela stopped in her tracks and helped Charlotte down to her feet. The group kept on riding but watched as the last troll cackled with glee as he came upon the two who decided to stop.

"Yummy, sweet woman meat!" it barked.

Jacob watched Charlotte place her hands into the snow, and upon touching the blanket of white he felt a surge of energy even from the distance he was at. It was as if all the snow around him had suddenly turned to water, gathering into a great wave ready to crash down upon him and everyone else. Everyone stalled their horses and watched in awe as the snow around Angela and Charlotte began to rise up like sprouts, reaching up towards the sky and crystalizing into floating icicles. When the troll came closer, the wind suddenly changed with the violent ferocity of a storm breaking free of its bonds at sea. Snow and ice rushed at the troll with so much force that it was blown back off the road, most of it's body haven been ripped to shreds by the shards of ice which sliced through flesh like hot knives through butter. The troll was dead before it even struck the ground and became completely blanketed with snow. Other than perhaps a slowly growing spread of crimson in the snow, there was no sign of the beast.

"Go, go!" Angela loudly commanded them, and spurring their horses, the group took off back down the road away from the carnage; not wanting to draw the attention of the third troll who was no doubt pillaging the dead. Just because they had managed to kill two doesn't mean the other wouldn't give up. A berserker such as that one would prove to be a more formidable foe; best to leave it to enjoy the easier pickings.

Angela then whistled and a few minutes later her own sleek black horse emerged from the white thicket and jumping up she nimbly landed on the back of the horse before gently placing Charlotte in front of her. With all horses and people accounted for, they rode. They rode and rode as far away as they could wanting to create as much distance between them and the troll's rampage as possible.

Even as they rode, even as they rode far enough away by now, every so often, the piercing scream of a man who had been discovered and no doubt being ripped apart could be heard all throughout the valley. The trees of the condemned spirits all screamed their own silent responses, as if in mockery.

In the sky, hiding against the face of the mountains as the mouth of the valley began to cast a great shadow across the forest due to the sun dipping beneath the horizon, Carmilla had watched from her broomstick the conflict between the Hunters and the trolls. The soldiers of the Empire had been decimated in a matter of minutes, but the group of Hunters had escaped-thanks to that one girl, that one child who appeared to have made the snow rise. It puzzled the witch, and greatly coaxed her interest greatly.

Could she be...

Carmilla watched as the whole valley was slowly becoming painted in shadow. It was still late afternoon and the sun still shone overhead, but the mouth of the mountain would not let any more light come in than just a dim reflection against its snowy peaks. It would be at this time, when her children went out to hunt their prey. But still, after watching the group, Carmilla wondered if she should stay close to help them.

Not only that, but that girl... could she be-

"An Ice Walker?" Carmilla hissed past her rotten teeth. If she was- then that had to mean that she was the last Ice Walker in the entire country- if not the entire world. The children had left the mountains long ago, that much Carmilla remembered. But to return- and to reveal herself as such... was the curse of the lake still alive? Was the curse... was the curse still there, after all these years? Was she, the goddess in human flesh- the bane of the sun? Carmilla didn't know the answer to this.

But the thought of the possibilities sent shivers down her spine, and made her grin from ear to ear. She wanted those Hunters- she wanted them all for her and her children.

But more importantly, that little girl... she wanted her. She wanted the Ice Walker.

Te

During that same afternoon, Matei had been summoned to meet with Velinar back at Shadowfort Castle. He had been instructed to grab his gear, and he groaned all the way down to the meeting hall at just where he would have to go at this ungodly hour.

He had slept most of the day away, having gone to bed immediately after seeing Sabina off. Without her to help warm their sheets, his room was cold. Nevertheless he was so exhausted that he slept the whole day away, and it even took the possessed armor set a good long while to wake him up from his slumber. As he slinked down to the Great Hall, he wondered how Sabina was doing as well as the rest of the group up in the nether of the Stonehollow Mountains. He also wondered how Angela was doing; being a Dhampir among humans and all, but this concern was minor compared to his worry about his lover and the rest of the guild- even Jacob Tepes.

He finally arrived in the Great Hall, paying no heed to the suits of armor standing guard or their Hellhound companions. He saw that Velinar was sitting on one of the tables, talking to Dr. Jecklyn who was smoking a cigar. There was no sign of the Ghoul butler at the bar, nor the maids who would normally be cleaning at this hour. The two suddenly hushed as Matei came to them, and the Hunter bowed his head to Velinar.

"You summoned me, My Lord?" he asked as he brought his head back up.

Velinar nodded, smiling softly. "Are you rested?"

"I'm awake," Matei answered. "Is there a contract?" He suspected this to happen. With all the other Hunters still on jobs or off in the mountains with those kids, and 'Bram and Adriana mending the wards around Shadowfort, he was the only one here at the castle. He figured that if any contracts came up, he would be the first to know. He just didn't expect it to happen immediately after a single day, especially given how vehement his master had been about no one Hunting alone anymore.

"Good," said Doctor Jecklyn, shifting in his spot and tapping some ashes into a ceramic tray. "We hate to call you at this hour, but it's important."

"It's not a contract either," said Velinar hoarsely. "It's something for the Black Hand."

"Okay," Matei said slightly curious now. He wondered just what the deity of death might want for the Black Hand. Such jobs were only offered to the oldest in the guild; being Vladimir or even 'Bram. It would have been Luca as well this year, but unfortunately...

"It is about those two children." Velinar said, then nodding to Jecklyn.

"I got to talk to them a bit while checking on them to make sure they did not catch a cold in the storm," the professor said around his cigar. "They said they had come from Firedell, at the base of the volcano. They had gone to live there when that Charlotte girl was just a babe. Before, however, they came from this very village they wanted to be escorted to near Snowcap Lake. The Black Hand might not have been on this mountain for as long as the natives had, but we were sure there was nothing else out there, until now."

"When you say 'natives,' said Matei. "You mean Nisthgúlians. Like there was a tribe in these mountains beyond the boundary of where we have access to now. There shouldn't be anything alive out there, not with how terrible this long winter has become."

"There shouldn't," agreed Velinar. "But I am not so sure."

Matei looked between the Fallen Star and Dr. Jecklyn. "So, why do the children need to be up there?"

"That is what we want to find out." Velinar said. "I have my... *suspicions*, that that little girl might be an Ice Walker."

Matei blinked. "A what?"

Velinar gestured for Jecklyn to explain.

"An Ice Walker is a child born from snow. Or so the legend goes, interpretations lost in translation, all of that shit. It's not uncommon when it comes to deciphering legends and religions of a nation with multiple tongues and hardly any legible texts, but I digress. Before the occupation of Balkeñoir, obviously this land was occupied by a bunch of native tribes who believed in many gods rather than the one true God. With this came different tongues, different traditions, etcetera, all of course was grouped together when the land was first named Nisthgúl.

"The Stonehollow Mountains are exceptionally sacred to the tribes who lived among them. They were the ones who warned many of the Noyiian soldiers occupying the new land about stories of the Wendigo Demon, as well as many others who still haunt the lands. Most of these tribes had been wiped out or driven off, eventually those who survived ended up in the reservations to this very day. But there is another legend in these mountains, before the building of Shadowfort; before the rise of the Black Hand."

Matei nodded, intrigued while Jecklyn continued.

"There is a legend among the mountainous tribes concerning a particular tribe somewhere in these mountains, who believed that their sun god is born from fire, and the only one who can coax him back into the world to bring spring, is the goddess of winter, who comes in the form of a woman who drowns in the lake they live among, you can probably guess which one. Anyway, the ritual was barbaric, as a chosen virgin or even a pregnant woman is taken to the lake and drowned in it to gain the attention of the goddess. When they do, the women usually come back with the power of winter, as the goddess takes the season away and transfers it to a guardian of the cold. Reports and notes on such things do describe women across the mountains who walk across rivers and lakes with the ice they create and harness the power of winter itself."

"Hence the name, 'Ice Walkers,'" Matei guessed.

"That's right." Jecklyn said around another puff of cigar smoke.

"But there is no such creature that was formally documented," argued Matei. "Wouldn't it have been in the bestiary?"

Jecklyn shook his head. "The bestiary contains what the Black Hand knows be it through contracts or from the exchange of information with other guilds. If no one has ever experienced something they read about, then you don't write about it. Hence why Ice Walkers are not common knowledge among Hunters, or most of the commonfolk for that matter. All we have that is concrete what we have in articles and what the old books say in our library. There is sure to be more about the legend, but even then, we are unsure as to what the complete story says, again considering so much of Nisthgúlian culture is lost in translation, and those who still remember the Old Ways refuse to speak to outsiders such as us. What makes us confident of what Ms. Charlotte is, are the texts that mention of those who are Ice Walkers possessing the Eyes of Ice, similar to that of which you saw when you met Charlotte and Morgan. This of course doesn't completely prove anything, at least in my opinion. Could easily just be a curse or some disease."

"Regardless as to what it is," Velinar cleared his throat. "We can't ignore the fact that someone with those eyes is going back to Snowcap Lake, where the tribe may still be in hiding. And if so, *why* are they going? What is waiting for them up there?"

"We promised not to get into their business, but my mind is troubled as to what this could mean," said Jecklyn. "Even if the legends aren't true, to know that a Nisthgúlian group is active in Balkeñoir and right at our backdoor step, it could lead to trouble."

"What do you mean?" Matei asked.

Jecklyn looked at Velinar, who shook his head solemnly. "I don't know," the deity said, but Matei knew this was a lie. However he didn't dare question his lord. "It is a hunch, nothing more. I just pray that I am wrong…"

Jecklyn cleared his throat. "In any case, we want to find out if there is a reason why they went to Firedell; and why Charlotte was an infant. Ice Walkers are not hereditary, they were specifically documented as 'chosen.' It doesn't seem to add up. Are they running back to Snowcap Lake just to hide from the Empire who may or may not have known what she is, or are they looking for something? Either way, it's a question that makes us curious. So, we'd like you to head to Firedell, and meet with a friend of ours; a priest at the Firedell Cathedral of the Nine. Morgan mentioned a church, and that is the only one in Firedell. We want you to go check it out, talk to the priest at the Firedell Cathedral, and see what he thought of the children, as well as their sudden arrival and departure from the city. Velinar and I will continue to work things out here on our end, and will await for your news."

"Does anyone know what causes the lake to create Ice Walkers?" Matei asked. "If this tribe or those in the mountains were the only ones who practiced this… ritual to create them, could it be just the lake?"

"That is why I sent Angela with the Hunting party," Velinar answered.

Matei was surprised. "Angela?"

"She knows what an Ice Walker is, we had discussed it before they had left. She knows of the lore behind the Ice Walkers among other Nisthgúlian legends. So I presumed she would investigate when they took the children to the lake itself. This could create a major opportunity for the Black Hand, and try to understand as to why the Empire was so keen on capturing the children."

"As well as confirm or deny any of your concerns, master," said Jecklyn eyeing the deity knowingly.

"Aye," Velinar admitted with a small hint of a cold smile. "That it would..."

Matei then asked, "Is she dangerous? The Ice Walker, I mean?"

"Probably no more dangerous than a Dhampir Huntress," Velinar smiled. Matei, did not. Seeing that the Hunter was not amused, Velinar continued after clearing his throat. "Ice Walkers are rumored to have the power of ice and snow. Matei, do you know who else has such power?"

Matei thought about it. If one looked at it from a supernatural point of view, technically Vampires could change the weather if they were powerful enough to do so, but he figured that wasn't the answer Velinar was looking for. Some sprites and fairies could harness fire, those who were still around and not extinct, but that didn't could either. So then, Matei thought about the Stars and their Fallen Brethren. He thought about those who had fallen to Lunokean along with Velinar, and when he recollected the one who had influence over ice and snow, he felt a surge of excitement.

"Dullahan the Wild?"

Velinar nodded.

"You don't think-"

"We don't know yet," said Jecklyn. "It could be a mere coincidence, but we want to make sure we do not just cover our mortal world, but others as well. Until we know for certain, it is all speculation, and we will expect you to do the same and to keep it quiet."

"Understood. But what will happen to them, the kids, I mean? What if there is really nothing for them there? What if that tribe is gone and they can't find anything up there? This Eternal Winter has been cruel, I wouldn't bet on anything staying alive further up the mountains."

"If there is nothing up there, then we will leave it for them, and our Huntsmen to decide," Velinar said with a shrug. "That is all we really can do. An Ice Walker is no different than a cursed human being. People will fear her and try to study her. That is simply something no one should endure. If she really is the last Ice Walker, we must protect her if she so chooses to come to us, or remain in the mountains forever. Hopefully by then, we will know what her very existence means."

Jecklyn spoke up then. "Head to Firedell, Matei. Find out what you can, about the children, and the Empire's desires. We'll do what we can here, and hope and pray for the best."

Matei took his leave, hurrying to prepare for the ride to Firedell. As soon as he reached the desert, traveling would go by a lot faster provided he remained weary of the wildlife. It would be at least two days on horse and possible another as soon as he reached the city. There would be heavy occupation of the Empire there as well, so he would more than likely not have any trouble trying to find out anything about any plans that the Emperor had for the country. Matei was no expert on the traditions and cultures of the natives of the land before Balkeñoir, having most of it destroyed or soiled by the Wildesding Cult who took after the practices of witchcraft by the servants of Kawfka- the same religion that the Ravens were now practicing. But he worried that if a tribe *did* exist in these mountains, and they saw that an Ice Walker has returned, what that could possibly mean for Charlotte, her brother, *and* his fellow Huntsmen.

But if the tribe didn't exist, he wondered and worried what could possibly remain still at the lake, and what that could mean, should an Ice Walker have to return to the world of Man.

Most importantly, if there was something else, something possibly worse that Velinar had in mind concerning the return of an Ice Walker, what could that be and how it would involve the Black Hand, who already had it's hand deep in the affairs of not just men, but fallen gods.

Ti

The group stopped at a small meadow where a frozen pond laid beneath the limbs of a great tree. The trunk was wider than all other trees and upon looking up it, Vladimir thought it was the tallest in the entire forest as he allowed Sabina to bandage his hand where the war dog had snagged him.

The group had managed to catch their breath after leaving a considerable amount of distance between them and the troll who had no doubt called whatever other brethren were hiding out in the forest for assistance rounding up their kills and taking them back to their caves. Other than Vladimir's injury, Jacob had been shot in the shoulder. The bullet splintered the scapula, but it had healed surprisingly fast, and while this was a miracle for the group, it wasn't for those who didn't already know. For good measure, Angela had helped bind the wound. She was glad that Jacob was far too tired for any jokes. She was too, although she would never admit this to anyone, especially him.

Morgan was giving Charlotte some water, and the girl was panting heavily as her eyes that were previously glowing bright and blue slowly died back to normal- at least by her standards. When she had caught her own breath, Sabina stood up and marched towards the children, who tensed up under her gaze.

"You both all right?" she demanded. "Either of you hurt?"

"No," said Morgan. "We're fine."

"You," Sabina said pointing at Charlotte, straight to business. "Explain yourself."

"Back off," Morgan hissed putting himself between his sister and the angry Vampire Hunter.

"What was that?" Sabina demanded ignoring the boy. "What did you do?"

Morgan glared at Sabina defiantly, whereas Charlotte seemed to merely shrink into her own hood.

Angela began to approach them but Vladimir had reached them first. He brushed right past Sabina and removing a pistol from his belt, he pulled back on the hammer and took aim right at Morgan. The kid didn't even flinch.

"Listen carefully, kid," he said in a low voice to Charlotte in particular. "If you don't start talking, I'll put a bullet right between your brother's eyes here. You have a lot of explaining to do, so start talking. Last I checked, as long as one of you make it to Snowcap Lake, we've done our part. So tell us right now: what are you?"

"If you shoot me," Morgan said not backing down in the slightest. "You'll be dead."

"No…" Charlotte whispered shaking her head. "I don't want to kill him… I don't want to kill anymore people…"

"Charlotte…" Morgan pleaded.

"What are you!?" Vladimir shouted, his patience strained.

"She's an Ice Walker," Angela suddenly said from where she stood just a few feet away from this confrontation. The Dhampir had been quiet since their arrival here, and to hear her speak now made Vladimir's very spine tingle unpleasantly. By the look on Charlotte's and Morgan's, they were surprised that someone in this little troop apparently knew the truth; even with a gun pointed at one of them.

"And what in the hell is *that*, exactly?" demanded Sabina.

"It is a person chosen from an ice spirit common among the old Nishgúlian tribes who resided in these mountains." Angela was looking directly at Morgan now who looked on the verge of panicking. "Am I right?"

Morgan stared at Angela, and then looked at Vladimir who kept the gun aimed right for him. He then looked at

Charlotte, who nodded her head, slowly, giving in to whatever pressure was upon her.

At last, he said, "It's true."

Vladimir lowered the gun, apparently seeing that the boy was telling the truth now, and taking the girl's word that she didn't want to hurt them. He did not however put it away, not yet.

He looked at Angela. "What else do you know about them? Her kind, I mean?"

Angela looked at Charlotte, and the girl averted her eyes. She turned back to Vladimir and said, "Nothing concrete."

Vladimir narrowed his eyes. "Are you sure?"

"Yes. I know of the legends, but that is all I know. *If*, they are indeed legends." She added this last sentence specifically for the two children.

"Not *all* of them," said Morgan albeit hesitantly. "We… she…" He looked at Charlotte for help.

The child spoke. "When I was born, my mother took my brother and I out of these mountains. She said we lived in a small village, hidden from the rest of the world next to a great lake. This lake, there is a legend, that those who drown in the waters and come back up, come back with the power of the goddess of winter. They have the power over the frozen water that covers the mountains. Our village, they honored such tradition by drowning themselves in the lake water."

"Goodness," said Sabina in unveiled disgust.

"Our mother," Morgan continued. "Was to sacrifice herself, before she gave birth to Charlotte."

"She survived," Jacob said. "And took you away."

"She was one of the few lucky ones," said Morgan. "Or, so she said.

"When I was born," Charlotte continued. "She baptized me in the waters of Snowcap Lake. But she said, something happened. She said, that after I was brought back up out of the water, my eyes were not the same as they were when I was born. They were blue, like this. As I got older, she said I would freeze up my room and the chief had begun to grow suspicious."

"She was afraid of what this could mean for Charlotte and the rest of the family," added Morgan. "I remember when she came home and told me to pack up everything. We escaped into the night, running away from the village and those who were already preparing to… to sacrifice her."

He gestured at his sister.

"We fled to Firedell, where our mother could care for us. It was on her deathbed, when she decided to tell Charlotte the truth; what she was and why the priests feared her. It was around the age of ten when she started to show even more signs of her power. She froze water from the shrines, crystalized any rain that happened to come through."

"In other words," Charlotte said with embarrassment. "I gained attention."

"So you left," said Angela. "Left to protect yourselves. So why go back to the village if they meant you harm?"

"Where else can we go?" demanded Morgan. "We're Nisthgúlian, this country doesn't like our kind and would fear Charlotte even more. And I refuse to risk us getting sent to the reservation."

"And besides," said Charlotte. "I want to go back. I want to see what our home had been like, and… I want to know why I am this way. I want to know… all of this."

She held out her palms, and to the Hunters' surprise, ice began to form within the lines of her palms and between her fingers, and continued to accumulate until it looked like she was wearing a pair of glass gloves.

No one said anything for a long time. All eyes were on the children, especially Charlotte whose ice gloves began to melt and drip into the snow, leaving a pair of hands that were small and untouched by frostbite. The cold didn't bother her any more than it bothered Angela.

"There's… one more thing, too," Morgan admitted to the Hunters.

He looked to Charlotte and nodded. The little girl then reached into her little backpack she kept under her cloak at all times, and from it removed a small silver urn with ancient writings along the side.

"We want to scatter our mother in the lake."

Vladimir's expression remained neutral but his eyes had softened. He looked back at Sabina and then to Angela and Jacob who now stood together. Then he looked back at the children.

"And the Empire…" he dared to ask. "They want you, because of your power."

Charlotte nodded and Morgan said, "That is why we hid in Firedell. Mother said the priests would keep us safe. But… one of them contacted the Empire, just when we had Mother cremated. We had to leave, and had been chased ever since. That is… until we came across you guys."

Morgan looked at Vladimir suddenly. "I still promise that we'd pay you. There is a temple, in our village. You can take the silver we have stored in there."

"You'd steal from your own gods?" Angela asked in a curious tone, as if she was testing them.

Morgan spat on the ground. "Any god who makes you sacrifice your own flesh and blood and allow you to kill to bring back winter, is no god of mine- or Charlotte's. We know the One True God, and He is a greater deal than what our ancestors believe in. They don't sacrifice for a god, they sacrifice for whatever demon haunts that lake and gives the power to those they see fit."

Angela thought to herself, *You just might be right about that.*

Vladimir nodded. "That's very noble of you." He crouched down and patted Morgan's head, which shocked the boy. "I had to do the same thing to my own mother, back when

I was a boy- before I went to look for the Black Hand to become a Werewolf Hunter. I know what it is like, to travel in order to spread your mother's ashes." He turned to Charlotte. "And you, knowing the dangers those eyes have upon entry to your homeland, and yet still willing to carry your mother back home. Most men would call you stupid, or insane. But you're a very noble girl to take on such a task. You both are strong, and as our Lord Velinar has said, we will make sure you get up there. That there is a promise."

Charlotte beamed and Morgan smiled bashfully. "Thank you, sir."

Jacob smiled. "We made it this far, and we've all dealt with worse than a couple trolls. Thanks to you, Charlotte, I know we'll be okay."

Charlotte blushed at that. She seemed genuinely happy, as if a heavy weight had finally been lifted off her shoulders. Despite the journey that still lied ahead, she was willing to keep on going, and bury the hatchet to create her own future. Vladimir, for the first time since leaving Shadowfort Castle, appeared happy as well. Though his heart was burdened with his lie to connect with the children, as well as Luca's own weight upon his shoulders, he respected them. These children had lost their mother. He lost his best friend and partner. He had kept his thoughts to himself, for he didn't want to lay his burdens upon anyone else or appear weak.

But these children... they showed him just what the heart really was capable of. What he himself, was capable of.

Someday, I will have to bury Luca as well.

With a sigh, Vladimir stood up and nodded. "We will all go soon." He gripped his pistol tighter, and then turned to Angela. "But first, we have some business to attend to." Angela merely raised an eyebrow, as Vladimir turned to her. "That Raven, why didn't you kill her? Why did you hold back? You could have destroyed her as easily as you did all those men yesterday."

"I didn't," Angela said.

"Didn't what?"

"I didn't hold back. I couldn't."

Vladimir shook his head. "Bullshit."

"She's telling the truth," Jacob said coming up to Vladimir's side. "I saw her fighting when you grabbed me on our way out. She wasn't holding back. The Raven was just keeping up with her."

"I don't *believe* she is human," Angela said. "Her scent, everything about her was wrong."

Vladimir ran a hand over his head. "You think she's dead? That the trolls have gotten her?"

"I doubt it would make much of a difference," Angela said. "She might still be alive."

"Shit..." the Werewolf Hunter groaned. "This just keeps on getting better and better. So you're telling me, that the Raven is still after us, and she is still out there?"

"I believe so."

"Shit," he said again, kicking aside a small pile of snow. "You shouldn't have messed around. You should have killed her."

"Give her a break," Jacob said. "She did what she could in the time provided."

"That's no excuse." Vlad snapped suddenly. "Although... I'll admit if she isn't human, then not only does that make our situation worse when it comes to the Ravens, but the immediate problem still stands. If she is still alive out there, we have to make sure she doesn't come back after us. The next time she shows her face, we *all* kill her. Then and there."

"Alright, alright," Jacob said raising his hands in surrender. "I was just saying."

Sabina looked up to the sky beyond the crevice. "We still have a few hours of daylight. We should keep moving."

"Agreed," Angela said. "If we can get just a little further, then we'll be closer to the end of the valley." She turned to Morgan. "Is that right?"

"Yeah, we've come a lot further than I thought we would," the boy answered.

"Angela," Jacob said coming up alongside the Dhampir. "What about the Raven? Do you have any idea what we might be dealing with?"

Angela looked at Vladimir for some reason, and then shook her head. "No. There are too many stenches on her, it is difficult for me to tell just what she is. However… I *did* catch a familiar stench. I caught the smell of Zoser on her person."

Jacob's eye went wide. "Wildesding."

Vladimir swore again and Sabina shook her head. "So, what?" She asked. "Are the Ravens working with the Cult now?"

"No," Angela answered. "They hate the Ravens almost as much as we do. I can only imagine that they struck a deal with this Raven. What that may entail I don't know. I don't even know what the Empire even wants with Charlotte."

Vladimir groaned, only now at last putting away his pistol. "Is there anything that you do know, Angela? Other than what you know about Charlotte already. Makes me wonder what else you kept from us."

"Will you lay off already?" Jacob said in an exasperated tone. "You're being unfair."

"Oh, I'm sorry," Vladimir said sarcastically. "I didn't know I had to be fair with someone who is withholding information she does have, and is absolutely useless with other information."

Jacob looked ready to stick a knife into Vladimir's throat. "Knock it off. Angela isn't a-"

"Jacob," Angela said in a cold tone. "Don't."

"Yeah, Jacob," Vladimir said in a tone just as cold and without breaking eye-contact with the Witcher. "Don't."

Jacob glowered at Vladimir, adjusting the scarf on his neck as if he needed room to breathe.

"Please, don't fight," Sabina said. "We don't have any time for this."

"That's right," Angela said. "We all need to keep moving. We should-"

She suddenly stopped and turned to the east. When Jacob started to ask what was wrong, the Dhampir shushed him with a hiss. Her head turned slightly to her right, and Vladimir noticed that she was now breathing in deeply, smelling the area around them. Her expression suddenly turned dim and she turned to the others as she unsheathed her sword.

"We're still being hunted."

Di

At the mention of these words, the Hunters all drew their weapons. Vladimir drew his second pistol and they all gathered in a circle around Morgan and Charlotte; their eyes scanning the forest before them. With so many faces looking back at them, it made the sense of being watched even more overbearing.

"Where?" Jacob demanded, an arrow fit to his bowstring.

"I'm not sure," said Angela, eyes darting. "Sabina, do you have any garlic powder on you?"

"A whole bag," said Sabina her eyes scanning the trees. "What are you thinking?"

Before the Dhampir could answer, a pair of childlike laughter echoed throughout the forest. Vladimir thought he saw a shadow to his right but immediately the figure vanished in an instant, followed by more of the chilly laughter. The darkness of the forest seemed to come to life, making the laughing sound more horrifying like children playing among the trees of screaming souls. Likewise the temperature seemed to plumet, the snow now frosting over with ice.

"You all are so loud," Vladimir heard a voice whisper right into his ear. He started and saw that only Sabina stood beside him where he had heard the voice, which was feminine, and that of a small child.

"We could hear you from back home," another voice whispered in Vladimir's other ear, this one obviously belonging to a boy. Jacob looked uncomfortable, the Dhampir remained stone-faced.

"Why are you acting like that?"

"We just want to play."

Angela spoke up, her voice surprisingly mellow and yet soft. "Where are you?" she asked. "Come on out."

"What do we do, Brother?" the feminine voice asked softly from somewhere within the forest.

"I don't know, Sister," said the other. "Isn't she one of us?"

"She smells like us, but she also smells like a human…"

"Should we wait for Mother?"

"I don't know…"

One of us? And Vladimir realized with a start and tightened his grip on his pistols. "Vampires."

"Save your bullets," Angela said stepping away from the group and standing apart from them. Jacob had started to follow but Sabina held him back, shaking her head vehemently.

"Let's see what she's doing," she told him and Vladimir both.

"Come on out, Angela repeated. "I know where you both are hiding. I won't hurt you if you don't hurt my companions. Come on out, don't be afraid."

Don't be afraid? Vladimir wondered in astonishment as he felt his breath get stuck somewhere in his throat when he saw the shadows beneath the limbs of the trees slowly converge as if in longing. The darkness then materialized into the shapes of two small children identical in appearance apart from sex. The two wore matching outfits of black and white, the girl in a small dress with a frilled white skirt. The boy wore a small suit with a black bowtie and both of their hair was as blonde as a field of wheat and of the same length; shoulder-length and as smooth as silk.

And their eyes… Dear Yohnah and the Nine, their eyes. Vladimir could not look away from them. They were glowing silver like molten quicksilver, and seemed to study the group behind the Dhampir like they were animals. Vladimir kept his guns on them despite Angela standing right between them. Jacob had done the same, drawing the bowstring to its full length and watching the boy in particular.

Both Vampires admired the Dhampir, who stood calmly before them.

"Who are you?" the girl asked.

"*What* are you?" the boy asked intertwining his fingers within the girl's. Holding hands, the two appeared elegantly churchbound.

Angela didn't answer, her own eyes seeming to glow bright and illuminating across her face. Though the two Vampires stood in the light, the sunlight could not reach them. The reflected light off the snow and rocks high above was not enough to cause them harm. From down here in the valley, they all might as well be traveling at night. The Vampires didn't have to wait until darkness. In this valley, time was not on the Hunters' side.

"Why don't you answer?" the boy asked.

The girl nodded. "Yes, why don't you answer?"

"Who are you?" they both then asked in unison. Their voices together sending chills down Sabina's spine.

"Who are *you*?" Angela asked instead. Though she remained as still as a statue, her sword remained drawn, hanging at her side and glistening as silver as the two's eyes.

"I am Lithus," the boy practically sang.

"I am Mithus," said the girl.

They both demanded in unison, "Who are you?"

"I am Angela," Angela answered with a dip of her head. "An honor, and a privilege to meet you, My Friends."

"What is she doing?" Morgan hissed. Vladimir wondered the same.

"It is a respect thing," Sabina answered. "When Immortals meet one another, they regard each other with high respect. Which means those two are not just normal Vampires; they are Immortals."

"That young?" Jacob asked pulling an arrow back on his bowstring.

"They were probably born," Sabina muttered. "Purebloods."

"You are one of us," Lithus said tilting his head.

"And yet, you are not." Mithus said tilting her own head in the opposite direction, her bright braid dangling over her shoulder.

"You are right," said Angela. "I am, but I am not. I am not an Immortal, but I am also not a human. I am a Dhampir."

The two's eyes widened and their mouths opened into the shape of an 'o'. Past their ruby-red lips, Vladimir could see their fangs glistening in their mouths. The two children looked so much alike in the way their facial expressions stretched that they could have been twins for all he knew. The twins then looked past Angela, and then back at her.

"They are… your comrades?" Lithus asked.

"That is right," Angela said. "We are just passing through."

"No one is allowed to pass through," Mithus said sadly. "Mother said so."

"Where is your mother?" Angela asked, obviously wondering the same thing everyone else was. They had mentioned a mother, which meant either another human, or worse, a full-grown Immortal was around.

The twins sniffed the air as they looked at the other Hunters again. The girl then lifted up a small pale finger and pointed right at Jacob. "That one there… he is yours?"

Angela tensed and Vladimir wondered why.

Lithus nodded, after following the direction his sisters finger was pointing. "They are all clean… but his blood is marked. Is he yours?"

Marked? Vladimir looked at Jacob, seeing that the Witch Hunter looked frightened. His Adam's apple shot up and down his neck as he swallowed again and again. *Could it be…?*

"Where is your mother?" Angela asked again. "We are of no threat to either of you, or her." She then raised her right hand, showing them her ruby ring. "I mean you all no harm."

"We don't know what that means." Lithus said, barely glancing at the ring but obviously understanding that Angela had expected them to know something.

Angela dropped her hand. "You don't recognize the sigil? The house marking?"

"We don't know anything about the nobility of our ancestors," Mithus said.

"It is just us three up here," they then said in unison. "Us, and Mother."

Jacob suddenly gasped, and he turned one of his frightened blue eyes towards the sky. "Something is coming…"

"Where is your mother?" Angela asked again. "Please, allow me to speak to her."

The Dhampir suddenly tilted her head, and then fast as lightning both her and the two children leapt out of the way just as a fireball splashed the ground just where she was once standing. She then looked up towards the sky as the children leapt as nimbly as grasshoppers onto the boughs of nearby trees. They turned their catlike eyes to the skies crouched like gargoyles from their perch and Vladimir looked up and saw where the fire had come from.

His heart sank then at the sight of the witch that Jacob was now gaping at with his bow drawn and aimed right for her.

Jacob had felt this sort of power before. He had sensed it, little by little as they ventured deeper into the woods. But now, the same sensation he had felt for so much of his adolescent life came crashing down like a waterfall upon him. The darkness, the sick feeling of dread and destruction, flooded his senses and made him sick to look upon the witch that floated just above all of their heads on her old and battered broomstick.

The witch appeared young and beautiful, but that hardly mattered. For all he knew, she could have been over a hundred years old or even younger than he was. She was bald and when she grinned her teeth looked like tombstones. She was garbed in a tattered dress under a cloak of red, her entire face and pale arms were covered in rune marks and tattoos of snakes curled around her forearms down to the tips of her fingers. Her left hand was covered by a gauntlet with log talons of what looked like iron, and her eyes glowed pale green like a cat's as she held another ball of fire in her free hand; the flames dancing around her slender fingers like worms around a decaying flower.

"Lithus, Mithus," the witch crooned in a voice that seemed to be overlapped with that of a child and some unseen demon within that body of hers. "What is the meaning of this? Why do you speak to these intruders?"

"She is one of us, Mother," Lithus answered, his silver eyes now glowing dangerously bright in the direction of the group.

"She is a Dhampir," Mithus answered her own eyes staying on Angela who glared up at the witch who remained floating just above their heads. "She has our blood within her."

"She also has the blood of your very own food," the witch said though she smiled seductively those rotten teeth like mold on a portrait. "Although, she really has a beautiful face. I would like to have a face like that- maybe I will keep you after all."

"Who are you?" Angela demanded.

"Guys," Jacob whispered reaching for one of his leg packs and removing a vial of clear liquid. "Spread out, keep her busy."

Vladimir smiled. The retired Witcher was about to begin his hunt- and it was their job as fellow huntsmen to assist. "Sabina, rush to Angela when you get a chance. You both are gonna need each other to deal with the Immortals. I'll help with Jacob."

"What about us?" Morgan asked.

"Make a break for the trees. You can handle yourselves but be careful."

"Who are you?" Angela asked again, this time a little louder.

The witch smiled, and raised her flame-filled palm. "I am Death. Lithus, Mithus, kill-"

Twang!

Jacob's arrow flew straight up, right through the ball of flame and right into the neck of the witch. Bright green flame erupted upon contact with her skin, and she shrieked like a crow wounded by a child's slingshot. The liquid he had slathered onto the tip had ignited the fire and mixed it with the extract of iron. Upon contact with the blood of a witch, she burned from the inside. As Jacob lunged forward and reached for another arrow, he saw the two Immortals lunge for Angela simultaneously. The Dhampir sidestepped out of the way just before she could get torn to shreds by their talons of shadow. Vladimir and Sabina had both moved out as well, firing their own guns at the witch who in her panic willed her broom to move- right towards the woods far away from the rest of the group.

"Kill them!" she screamed just as she crashed into the trees beyond.

"Sabina!" Jacob shouted and Sabina turned away to help with Angela who was now leaping away from the snarling Immortals- drawing them away from Morgan and Charlotte who ran off in the opposite direction.

"Go!" Vladimir shouted to them as he followed Jacob close behind, who kept his focus on the smoke rising in the woods. The wound the witch had received would not kill her- no, that would be too easy. To kill a witch, you had to render her immobile.

Then, you had to burn her.

"C'mon!" Morgan shouted, taking Charlotte by the hand. They had left the Hunters behind, who were now dealing with the Vampires and witch who had seemed to come out of nowhere. It was as if the forest really was cursed, and had no intention of letting them get to their old home alive at all.

They ran and ran until they came upon a small ridge, and took cover behind it. They didn't know whether or not they were safe, but for the time being, they would be okay. In the confusion, the horses had all fled once again, this time nowhere to be found.

"We should have stayed," Charlotte panted heavily. "We should have helped them."

"There is nothing we can do," Morgan said not looking at her, and keeping a hand on his rusted sword. His eyes darted from side to side, keeping an eye out for anything else that might come out of the woods that continued to laugh and moan at them. In the far distance, the two could hear fighting. A shrill shriek sent a ripple of gooseflesh along Morgan's arms and back. Charlotte however was unaffected.

"You already used your power once today- you're exhausted," Morgan was telling her. "We can't have you collapsing and becoming helpless. Besides, they are Hunters. They are used to this stuff."

"That was a witch though..." Charlotte frowned. "A witch, and two Immortals. Can they really fight them off?"

Morgan's mouth twitched, but he nodded confidently. "They live for this kind of work. I know they will come back to us victorious. Don't worry- they'll find us. They have to."

Charlotte looked down at the splotch of powder at her feet. She was thinking of how much the Hunters were also good at fighting one another. Especially with most of the hostility towards that one, that Dhampir.

Charlotte sympathized with her.

Charlotte buried her face into her brother's back. She had done this her whole life, to hide from the monsters that haunted her dreams, as well as the ones in the daytime. All the people who treated her like an animal, calling her a witch or a demon because of her eyes and her powers. All the whispers of the priests back in Irondell, calling her a wretched child. There were times when Charlotte wished she had never become an Ice Walker. It was only because of Morgan, and Mama, that she was able to endure it. It was here in their arms, where she felt safe; where she felt at home.

Even now as they listened to the fighting still going on, she felt at home being this close to her last living relative that she knew of.

"I hope they come back…" Charlotte whispered. "All of them.

Morgan nodded, despite his sister's frigid breath making the back of his neck freeze with discomfort. "Yes. Me too."

Angela bounded away as swiftly as a leopard as the two Immortals tried to corner her from the darkness. In flashes of black and shadow the two beings kept on chasing her, leaving Sabina to only follow from far behind. No matter how hard they tried however, they could not catch up with the Dhampir, nor could they provoke her into turning around and attacking them.

"Come back!" Lithus hissed.

"It's not fun if you run away!" Mithus screeched as she lunged once again, lasing out with a clawed hand and missing Angela who ducked just at the right moment before planting a heavy boot into the girl's belly. Mithus went flying right into a tree and her brother was by her side in an instant.

Seeing that his sister was unhurt, Lithus growled at Angela, who for the moment stopped running and regarded the children with cold eyes.

"Such a pity," Angela said starting towards them. Her words sounded regretful as she stated, "With no other Immortal to raise you. To train you how to use your powers properly. You have been living it far too easy in these mountains it seems."

"Shut up!" Lithus hissed standing up, his silver eyes glowing brightly. "You who share the blood of a human have no right to talk to us that way!"

"And yet you are being cared for by a human," Angela challenged which left the young Vampire in stunned silence. She stopped before them, no longer advancing. "Is she *really* your mother? I'm surprised she is still able to walk."

Mithus groaned as she sat back up against her brothers wishes. "No... she found us."

"Oh, I see," Angela said. "You both were abandoned, is that it?" When the two didn't answer, the Dhampir merely sighed. "I have no reason to hurt you. I do not want to. My companions and I just need to get to Snowcap Lake. If you let us proceed and mind our business, no harm will come of you or your mother."

Lithus looked at Mithus, then back to Angela. "She wants you all dead, you know."

"That's for her to decide," said Angela. "I'm telling you and your sister to decide for yourself. If you two leave us be, we will leave you be. If your mother cannot leave us be, then she will die. Such a fate doesn't have to be shared with you two."

Lithus growled and he stood up fast, clenching a fist of shadow as his primal instincts began to take over. How dare this thing, this *halfbreed* threaten Mother?

"I'd like to see you try!" With that, he lunged forward so fast that any normal person would have been overcome by the Immortal. However, Angela was able to sidestep the boy and trip him before elbowing him in the back of the head, rendering him defenseless on the ground.

"Lithus!"

Angela turned an eye to the spot where Mithus once laid, and following the scent she saw the young Immortal perched on the limb of the closest tree before the Vampire leapt down and came upon Angela fangs bared and claws ready to tear. Angela merely stepped aside and with one quick slash of her sword, severed one of the Vampire's legs right at the knee. Mithus screamed out loud as she collapsed to the ground mere feet away from her brother, her blood now spilling onto the ground as her leg collapsed just behind Angela.

"Mithus!" Lithus groaned hearing his sister's screams and seeing her severed leg. He was grasping the stump with both hands, causing both Mithus to scream and blood to bubble between his pale fingers.

"A pity," Angela said somberly. "You can't even shift into your beastly forms. You don't even know how to summon your familiars in order to heal your severed leg to walk. You two have been rendered nothing more than beasts to a witch."

Lithus hissed at Angela angrily. "I'll kill you!"

Angela sighed and scooping up the severed leg, she tossed it over to the twins as casually as if she were tossing a dog a bone to chew on. "Use your own blood to connect your leg back on. Don't worry, you won't die. Though I pity you. You both could have been powerful, dangerous Immortals. Even by now you both should be feared and preying upon the meek. But instead you have become wolves without fangs, forced to wait up here in these mountains until a traveler comes by, owned by a witch. Tell me, what use does such a woman have with two Immortals?"

Lithus placed the leg back onto Mithus' stump, and told her to try to get it back on. He then stood, and regarded Angela with cold silver eyes. He then began to growl, as his skin turned from pale white to ashy gray, his fingers curled into talons, and his very fangs seemed to grow and sharpen as did his face which was drawn into a shriveled snarl.

"Damn you, Dhampir. I'll kill you for what you did to my sister. And Mother is none of your concern. She cares for us, helps us to grow. As long as we have her approval, we don't need to be feared by the meek humans you've allowed *yourself* to be tamed by. You are a hypocrite- a filthy human-bred hypocrite!"

Angela showed no fear or concern of the boy's transformation. "If your ancestors could see you now," she said in an attempt to break his spirit just a little more for him to open up to reason.

"Our ancestors can burn in Oblivion and you with them! *Die!*" And with that, Lithus lunged forward, ready to rip Angela open from groin to throat. The Dhampir tensed, ready to sidestep and subdue the boy rather than hurt him too bad or kill him.

Click!

Angela lunged forward. "Don't!"

Bam!

Angela heard the shot coming before Sabina's gun even went off. The silver bullet tore through the boy's body, staggering him and causing him to crumble to his side. Turning his gleaming silver eyes towards Sabina who had managed to catch up, the Vampire bounded from tree to tree dodging her bullets while coming in close enough to be ready to claw her.

But then Sabina removed what looked like a fireplace bellow, and clenching the two handles together, a green mist sprayed out and collided with the Vampire as she dove aside. Lithus immediately began to scream and bark like a wounded wolf, rubbing his face into the snow as the distinct scent of garlic filled the air. Sabina immediately drew her silver sword swung it. Lithus saw it coming and bounded back and far away from the Vampire Hunter, retreating back to his sister while Angela tried to intervene.

"You cheated!" Lithus snarled loudly.

"No," Sabina said raising her sword. "You are just clumsy." She would have kept on going, right towards the Vampires if she had not been stopped by Angela's hand.

She glared at the Dhampir, who merely stared at her with somber eyes. Her sword had been sheathed but her grip on Sabina's arm was unbreakable. "What the hell are you doing?" she snapped.

Angela looked at the two children with a look of pity as Mithus was still unable to reattach her leg. Lithus remained standing over her, looking like a savage wolf trying to defend their pups. She considered them for a moment, and then Sabina saw Angelas eyes harden and the Dhampir turned around almost immediately, releasing Sabina's arm.

"Do what you want. We don't have time for this."

"Hold on a second!" Sabina said. "They are Vampires! We need to get rid of them, here and now."

"As I said: do what you want." Angela said starting forward still without looking back. Right now we have a bigger problem to deal with.

"But-"

"Rrreeeaarrgh!!" Lithus snarled as he suddenly leapt up and came upon the distracted Vampire Hunter with fangs glaring. At that moment, Angela had spun around and hurled a silver throwing knife towards the vampiric child, impaling him right through the chest and making him fall back into the snow just as Sabina got out of harm's way.

"Lith!" Mithus screamed, her leg now on but still slowly mending as blood continued to spill. As she tried to get up her flesh split once again and she staggered onto all fours.

Lithus coughed out blood, the dagger having gone right through his body without hitting his heart. Angela stalked over to him, and planted a heavy foot upon his right shoulder, pinning him down as she grabbed ahold of her weapon. The snarling wolf on her pommel of the sword peeking over her shoulder matched her expression, as she looked down at the Vampire who tried to stare back defiantly, but unsuccessfully.

"I warned you," she told the Immortal child. She then looked up at Mithus, who stared in horror at the Dhampir who held her brother down. "You both are a disgrace to your bloodline. Sabina."

Sabina joined her side, her sword ready.

"What say you?" she then asked the Vampire Hunter.

Sabina scoffed. "As if you need to ask."

"Very well." She looked to Mithus and said, "Let this be a lesson for you before it is too late. Go ahead, Sabina."

Sabina raised her sword again, the point aiming directly above the Immortal's heart.

"Wait!" Lithus hissed, his bat-like features morphing back to that of a frightened child. His eyes burned bright with terror. "You are one of us! Why are you doing this?"

"No," said Angela. "I'm not. Sabina."
And with that, Sabina had plunged her sword down, driving the silver right into the heart of the Immortal and causing the creature to scream as snarl like a wild beast. Mithus screamed as well, as she watched her brother turn ashen gray and slowly crumble away to dust, only to lightly dust the snow around his final resting place if he would have anything left to rest.

"Brother!" Mithus cried glaring at the Dhampir hatefully. She tried to get up, then she tried to crawl. But the injury to her leg made impossible and she remained where she was, sobbing hot and angry tears. "Damn you Dhampir. Damn you, Huntress…" Then shrilly, "Damn you both to hell!"

Angela sheathed her dagger, and turned her head to the north. There was nothing left of Lithus now, and she looked to Sabina. "Come." She started to go.

"What about her?" Sabina demanded, gesturing towards the still wounded Mithus who stared at the ash pile that was now what was left of her brother.

"Do what you want," Angela said. "She has been warned by me, but not by you. Do what you want, but be quick about it. The men need our help." She didn't even look back as she kept on going.

Sabina was frustrated as well as outrage. "You'd allow het to grow up and be a predator of man?" she demanded. When Angela didn't respond or look back, Sabina swore and looked at the ash pile, and then looked at Mithus, who continued to seethe at her.

"I'll kill you…" she snarled. "I swear, I'll come after you and kill you myself! Hunters!"

Sabina threw a look of disgust her way, and she started when she heard Angela telling her to hurry up and decide. This was almost as bad as letting some tiger cubs live after hunting the mother who had begun to prey on humans. There was instinct and nature that could never be changed by good deeds or mere pity and mercy. Immortals were of course no exception- no vampiric beings were.

With a shake of her head, Sabina spat into the ash pile, and turned away. "You've been warned," she decided to tell the Immortal child. She sprinted after Angela, leaving Mithus alone to heal her leg and stare at the defiled ashes of her brother. As she left, the young Immortal was still screaming, cursing them, swearing that they would all die.

When she finally caught up with the Dhampir, Sabina kept up with her pace as she walked alongside her. "Why didn't you just destroy her as well?"

"Why didn't you?" Angela asked which left Sabina at a loss for words. "They pose as no threat to us as of yet."

"Not yet," Sabina corrected. "Once they grow up, they will become dangerous- a threat to all living things."

"They were just children."

"Then why not stop me?"

"Because that's your decision."

Sabina stared at the Dhampir, thinking, *No. No, you just didn't want to be responsible for it.*

She said instead, "That doesn't change the fact that the girl won't grow up to be a killer. She'll grow up to be dangerous."

"So will humans," Angela countered which once again surprised Sabina. It also made her think about how it was raising dogs.

She decided that if they finish their business with the witch, wherever Jacob and Vladimir were now, she would discuss this further with Angela if she got the chance.

In the meantime, they were still being hunted, and they still had a witch to deal with. This was no time for more discussions.

It was time to hunt a witch.

Do

Jacob rushed to where the witch had landed only to find her in a small clearing next to a couple of small ponds that had been long frozen-over. She had her hand at her neck, and she was breathing in deeply as her magic seeped from her hand and into her wound. She hissed like a snake, when she turned those cold eyes upon him and Vladimir as the two emerged from the thicket.

"That wasn't very nice," the witch said standing up and removing her hand from her neck. With a turn of her head, her neck cracked back into place. The wound was gone, but there were still splotches of burns at the base of her jawline. "You could have killed me."

"Too bad I didn't," Jacob said tightening his grip on his bow. The witch's very aura... it was pure evil. Black magic seeped from her body like body odor, bringing with it horrible memories of the past as well as the possibilities of a twisted future.

She had started towards him.

"Not so fast," Vladimir purred as he took aim at the witch with both of his revolvers. "Put your hands up."

"Such a big strong man, hiding behind little guns," the witch purred as she raised her hands right up to the height of her shoulders. "I'll play along, for the time being. I'm sure my little darlings are having fun with your companions."

"I wouldn't worry about them," Jacob said sheathing his bow and drawing his sword in one hand. Then with his teeth he began to pull off his glove. "Vlad," he said past his clenched teeth as he pulled the black leather right off his fingers. "Don't let her get away."

The glove then fell away, revealing his discolored hand and the Mark within his palm. Vladimir only saw a frail-looking hand, whereas the witch's confidence quickly diminished from her expression, turning it cold and cunning. Thoughtful, Vladimir thought.

"I *knew* I felt something coming from you," she said eyeing Jacob now with intense interest. "But I didn't think I would see something like *that* again. The Eye of Kosm… tell me, Hunter, where did you get that?"

"Doesn't matter," Jacob said approaching the witch with his palm facing her and his sword ready. "But she is now with her dark lord in the depths of Oblivion; You can ask her when you get there."

The witch smiled with a mouth of rotten teeth and iron fillings. "What an interesting creature you are."

"Don't move, witch," Vladimir said now circling around and keeping his guns trained on the woman. "No tricks."

"Tricks? Now why would I have any tricks?"

Jacob got within ten feet of the witch before he stopped and began willing the energy circulating through his body to concentrate into the mark on his hand. "That's enough coming from you. I'll make it quick, which is the least your kind deserves."

"Sorry," the witch said immediately clapping her hands together. "But I have children to look after." Immediately, her body dematerialized into a swarm of thousands of black rats just as fire erupted from Jacob's palm, roasting a few but not enough to stop the swarm now coming his way. He ran back as the swarm chased him and charged towards Vladimir, who began shooting them one by one into bloody chunks. Jacob blasted more fire across the swarm and a good many of them slipped back and away and rematerialized into shadow which formed the shape of the witch who reappeared and came at him with the clawed gauntlet.

Jacob managed to get his sword up to stop the claws from digging into his face, but he felt his knees buckle against the force of the attack. He gritted his teeth, not at all surprised by the witch's strength. He then gasped out loud as she planted a strong knee into his groin, and then seizing his throat with her free hand, she hurled him across the meadow with inhuman strength, sending him tumbling across the ground and sliding across one of the ponds.

"Fuckin' slag!" Vladimir swore as he fired his guns at the witch. The bullets punched right through her, painting the landscape around her in mists of blood. She bounded away like a cat and muttering some curse in an ancient language, and a strange mist seemed to materialize from her fingertips and float towards the shooting Hunter. Upon closer observance, he realized that it was a swarm of wasps, and he was quickly swarmed by the many stinging insects and was forced to wave his arms about to swat them away.

"A *slag*, am I?" the witch hissed as the bullets stuck in her arms and body slowly began to get pushed out and the holes they created closing like shifting clay. Her eyes then glowed bright as she extended the claws on her gauntlet, aiming for the flailing Hunter. "I'll show you-"

Shurk!

"Gah!" the witch snarled as she clutched at the arrow that had pierced right through her right knee. She then turned her eyes upon Jacob, who nocked another arrow and took aim at her, this time aiming for the hand she was extending towards him. The second arrow stuck right through the palm and the silver-tip just barely piercing the flesh on her forehead. As she wrenched the arrow out, Jacob had already nocked another arrow and took aim again as the swarm of wasps finally disappeared like smoke around Vladimir, her spell breaking with her concentration.

"This arrow here is iron-tipped," Jacob warned her. "Blessed by the holy waters of Yohnah."

The witch snarled. "That bastard..."

"It'll burn just like before." Jacob warned her. "Worse than fire. But one shot and it will be over. Don't fight any longer."

The witch breathed heavily, more angry to be hearing the name of Yohnah than she was of the pain caused upon her body.

"Do you have any last words, witch?" Jacob muttered, his blue eye cold and hard as he stared at her. His glare was so intense that even Vladimir was amazed at the Hunter. He wasn't just some rookie anymore, but a bloodthirsty Hunter who wished to end the life of a miserable witch.

The woman then began to chuckle, which then turned immediately into chortled laughter. Her cackle carried throughout the trees almost manically as she remained where she was.

"You *really* think you've bested me? I don't have any last words, Hunter. But I *do* have the last words you're ever going to hear." Suddenly her eyes flashed bright and green as she practically hissed like a snake. "Yohnah, is dead."

"Jacob!" Vladimir cried out and Jacob didn't think of questioning as he threw himself aside just as the witch's broomstick whizzed past him like a spear. If he had not jumped, he would have been run through and would probably be dead when the broom brought him close to the witch to rip his throat out. The witch then grabbed ahold of the speeding broomstick and mounted it like a horse. She then came barreling right after Jacob with her claws extended. "Let me hear you squeal, pig of Yohnah! *Squeal*!"

Jacob pushed himself back up and wrenched his eyepatch right off his eye. Upon seeing what lied beneath the leather binding, the witch banked around, desperate to get her eyes out of the line of sight of the-

By the gods, that had been an Immortal Eye!

Unfortunately, her evasion caused her to bank in the direction of Vladimir, who had been firing at her. She spun on her broomstick to maneuver through, but now Vladimir had dropped his pistol and went for his sword. He swung as she came barreling past. He had missed her body but the sword cut

deep across her arm, the tip gliding across bone as she swooped back up and out of harm's way. She snarled at the two, her hand over her bleeding arm where droplets fell like rain.

A piercing scream suddenly sounded across the valley, and the witch turned her head towards the direction it came from. Jacob had heard such a sound before, echoing throughout the city of Irondell, during the Plague of the Dead.

The witch turned her evil glare back to Jacob, who was now accompanied by Vladimir, ready for another go at her. "Don't get so cocky, Huntsmen," she hissed, her eyes glowing with hatred; enough to almost pierce right through the Hunters right down to their souls. She removed her hand from her arm. Though blood had smeared all across her tattooed skin, the wound from the sword had healed.

"What the hell..." Vladimir cursed in a low voice. "What do we do, Jacob?"

Jacob answered without taking his eyes off the witch, "Only fire and holy relics can kill her. But fire... she just needs to burn."

"Jacob..." the witch hissed, her broom slowly lowering back down towards the earth but still being far enough as to not get attacked so suddenly again. Should either Hunter try to shoot at her she could easily just maneuver away from this distance. She also kept her focus on Vladimir it seemed, as if to avoid Jacob's gaze despite talking to him.

"That is your name, right? Such a handsome one at that... I really want to keep you now."

"Well then come down here, and we can talk," Jacob said.

"I *would* like to know about how you came across that Mark," the witch purred. "However, I do not want to waste any more time. You've trespassed in my domain, and all of you shall be punished. You, though," she added pointing at Jacob and looking at him at last. "I will have you *and* the girl."

"The girl?" Jacob demanded.

"What do you mean?" Vladimir added.

The witch smiled as she raised her clawed hand above her head. "You'll find out!"

Upon thrusting her hand down towards the two, a current of green lighting flashed down and blew the two Hunters away. The witch then cackled as she swooped in and charged for Vladimir who was just barely getting up. He managed to lean back to keep his very head from getting sliced off by her talons, but the claws had cut his cheek, shredding four deep cuts across his face. The witch banked back around, sucking the blood off every talon as if slowly savoring cherry syrup.

Vladimir, cut and bleeding, pulled his gun again and fired it at the witch until the cylinder was emptied. Only four bullets had lodged into her body, but the witch just continued to laugh. That hideous and terrible laugh that destroyed whatever beauty she once had, echoed in Jacob's ears like a horrible nightmare. When his gun was out, the witch lunged right for him again, this time her eyes flashing bright and green as her faced seemed to morph into one that even Jacob could recognize. For lunging at Vladimir with claws outstretched and fingers crackling with green lighting, was none other than Luca Harker.

"Squeal for me, *pig*," Luca called out as he rushed at Vladimir. His face began to molt and blacken as if he were a rotting fruit, and parts of his skull was visible in his peeling skin. He pulled his lightning-coated arm back, ready to blast Vladimir before he sliced him to ribbons. "Squeal!"

Jacob turned his eye upon Vladimir, who saw the Immortal red flash, and shouted, "See!"

Immediately, the veil seemed to have fallen from Vladimir's eyes as he saw past the witch's spell, and with a loud cry, he scooped up his sword and slashed right at lightning-coursed hand that was just mere inches away from burning a hole right through his body. The hand of the witch went flying and a shrill and terrible cry pierced the ears of the Hunters, causing them to collapse to their knees in incredible pain. It felt to Jacob like his very eardrums were about to get blown out as his mind was rocked by the inhuman howl that came from the magical being. The witch had crashed down into the snow, and still she cried out clutching her bleeding stump as her hand landed just a few feet away from her. Vladimir turned an angry eye towards the witch, who looked upon both Hunters with the hatred of a wounded dog against its former master.

"You stupid boy!" the witch snarled, her voice layered with a monstrous growl like a wild beast as she clutched at her bleeding stump.

"Fuck you too," Vladimir growled, his teeth clenched so hard that they looked like they might just shatter beneath the pressure of his jaw.

The witch seethed as the two men picked themselves back up. Jacob had drawn his bow, but already Vladimir was already starting for the witch, his bloody sword clenched tightly in his hands.

"You *dare* show me his face," he growled with every step he took towards the witch. "You dare wear it like a... like a *mask*? You're *dead*, you bitch. I'm going to enjoy bathing my sword in your blood!"

The witch swiped her arm before her, splashing her blood across the ground which somehow caused black smoke to erupt as if it was acid burning the dirt. Jacob warned Vladimir to get back as he loosed another arrow into the plume of smoke. He heard no sound and looked up to see the witch back on her broomstick and sailing away with her severed hand in her claws.

"*You* are dead!" she swore as she sailed off and away from the two. "You will all pay with your blood! You will all pay!"

With that, she disappeared from view above the trees of the damned, leaving the two Hunters gasping for breath as the smoke seemed to spread like wildfire, consuming all sight and taking the air right out of their lungs.

"Don't…" Jacob coughed out as he collapsed back onto his hands and knees, the smoke seeming to coil around his neck like a serpent. He could barely see a few feet in front of him the smoke was so thick, and within the darkness he thought he could see the souls of all the witch had eaten, screaming at him, begging for him to let them in.

"Don't… breathe…"

But he collapsed face-down into the ground, seeing even Vladimir succumb to the strange smoke. His vision blurred and all sound turned to white noise like a drowning man whose ears were filling with water. He then saw nothing but darkness, and he knew no more.

Di

Carmilla arrived, both hands attached, but she would have rather lost both never to have use of them again, than to arrive at the terrible scene that was her distraught daughter and the ashes of her son.

Yes, her son and daughter. Because although they were taken by her, used for her experiments and study, she cared for them still as if they were her own. Her womb had been destroyed along with her soul when she had joined the Coven, but as black as her heart was, she still found love in it for the children, one of whom was dead. It was unbelievable, unfathomable, really, and yet here it was. Her Immortal child had been killed. Slain.

Murdered...

She stared down at the ash pile that Mithus had thrown herself in, holding the ashes of her brother in her hands and crying in anguish, her tears clotting up the ash like raindrops after a forest fire. Carmilla had said nothing upon finding her children, but a monstrous growl threatened to rise from her chest and escape her throat. While she had been healed from the gunshots and her severed hand, no spell or herb could heal the terrible pain in her heart. She had not felt this way in a long time, not since she could really be considered human. The anguish was as sickly as a disease, and it seemed to grow worse and worse as she dropped to her knees, exhausted from her fight and now seeming to lose to this anguish that held her tightly like a rapist.

And now... now Lithus was dead.

Having been granted immortality at such a young age, Carmilla never quite understood death anymore. Death was just a distant memory for her; a childhood memory she was incapable of catching. All of her family was lost in time, and she had vowed never to start again. But all that changed when she stumbled upon the Immortal family, and stole the infants away from their wetnurse like a thief would diamonds from an aristocrat. Raising them specifically for power, her heart had changed. She had grown to love the children, and it pained her miserably to see one of them dead. She never expected to be affected by such pain again, and yet here it was, seeming to have laid in wait for the right moment to pounce.

This isn't right... she found herself saying to herself again and again. Unwilling to accept the harsh reality in front of her. *This isn't how it was supposed to be... we were supposed to grow together here, live together here... away from the rest of the horrible world beyond the mountains... why...*

Why...

... why...

Carmilla suddenly threw her head back violently as she howled up to the skies beyond the crevice and far beyond this world of Lunokean. Like a chorus of crows screaming at a deer to just give up and die, her voice carried across the valley, shutting all sounds of the night into silence. She tore at her own clothes in anguish and anger, tearing it all down until her marked and rune-covered flesh was visible to the setting sun's rays. She screamed to the heavens and whatever Stars were listening into the abyss beyond, proclaiming her hatred for the ones who had killed Lithus- her one and only son.

When she brought herself back to the world she was on, she stalked over to the ash-covered Immortal and snarled at her. "Get out of the way."

Mithus looked at her with wide silver eyes filled with tears. "Wh-"

"I said *move!*" Carmilla snapped grabbing ahold of the Vampire by the scruff her of dress and throwing her aside. She then scooped up a handful of Lithus' ashes and held it up to her eyes. She thought that she would never have to do this; never having to do what she had planned to in the very beginning. Her heart had softened, and the thoughts of such a spell had never crossed her mind in the twelve years she had the children.

But now... in order to avenge the death of her son, Carmilla decided that it was time.

Those Hunters would pay with their blood and flesh. That Witcher in particular, would drown her misery with his blood and the flesh on his bones would feed her belly. The others, would feed Mithus, and she would grow stronger with human blood instead of the tainted blood in her own body. They would both take chances, they would both sacrifice in order to kill them.

This, upon Lithus' ashes, Carmilla swore. "Come," she told Mithus standing up. "We are returning home."

The young Immortal was crying, her tears glistening with the glow of her beautiful silver eyes. "But... Lithus..."

"He is *dead*!" Carmilla snapped, impatient with the Vampire's crying. She felt sorry for yelling, but her rage was justified, and soon Mithus would understand. "Unless you want to join him, you are coming with me." She stalked past Mithus, threatening to leave her behind unless she got moving.

"What are we going to do, Mother?" the Vampire asked as she scrambled to her feet. She was alongside Carmilla in an instant. Good.

"Something I vowed I'd never do," Carmilla muttered, clenching the ashes tighter in her fist. "We are going after those Hunters- soon."

"They'll kill us," Mithus said following close behind. "Just like they killed Lithus."

"No. We will kill *them*. You and I both will bathe in their blood, and we will make sure Lithus is able to rest in peace at last." Carmilla stopped, and after thinking about it for a moment, turned and embraced Mithus around the neck. The Vampire was surprised at first, but then released her anguish into soft sobs which drenched what was left of Carmilla's shirt, her cloak offering what little warmth her body could not.

"I'm sorry," she told her daughter. "I promised I would protect you both. I couldn't keep my promise."

"Mommy…" Mithus cried softly. "Please, no…"

"It was my fault I couldn't protect you. I thought we would be safe. I thought, I could protect you both until you were at an age where you would be able to. Unfortunately, I couldn't do it for Lithus. But I won't lose you too. I can't. We will kill those Hunters, and then, you and I will continue to be together, forever."

Mithus sniffed. "You promise?"

Carmilla tried to swallow the lump that had formed in her throat. She knew the words were coming. Though Mithus was an Immortal; a Vampire, she was still but a child. Ignorant of the ways of the world, and what it can do to people both and high and low on the food chain. It ate you up, and it didn't give a damn what you did or didn't do. It didn't give a damn about Carmilla, or poor Lithus.

But Carmilla would walk through the fires in deepest pits of Oblivion, before she allowed anything or anyone to take Mithus as well.

"Yes," she nodded to her only child. "I promise."

"Come on," Luca said to Vladimir taking off and stopping at the ridge, overlooking the city of Dragondell.

The tall brick chimneys of the sandstone buildings belched black smoke, and the Núul River snaked right through the city's heart, with boats of all sorts traveling up and down carrying goods, passengers, and the occasional gondola containing lovers as men sang in deep tongues. Vladimir leaned up against the chimney, joining Luca in taking in the view. It was night time, and the moon shone bright over the city which seemed to never sleep. Ships full of crates were being unloaded at the docks, and the butchering factories were getting ready for the next morning. Some housewives were putting up their laundry on lines between some of the smaller buildings, and the chimney-sweeps were dancing along the rooftops to the music being played outside the many bars and stages in the streets far below.

"It's beautiful," Vladimir muttered, lost in the memories of standing on rooftops just like this one, except alone and not with a partner. How long had it been since he had paused during a contract to just love on the world and time he was living in? It felt like an eternity.

"Isn't it?" he asked Luca.

"Just goes to show how big the world really is," Luca replied smiling. "Though, I miss the farmlands. Everyone here seems too close together."

"Well, that's just the way some of them live," Vladimir said. "It's the way I used to live."

"I can tell."

"Cheeky bastard."

Luca laughed. Luca turned to him then, considering what his friend had said. Vladimir hardly ever talked about his past. There was nothing left, so there was no point in talking about it. But the two of them had been working together for about a month now, and together they had brought down ten werewolves and four Lycans. All of them were forces to be reckoned with, but they all fell at the hands of the Hunters.

"Oi," Luca then said, breaking the spell which the city had put Vladimir under momentarily. "We should get going. The night's still young."

"That's right," said Vladimir, turning his eyes up to the moon far above. The moon was not only the light of the world when night falls, but also the bane of humanity. For this was when monsters emerged, and fed on the people of Balkeñoir. He turned his head as a howl sounded in the distance, to the east of the city. The howl was low, lonely, and afraid.

The beast they hunted, was there.

"Come on," Vladimir said placing a hand on his gun as he began to slowly make his way down the length of the rooftop with Luca in tow. *"Let's go hunt some dogs."*

Vladimir slowly began to stir. The blackness of the dream he had begun to fade away, turning into thin slits of light that revealed a small crackling fire. He groaned, and tried to sit up only to be pushed back down by a gentle hand.

"Stay down," an angelic voice said to him. "You need to rest."

Vladimir willed his eyes to open more, causing him to be blinded for a moment by the firelight. He saw the pale hand with black nails holding him down, and he followed the arm with his eyes until he saw himself looking into hard, purple eyes.

"It's okay," Angela said. "You're safe now."

"Vladimir..." Sabina's voice said coming up to him opposite of Angela and placing two fingers beneath his jaw. Appearing satisfied with his pulse she asked, "How are you feeling?"

Vladimir parted his lips to speak, feeling them crack upon movement. "Like shite," he answered, suddenly aware that he was speaking in his old lingo growing up. He turned his head to his right, to see Jacob laying right beside him, his body concealed in a bedroll and his eyepatch returned to his eye. Had what he saw and experienced... had all that been real?

Yes, he believed it was, and he realized he didn't care about it, not right now, anyway.

He looked up, to see that they were all sitting in a small dugout that held a person-sized statue of some man wearing a blank mask and carrying a bell between his hands. He was robed, and Vladimir's head was propped against the feet of the statue. The world outside the ridge was dark and a light breeze rushed through the dugout, sending his body into a world of chills. He reached up to his face which was itching, and felt that a bandage had been wrapped around his scratched cheek where the witch had gotten him.

"Don't touch," Sabina said gently pushing his hand back down to his side. "The medicine will help it heal."

"Where are we?" he groaned.

"Some old shrine," Angela answered, now sitting in a different position, perched on a rock facing the mouth of the strange cave they were in. "The Bell-Ringers probably used to come up here to meditate and pray. We got out of the area just in time, picked up Morgan and Charlotte on the way up here. Our horses are just outside."

Vladimir sighed with relief, and allowed his head to gently fall back. "The witch?"

"Gone," Jacob's voice croaked, pulling Vladimir's attention to the Hunter who was just laying still staring up at the rocky ceiling. "Gone, just like the Vampires, according to Angela and Sabina."

"They might come back though," Angela warned them all.

"If she does, I'll kill her," Vladimir groaned. "Me and Jacob both."

Jacob grunted in reply in a way that made Vladimir think of Luca again. "Let's just focus on resting up. Angela found the herbs in my bag and mixed up a concoction for our wounds- as well as an oil for us to breathe again."

"What was that shit anyway?" asked Vladimir.

"Dunno," said Jacob. "Some call it Black Death, but no one has been able to recreate it. In fact, that's only the second time a witch had ever used that spell on me."

That sounded funny to Vladimir somehow, and he laughed. "Only the second time..."

Jacob smiled but said nothing.

"We found you both all blue and coughing up blood," Sabina said sitting back and picking at her nails. Somewhere behind her, the children were snuggled up in their respective bedrolls, sleeping soundly. "Angela carried you both here by herself."

"Did she now?" Vladimir's gaze lingered over to the Dhampir who gave no indication whether or not she had heard them. "Why didn't she just get the horses?"

"You were both dying," Angela said without looking back. "We had no time. We had to get you somewhere safe, and apply the salve and make you sniff the oils. You would have died if I waited to find the horses. I did that after I was sure you would both survive."

Vladimir pouted and looked up at the ceiling deep in thought. "Why?"

"What do you mean?" Sabina asked. "You both would have died if we hadn't-"

"That's not what I mean," Vladimir said rubbing his sore shoulder. He thought of just letting it go. Then he decided otherwise. "I mean, why me, Angela? Why would you try so hard to get me here? I don't deserve it from you."

"As Sabina said," Angela said simply. "You would have died if I hadn't. We are all on this job together, and we all need to return together."

Vladimir turned his eyes to the Dhampir, and she still had not moved from her spot. Movement caught his eye and he turned to see that Charlotte had roused and was now at his side where Sabina had been before and looking at him. Her hood was off, revealing her large bald head, making her appear more alien than before. In her hand, she held a small piece of cooked meat. She offered to feed Vladimir, holding it close to his mouth.

Didn't even hear her coming...

Not knowing what to say or whether even to accept it or not, he gave in and opened his mouth. When the succulent meat met his teeth, he pulled it off slowly as to not spill on himself. He chewed it without tasting it, and swallowed.

"Thanks," he said reaching out. "I'll take care of myself now."

Charlotte smiled, and then turned to look at Jacob who was chewing on a piece of meat of his own. The Hunter was smiling at Vladimir.

"What?" Vladimir demanded.

"Nothing." Jacob shook his head. "You just look so nice when you are helpless."

"Fuck off, will you?"

Sabina slapped his leg. "Vlad!" she hissed gesturing to Charlotte who had returned to the sleeping Morgan. Jacob was chuckling, content with the reaction.

"It's okay." Charlotte assured her when she got settled back in. "We've heard worse in Firedell."

While munching on the rest of the meat, Vladimir turned his attention back to Angela who remained where she was. She never once looked back, always on alert and watching the world beyond the cave.

"Angela," he called out to her.

"What is it?"

"This doesn't change anything between us," he told her. "But... thank you, for saving Jacob and I."

Angela made no movement whether or not his words had bothered her or not. She just simply said in an almost bored tone, "You're welcome."

"Heh," Jacob chuckled bemusedly. "That's funny. 'This doesn't change anything between us'... That's a hell of a thing say to her."

Vladimir sighed. "Let's not do this now."

"Why not?" Jacob demanded sitting up and glaring at him. "You've been giving her nothing but shit since we left."

"Jacob," Angela started. "Please, not now."

"No, I wanna hear it. What is your problem with Angela, really?"

Vladimir groaned as he laid back down. All at once he felt too tired to deal with anything else. "Drop it, Jacob."

"She's never wronged you, has she?"

"Jacob…" Angela said in a low growl. She was losing her patience almost as fast as Vladimir was. Almost, but not quite.

"Cmon, then," Jacob persisted like a child. "Let's hear it- and don't just say 'she's a Dhampir.' So what? She hasn't done anything to you, has she?

Vladimir's patience finally snapped like a frayed viola string and he snapped in a hiss, "Her kind has!"

Despite his care however, Morgan was rousing, asking what was wrong as Charlotte tried to assure him everything was all right despite everything not going in that direction at all. Vladimir was glaring at Jacob with a look which he realized was hatred, and although it might have been wrong to hate the young Hunter, such concerns were the last thing on the Werewolf Hunter's mind. Jacob meanwhile appeared perplexed, not ashamed but perhaps considering. Angela meanwhile, only watched the two curiously, not speaking up but instead seeming to wait back and see what would unfold. Sabina and Charlotte meanwhile, appeared very uncomfortable, and both wished they were not here.

"You want a more satisfying reason?" Vladimir was demanding. "Ask Sabina, why she became a Vampire Hunter in the first place. Ask her what she feels working with someone who shares the blood of a Vampire in their veins. Ask me why I became a Werewolf Hunter- better yet, why did you become a Witch Hunter, Jacob? Not for sport, that's for damn sure. All beasts no matter the breed are a plague on the world, and they all need to be eliminated. They deserve no more sympathy than rabid dogs. Yes, I admit, Angela had done nothing to me personally, but I cannot bring myself to ever truly trust her for what she is. As long as my heart still beats, I will always hunt the beasts of this world, and I will *never* trust one, regardless whether they are feral, or docile."

He ended this while looking at Angela, seeing that the Dhampir was now looking at him with those cold, purple and inhuman eyes of hers. It was impossible to tell what she was thinking. Such a beautiful face, always cold and rarely showing any happiness, or anger. Whenever he saw it, her anger was like a whirlwind. In fact, there were times when Vladimir hoped she would snap so that he would have a chance to just have an excuse to get rid of her. But that wasn't because of her personally, and he knew it. It was a prejudice he simply could not let go.

"It has nothing to do with you," he added to Angela. "I hope you at least know that."

"I doubt it matters," she said simply, and thankfully not sullenly.

"You're a real bastard," Jacob finally said to Vladimir. "You know that?"

"Maybe I am," Vladimir admitted. "But I'd rather be a bastard, than share my blood with a monster."

Angela's eye twitched at that, and for a second, it looked like the Dhampir would indeed react. For a moment, Vladimir thought his time was numbered. She saw the real anger in her eyes then, that was barely held back by some desire or need to hold on. But that didn't stop her from speaking her mind at last, much to everyone, especially Jacob's surprise.

"Do you really think your kind is any better?" she then said, her voice barely above a whisper. No one said anything as they just stared at the Dhampir, her words while quiet, laid on a heavy weight upon them all. "Do you really think humankind is any less monstrous than the beasts that walk the planet?"

Vladimir swallowed. "That's not the point..."

"Is it not?" Angela challenged. Her voice was set, her eyes furious, and she *would* be heard. "You blame me for the acts of those who share my blood, but let me ask you this: Can I blame you for the actions of your own bloodline? What you humans are capable of?"

Vladimir said nothing. He wouldn't be able to even if he had something to say.

"You kill your own kind. You war with one another, you butcher and tear each other apart through discrimination, hatred, and all the sins you are capable of. I've seen many humans slaughter the innocent in order to obtain land, riches, or even fame. You have your own thieves, murderers, whores and cultists. You humans look down on me because I share the blood of Vampires, but I never once saw one Immortal feeding another to the wolves. Sometimes, in my experience with both Vampires and humans, it is impossible for me to tell the difference anymore."

Her words, they struck without mercy. Though they were directed at Vladimir, everyone heard them and were found contemplating. Despite them being spoken in a calm matter, the force behind them threatened to tear all the Hunters apart. Everyone simply stared at her, unsure what to say or do after hearing such a thing. She had given away nothing of her personal experience, nothing of her treatment. But still her words sunk deep like knives.

To everyone's surprise, Sabina was the first to break the silence. She shifted in place and rested her back against her pack before crossing her arms and speaking.

"I sympathize, I really do. Maybe we humans can be just as monstrous as Vampires. You know both sides better than anyone, there's no question. Perhaps it is wrong to lump you in with the rest, but you have to understand that there are things that cannot be forgiven. Families have been destroyed by the Immortal Nobility, even after their hierarchy had fallen. So many lives are lost to vampiric beings, Dhampirs included. I understand your pain and apologize for all mistreatment on my part. But the things we've all seen and had to deal with... it is...

difficult to truly forgive Vampires. I'm sure to them we are just like the cows and sheep that we slaughter."

Angela nodded. "That might be true. But if you think I have any connection to the world of Immortals, however much smaller it is now, you're wrong. They don't like me any more than humans do."

Vladimir frowned at this. "Well... even so, it is difficult to ignore our own instincts. We're human, we fear the dark and those who control it. I have no doubt that you're a good person, Angela. But still... in the end, you are still a Dhampir. Our kind... we aren't meant to get along with you."

Sabina added, "What Vladimir said, it might be cruel, but it is true. You're still a creature of the night, and we are of the day. We aren't meant to coexist, no matter how unfair it may be."

"You're so full of shit," Jacob snapped angrily; frustrated and tired of hearing all of this. "All of you. You can't even-"

"Jacob." Angela then said turning her head away from the group. Her voice carried no malice nor cruelty, it had become just as tranquil as it had been before. "Don't waste your breath."

"But-"

"I said: Don't." Though her voice was stern, it was quiet and her tone was bored. It was like she was trying to be serious, but just didn't care.

Or perhaps, Vladimir wondered, she's just trying to hide it again, reel back the anger and frustration that had been there momentarily.

Jacob looked like he wanted to argue but simply laid back and crossed his arms. Vladimir felt bad for the guy, but there was no changing his mind. He meant what he said to Angela, both the thanks and where he still stood with her. Although like Sabina, he sympathized with Angela concerning how unfair it was to be treated as a hostile, but there was nothing that could be done. How could he make it any simpler to understand?

"It's nothing against her personally," Vladimir said to Jacob but loud enough for even Angela to hear. "But what she is, and who we are, it's never meant to be. I can never trust a Dhampir, not me personally. That's just the way it is."

What she is… and who we are. What a shitty way of putting it.

"Whatever," Jacob said crossing his arms.

"Can I ask you something?" Sabina then dared. "What if she is a witch?"

Jacob's mouth twitched, but he didn't say anything.

"Exactly," she said. "We all got our prejudices, and sometimes… sometimes they are justified."

She looked up as Charlotte then walked past the group and stopped before Angela. She then closed the rest of the distance between them and stood right beside the Dhampir. Everyone watched as Angela turned her head to the girl, who tightened her coat around her little body.

"May I… sit with you?"

Angela blinked at her, but then scooted to the right, leaving room on the rock for Charlotte to sit and curl up beside the Dhampir. It amazed everyone, especially Vladimir that the little girl could sit next to a creature possibly more dangerous than a Vampire. That, and the fact that Angela had allowed it. She obviously meant no harm to anyone here, but still… the gravity of the dangers was immense. He looked at Morgan, who was still deeply asleep.

She knows what it is like, Vladimir realized. She wasn't completely human either. *The two of them… are almost the same.*

After a long time of silence, Vladimir called out to Charlotte. "You need to get some sleep too. We need to head our first thing in the morning."

"O-kay," Charlotte said. She bade Angela goodnight and rushed to her brother's side and getting ready for bed.

"Yeah," Sabina agreed nodding solemnly. "We should all get some sleep." She turned to Angela. "Do you want to sleep?"

"I'll keep watch," the Dhampir replied, not looking back.

"You sure?"

"Sleep. I'll keep watch," she repeated.

Sabina looked at Vladimir, who shrugged and proceeded to lay back in his bedroll. "We leave at first light," he announced.

"Right," Jacob said turning in his roll so that his back was to Vladimir. The Werewolf Hunter was glad the conversation was over, but at the same time, it felt like he was simply dropping something on the floor, when eventually he would have to circle back to pick it back up. It only made it more difficult, as only the crackling of the fire sounded in the cave and lulled him back to sleep. Until he finally closed his eyes, he had always kept an eye on Angela, sitting on her rock.

The Dhampir never stirred.

After a period of time, Sabina rose from her bedroll. She checked on the children and then watched Jacob and Vladimir to ensure that the men were likewise asleep. When she was sure of it, she quietly crept over towards Angela who heard her coming.

"I told you that you could sleep," she told Sabina.

"I need to talk to you."

"Can't it wait?"

"No."

Angela sighed. "What is it?"

"We should have killed those Immortals."

"Hmm."

"You could have done both of them yourself."

"I could have."

"Yet you told me to do the boy, and you didn't bother with the girl."

"I gave them both my warning, and the boy didn't take it."

Sabina grew frustrated and had to constrain herself to keep her voice down. "That doesn't explain why you didn't kill them yourself."

"They were only children," said Angela. "They don't know what they are doing."

"That girl, if she doesn't come after us because of what we did to her brother, she'll grow up to be a killer of men anyway."

"Perhaps."

Sabina snorted. She couldn't help it. "'Perhaps'? Why did you spare one and not the other? Why didn't you kill them?"

Angela didn't answer. Not only that, but Sabina realized that Angela didn't once look at her since she had been approached. The Dhampir kept her eyes on the frigid winds blowing fresh powder across the mouth of the cave.

So, Sabina asked, "Do you pity them?"

No answer.

"Angela?"

"Maybe I did," Angela admitted. "I found it difficult to murder those children just as any human would when children are in question."

"They aren't children though."

This time, Angela did look back at Sabina. Her face showed no real emotion, but her cat-like eyes contained something along the lines of... of...

"To you, perhaps not. To me, what's the difference between a human child and a vampiric child, apart from their biological makeup?"

Sabina frowned heavily. Now she understood.

"I get what you're saying," she said. "But you can't save everyone. In the end, it's always one or the other. Vampires and humans no matter how similar we are in looks and nature, we are never the same. You might be the same because you are part of both. I… I also understand that you struggle with us because we are human and quite frankly, we fear you. You said the Immortals despise you. So why help either? Better yet, why hunt monsters for mankind and yet spare two… two children as you call them, who might have grown up to be murderers."

"It's complicated," said Angela.

"Like hell it is," said Sabina. "I understand your hesitation. But it isn't the same way as it is for us. You obviously chose to help mankind. Then help us. You can't be on the fence when it comes to stuff like this."

"I'm not," said Angela. "I understand everything that Immortals are capable of. If their noble houses had not been destroyed long ago, they might have very well overtaken this country for themselves. As mankind advances, as they evolve, they will soon inherit Lunokean and everything in it. For that to happen, I know Immortals have no place here any more than any other beast will one day. But that doesn't mean it is always easy. It is easy for me to stop an Immortal trying to take over a city, or plaguing a village or haunting the night. It isn't so easy to condemn children who don't know any better. It's like punishing a tiger cub because they might become maneaters. Immortal or not, that doesn't make it easy. But, I understand that my actions today might have put you and perhaps us all in danger. We are in danger still as long as that witch is alive. That still doesn't make it easy."

Sabina was quiet for a while, digesting the Dhampir's words. When she spoke again, her voice was softer, kinder. "Well, it is good neither of us guaranteed that we killed both of them. If they ask we can say that the girl got away. But if she ever comes after us, and you have to cross blades with talons, you can't hesitate."

"I don't need you to tell me that," said Angela.

"Maybe not," Sabina agreed. "I'm not saying you need to pick a side here, but understand that not every monster is worth saving. And quite frankly, I don't understand why you would protect the children of the very race who scorned you."

"Just as you don't understand why I chose to hunt beasts for the sake of mankind, who likewise scorn me."

Sabina nodded. "Touché. But I–"

"I understand," said Angela. "Trust me, I already know. As for those children, understand that it is difficult for me to condemn them when they didn't choose to be what they are."

Sabina was offended but she didn't let it show. Angela's last saying regarding the kids struck home and while Sabina could understand and sympathize, it didn't make it easier. She also wondered if Angela was partially talking about herself as well.

But she didn't hound her on the matter. She knew deep down that the Dhampir already knew the possible consequences of her actions today, and those actions were of her choice. She was no doubt much older than Sabina and perhaps wiser in regards to Hunting Vampires and other monsters. But she also knew and she wasn't going to say this, but she knew that sometimes people needed to hear something in order for it to sit in. She had no doubt that even Angela, a Dhampir who was human enough, needed a reminder as well.

"That's good," she said to the Dhampir. "Let's just hope we finish this contract scot-free." She paused and then asked, "Are you sure you don't want to rest?"

"I don't need to."

"You know, it wouldn't kill you to try to rest like the rest of us."

"I know."

"Also, before I go, I just want to say I'm sorry."

Angela turned to look at Sabina again, looking puzzled.

"For the things I've said in the past. I meant what I said earlier. Ever since you came back and saved Jacob... it made it a lot easier to trust you, I hope you know that."

"That's... kind of you."

Sabina nodded.

"Your family," Angela suddenly asked. "Were they the victim of Vampires? Is that why you chose to specialize in them?"

Sabina didn't answer. She stared out at the snow, her arms crossed. After a while, the Huntress asked, "Why do you care? We all have our reasons for being Hunters, right?"

"Perhaps."

"My father was kidnapped by an Immortal. None of the villagers would go after him. Shortly after, he came back, but he wasn't my father anymore. He came and took my mother from me. The priest there killed them both."

"I see."

Sabina looked at Angela. "Do you?

Angela nodded.

"Hmm." Another pause, and then Sabina revealed, "I left the village when I was old enough. I prayed to Velinar and one of the old Hunters came and took me to Shadowfort."

"You became a Hunter to avenge your parents," said Angela.

Sabina chuckled humorlessly. "A lot of good it does me. I still see families destroyed and people ruined by Vampires. They say that the time of the Vampire War was bad, but I think it always has been. You have your werewolves and Lycans, and other old beasts who do the same. But Vampires... there is just something that cannot be ignored with them."

"I can understand your hatred then," said Angela. "The life of a Hunter is never easy. At least you have good memories to return to when you complete a job and manage to save those who count on you."

"I suppose. Why did you become a Hunter though?"

Angela answered, "Because I'm a Dhampir. I don't get to have a life like a normal person. I didn't get the luxury of a happy memory to return to. But let's just say I made my peace with it."

Sabina wondered what that meant. But she didn't have the words to express her questions that went through her head, they mingled and clashed with the cold truth that Angela had stated. She really didn't get to have a life like a normal person. She couldn't go to the Immortals for reasons of their own, and she no doubt found it difficult to live among humans. What she had said about a memory to return to... What had that meant?

"It is late," Angela said. "You better go rest. Don't worry about me."

"All right," said Sabina. She turned to go, stopped, and looked back. "Goodnight."

There was a short pause and Angela's response was almost carried away by the shrill howl of the wind outside. "You too."

Sabina had gone away. She had crawled into her bedroll and covered her face with the inner lining to keep it warm. Angela listened to the breathing of all the Hunters, and only relaxed when she knew they were all asleep.

Well, with the exception of one restless soul, who seemed to be outright refusing to go to bed in order to listen in. Or perhaps he just wanted to make sure she was all right. In any case, she was sure it wouldn't take long for him too to fall under the Flutemaster's lullaby.

Ti

When he was sure that everyone else had fallen asleep, Jacob slipped out of his bedroll and quietly crept past Vladimir and Sabina who were slumbering warmly.

The two kids were huddled close together on the other side of the Bell-Ringer's statue, Morgan holding Charlotte close as if afraid to let her go. Ignoring the pain in his side, he crept over to Angela, who remained where she was as still as a statue. He knew that she could hear him and didn't bother to say anything until he reached her.

"Hey," he said taking a seat beside the rock without getting too close to her.

"What are you doing up?" Angela asked, her eyes still fixated on the cold world outside the cave.

"That's a fine 'hello,'" Jacob said smiling. "I couldn't sleep, so I wanted to come join you."

"You were trying not to."

"How can you… whatever. Of course you knew. To be honest I was going to offer to take your place so you can get some rest."

"I'm fine."

"Sure. But would you still like some company?"

"… Do what you want," Angela decided.

Jacob turned his attention forward. "Very well, I will."

They both stared out into the night together. They didn't talk, at least not for a while. They simply shared the silence that the two had for this moment, as the wind howled somewhere far above the valley, and the howl of wolves sang chorus' that could be heard for miles around. They just sat there, two very different people, having at least something to share in a world that only knew how to take. Angela had been sure that Jacob was going to try to lecture her about how she just let Vladimir say whatever he wanted, or worse, bring up the

Immortal child still alive out there. For a long time however, he did not speak, and it wasn't awkward or uncomfortable for her. It was comforting, just sitting here for now.

In reality, Jacob did want to talk to Angela about that. But he didn't feel it necessary because there would just be no point to it. Whatever reasons Angela had, were her own. Regardless of what he thought of it, his only job was to support her as best she could. Also, considering their current predicament with one another, he didn't feel like he had the right to. Whether he felt that he had been in the wrong or not, he had plenty of time to think during this Hunt, and decided that he could have been a bit more sensitive. Angela was no fragile being, but even the strongest metal in the world could be tampered and worn, even the silver which fell from the moon. He just didn't think that their last conversation had really ended, and he didn't want to make cracks in something that had possibly been mended.

Eventually, after minutes of silence, Jacob dared to speak. "I don't believe them, you know."

"What?" Angela asked turning an eye to him.

"You know what," he said. "What the others say."

Angela frowned. "You say that but you wouldn't mean it when it would matter most."

"Like when?"

"When I show my monstrous side."

"You don't have one."

"Jacob…"

"I don't care," he said. "I don't care about what you are or even about your past. I only know you now, and that is all I need to know."

"That isn't true. How can you trust someone without knowing everything about them?"

"I don't have to. Do you?"

Angela didn't answer. She looked forward again towards the snow.

Jacob swallowed, as he struggled to confidently say something that would reassure Angela but at the same time bring this conversation to a close. "I'm not going to get preachy with you on the subject. I'm just saying I don't care about what the others say. I know you, and that's that."

"You don't even know anything about me."

"Other than you are a good Huntress? Lemme think…" Jacob tapped his chin with a forefinger as if actually pondering. It looked ridiculous to Angela when she noticed. "You have a cat, you love to read, you obviously play piano, and you like your privacy. You're not defined by your heritage, Angela. Just like those kids aren't."

Angela eyed him suspiciously and he raised his hands.

"That ain't any of my business," he said. "I'm not saying anything on that matter."

Angela watched him for a moment before bringing her eyes back forward. "All right."

Despite what he promising himself he wouldn't do it, he did it anyway. "I'm glad you finally stood up for yourself earlier."

"I didn't do anything."

"You sure got *someone* to think at least," he pointed out referring to Sabina.

"It doesn't matter," said Angela. "I know what I am, and who I am. Why do I need the approval others, when it never mattered before? All I can do is satisfy myself." What she didn't add was that she had Jacob too, but that wouldn't do to say here.

"But you aren't," Jacob said staring at Angela. "You aren't satisfied."

"You don't know what you're talking about."

"Really? If you really meant that, then you wouldn't be trying so hard to please Velinar. If you were satisfied with yourself, you wouldn't have tried to justify how monstrous humans can be. You wouldn't… you wouldn't have saved me back in Irondell, or again with me and Vladimir both."

Angela's mouth twitched, but she refused to look at the Hunter.

Jacob smiled. "You're not slamming me against walls. I guess that means I'm right."

"You're not," Angela denied.

"Yeah, right." Jacob chuckled. "I just… I can't stand you being treated like that, and I'm glad you at least *started* standing up for yourself."

"Because I am your 'friend', or because you see me as something else?" Angela asked looking at him. "You say you see the human side of me, and so you treat me like an equal. But, is there not a more… valid reason?"

"Does there always have to be?" Jacob countered, to which the Dhampir had no answer for. "At least when someone saves my ass, I give them a chance."

Angela turned away. "You just don't understand…"

"I don't? Or do you not want to understand?" Jacob shifted in his seat, and removed his glove to reveal his deformed hand. He flexed his fingers, which had all gone numb after casting his fire spell, twice. Angela noticed, and didn't peel her eyes away as he was often afraid most would. The idea that Vladimir had seen it too only made the feeling more prominent, and he felt a need to speak of something else.

"When I met you, I saw myself. Feared, hated, because of my magic. But… I also saw a fighter. Someone who had seen the blood, and had fought against it. Someone, who cares about others, more than herself. You showed me how to hunt Vampires, but you also showed me how important it is to have the back of your comrades. I would never allow harm to come to any within the Black Hand, not after you guys allowed me to come in. But you… you've set the standards in a way. Despite how others fear you, you still do your best. I can't help but admire you for that. You showed me all of that throughout our struggle in Irondell. That is why, I trusted you when you gave me the Immortal Kiss, or whatever it is they call it regarding Dhampirs."

He looked at Angela, to see that Angela was now looking at him again. He added at last, "I still trust you now, and hope that you can one day say the same to me. After all, what's the point of partnership or even friendship if we can't trust one another?"

He realized he *had* sounded preachy despite also telling himself that he wouldn't. He was breaking a lot of promises to himself, although that was no surprise he supposed.

Angela stared at him for the longest time. When she finally spoke, her voice was hollow. Not demanding, or calm, or indifferent, but instead, that of a lost soul; tired of wandering, and just finding home. "Vampires, and humans, don't belong together. Night and day cannot mix. Your words, they are kind and I appreciate them, but that doesn't erase the fact that I am the product of a forbidden abomination. I should not exist."

"And yet you do," Jacob countered. "And I say you are doing as good a job as any who is alive today. All I'm saying is you do not have to deal with it alone."

"People who try to make friends with monsters, end up getting eaten," said Angela. "Isn't that what they were supposed to teach you when you were adopted by the Bell-Ringers?"

"They did," Jacob chuckled. "But they also taught me to treat others the way you want to be treated. That's what friends do."

Angela looked away and shook her head. "You really are annoying. You know that?"

Jacob smiled. "That only means I'm getting through to you."

Angela grunted in reply. "How is your hand anyway?"

"It hurts. But I'll live. I only had to use my eye once as well- on Vladimir."

A thoughtful pause, and then Angela asked, "Does he know?"

"I'm sure he does. And I expect him to ask about it sooner or later. But for now, we just need to focus on getting to Snowcap Lake. We are almost there, and I say the sooner the better we get Morgan and Charlotte there, the sooner we can get out."

"Aren't you afraid we'll run into that witch again?"

"Not as afraid that we might run into that Raven again." Jacob looked at her. "But no matter what we come across, we are all going home again, right?"

Angela nodded. "Right. We are all going home."

Jacob smiled once again. "Then that is all the reassurance I need." He then faced the mouth of the cave again, once again joining Angela in the comfortable silence of each other's company; two beings alone in the night to share one another's silence. Jacob felt bad for hiding so much from the Dhampir, as well as the rest of the group, but he had spoken from the heart, and meant every single word he said to Angela.

He was not aware, but Angela knew, that Vladimir had awaken, and he had been listening the whole time.

Meanwhile, the spirits of the forest were stirring, circling like vultures as they neared the source of power growing steadily beneath the chilled skies. Like shadows, they crept and slithered into every nook and cranny in Carmilla's homestead, settling down in a sense of dread that fed them almost immediately. Any Sprites that were in the vicinity avoided this general area at all costs, for fear they would be corrupted against their will like some of their lost brethren, who fled to the Reservation deep in the south.

The witch had spread Lithus' ashes across a table where she had drawn a magic circle with her own blood. She then ground up salt, black tuber root, and the wings of a bat. She ground it all up and mixed it among the ash. Carmilla then crossed the room over to her cauldron, where a vat of various oils, potions and other ingredients were starting to boil. The smell was foul like a decaying animal, and the little mixture that spilled over the rim turned the fire almost bright red upon contact. The mixture only bubbled more when Carmilla added a dried white rose she had picked the last time she had gone down the mountain. At the sight of the flower, Mithus hissed in displeasure.

"Hush," Carmilla hissed back as she spread her hands over the bubbling cauldron. Then taking in a deep breath of the fumes emitting from the liquid, she began to chant the words of ancient power, left behind by the servants of Kawfka. She could feel many of them now, watching her, guiding her hand as she worked. She ignored them all however, as well as her daughter's obvious displeasure of the negative energy in the workshop. Having grown up with no parents to disclose the secrets of the Immortal Nobility, she couldn't have known that Kawfka and his coven despised the vampiric almost as much as their more blessed counterparts.

Carmilla's many runes marked upon her flesh began to glow bright and red, and the talons on her gauntlet began to shimmer and shine as she poured her own enchantments into the mixture. Then, when it was all ready, Carmilla took a wooden bowl, scooped up some of the mixture, and then taking it over to her table, she poured it over the ashes of Lithus.

Awaken, the demon you were meant to be... she prayed as she soaked all the dust within the magic circle with the liquid. The ash bubbled and clumped together like sand, turning into a tar-like substance that slowly stretched out along the lines of the magic circle. Carmilla then took an emptied vial, and then willing the air around the circle to move, she made the blackened liquid flow like a miniature river into the bottle; slithering like a snake down the neck until it filled the vial completely. As Carmilla studied the liquid within, she could have sworn she saw a face, morphed and unrecognizable, smiling at her. Smiling, but with no kindness.

She smiled right back at the soul within. "Don't worry, I'll take proper care of you."

Mithus, who had been hiding back, dared to approach Carmilla. "Mother, what is that, exactly?"

She and Lithus hardly ever asked Carmilla what her potions were for. In fact, they never asked about anything that Carmilla worked on here in this workshop. She always knew they had been watching, curiously wondering, but they never approached her. Lithus never had the chance, and the fact that it was happening now with Mithus, puzzled Carmilla for a moment.

Nevertheless, she answered.

"This, is a potion made specifically for a Vampire. According to the old legends, before the war with the Immortals, there was a hidden form hidden inside the bodies- a demonic being, sort of like a wolf in a Werewolf or Lycan. Today, many Vampires and Immortals can shift into the form of animals and whatever familiar they come into contact with- even shadows. But this particular form is... monstrous. I was experimenting on Vampires who tried to come and suck my blood. Using some of the old books I got from the Yom Univeristy, I managed to find some old records of an Immortal alchemist who created a potion that could draw out the beast most Immortals have forgotten about."

She didn't bother to mention that many Immortals had not forgotten but in fact refused to shift into their demonic form; the form of which Kawfka had granted them in order to become the most dangerous predator of Man after his gift of life had been scorned by the other Stars. This was of course before the Immortal in question had betrayed Kawfka and denied him as a god, which was as equivalent as grinding salt into an already festering wound.

But that wasn't important right now.

"I have a confession. I had planned to use you and your brother, two Pureblood Immortals to test this theory on. One of you would help me create the potion, and the other would receive it. But... I couldn't go through with it."

She looked at Mithus who was looking at her with solemn eyes that were tinged red from tears.

"So... We were to be used as experiments?"

The truth had to come out. There was no going back now, no matter how much it hurt.

"That was my intention at first when I found you both," said Carmilla. "But then... I fell in love with you both. You completed me, and so I abandoned my hypothesis. I abandoned my original plans, and decided to just raise you both here in the safety of the mountains. Unfortunately, I failed you both."

Mithus looked down at the floor, unable to look at her mother whom she thought would never harm her.

"I can do nothing for Lithus now," Carmilla said, approaching Mithus and dropping to one knee to meet the Immortal eye to eye. She took up Mithus' chin and raised it. "Hey, I promise you that if I could save him or bring him back, by the Stars and the Ancients in the deep seas, I would do it. I can do nothing for him now, but you and I can avenge his death. Do you want that?"

Mithus sniffed but she didn't pull away as her face crumpled into an expression of pure hatred. When she thought about it, sure, perhaps her mother had the worst intentions at first, but she had treated them good all these years. Now that her brother was gone, thanks to that Dhampir...

That demon...

"I want to," she answered. "I want that... that thing dead."

Carmilla smiled softly. There was no pride in it, only bloodlust. She had Mithus on her side. Good.

"So do I. Mithus, I know I will be asking much of you. But I need you to drink this potion."

Mithus looked at the vial, and then looked back at the witch. She was hesitant, as expected. She would be drinking her own brother's ashes among other things that alone are harmful to Vampires. "What will happen to me, when I become a beast?"

"If I'm correct, you'll still be the Mithus I know and love," Carmilla said and prayed for. "But… you will be able to shift not just into shadows anymore, and the chances of you being able to control familiars are slim in the demonic form."

"Will I… be able to come back?"

"Yes."

But this had been a lie. In truth, Carmilla didn't know for certain. Though she certainly hoped so. If she truly acknowledged any gods anymore, she would have prayed it be so.

"Will this… will this make you happy?"

Carmilla paused for a moment. She could still be happy, but after what happened to Lithus…

No. No, the Hunters had to pay for their crimes. When Carmilla was an officer in the Witches Covenant, she would never allow even a rude gesture from a man to go unpunished. In fact, there was once a time when a Lycan howled a mating call at her, and she responded thusly by ripping the creatures guts out before he could even shift into his beast form. This was how you dealt with defilers both who covet and those who act. The only way to avenge Lithus, was to have the Hunters pay. She had to use Mithus, in order to satisfy the roaring rage inside her heart, and she knew that regardless of whether it made herself happy or not, her now only child would perhaps wish the same upon them regardless. She wanted revenge, and that was just as well.

"Yes," she responded at last, holding out the vial. "Please."

Mithus looked at the vial one last time, and then took it into her small hands. "Okay," she said adding a small smile. "If it will make you happy, Mother, then I'll do it." She hesitated again however. "But that Dhampir… she said she would kill us both if we went after her or her friends again."

"Then I'll leave her to you," Carmilla said. "That is what you want, isn't it?"

Mithus' fist clenched the vial tighter, her knuckles growing paler, and for a moment, her mother worried that the vial would shatter.

"More than anything."

Carmilla nodded, satisfied. "As a Vampire, you are superior to her. She is just a half-breed sow. She shouldn't be a problem, not in your-" She stopped as Mithus suddenly snapped her head to the side, her eyes piercing through the window behind her. Her ears had twitched ever so slightly like a cat who had caught the minute squeak of a dormouse. "What is it?" She asked.

"There is someone out there…" Mithus told her, and immediately, Carmilla extended her talons and started for the door.

Healed after her encounter with the trolls, Sorina limped through the woods following the scent of the Dhampir she had fought before they were interrupted. Her cloak was torn to shreds but it still hung on her shoulders and stayed the cold of night. Her mask was bent, but she kept it on to keep her face from developing frostbite. She had followed the scent all this way, knowing that the group had to be about a mile away from here.

As she moved through the haunted trees, she noticed a small crumbling tower to her left. The decrepit bricks laid in ruins at the base, and a few holes were in the roofing. But what really caught her attention was the orange light peeking through the shutters of the lower part of the building. Sorina sniffed deeply, catching the smell of blood, rotten decay, and something else… something pleasantly foul like rotting fruit. She wondered what it was. The cold made it difficult to tell exactly what it was, but her senses weren't completely dulled, and as she listened, she heard talking. Two feminine voices...

"Tch," she sounded, releasing a stream of vapor from her breath as she trudged along. They were probably just mountain hermits, living away from civilization. Let them. They were probably worthless trash to begin with. Sorina couldn't dwell on who was living here or not. She had to catch up with the Huntsmen and kill them all.

With her platoon slaughtered and most of the war dogs dead or scattered, there was only her left. The only good thing being that there would now be no witnesses to be concerned with before leaving to Goldendell- she was to ensure that no word slipped away and got back to Emperor Ion. She could return to Goldendell and report to the High Raven that they had failed, and she herself had survived the monstrous attack by the Black Hand. She was sure that the Thunder of Ravens would love to finally know about the location of the evil guild. Maybe she *should* have sent a messenger back down the mountain...

Oh well. There was no point in dwelling on that. That was the only con- aside from the fact that Sorina was now on her own. She wouldn't be able to rely on the stupid and slow creatures who served her. In order to restore the peace and keep the Thunder of Ravens from delving too deep into the utter abyss of Oblivion, the Ice Walker had to be captured. She had to die.

And Sorina herself, would teach that annoying Dhampir a *personal* lesson on respect.

Sorina stopped suddenly, catching that sweet but rotten scent again. She snapped her eyes immediately towards the source, and saw just what gave off such a pleasant but awful smell. Like a shadow with glowing green eyes and her red cloak indicating her high rank, the witch seemed to have appeared out of nowhere. The talons on her gauntlet dug into the nearest tree, the face within the trunk seeming to scream at her touch.

Realizing just how much trouble she was in, Sorina reached for her weapon, only to feel cold hands grab ahold of her shoulders.

"Move, and you are dead," a young child's voice hissed into her ear, sending chills down Sorina's spine.

Nevertheless, she smiled. "Try it, and I'll rip you in half, underling."

"How vicious," the witch said stepping forward, scratching the entire face of the trunk as she neared the Raven and the Vampire that had her hostage in a cloak of shadow. As she stepped closer, Sorina realized just how beautiful she really was despite the many runes and tattoos along her body- along with that horrible smell that seemed to get stronger with each step into the snow. The bald witch paused before Sorina, looking her up and down with feline curiosity. She then reached out, and slowly removed the Raven mask, revealing Sorina's face.

Sorina, despite her hatred for the witch, flashed her a smile. "Not what you were expecting, huh?"

"If I would have known any better, I would have said you look like a noblewoman."

"I'm *anything*, but a noblewoman."

"That's right, and so you became a Raven. A... copy-cat, of the followers of Kawfka." The witch chuckled, trailing a talon across Sorina's cheek, causing a thin stream of blood to spill. "I suppose this is your first time, meeting a true warrior of the Dark Lord?"

"I think you're a piece of filth," Sorina said, feeling the hands tighten around her shoulders. "Though I have to admit, I am surprised to find anyone else here in these mountains."

"The mountains hold many secrets..." The witch looked Sorina up and down. She grinned, exposing those blackened teeth. "As do you."

"Tell your devil-spawn to release me, or I'll rip your throat out."

"Is that a threat?"

"A promise."

The witch chuckled. "I like you. You are something else. I'm sure you could, given how close I am. But might I ask, what are you doing here, in *my* forest, Raven?"

"Hunting," Sorina answered spitefully. "I thought that would have been simple to guess."

"*What* are you hunting, exactly?" the witch asked seeming completely uninterested in Sorina's sarcastic reply.

"I hardly believe that is any of your business."

"Oh, come now," the witch chuckled, revealing those teeth stuck in her putrid gums. "As followers of the Dark Lord, we should be able to see eye to eye, yes?"

"There's nothing to see eye to eye to," Sorina spat. "And I'm no follower like the rest. I am a warrior of Yohnah, and the people of Balkeñoir."

"A god who has abandoned you, and a people who fear you." The witch smiled sarcastically. "How noble."

Sorina sniffed, irritated at the witch's snidely comment.

"What do you hunt, Raven?" the witch demanded, her eyes glowing bright and green. "You might be a very dangerous beast, but I am a witch. I've lived on this world long before you were even a pup. Now answer me or I'll make sure you meet the Dark Lord and see for yourself what he is capable of."

"I might just take you up on that," Sorina spat. "I am ready to die. I am prepared to go to Yohnah."

"And abandon your hunt?" the witch countered.

Sorina's mouth twitched. "What business does a witch have with mine anyway?" she asked trying to buy herself some more time. Though she could easily dispatch the witch or even the Vampire holding her steady, the other would immediately retaliate, and she would be dead. The witch was calling her bluff, and she was damn good at it too.

"There aren't any troublesome beasts here in this valley," the witch replied and Sorina wondered if she was joking. "So that means you're hunting something else. *We* are about to do a little hunting of our own. So, I got myself thinking: maybe, we can work together."

"I'll die before I work with a witch."

"Is that you talking as a Raven, or a savage beast who is used to getting out of scrapes with teeth and claws?"

Sorina growled despite her efforts to remain calm. "Watch it."

The witch smiled, knowing that Sorina had nothing on her. "Make me. I *dare* you."

Sorina thought about it, her heart rate accelerating but only a little at last. She really wanted to kill the witch. But if she did that, the Vampire would fall on her. On the other hand, if she attacked the Vampire, the witch would kill her. The witch had to have some other trick ready for her. They were crafty, evil creatures.

Worse than her.

"What are you hunting?" Sorina asked, deciding to just hear her out.

"What are *you* hunting?" the witch asked with a toothy smile. "I asked you first, you know."

After some thinking, Sorina relented. "I'm hunting some Hunters. They have a girl with them, and I am to find her."

"Hunters..." the witch purred, her smile stretching clear across her face. There was no glee or excitement, only rage. Predatory rage, and it made Sorina's skin crawl. "What a coincidence. Mithus, release her."

"But, Mother..." the Vampire being Sorina murmured uneasily.

"Fate is smiling upon us," the witch said and then repeated, "Release her."

The small hands released Sorina, and she found herself able to breathe again. She turned and snarled at the little girl behind her, who likewise hissed agitatedly, displaying her elongated canines.

"Those Hunters you seek," the witch said stepping between Sorina and the Vampire, her eyes glowing bright green with greedy desire. "They killed one of my children. I want them all dead. I am sure you already know where they are going, and so do I. So why not strike a bargain? You help me get what I want, I help you get what you want. I have no need for such a pathetic little child. You help me find and kill all the Hunters, and I will allow you and the child to make it out of my mountain alive."

This last part was a lie of course. Carmilla was not about to let the Ice Walker escape these mountains. What ancient secrets did that little Nishthgúlian hold in that tiny body? What could Carmilla learn, regarding the old legends of fate including the possible causation of this Eternal Winter?

"And if I refuse?" Sorina asked taking a step back. She in turn didn't want anything to do with this witch. She would be working close- too close to an actual servant of Kawfka, unlike the bastardized rituals performed back in Goldendell by the rest of the Ravens. She had no reason to work with this woman. It went against everything Sorina believed in- and more. True, she had plenty to gain. But to strike a deal with a witch was like shaking hands with the devil himself. And Sorina had played her cards close to her chest too many times to count.

The witch grinned. "Then I'll let you go find them of course. And if the Hunters don't kill you first, I will. I'll make sure that even if you survive and escape with the girl, I'd never let you leave these woods alive."

Sorina almost chuckled. This witch couldn't be that powerful. Despite having a red cloak, no one could have enough power to make such an idle threat. She was either a very convincing liar, or she was dead-serious.

"Is that so?" she asked. "Have you even met someone like me before?"

"More: I've killed many too." The witch grinned. "Your meat… it's a little tough for my taste. But… still, it is delicious to sink my teeth into."

"I'd kill you."

"Maybe. If- and only if -you succeed in killing four Hunters before they kill you."

The witch had a point. Sorina was on her own now. She had no useless sacks of flesh to help her now, and they couldn't even do it before. Not only that, but her desperate and idiotic choice to use troll piss to bring in a pack only backfired on her. Even if Sorina used her beast form, she would still have terrible difficulties with the Hunters. Especially that Dhampir…

"Come now," the witch said extending her hand- the one without the clawed gauntlet. "What do you say? Together, those Hunters don't stand a chance. And if you help me, you get to walk out of these woods without becoming one of them."

She said this with a knowing smile, and Sorina thought that just for a moment, she heard the cry of a young girl.

She turned to the sound, only to see a face in one of the trees looking at her. The bark-covered eyes made her skin crawl. She turned back to the witch, while reaching into her pocket beneath her cloak, grabbing for her pocket watch. She felt the cool metal and etching across the lid; its touch somewhat calming her from the terrible sensation she felt growing all around her like a cancer. The pocket watch… the only thing of comfort that she had in a world that had taken everything else from her. She should have left it behind, she should have let the other Ravens destroy it.

But… she kept it. All because she couldn't have anything else to hold onto if she didn't have it. If she gave up on the watch, she'd be… giving up on them all. Despite becoming a Raven, despite what she was, Sorina just couldn't let it go. She promised to make the world a better place. And it starts, with that Ice Walker…

What have I got to lose? She extended her hand out, but immediately pulled away when the witch reached closer. "Swear it."

The witch blinked.

"Swear that you'll let us walk. Swear upon your god."

The witch smiled, and kept her hand straight out. When Sorina reached for it, the two women clenched each other's hands firmly. "You mean, *our*, god, yes? Well, I, Carmilla the Red swears upon my lord Kawfka of Oblivion, you will leave these woods one way or another."

Sorina narrowed her eyes at the witch and her vow, but nevertheless, she nodded. "And I, Sorina the Raven, swears to join you in our hunt until our prey is slain."

The witch, Carmilla, grinned. Those horrible, horrible teeth, made Sorina's stomach clench at the sight of then. "Excellent," she said. When they released each other's hand, Carmilla looked to the Vampire who had been watching with large silver eyes the entire time.

"My broom, my dear?"

The Vampire nodded with such innocent enthusiasm. She then disappeared in a flash of darkness, and then reappeared in the same spot; this time holding a broomstick.

"Thank you." The witch took her broom gratefully. "Shall we go then?"

The Vampire nodded again. "I'll do whatever it is you need me to do. If it will make you happy, Mother, I'll do it."

Sorina frowned. Even as a Vampire, Mithus was just a little kid still. Owned by this witch, who either really was or wasn't her mother. Nevertheless, she was still innocent; a child just wanting to make their parent happy. But what she would be asked to do...

The witch, Carmilla, looked back at Sorina. "You are on the path. You will lead us there."

Sorina bit her lip. "Of course."

Carmilla smiled again. "I think I like you," she said again. "You have such... potential. I can see Kawfka really-"

"Don't," Sorina warned the witch before trudging forward to leave the two behind unless they caught up. "Do not pull me in as one of your kind. I have *nothing* in common with you."

"Oh, you wear more masks than one?" Carmilla asked from behind. "You really are... interesting."

Sorina almost laughed. *No, I'm really not. I'm just someone, trying to make sense of this world.* In order to rid the world of evil, the curse upon Balkeñoir had to be broken first.

That was why the Ice Walker had to die.

"Hey girl," Carmilla said appearing right beside Sorina, making her jump. "What did you say your name was?"

Sorina looked at the witch, those inhuman eyes bearing right into her soul. "Sorina. Sorina Narcisa."

"Narcisa..." Carmilla purred, her bare thumb hovering over her lips in thought. She then looked at Sorina, not with feline curiosity, but something along the lines of intrigue and hostility. "You wouldn't by chance be related, to Sokafia Narcisa, would you?"

At the mention of her grandmother's name, Sorina felt her blood stop cold. Wishing her mask was back on her face and not in the witch's claws, she wondered what expression Carmilla was looking at.

"Who is that?" the Vampire asked taking ahold of Carmilla's hand, taking the Raven Mask from her mother.

Carmilla, seeming not to notice that the mask had been taking from her, nor that her daughter had even taken her hand in place of the mask, kept those hideous eyes on Sorina like a predator eyeing prey. Sorina knew that look all too well. She's seen it her whole life- and even gave it to so many herself.

"Well," the witch said without so much as a glance away from Sorina. "She was a terrifying creature of both beauty and power. Having being a native of these lands long before it was even called Balkeñoir, she struck fear into the hearts of men and women alike. Even the witches who crossed the seas here admired her and heard of her legends around small campfires during the siege of Woodendell. I knew she courted many men throughout history, but I never would have guessed that she would bear any children…" She smiled at Sorina. "I thought I recognized your scent."

"You knew her?" Sorina asked, immediately on her guard. Her hand was on one of her swords, but other than that she kept still as she trudged through the snow with the witch who didn't appear alarmed in the slightest.

"I never met her," Carmilla replied. "But I heard of her, back when I was but a chick climbing the ranks of the Covenant. You and I, Sorina Narcisa, may have a lot more in common than you realize. I would venture a guess then, that you are here to complete her work?"

Sorina's eyes narrowed. "She came for the Ice Walker?"

"Long ago," Carmilla nodded. "But by then, the brat had escaped along with her brother and mother who took them away. Where they went, I do not know. But now they have returned- and they have those Hunters to protect them. If you wish to finish your grandmother's work in order to purge the world of Winter, then you and I need to be rid of those Hunters."

They started to go.

She caught a scent as a light breeze managed to be caught in the valley and Sorina turned to her right where the young Immortal walked alongside her, putting herself between the she-demon and the witch. Mithus stared up at Sorina with those large inhuman eyes of silver which seemed to reflect the moon peeking past the peaks far above like small pools. Sorina tried to remember what those kinds of eyes can do, but she couldn't recall what kind of Immortal Eyes had what anymore. She found herself lost in the child's eyes; a prisoner without chains and shackles.

Mithus presented Sorina with her mask, offering to return it. As soon as Sorina touched her mask, the Vampire said, "You look prettier without a mask."

Sorina swallowed as she snatched the mask out of the Vampire's tiny hands. Such filthy demonic spawn... the child should never had been born. But those words... they got to Sorina, and she could tell that the witch was watching closely. Without so much as a glance, Sorina placed the mask back over her face, returning her demeanor to that of a Raven; a servant of the Empire and a slayer of beasts through the power of darkness.

What... she thought as she trudged through the haunted forest with the witch and her child in tow. *What is pretty about me?* She tightened her grip around the watch in her pocket, and prayed that her grandmother was watching over her now.

Te

Matei arrived in Firedell before the sun rose in the east, the sky being overcast with black clouds rolling in from the Dead Sea.

The Anguis Express had gotten him to the city of stone much faster than anticipated; having hardly any passengers to board upon the train he got on as soon as he got to the station in Shadowfort Pass. With fewer stops having to be made, he made it to Firedell in almost no time at all; only a day and night long ride across the snowy landscapes of southern Balkeñoir where the Deepland Barrens laid as an ocean of frigid sand.

Firedell, the city of stone, sat at the base surrounding a dormant volcano; Mr. Stronghaven's mouth without fire opened to the skies above. Buildings and homes of stone climbed the feet of the behemoth, the railroad circling the mountains from the south before banking back towards Mistendell to the north.

After getting off the platform, Matei hails a coach and gets a ride down to the heart of the city, where the Firedell Cathedral stood among the shops and apartments of stone and igneous rock. Crystalized bedrock containing gold and iron were carted from Mt. Stronghaven on large barges that flew down chutes before coming to a halt at one of the many factories that smelt and chip at the gold. This was also the city where any silver found to have crashed to Lunokean from the moon was brought to be harvested and tempered not just for riches, but for weaponry as well. Count Igníl Vaas was certainly making a huge profit not just with the manufacturing of gold, but with the recent uprising of the Thunder of Ravens, this would prove to be his city's most profitable year to date.

It appeared as well that the count had taken to more severe punishments than what was often seen in Balkeñoir. Here and there among the gas-fed lamps, tall crucifixes had been placed and hanging from them were a few men and women, all with their crime posted right above their heads.

There were some who were illegal aliens coming in from countries like Noyii and Ukusvit and tried to avoid customs. There was one or two for theft, and Matei noticed one that had been called 'illegal hunting' which was not about poaching at all. The man who hung from it wearing only a loincloth, his feet and hands covered with brown stains of dried blood, had once been a Hunter from a different guild. His head hung back and a crow was working on the gelatinous eyes in the flayed sockets. Matei couldn't remember the last time he saw public crucifixion but he didn't want to stay in Firedell too long to end up like them. Among the hanging dead and dying, flags bearing the city's sigil; a bull's head circled in a ring of fire flapped in the winds coming in from the sea. Storm clouds were gathering in the north, past the volcano itself which towered above the city.

"More fuckin' snow…" Matei grumbled as his coach stopped on a roadway close to the Firedell Cathedral. Feathers of ashy snow was drifting across the city now, polluted by the smog. He tipped the coachman an extra florin for the ride.

The church itself stood more like a castle than it did a normal dome that was popular in Balkeñoir. Tall towers of sharp spires reached for the sky like spears pointed towards the heavens, and the keep itself stood as a giant form of frozen frock. In fact, the entire church looked more like a wave of frozen lava than it did brick and mortar. Hawks and ravens circled the highest towers, and just outside the steps leading to the front doors of the church, two Bell-Ringers stood ringing their bells with poor-boxes next to them.

The men were tall, garbed in white robes and wide-brimmed hats. Their faces were covered by masks of gold formed into expressionless voids. In their gloved hands, they rang small silver bells to and fro, gently weaving their strange music into the sounds of the city around them. As Matei approached them, he muttered a hello while dropping a few coins into one of the boxes. He didn't allow his eyes to move away from the guns strapped to the belts of the men's robes.

Nevertheless, they nodded to him as he ascended the steps, and pushed through the large wooden doors of the cathedral and entered the building.

After passing down a corridor of statues depicting nuns and other women of Yohnah holding candles, Matei entered the main sanctuary. The pews were all laid out in rows with large sconces at each end to provide light in the evening. Large painted glass windows let in light on either side of the sanctuary, depicting many legendary scriptures in brilliant colors. At the end of the sanctuary, the Dove of Yohnah hung on the wall holding an olive branch in its little beak just above a large podium seeming to be held up by two more statues that almost resembled the Bell-Ringers outside. Next to the podium, a pool of holy water reflected against the surrounding walls sending out brilliant colors everywhere. Matei stopped before the alter, and bowed his head in a silent prayer, thanking Yohnah for his safe travels before dipping his fingers into the pool of water and crossing himself in a matter that represents a dove taking flight.

The sound of someone clearing their throat alerted him after he had raised his head, and Matei turned to see a priest standing there with his arms behind his back and a smile on his face. The man was old, with a beard as white as snow trailing down to the belt of his robes. His head was bald, and his eyes appeared milky white.

"Hello," he said in almost a whisper. "Pardon me for saying, but you do not look like one of the locals who come here."

"I'm not, Father," Matei said reaching his hand out to shake with the priest, admiring the many rings on the bony knobs that were the man's fingers. "I am a Hunter who has traveled here seeking your aide."

"Ahh…" The priest smiled warmly. "A Hunter, are you? Well welcome to the house of worship. Please, come, and leave of some of the happiness you bring." He gestured to one of the pews and after the two had taken a seat, the pastor turned his complete attention to Matei.

"I would be weary of whom you disclose such information if I were you. These are dark times for those who like to hunt beasts. Count Vaas is certainly not forgiving of those who defy his decrees given by the Emperor."

"I'll keep that in mind," said Matei. "But I trusted a man of Yohnah would not be so willing to assist those who shake hands with the devil."

"For some," said the priest. "There is little difference between the dove and the crow. But, you were right to speak to me at the very least. I am Father Cephas. Tell me, what can I do for you, mister…?"

"Matei, sir." Matei replied. "Matei Coventon. I am here regarding a supposed visitor of your church."

"Oh?" Father Cephas said with soft eyes. "You will have to be more specific. We get many visitors within these sacred halls."

"It is just a simple question that I hope you can answer."

"I'll do my very best."

"Have you been a leader of this church long?"

"Nearly fifty years," Cephas said with a touch of pride. "I was called to lead the people of Firedell to Yohnah, and the Lord has blessed me greatly."

"That truly gladdens me to hear that," Matei said meaning it. "So then, do you remember taking in a family of three in your church? A mother and her two children? Nisthgúlians to clarify? Perhaps in the last five years?

Cephas thought about it for a moment. "Come to think of it, I did. Long ago, but the mother had died, the poor thing. Her children had gone off on their own, and no one in Firedell had seen or heard from them again." He eyed Matei curiously. "The poor dears… Do you know if they are okay?"

"They are safe," Matei assured the man. "My companions are taking care of them now. My guild master simply had a few questions regarding the children. Were they named Charlotte and Morgan? The children, I mean.”

“Oh, yes,” Cephas said without hesitation now and a smile on his face as his recollection rewarded him with some happy or perhaps cherished memory. “Their mother, sweet and pretty little thing she was...”

Cephas closed his eyes, as if picturing the woman now. “Her name was Aushra. She came here, begging for a place to stay and work to do. It’s a terrible shame, really, the treatment of any Nisthgúlians regardless of citizenship. At any rate, we took her and her children in. We taught them the alphabet, how to read, the necessities before they would have to go to school. Aushra worked as a servant here; cooking and cleaning and offering to help with seminars within the cathedral. She was a wonderful woman, raising two children on her own.”

“Did she say where she was from?” Matei asked.

“No, she didn’t,” Cephas frowned. “In fact, whenever we did ask, she would immediately grow sad, almost to the point of tears. Therefore we never pushed the thought.”

“Was there anything strange about the children themselves?”

Cephas thought about it. “Morgan... he was just your average young boy. Oblivious about the world, uninterested in the search for Truth, and, of course, rejecting all of my and my elder’s guidance’s. There wasn’t anything particularity strange about him. His sister however... we knew that she was special in her own way.”

“In what way?”

Cephas hesitated.

“Father Cephas,” Matei insisted. “I know what she is.”

Cephas looked at him more nervous than ever. His features relaxed little by little however as he said at last, “Yeah... Yes, I suppose you would know. Yes, it is true. She held the eyes of an Ice Walker.”

Matei nodded. “You believe this for certain?”

"We didn't know for sure, but there was no doubt in my eyes." Cephas nodded. "Her eyes, such a thing is recorded in the book of Yohnah, as well as the ancient writings of Balkeñoir before the land was occupied by the Empire. The eyes of the one who controls the very spirit of Winter. Though some records conceive them as offspring of a water goddess by the natives. But as she grew older, she begun to show more and more symptoms that only solidified our guesswork. So we protected her, and the rest of her family, for fear one might mistaken her for a beast. It was not shortly after that when Aushra passed on, and immediately after, the children fled. Perhaps they thought we would abandon them as well, or worse, surrender them to the Empire. At any rate, it saddened me when we couldn't find them anywhere, I honestly suspected the worse."

The priest then looked to Matei. "Tell me, Mr. Coventon, is she really an Ice Walker?"

Matei swallowed before answering. "That's why I am here. What if she is? If she really is an Ice Walker, what does that mean for her?"

Cephas frowned. "Then that would only mean that she came down from the mountain... Aushra took them both down from the mountain, and fled all the way here..."

"Where does this curse or whatever it is come from? Is this really a miracle of God, or a curse? Or is it something an alchemist can explain? Just... what is she?"

Cephas was silent, deep in thought for a moment. But eventually, he spoke in a low and quiet voice. "This is only my point of view, but the old gods worshiped in these lands, I do not believe they exist. At least, not as gods anyway. That being said, there are still many things we are not sure of here in Balkeñoir. Ancient beasts, curses, all still weave into the new history of the country. But whatever it may be, Charlotte just might be the key to this strange curse of Winter that had fallen upon us."

"How so?" Matei asked.

"The curse had brought winter here for many centuries," the priest said. "Here, and no where else in Lunokean. An act of God, I don't believe so. No one knows how or why. But, according to the ancient writings of the natives of former-Balkeñoir, there is a goddess who can bring back the sun and with it, spring. Such a goddess, possess a similar magic to which Charlotte herself has, as well as many people recorded in history. Unfortunately, many of the tribes who once lived here no longer exist, so the chances of a goddess coming again might have become slim. However, if I am right, then Charlotte may very well be the last Ice Walker in existence. Not a god, or a goddess, but a human being capable of controlling Winter. Sending reel it in like a fisherman's line, and bringing forth Spring. Or so the legend goes."

"How does this apply to Yohnah?" Matei asked looking up at the statue of the Morning Dove.

"Maybe it is a test," Cephas shrugged. "The Lord works in mysterious ways. He gives some people the ability of magic- pure magic that no one else can possess, unlike witchcraft to which anyone can do it- under the guide of the devil himself. Tell me, have you ever heard of Fire Weavers?"

"No, I haven't," Matei said deeply intrigued at what he was learning now.

"Fire Weavers were known as human beings capable of creating fire out of the exposure of sunlight. They used to be very common here in Firedell when Mt. Stronghaven was active, until the occupation of Balkeñoir began. Many magic-users possessed pure elemental magic. Fire, earth, water, air, the four elements written in the ancient texts by the tribespeople who once lived here. Ice Walkers, are probably no different. They are magic-users, capable of changing water into their heart's desires."

"So they aren't gods at all."

"No," Cephas replied. "Just human beings, blessed with magic. However… the methods to awaken such a power, are done in… quite barbaric ways."

Matei waited patiently, for the priest to continue.

"We once had a visitor here, back when I was just a decan training to become a missionary." Cephas eventually said. "He said he was an Earth Shaker, and a native of a tribe in the southern wastelands. He came to us, seeking protection from his tribe who were trying to see who had the magical power of earth and stone. Their methods… they would drop boulders on men stuck in a pit, and if one was able to break the stones and use them to climb out, then they had the ability. If not… well… they got crushed. He didn't want it to happen, so he fled. He fled and left his home and sought protection in Firedell. We accepted him, telling him he was safe as long as he never caused trouble. We even alerted the Empire that his tribesmen would be coming to Firedell to search for him, and the Emperor called for the Ravens to slaughter them all. They even went back to the main village, and killed all the natives. It was a bloody massacre; no one survived. Men, women, and children… they were all killed. We told the Earth Shaker, who appeared to be glad that his pursuers were gone, but understandably, he was heartbroken at the news. We tried to console him, but he insisted on being left alone."

Cephas looked down, the memory seeming to wear him down. "But one day, we found him in his room. He had somehow managed to get a gun, and shoot himself in the head."

"Did he show any of these powers?" asked Matei.

"No. So we don't have any record of him exactly being that at all. Again, you have to consider how much stress such barbaric rituals can put on the human body."

"So other than what the Nisthgúlians know, there isn't much we can learn about these elementals or whatever they are called, or Ice Walkers in general."

Cephas shook his head. "One people's interpretation does not always correlate with another's. An interpretation from the Book of Yohnah may not always have the answers set in stone. Which would lead to what you said before: a curse or some other form of magic. But perhaps that isn't the case?"

"What do you mean?"

"What if it isn't Yohnah who has the answers for us, but perhaps one of the other Stars?

This made Matei think of Velinar and whatever other Stars both Fallen and still beyond the Veil. There were many, but hardly any with the exception of Kawfka got a lot of recognition. You had the Flutemaster and Gotteschalk, as well as a few others that are mentioned in the Holy Book but never described in detail. But if Cephas was mentioning the possibility of another godly being having the possible answers, might not Velinar himself possibly know where to begin? Matei then thought that Velinar should have thought of that in the first place, but then again, the Fallen Star did not keep company with the other Fallen nor those beyond the Veil.

"You've given me a lot to think about," said Matei. "Hopefully these questions will help lead us in the right direction to keep the children safe. I do have one last question, Father: Did anything happen after the children left? Anything... suspicious or concerning?"

Cephas scratched the top of his dome. "Well... A Raven, came into our church the morning we found that the children had escaped. She demanded where they were, and when we couldn't find them, she sent out soldiers to patrol the streets. She stayed at the church until she was informed that someone saw them taking a train back to Dragondell. They wouldn't give any details nor would they respect our church." Cephas shook his head then, adding grimly, "They wouldn't allow anyone to come in and worship or meditate."

"Typical. Did she say why she was looking for them?" Matei asked.

"No, like I said. She didn't say. Only said that it was business of the Empire."

Matei frowned. Though there was no telling just what source of power Charlotte had in her possession nor was there a way at the moment to see how or why she has elemental magic, he figured it could not be good news if the Empire was looking for her. After their collaboration with the Ravens as well as dealing with some of the most powerful Immortal Lords of Balkeñoir, who knows just how much the Emperor would allow his hard-won Empire to dwell within the darkest parts of the country's strange history.

"Do you remember what she looked like by chance?" Matei asked.

"No. She never took off her mask," Cephas said. He then shook his head solemnly. "How far has our nation turned from the eyes of God, I wonder… Those heathens use the very evil that the Afterworlds are constantly at war because of. Trying to eliminate darkness with darkness… it never goes will, not for the Ravens or anyone who honors themselves in the name of Kawfka."

Matei couldn't agree more with such a statement. He wasn't surprised that Cephas didn't know what the Raven looked like. They seldom revealed their face.

"However," Cephas then said. "This Raven, I'll admit… she did act, odd."

"How so?" Matei asked.

"During her time here, she was polite," Cephas said. "Asked for tea, talked to the nuns in a polite manner, and even offered a tithe for the poor."

"Sounds like a general follower of Yohnah."

"Indeed. But what Raven follows Yohnah now?" Cephas asked. "It was a sight to see, that much is for certain. Though she wouldn't touch any of the artifacts, she did spend quite a bit of time here in this room, praying."

That was indeed strange. Becoming a Raven meant that you were turning your back on Yohnah, and accepting darkness in over to overcome the curses wrought upon Balkeñoir. That had been their calling ever since the guild had first been founded, long before joining forces with the Empire. To hear about this Raven doing unordinary things uncommon to that of her comrades, made Matei wonder just what kind of person such a Raven is.

"You said the children slipped out the morning the Raven came to see you," Matei said to the priest. "Do you think they knew they were going to be chased by the Empire?"

Cephas thought about it for a moment. "They couldn't possibly... But maybe Aushra..."

"Did she think someone was looking for her?" Matei asked.

"Aside from her own people? She was always conscious of her surroundings. Whenever she was outside, she always kept her head on a swivel. She would always go to sleep with a candle burning by her bedside, and she would never go anywhere alone or allow her children to either. She always behaved as if she was ready for anything and anyone to come her way."

"Hmm..." Matei sounded rubbing his chin in thought. "Do you have other information you could spare, Father? Anything would be appreciated, considering Morgan and Charlotte both."

"Are they all right?" Cephas asked instead. "The children... are they well?"

"As said before, my companions are attending to them. As far as I know, there isn't a safer place for them to be than with my guild."

Cephas smiled. "I am... happy, to hear that. Truly, I am. After Aushra... I worried about them. Wondering what I would do, as a pastor and a man of God, to take on the responsibility of caring for two children..."

"I'm sure you would have been incredible." Matei assured the man. "Those two, are very strong now. They will be okay. I know not where their path will lead them, but I know they will find peace one day."

Cephas then leaned forward, his milky eyes stabbing right into Matei's own. "Please, make sure the Empire never finds them. Whatever it is, it can't be good. You've seen this city. Things are getting worse. Make sure, they never go back to where their mother ran from. If the legends are true, then Charlotte will always be in grave danger. If they really did come from a tribe lost in the mountains, then as much as I hate to say it, I pray that such a place exists no more. Because if they do, they will sacrifice Charlotte."

"That won't happen. We'll protect her," said Matei. "You have my word. We won't let any harm fall upon them."

Cephas nodded. "Thank you, you bless me with such words." He then smiled and said, "You know, I wonder sometimes. Everything, and everyone on this planet... we are all here for one reason or another, to proclaim Yohnah's glory. All we have to do, is submit to His will and become one with Him. We all have a reason to be here, even the natives who once ruled this country. So I wonder... what could Charlotte's reason be?"

"I don't know," Matei admitted.

Cephas sighed. "Winter, it gets tiresome, after so many years of cold and snow."

Matei couldn't agree more.

But now he had more work to do; his job wasn't over yet. "Did the Raven say, just where she was stationed at the time?"

Cephas thought about it for a moment. Somewhere in the city, a clock tower chimed the 18th hour; its loud and hollowed chime echoing through the walls of the church. "I think it was at our great Count's palace. Count Vaas always offers sanctuary for servants of the Empire, even Ravens-unfortunately. I would check there, though I doubt they will let you in the moment they know of your profession."

Matei nodded. "What they don't know won't hurt them." He stood up from the pew, Cephas likewise rising with him. "Thank you, Father. You have been most helpful." With a bow, he turned and started to go.

"Mr. Coventon," Cephas called to Matei, who turned at the mention of his name. "I may not agree with what the Empire has become, nor do I have anything against Hunters in general. But... you are of The Black Hand, aren't you? That castle in the mountains... Even though you hunt for the people, you are in danger should you decide to get too close to the Count and his soldiers. And if members of the Empire are still lingering about, you are in much more danger, that I cannot stress enough."

Matei chuckled at that. "Believe me when I say I dealt with worse. Don't worry, I'll be fine." And with that, he started for the exit once again. He had managed to get whatever information he could out of the pastor and his church.

He stepped out just as another soul was being nailed to a cross.

The man had been dragged out into the street, stripped and beaten within an inch of his life by Firedell Watchmen. Heavy gauntlets split open his lips and the side of his head while two strong men dragged the wooden beam from across the street, holding up a carriage whose driver was cursing the lot of them for making him late. Matei cringed as he saw the screaming man's arms being stretched out to the ends of each branch and a large nail was driven through just below his wrists. Another was driven into his feet as a sign was being fastened right above his head. The cross was then raised up and stuck into a hole recently dug specifically for this punishment on the side of the road and the man was hoisted up, moaning and begging for someone to help him.

The sign above the man's head read, 'traitor.'

Overseeing all of this as the Watchmen laughed and jeered at the man and encouraged onlookers to join, was a Raven garbed in the signature feathered cloak and the beaked mask of tin. The man, perhaps sensing being watched or merely curious, turned and happened to lock eyes on Matei, looking like a large bird of prey spotting a potentially tasty treat. Matei kept his head low and his cloak tight about him to hide the weapons he brought with him, but did not leave. He did not leave until he was sure the Raven was no longer interested in his general direction and then he quickly left the scene, hearing the man crying out for aid that would never come.

"I'm not a traitor!" he insisted shrilly. "I've done nothing wrong! I am a man of Yohnah- that Raven lies! He lies! He lies!"

Matei, wishing he could have done something, stuck to the task at hand. He had some more digging to do before he returned to Shadowfort. If he lingered too long in Firedell however, well, he might just be joining that poor 'traitor' if he wasn't in and out and careful enough to do so.

Angela woke up from not a dream, but a vision of gruesome and terrible memories she longed to forget.

It was the same horrible nightmare that has haunted her ever since she had fled Noyii and eventually made it to Balkeñoir. No matter how far across the country she went, no matter how much she exposed herself to the horrors of the world, nothing could rid the nightmare from her brain that absolutely refused to let her go. There were many bad things that she remembered, but this one stubbornly refused to be shoved into a corner and left alone until she inevitably brought it back to examine and pick at, as most bad experiences are. Like a leech upon prey, it remained on her to the point where it practically became a part of her. If Dhampir's could dream as simply as human beings would, it wouldn't be so concrete, so persistent almost. But then again, could she call what she did as she slept really dreaming?

She didn't know how long she had been asleep, having dozed off long after everyone else had retired, but even still the vision had found her in the few hours she must have gotten. This Hunt was really beginning to tire her out, she thought.

With a shudder, she remained where she was sitting on her rock, still watching out into the world outside the mouth of the cave. She heard the deep and slow breathing of all the other Hunters behind her as she looked at the fresh powder that had blanketed over the ground and trees in some areas. The air was crisp and cold, and warm vapor plumed from her mouth as she breathed, calming herself as she tried to get rid of the image still flashing in her eyes. That same bed, the eyes of a beast that belonged to a man... Angela would never forget such a look. It frightened her even today, despite all the horrendous beasts she had come across in her career as a Hunter of the Black Hand.

Someday, she reminded herself. *Someday...*

She heard movement and turned her head slightly to see that Charlotte had slipped out of her bedroll, immediately jamming her fingers into her armpits while her brother slumped against the feet of the statue they were sleeping under. Next to them, Jacob slept soundly having gone to bed after staying with Angela for a few hours. With some effort, the Ice Walker escaped her roll and crossed over quietly to Angela who watched her like a hawk the entire time.

"You're up early," she stated as the young girl stumbled over.

"So are you," Charlotte said rubbing the sleep from her eyes. When she opened them up again, she looked at Angela. "Have you been here all night?"

"Yes," Angela answered. "I got a little sleep, however. I'm fine."

Charlotte looked at the rock the Dhampir was sitting on like it was the most uncomfortable thing in the world. In all honesty, she wasn't wrong. Angela would much rather prefer her own bed with her books, and Sebastian.

"Aren't you cold?" Charlotte then asks.

"No," Angela said. "The cold doesn't affect me that much."

"Oh," Charlotte said, those inhuman blue eyes looking Angela up and down once again. "Just like the sun doesn't affect you..."

"To a point anyway..." Angela said this now getting nervous. It was strange, she almost welcomed it. How long had it been since Angela had felt nervous? And because of a child no less?

Charlotte pursed her lips. "How did you do it?"

"Do what?"

"How did you become so strong? I mean... everyone, is scared of me, because of what I am. All the nuns and people back home, they were afraid of me. Everyone except my family and one other. When I look at you, I see how you are treated. It… reminded me of what it was back in Firedell. But… you never seem bothered about it.”

“I never said it didn’t bother me.” Angela said turning her eyes back to the outside world. “I would think that my argument with my comrades last night would have proved that. I just learned to deal with it.”

“That doesn’t seem fair…”

“It isn’t,” Angela agreed. “But people are going to say whatever they want about you. You only have two options at that point. You need to either do something about it, or ignore it. That’s just the way it works.”

“But why didn’t you do anything?” Charlotte asked. “When people get called bad names back in Firedell, fights break out. Duels get challenged… people always do something about people they don’t like. Why don’t you?”

“Because sometimes the best thing to do is to do nothing,” Angela answered. “My comrades, they might look at me like I’m a monster, but they are still the closest thing to a family I have. And so I will protect them to the best of my ability, so that we all can return home safely. I may hate them, just as they hate me. But in the end, the best and right thing to do, is to make sure we all get home safe. That’s what being a part of a guild is all about.”

Charlotte’s mouth opened into an ‘o’ in thought. “I guess that makes sense… But doesn’t it get hard sometimes?”

“It always is,” Angela admitted.

“Especially, when Mr. Vladimir is rude to you?”

“I’ve learned to ignore it,” Angela said. She thought about what Jacob had said last night and added, “Sometimes, anyway. He is a good man, and a skilled Hunter. I expect him to be the backbone of the guild, that is what everyone sees him as. I might be a Dhampir but that doesn’t define who I am. Vladimir, he is sometimes cynical, and crass. But that doesn’t define who he himself is. He risked his life for his comrades when he first got started. His partner was a strong warrior. He protected the man with his life. And… it pained him terribly to find out the man had died on a Hunt. Vladimir cares for his comrades, and would risk his life for them all. Such a trait, is not common in Balkeñoir or the world of Man. But when your time rises from the ashes of Winter, then the world will need men like him. That much, I know for certain.”

Charlotte asked, “How can you be so sure?”

“I've seen it,” Angela said this looking back at Charlotte, her bright purple eyes flashing almost as she observed the girl before her; what sort of woman she would become in the near future.

Charlotte, looking right into those eyes without fear, said, “Vladimir may care for his fellow Huntsmen… but what about you?”

Angela looked away. “That is for him to decide.”

Charlotte pouted, clearly unsatisfied with Angela's answer, thankfully accepted it. She joined Angela in watching the outside world, which was now sprinkled in a blanket of powder. “At least you have Jacob.”

Angela looked at the girl.

“Just like Morgan has always been there for me… Jacob is always there for you.” She then smiled at the Dhampir. “So at least you're not alone.”

“… I suppose not,” Angela finally decided, returning her attention to the outside with Charlotte who began humming some light tune to herself.

“It snowed last night…”

“More outside than down here in the valley,” Angela agreed.

“I know. I felt it. I dreamt it.”

Angela looked at Charlotte, curious about the Ice Walker. “Do you dream of snow often?”

“Almost every night,” Charlotte nodded. “Not every night, but mostly. Sometimes I see someone in the snow, but he's never close enough for me to see who it is or hear what he is saying, but I know he talks to me."

Now Angela pursed her lips. She wondered what Professor Clockwork would think about this.

Charlotte turned to Angela and smiled. "Do you want to see something?"

"Like what?" Angela asked just as Charlotte rushed forward without warning. She stepped out into the cold, and stopped near the largest collection of white powder where the winds that managed to make it into the valley had blown it into a wave-like dune. Angela, concerned, stood and stepped out into the cold. The thin rays of the sunrise shined through the crevice far above, and reflected off the mountainsides in blinding rays of rainbows. Her breath blinded her in white vapor momentarily as she neared the Ice Walker, who waited patiently while rubbing her hands together as if they were cold.

"Watch this," the child said enthusiastically. She clapped her hands together one last time, and Angela thought she saw those icy blue eyes flash like a lantern had suddenly turned on inside her head. She then began to raise her hands up and move them around her as if she was swimming, and before the Dhampir's eyes, Angela watched as Charlotte made the snow all around her condense and slither around her like ribbons around a dancer.

The snow then rose towards Charlotte's head, and it appeared to clump together into string-like shapes that stretched from the top of her head down to her shoulders. Shaking her head back and forth, she showed off her new snowy locks with a smile on her face. "Look; I have hair like you!"

Angela couldn't help but relent a smile to the girl. "So you have."

Charlotte raised her hands and immediately the snowy hair disintegrated and began to swirl around her like the rings of distant planets discovered in the Great Library.

"I wish I had hair like yours. It's beautiful."

Angela didn't know what to say. She had always been called beautiful, simply because of what she was. She was never one to worry about her looks. She just didn't care about anything about herself. To be called beautiful, was never a compliment to her in any way shape or form. She despised men who looked upon her lustfully, even women who gawked at her before they realized just what she was. But to hear Charlotte say such a thing... it gladdened her, immensely. It was a pure and innocent compliment, untainted as most children ought to be.

"... Thank you," she eventually told the child.

"Were you born in Noyii or just your parents?" asked Charlotte.

"I was born there."

"Why did you come to Balkeñoir?"

Angela paused and then said, "I just wanted to."

Charlotte nodded and smiled wider. "Want to see something else?"

Without waiting for Angela to even respond, she began to mold the snow in midair once again, this time making the snow form into the shape of a sword which solidified and crystalized with ice around it. She grabbed ahold of the hilt and pointed it at Angela, to which the point then molded into the shape of a face that stuck its tongue right at her. Charlotte laughed and Angela smiled at her.

"You are quite the jester," Angela said to her.

She turned her head to the few horses they had left, who were now nickering at the sight of the two supernatural beings laughing amongst themselves. With only four horses now, two of the Hunters would have to allow Morgan and Charlotte to ride with them. It was a miracle that no more had been lost. Finding Midnight was no problem; the horse always returned to Angela no matter the danger. At least they would all be able to still return from Snowcap Lake when Charlotte and Morgan finished with their business.

I wonder what they will do afterwards... Angela said to herself as she watched the young girl continue to shift the snow into whatever shape or form her heart desired; a goddess of ice creating and uncreating in mere moments.

After the other Hunters had awakened and they all packed up their gear, the group started off once again. Morgan sat behind Jacob who rode ahead of the group while Angela rode behind him with Charlotte holding onto her waist. On either side of the two Hunters, Vladimir and Sabina kept watch for any creatures who would try and come for them again.

The cold never relented, even as the sun finally peeked its face through the crevice high above. Some wolves passed by the group but they gave them a wide berth; probably deciding that it wasn't worth to go against four horses and whatever strange creatures were riding them. Charlotte watched the wolves pass by with bright and curious eyes. She then brought her attention forward and asked Morgan how they were doing.

"The end of the valley is right over there..." Morgan said pointing straight ahead. What he said was true, for the very end loomed over them like a great behemoth, nearly as tall as a mountain itself. "There should be a cave at the end of this path... I remember we had to enter and exit a cave before we left this place for good."

"Good," Vladimir said keeping his eyes on one of the nearest trees by the road. "The sooner we are out of these woods the better. This place gives me the creeps."

"You realize we're going to have to go back through on our way home, right?" Jacob threw this question over his shoulder, which made even Sabina snicker.

"Thanks for reminding me..." Vladimir grumbled but nevertheless he smiled.

He appeared to be doing better since last night, having his bandages cleaned and reapplied. If Angela didn't know any better, nor did she smell the blood that was seeping into the wraps around his head where he had been struck, she would have never guessed that he or Jacob had been attacked at all by witchcraft. She could still smell the fear in their sweat as they moved however, their caution. Whatever they saw, whatever that witch did, the two would remember it forever.

She would never forgive her, and this Angela told no one but herself. Should that witch ever show her face again, Angela would aid in destroying her. Thinking of this however brought back the memory of that young Immortal as well... including as to what she would have to do should it ever reappear again with her monstrous mother.

Whether I admit it or not, she thought. *I shouldn't have let the child live. It was a mistake.*

"Hey, kid," Sabina called out and Angela turned to see that she was staring at Charlotte. "Are there any songs that they usually sing in Firedell?"

"What? Have you been living under a rock?" Vladimir demanded.

"Not all of us have been as far south as you," Jacob laughed.

Charlotte pursed her lips and Angela felt the young girl's little hands tighten around her waist. "The church sings many hymns... but..."

"There are a few songs sung by the soldiers and townspeople," Morgan spoke up looking at the group from behind.

"Well, let's hear it." Vladimir smiled. "It might help pass the time."

"I can't sing..." the boy squirmed in his seat which made Jacob's horse sputter in annoyance.

"Neither can we," said Vladimir and both Jacob and Sabina laughed out loud. Vladimir smiled. "C'mon, it might be something we might have heard before. Maybe we can start it off for you?”

Morgan pursed his lips in thought. “There is the legend of the Burning Bull... the song sung about what the founder of the city saw when he first made port.”

“Oh! I know that one,” Sabina smiled. “Matei and I heard it, when we took leave in Waterdell.”

“Well, let’s hear it.” Vladimir said with a smile.

“Yes, teach us,” Jacob chimed in. Angela remained silent, watching and waiting to see what the Vampire Hunteress would do.

Sabina looked at Charlotte. “Charlotte, can you start off for me?”

Charlotte pressed her lips tight against one another. “Okay...”

She thought about it for a moment, taking deep breaths as she did so. She then started to hum a tune loud enough for the group to hear, and snapping her fingers, Sabina slowly started to recall how the song began.

“There once was a hero
Named ‘Okar the Flame’,
Who was never once known
By any other name.
He sailed the Dead Sea
From a land far away,
Seeking fame and fortune
Wherever it lay.
He had slayed the mermaids
And the Ghouls of Sand,
But there was a beast he
Had not met on the land.
From the deep fires from hell
Came a bull so fierce
That no man would last long

Charlotte and Morgan immediately started to clap for the Vampire Hunteress, who bowed dramatically at her two loyal fans. Jacob gave her a thumbs up and Angela merely smiled at Sabina. The Dhampir was impressed. She had not heard such a legendary folksong in a long time. Maybe when she got to Firedell in the near future, but it was still a blessing to hear such words after so long.

"You sang off-key," Vladimir said with a grin.

Sabina responded by riding her horse close to Vladimir's and kicking him in the leg. The Werewolf Hunter laughed as his horse whinnied in annoyance. Everyone laughed at the two, even Angela couldn't hold back her own smile of amusement.

"Hey," Morgan then said up ahead. "Look, over there!" Angela turned back and peered past Jacob and the boy in order to see what he was referring to. "We made it…"

And sure enough, they did. The end of the valley was finally upon them, the road proceeding on.

Tall cliffs stood high above the Hunters, having appearing to be held up by two large statues of men garbed in pelts with bows at their sides. Their hair which if they were human would probably be red, was roped in thick braids that coiled across their opposite shoulders. In-between the two, they appeared to be holding up the ceiling of a tall cave that looked like something thin and sharp had just cut into the rock. The cave itself was only ten feet in width, but it was so tall in height that it was almost menacing just to peer into the utter darkness within. Angela had no problem seeing through to the light on the other side of the tunnel, but the other Hunters only saw pitch-blackness that felt almost alive; calling to them and beckoning them to enter into its embrace.

"This is it?" Sabina asked from behind.

"This is it," Morgan confirmed. "I remember this. The Wolf Twins, the cave, everything. This is where we escaped."

"How far is it?" Vladimir asked.

"I don't remember…"

"Two miles," Angela answered for the boy. "Give or take."

"Look at the toes," Jacob said pointing at the feet of one of the statues. "Six on each foot. Nephilem."

"Born as such, and raised by wolves," Sabina said her horse skittering to the side a bit. "They were actually the creators of the bow- or so the legend goes in the ancient lands."

"So many legends…" Vladimir shook his head. "Angela, can you see the end? How far do we got?"

"Not long. Half an hour, I believe," Angela repeated her earlier answer.

"Well, let's get moving." Jacob said spurring gently and getting his horse to move forward already. "We're burning daylight."

"Indeed," Vladimir said following close behind. He caught Angela looking at him as he passed by and he shrugged. "One person behind every two, aye?"

Angela said nothing. The man could do what he wanted.

"We're almost home…" Charlotte said. "I've never seen it, since I was a baby. I wonder… I wonder how it will look like…"

Angela could understand the child's hesitation. To return to a home that you never were once a part of, it was scary. Even today, Angela wondered how she would feel; what she would think before she herself returned to her homeland which only lasted about six years. Would it be the same? Would even she remember anything? As a Dhampir, her memory stretched for a long duration, but even she was capable of forgetting, she supposed. Charlotte was blessed to only be a child when her mother decided to run from the village. Who knew what sort of place this lost haven of the last free Nisthgúlian tribe had been reduced to over the thousands of years?

She started forward, following Vladimir close behind as they entered the cave and allowed the darkness to swallow them both; with Sabina right in tow.

Silence enveloped the group almost as much as the darkness, the sounds of the mountain muted by the tunnel. Jacob and Vladimir had lit some ancient torches hanging in stone sconces using oil and some branches found on the floor of the cave. The ancient lights of which appeared to have not been alight for eons lit their way now. No one said anything, as the long pathway of tight stone walls passed them by without any difference as the time went by. It looked as if the walls themselves had been smoothed over after being carved right through the heart of the mountain. Upon looking up towards the high ceiling, Angela could see that the walls remained smooth all the way to the top. It made her wonder how long it really took to carve out such a passageway; especially without the use of modern tools and machinery. Then she considered the possibility that this was not at all done by mortal hands.

Angela felt Charlotte tighten her grip around her waist, and she turned to look at the girl from behind. The Dhampir almost bristled at the touch but she managed to control her urge to squirm. Charlotte didn't mean any harm; it was okay for her to hold Angela like this. Surely it was.

"It feels hard to breathe..." Charlotte whispered. "It's like the walls may close in at any moment."

Angela's brow softened and she reached down with a hand and took Charlotte's in it. "Don't worry," she assured the frightened child. "They won't close in. I'm right here."

Charlotte took a peek up, but then resumed in resting her head against the back of the Dhampir. "Can you tell me when we get out?"

She must have closed her eyes... "Of course." she said.

Angela then became aware that no one was behind her, and she looked to her left to see Sabina riding very closely alongside her. With the tight space it made Angela desire for breathing room, but the way the Vampire Hunter was looking at both her and Charlotte made her hold her tongue- for a moment anyway.

Sabina then looked forward toward Vladimir and Jacob, who had ridden a little further ahead. She then looked back at Angela, and then without another word, she pulled back, once again behind Angela and Charlotte. Angela wondered just what was going through the Vampire Hunter's mind, but she didn't bother to find out why. If Sabina had something to say, she would say it; sooner or later. So she just kept on riding behind Vladimir and Jacob, her hand remaining on Charlotte the whole way through the dark and air-crushing tunnel.

La

Though Angela saw it coming already, no one else truly saw the light at the end of the tunnel until a solid five hours or so of utter silence that at this point had become unbearable.

But at last they all felt the sunlight touch their skin as they all ventured out of the other end of the tunnel. All breathed with relief and all the horses seemed to nicker in relief as their coats caught the sunlight glaring down at them without any mountain or cavern to hold it back. The group looked out into the land hidden from the rest of the world; a bowl-like valley where no man had seen or heard of in probably centuries.

To the left, a vast lake shimmered off the base of a mountainside that seemed to hold it all from falling over the side of the range. It was *huge*; surrounded by thick black pine that stood tall and dark across the valley and separating the lake itself from a small village in a clearing just ahead of where the path really began to carve into the woods.

The village itself was in a small clearing in the middle of the pine, and from where the group of Hunters stood they could see just how large it really was. Many small log buildings circled around a space between them all; including the largest building furthest away from the path leading into it. Tall totem poles stood by every home, and the two tallest stood on either side of the entrance steps leading to the largest building of logs and banners of pelts far beyond their former glory.

What Angela found curious was that there was no smoke rising from the village; no spot-fires, no chimney smoke, nothing. She didn't mention her curious worries as Morgan asked Jacob to start riding down the hill the group stood upon and then little by little, they all started to move. As they neared the forest of black pine, Angela as well as everyone else was relieved to see that no faces were within the trunks of the trees.

They were normal; clean and pure, their skin thick and ruddy. As they delved deeper within the wood, Angela's piercing eyes caught sight of a few Sprites who were watching the Hunters from the boughs of the trees. They didn't make any move to greet them as this was normal behavior for the little fairies, but something about how they looked at the Hunters made Angela wonder how long it had been since such beings that most didn't believe exist anymore had seen a living human being.

They all… they all looked upset; disturbed about something and not knowing the words to explain to the group who just continued on their way with two excited children in tow.

"We're finally home…" Charlotte said loud enough for her brother to hear up front.

"Yeah, but keep alert," Morgan said. "Who knows what the villagers will think about us entering their home."

"No need to tell me twice," Vladimir said already having his pistol primed and ready in his hand as they broke through the line of trees and finally entered the Snowcap Village. The horses rode between the two totem poles depicting the many animals and beasts that the people of this tribe valued and respected. There was the eagle, the bear, the tiger, the wolf, the Crota, Wendigo, and even the dreadful troll. They passed through this makeshift gate which hid no guards and they entered what would have been called the 'plaza' of village at last.

It was empty. Like a ghost town from an old story, the village appeared completely and utterly deserted. Snow completely covered the ground, undisturbed by man for what could have been for years if not months. Shutters and doors hung on their hinges, squeaking audibly as a cold breeze passed through the village, causing the logs the homes were built of groan as if in agony. Some actually had caved-in ceilings, letting in the snow that had collected right on the rooftop. As Angela sniffed the air, she caught no scent of anyone hiding, no dogs, nothing. The village was completely abandoned.

Morgan and Jacob dismounted and Morgan began calling out for anyone to come out. Jacob had his bow drawn and Vladimir began doing a sweep of the area on horseback. Angela got Charlotte off the horse and while holding the little girl's hand, began their own search around the homes.

"Hello?" Morgan called out, his voice echoing off the mountain range around them. "Anybody? Hello?"

As they passed a nearby house, Angela peered into an open window to only see a living room coated with frosty dust. Sprinkles of snow had fallen in, and the light from the sun revealed overturned tables and chairs that looked old enough to crumble into splinters. A child's pine doll laid like a corpse across the back of one of these chairs that remained standing. She looked down at Charlotte, who simply stared at her surroundings in wonder.

"Angela," Sabina said coming forward, her rifle in her hands. "Do you sense anyone?"

The Dhampir shook her head. "Not a soul, neither left behind nor present." She chose her words carefully in regard to Charlotte. "There's no one here."

"Where'd they all go?" Jacob called out after exiting another home he had searched. "Nothing seems to be missing, but there isn't any sign of anyone being around here for quite a while."

"The place is abandoned," Vladimir suggested dismounting his horse just as Morgan came out of another home. "There's no one here." He told Morgan.

"I..." Morgan sighed, looking defeated and on the verge of tears. "I know."

He looked at every Hunter individually, as if trying to find someone who would speak against such an assumption. That this was all possibly some cruel joke. When no one did, he shook his head and looked up towards the nearest totem pole.

The many carvings of animals were practically rotted and falling apart from the unmerciful weather, but you could still make out the animals and beasts it contained. Only a few animals were unrecognizable, to Angela as well as everyone else.

"Morgan…" Charlotte said. "What now?"

Morgan shook his head. He reached into his satchel and removed the jar of cremated remains. He appeared to have made up his mind about something.

"We came here to spread Mother's ashes. We didn't come here to return to the village. Mother warned us to never actually return to our home…"

"But… where did they all go?"

Angela had an idea, but she didn't dare speak the words.

"You've been brought here," Vladimir spoke up. "So let's get on with it. The sooner we finish your business here, the sooner we go home."

"Right…" Morgan said. He then turned to Charlotte who was now holding the urn that contained their mother in her hands. "Let's go, Charlotte."

And the two started for the lake, which was exposed by another narrow pathway cutting to the leftmost side of the village.

"Angela, Sabina," Jacob called to them. "You should go with them. Vladimir and I will scope out the area. Make camp. No sense leaving just yet."

"Right," Sabina said taking off after the kids while Angela merely followed at her own pace. She took one last look at the two Hunters staying behind, and then continued down the narrow pathway leading to Snowcap Lake.

They had arrived, but the journey here was far from over.

While the women attended to the children, Jacob picked up a broken sword that laid close to a nearby well. The water far below had been frozen for probably years and there was no chance for a drink. He then noticed the hilt of a rusted weapon and he stooped over to pick it up. The blade had been snapped off at the base, nowhere to be seen.

"Cryin' shame," he muttered tossing the hilt away. He turned to see Vladimir emerging from the last home they checked.

"Not a bloody thing…" the Werewolf Hunter groaned. He took a seat at the foot of the staircase. He sat his gun on his lap and then rubbed his unscathed cheek with his hand. "No bodies, nothing. It's like they all just up and disappeared."

"You think they left?" Jacob asked.

"No. Everything is still in place. Even the food stored in their pantries and bags are still there. Rotten now, but still full."

"So, *what* happened to them?" Jacob asked making his way over.

Vladimir took up his wineskin and took a drink of water. He belched into a fist and answered, "Could have been an attack. Trolls, maybe. Thing is, those things ain't exactly the cleanest kind of beasts. There's no sign of a struggle within any of the homes. No blood, no claw marks, nothing. Just a whole lotta nothing."

Jacob frowned. It didn't make any sense. *Where did they all go?*

"Well, in any case," Vladimir said capping his water source. "It's obvious we can't leave those kids here after they spread their dear mother."

Jacob looked back at Vladimir. That was right. The kids had nowhere to go after this. Not only that, but the Empire would probably still search for them if they returned to Firedell. It was safe to assume that they both left with the intention of never coming back. Even if there were people still around here, Morgan himself said that they wouldn't return to the village, just the lake. Even still, why did he hesitate? Was it nostalgia? The memory of living here as a young boy? What was going through the kid's mind now? What would they do after all of this?

"They would be safe with us," Jacob eventually said.

"Aye, they would," Vladimir agreed. "But Shadowfort Castle is no place for children. We are all Hunters, not capable of taking care of those who cannot hunt just yet." Vladimir shoved his wineskin away and grumbled to himself. "Even so... we can't send them back down the mountain. If the Empire ever finds out that their little platoon has disappeared going up the Thousand Steps, then we might end up having to deal with more soldiers at our doorstep. But until then, the castle is the safest place for those two."

"I'm sure Velinar will have an idea concerning the soldiers- if any ever do come back up the mountain," Jacob figured the undead deity would anyway."

"Maybe, I don't know." Vladimir shook his head, deep in thought. "We never had children at the castle. I'm sure they can be taken care of, but like... I don't know. We'll have to figure it out when we get back."

Jacob sighed. "The thought of going through that creepy forest again..."

Vladimir nodded. "Not to mention, we may or may not have to deal with that witch again."

Jacob bristled at the memory of such a woman. "If we do, we have to kill her."

It didn't take a genius to see that Vladimir agreed wholeheartedly. "I don't like the thought of having a witch sharing the same mountain as us. With those two Vampires as well... Angela should have killed them both when she had the chance."

Jacob looked at the Werewolf Hunter. "Yeah, he should have," he agreed. "But it can't be helped now, not yet. She did her best."

"Did she?"

"I know she did."

Vladimir looked at Jacob, as if trying to see something that he just couldn't at the moment. It occurred to Jacob, just how dark Vladimir's eyes were. Not just in color, but in depth. They were the eyes of a warrior; someone who has lost much and still stood tall today. How many Hunters has Vladimir seen fall to the creatures of night? Where did he come from, and why did he become a Werewolf Hunter in the first place? What went through his mind, hearing about Luca's untimely demise and then suddenly plunging right into another job?

"I need you to be honest with me," Vladimir eventually said to Jacob, breaking into his train of thought. "Between us, too. I don't want the women to be worried."

"What is it?" Jacob asked, curious as to why Vladimir had meant Angela as well as Sabina.

"Do you trust me?"

"Of course."

"Can *I*, trust *you*?" His stare never broke; it didn't even falter as he asked those two questions.

"I *hope* you can," Jacob replied, feeling very uncomfortable in his skin at the moment.

Vladimir didn't even bat an eye. "Take off your scarf."

Jacob blinked, trying not to react to the sudden stoppage of his heart. "Excuse me?"

"Take off your scarf," Vladimir repeated himself. "Now."

Jacob flashed one of his smiles. "You kidding me? It's cold out here."

Vladimir didn't even flinch. "Jacob…"

Jacob stared for a long time at Vladimir. The two men never blinked or broke their gaze. At last, Jacob sighed and then reached up to the black cloth around his neck. He undid the single fold, and then removed the scarf, exposing his neck and the Immortal Kiss still upon it.

"Oh, gods above…" Vladimir whispered, his hard and cold eyes set on the bite marks on the side of Jacob's throat.

"I can explain," Jacob said, replacing the scarf as best he could without taking his eyes off of Vladimir. "You asked if you could trust me, right? Trust me if not for a few minutes, to explain."

Jacob could see that Vladimir really wrestled with such a request. He absolutely hated Vampires; hated Angela for sharing blood with such creatures. To see such marks on Jacob's neck, probably unfolded many suspicions the man probably already had concerning him. Vladimir being the guy he was, Jacob figured he would have immediately done something. Whether it be holding Jacob down and begin the process to stop whatever infection was in his blood, or even attempt to kill Angela. Though Jacob had complete faith in Angela, it was still a mystery to him how amazing of a warrior Vladimir really was; what sort of potential he was hiding.

Eventually, Vladimir's eyes lingered towards the spot where the mark would be underneath the scarf, and then back to Jacob's imploring face.

"Explain yourself," he relented, placing a hand on the gun still sitting in his lap as he said so.

And so, Jacob told him. He told him everything that happened in Irondell, leading to the slaying of Count Horla the Great Illusionist. He told Vladimir about how both of them were badly hurt, and were almost killed. In order to save them both, Jacob offered his own blood to Angela so she would be able to finish the hunt. If he hadn't, both he and Angela would most likely no longer be alive.

"We informed Velinar," Jacob said finishing up. "Angela, assured both him and me that I wouldn't Turn. That a Dhampir's bite is not potent enough to cause me to catch Vampirism. Velinar trusted her, didn't even bother asking for me to be put under vaccination. I promise you, Vlad, I am not a threat. And neither is Angela. She bit me, because I offered myself to her. Otherwise, she wouldn't have done it. I promise you, Angela isn't the kind of monster you make her out to be. She isn't a threat, to me, or any of you. She did it because I told her to. It was my choice, otherwise we wouldn't be here right now."

Vladimir remained silent after Jacob said his piece. He remained that way for a long time. Then he sighed and ran a hand over his face, contemplating everything he had just heard, seeming to soak it all in like a sponge absorbing dirty water.

"Are you sure?" was all he said after everything.

"Am I sure of what?"

"You know what."

"Yes," Jacob said with no hesitation. He did in fact know what Vladimir was referring to. "No one else knows, except for you and Velinar now. We were told not to tell you guys."

Vladimir nodded. "Figures. I can understand why. Velinar... what are you thinking..." He seemed to be talking more to himself than he was to Jacob. He then turned his face back to Jacob and said, "I believe you."

Jacob felt relief wash over him like a tidal wave. "Thank you..."

"But I still don't trust her," Vladimir added broodingly. "But if all that you say is true, then I'll believe you. But, I will have to let Velinar know that I am aware of what happened. And it might be best if you keep that a secret between us three. I don't know how well the others are going to take it. They might not even believe you, and vouch for Angela to leave the Black Hand."

"They'd do that?" Jacob asked.

"Have you ever heard of Damion?"

"I heard it mentioned once... I think."

"Don't play dumb, have you or haven't you?"

"I'm not sure, honestly. Was he a Hunter?"

"Demonologist," Vladimir pointed out. "The only real one in Shadowfort's history, or so I've been told. He was... an odd fellow. But he was a good man, and a great Hunter. At the same time however... he wasn't completely human either. One might, he attacked one of our own. He was exiled by Velinar, despite the old man trying his best to let the Black Hand keep him. In the end, he was exiled forever."

"Where is Damion now?"

"I don't know," Vladimir admitted. "I miss the old bastard, now that I really think on it. He was... Anyway, who knows where he is now. There are rumors here and there throughout the country, but other than that... nothing. But yes, if the other's found out that Angela bit another member, even if she has no toxin to Turn you, she might be exiled nonetheless and you might be taken into precautionary care, if not worse."

"It's been weeks though since that night," Jacob argued. "Wouldn't that be proof enough that-"

"No, it wouldn't," Vladimir said sternly, almost impatiently. "Depending on the Vampire, it could take a few hours, or even a month to completely Turn. And for a creature who is only half Vampire, who knows? So, no. It wouldn't matter. Just promise me, brother to brother that you'll keep it a secret and go straight to Velinar if you feel any changes."

Jacob wanted to argue further, but knew it would be pointless. Vladimir was an experienced Hunter, and his mind was set. "Fine."

"And Angela has not bitten you since?"

Hearing that made Jacob think that the two of them were talking about a misbehaved dog rather than a person. It made him angry, but he swallowed that anger not necessarily for his own sake, but for the one who mattered in this conversation.

"No."

Vladimir eyed him disbelievingly but then nodded, almost with relief. "Good... good."

"Why can't you just give her a chance?" Jacob asked. "Is it really that hard? Or have your years Hunting only gotten you to see the worst she can be? Or..." And Jacob realized this just now. "Is it because of Damion? Is that why you can't trust her?"

"Don't," Vladimir warned Jacob. He didn't look angry, just weary. Tired. "Don't go there. You see what I see, and then you *might* understand if you are thinking clearly. No matter what intentions Angela had, no matter whether she was in the right or wrong, or even you for that matter, I will *never* trust someone who has the blood of beasts in them. And that is *final*."

"What if it was you?" Jacob demanded unwilling to let this one go. "What if you were on the ground, sword having gone through you and your own blood spilling on the floor? Angela is hurt, and the only way to get her to slay the beast was to give her your blood? What would you do?"

"I wouldn't let her bite me," Vladimir said. "I'm sorry, but that is too much for me. I would rather bleed out and die, than give myself to a she-demon."

Jacob felt a flare of anger rumble somewhere inside him. "Don't call her that."

Vladimir held up his hands in pitiful surrender. "Fine, fine, whatever. My point is made though. I wouldn't give myself to her. I don't think you understand the gravity of your situation, Jacob."

"I thought I told you, I'm not going to-"

"It's not a matter of your Turning or not," Vladimir snapped. "Just shut the hell up and listen for a moment, wouldja? It will do you some good if you quit asking and asking and just listen to what's being given to you."

After taking a deep breath, the Werewolf Hunter continued. "Now listen, an Immortal Kiss doesn't just mean servitude be that as a Dearg or some other lesser Vampire. It means you are *owned* by the one who bit you. Even though Angela is only a Dhampir, who knows how deep her vampiric roots go? Whether you like it or not, you are now owned by Angela, a Dhampir, for the rest of your days whether mortal or immortal. You are under her control should she seize your will, and you will be feared by Man and Beasts as long as you bear that mark. That is why the bite never heals. You are hers, for life."

Jacob didn't know this. Angela didn't even mention such a thing; did she even know? Or does she know, and just refused to tell him?

"It is a burden to carry and any who sees it will think that you're infected."

Was *this* what she had meant on the train back home from Irondell? *If so, why didn't she tell me?*

Whatever her reasons may be...

"Then it's a good thing I trust her," Jacob said to Vladimir.

The Werewolf Hunter seemed to be at a loss for words. He stood up, his eyes not breaking contact with Jacob's own. "Do you really trust her that much?" he asked.

Jacob swallowed, the mark on his neck burning at the movement. "With my life."

Vladimir stared at him a moment longer, and then sighed as he started to go after his horse. "It's your neck-literally. Come on, help me gather the horses. We'll put them in one of the houses, away from the cold."

"Is that really a respectable thing to do?" Jacob asked looking at all the abandoned homes. "These all used to belong to someone..."

"Your point?" Vladimir demanded still moving without stopping. Seeing that the Hunter was not going to be swayed at all in this, Jacob relented and went to help him. Wrapping his scarf tighter around his neck, he felt glad that he finally got to tell someone and actually talk to them other than Velinar or even Dr. Jecklyn. But at the same time, he couldn't help but wonder what sort of consequences giving such information would bring.

What would Vladimir do, and what did he think, now that he knew the truth?

Angela and Sabina followed the two siblings from a distance. They both agreed that the two needed their space, for their moment together. With their mother held by the two of them together, Morgan and Charlotte plunged themselves into a world of respectable silence, saying whatever prayers they knew before they finished what they had come all this way for. The forest thankfully provided just the tranquility they needed as they made their way to the legendary Snowcap Lake.

However, that was what made Angela weary. Ever since they had gotten to the village, they heard absolutely nothing. But out here in the woods… there was no sound to be heard. No birds, no squirrels, nothing. It made her feel uneasy. She figured that it was probably because of the high altitude, but there had to have been something for the villagers to live off of here, especially if they had livestock of some sort. There was nothing to plant here, so they had to have relied on meat and whatever the forest itself could provide in terms. It didn't make sense, and the eerie silence made her wish she was back in the haunted forest of a Thousand Faces. At least there was actual wildlife in that creepy place.

She wasn't the only one who was uneasy. Sabina never once put her rifle away, always keeping it close and primed. Her eyes scanned the nearby trees and beyond, unwilling to be surprised by anything.

She caught Angela looking and shrugged. "I don't like places that are too quiet. I'm expecting *something* to jump out at us."

"I agree," Angela replied. "But I'll hear whatever comes at us, should anything actually take an interest in us."

Sabina looked at her. "Sometimes I wonder, just how useful it would be to have heightened senses like you."

"It isn't all it is cut out to be."

"What do you mean?"

"There are some things you don't ever want to hear or smell."

"… Fair enough." Sabina said deciding it was best not to ask for details. "Still, it's got to have some advantages to it."

"It does. But at the same time, it would be nice to be… normal."

Angela had chosen her words carefully, but it got Sabina's attention nonetheless. However, she didn't say anything about what Angela meant by that. Instead, she took the conversation into a completely different direction.

"Well, we are almost there. And you haven't gotten us killed yet."

Angela had to bite her cheek to keep her temper in check. "Indeed."

Sabina, perhaps sensing this a little more precisely, pursed her lips in thought.

"Look, for what it's worth… I don't like you. In fact I have to be honest, I can't help but hate you- probably as much as you me."

Angela turned her head at her, those lavender pools inquiring.

"But I *do* know that you have my back," Sabina said. "All of us. I know that if we are all backed into a corner, I know that you will help us get out. You have our backs. I may not like you, but you have my respect. I just… I wanted you to know that."

Angela's face gave no indication whether or not she liked or disliked this half-compliment from Sabina. She didn't give away that she had heard perhaps the one thing she desired most within the Black Hand. Her face remained neutral, careful.

"I am… I appreciate you saying that. It gladdens me to hear that."

Sabina looked away but said, "Anytime."

Angela had to put up a hand to stop the Vampire Hunter. Before Sabina could say anything, she saw why Angela had halted their progress.

Charlotte and Morgan had stopped right at the shore of a great lake, frozen completely over and reflecting the sun like a giant, frosted mirror. They stood hand in hand as if ready to plunge into the depths beneath the ice together. An eagle passed overhead, the only sign of wildlife in the entire Snowcap area; it's shadow sliding across the ice as it tried to keep up with it's master. The two didn't look up to see it. They didn't move at all.

"Should we…" Sabina looked over at Angela.

"No," the Dhampir replied taking a seat on a nearby rock. "Just let them be."

Sabina nodded and took a seat on a rock on the opposite side of the pathway. The two of them watched the two children, who now sat cross-legged on the shores of Snowcap Lake with their mother right between them. They kept watch, and let them do their deed.

And so, the moment began.

Morgan remembered this place. He remembered how it looked. He remembered being on these same shores, watching as people purposely plunged themselves into the depths of the water, while everyone else sang their prayers and hymns. He remembered he had bathed in this lake and had seen men and women fish in it. The lake provided them with everything they ever needed, including, he thought morbidly, a mass grave.

It even smelled the same here; lake water glassy with terrible cold. The only thing missing, were the chosen one's lumbering into the waters, naked and chained to the rocks that would hold them under. Regardless of the good that Snowcap Lake brought to his people, it always came back to the brutal and dark detail that this place was just another site for sacrifice. He remembered the sensation of dread whenever a sacrifice went in vain, and he also remembered just how much grief had been on his heart on the day his mother had been chosen to sink into the wake.

But then she came back up. Alive, well, and speaking of meeting one of the gods. Not the god that she and many others had prophesized about meeting should they be the one to carry the curse of Winter, but this was still met with great jubilation from the rest of the village. Morgan too had been glad, but simply because his mother was alive. It was not long before he too realized that the joy would not last, for the chief and his council had plans for his mother, and his newborn sister.

He was glad- no, he was *overjoyed* that Charlotte had not been around to see such horrible practices or see the end result just before his mother told him that she was taking him and Charlotte away.

Except, that wasn't what they had been called back then. Back then, back here, they were called something else. Their true names. What they had currently were their adopted names, and Morgan had adapted and accepted this change with some difficulty but now it was almost easy. Here, however, he knew that he would have been called his real name. His name of which he had been baptized with the blood of a hunted deer, what his father had given him before the pox had taken him. Charlotte never knew her real name, and for a moment, he had debated whether or not to tell her.

Looking at the lake now, it was just a frozen body of water. Dead, with absolutely no life able to quench. The terror, the feeling that something was in the water watching Morgan was long gone. All he saw now was ice.

He looked at his sister, who just stared out at the lake, mesmerized by its silent beauty that it now held. For Morgan, regardless of how long it had become or how beautiful the ice was, it would forever taint his memory as a stain of terror and hopelessness; the false hope to reach out to a fake god in order to bring back the sun's brilliant heat. The ice itself being nothing more than a scar hiding the wound beneath which would otherwise have festered and infected.

At least Charlotte could look at the lake with such a look of awe. By the way her terribly blue eyes seemed to soak up the view, she truly enjoyed coming here, to where her mother and brother once lived. He had warned her a little about what had happened here when he was a child; the reason Mother decided to flee down the mountain. But even still, to describe the horror that took place in this place, all the souls snatched by the waters of the lake, it was something that thank Yohnah above, that Charlotte never had to experience.

Nor would anyone else, ever again.

The last two descendants of the village were here now. The rest... they were all gone. Morgan didn't know how or where they went, but he refused to even consider such a thing. It was not his problem in the first place. They were here now, and together he and Charlotte would fulfill their mother's last dying wish: to be spread into the waters of Snowcap Lake where her soul should have departed years ago. She was happy she got to live, happy that she lived to raise two beautiful children, she said.

But in the end, the lake called to her until her final breath. It was pointless, given her soul had already gone to the place where it belonged in the house of Yohnah in the far reaches of Kawn, but her body...

It was the least her two children could do, Morgan had to remind himself of that.

Bury the past into the waters forever, and continue to live on. That was what their mother wanted of them. They were to chart their own course now, both of them.

Morgan reached out with his free hand and gave Charlotte's shoulder a squeeze. When she looked at him, he felt his very spine go cold at the sight of those eyes. It was a feeling that was normal around Charlotte, and at this point Morgan had accepted it.

She is still my sister; a sharer of my blood.

"Are you ready?" he asked her.

Charlotte nodded in affirmation, a look of determination on her face. She threw up her hood, revealing her bald head that never once sprouted a single hair. What color would her hair be? Dark like ripened strawberries from Ukusvit or Noyii like his, or light with streaks of gold that made red hair like that look like fire, like Mother's?

"I'm ready," Charlotte told him and breaking the stream of thought.

Morgan took the urn from her as Charlotte stooped down and removed her shoes. She then stepped upon the ice with her bare feet, unsurprisingly untouched by the bitter cold. She then clapped her hands together, and began breathing deeply as she closed her eyes. The very air felt to have gotten colder, and Morgan hugged the urn close to allow his arms to hold in whatever warmth he had in him. He watched as Charlotte then snapped her eyes open and slapped her palms right on the surface of the ice.

Almost immediately, the ice melted into water; the entire lake turned from reflective glass to a disturbed surface of dark water almost as black as night. Charlotte's feet dropped into the water but only up to her ankles. She gasped out loud as if she was suddenly cold and she smiled proudly at her accomplishment in melting Snowcap Lake after who knows how long of being frozen and undisturbed by the souls of men and women who drowned within.

Charlotte began panting, the toll of magic seeped from her body leaving her breathless from her fantastic feat. Still, she looked at her brother and smiled, proud of her accomplishment.

Morgan, while smiling right back, kicked off his own shoes and joined Charlotte in the water. The water was terribly cold, and it made his legs feel like they were on fire all the way to his hips and his toes had already begun to turn numb. Still, he and Charlotte both grabbed ahold of the urn, and after saying a silent prayer together, they both swung the silver jar and the ashes of their mother sailed through the air like dust; sprinkling across the still waters of the lake and slowly sinking beneath the surface. They watched them clump and sink, until there was nothing more.

Just like that, it was over. Their deed; the final wish Mother had for her two children, was complete.

After retreating back onto the shore of the lake and quickly putting on his shoes, Morgan looked at Charlotte who had stuck the urn right into the dirt so that it could mark the massive grave of their mother and the many who had sunk beneath the wake. After sticking it in, Charlotte fell back and sat down into the snowy sand, retrieving her own boots.

"So, what now?" she eventually asks.

"What do you mean?" Morgan said. "We pay the Hunters, we go back through the forest, and we part ways when we get to the castle."

"Are you sure there is a way to pay them in the temple?" Charlotte asked looking at her brother skeptically. "For there to be treasure, there has to be a temple, right? I didn't see any temple coming in here."

"Don't worry about that," Morgan assured her. "I know exactly where it is. We'll make sure those Hunters get paid and more. They deserve it, after all the hell we've put them through."

Charlotte smiled, seeming relieved that her brother hadn't flat-out lied about the method of payment. Though she was still skeptical, as she should be. He *did* say there was a temple, though he didn't say *where* exactly.

"They really are nice people…" she muttered just now working the laces of her boots.

"Yeah, they are," Morgan agreed standing up to stretch. "Though they *do* seem to fight a whole lot. Mostly because of that Dhampir…"

"But she really is nice," Charlotte said frowning as she stood up. "I wish they could see how nice she really is. She… admires them it seems, I don't know, but I have that feeling, anyway."

"Yeah… I suppose she is."

"I hope someday I can grow up to be as strong as she is," Charlotte then said.

Morgan smiled at Charlotte, and patted her head as he had done many times when she was being the naïve little girl that she was. But this time, he patted her head with a confident look of belief in her. "You will. I already know you will."

He said all this with a smile, regardless of the two icy spheres staring right into his own eyes. Regardless of the dread he felt seeing those eyes, and the thought of what Charlotte would grow up to become. He loved his sister, but what she was didn't just reflect on what this place, their spiritual home really was. It was also the unknown future before them, and what it would entail concerning the legends of the Ice Walkers.

Charlotte smiled gratefully at her brother. "But anyways… where will we go after this?"

Morgan sighed and shook his head. "Do we go back to Firedell… or do we go somewhere else…"

"The Empire will still be looking for us."

"… Right."

"So…"

"I don't know," Morgan said, running a hand through his hair. He had always known he would have to think about that, figure it out. But it was so hard when you were as young as he and was already undertaking a difficult enough task.

"I don't know," he repeated. "I'll figure it out, somehow." He waved his hand, wanting to dismiss the conversation. He didn't want to have to think about it, not yet anyway. "Come on, we shouldn't keep them waiting…"

His eyes lingered to the Huntresses waiting at a good distance on the path, sitting on rocks silently without moving.

"Morgan…" Charlotte muttered as the two started back towards them.

"What?"

"Do you… do you hate me?"

Morgan stopped dead in his tracks, turning to face his sister. "Why in the world would you think that?"

"Because of me, you have to deal with everything that has happened to us on our way here. Being chased out of Firedell, having to sneak on trains to avoid Empire Soldiers…"

Charlotte sniffed, clearly upset. How long had she been thinking all of this?

"The way the people looked at me, even the nuns… Even you… do you-"

"Stop right there," Morgan said knuckling Charlotte's pale and soft chin. "We're in this together. I don't hate you in the slightest. You're my sister, and nothing is ever going to change that."

Charlotte's face broke out into a look of joy and relief so pure that her eyes began to moisten with tears. Before any could spill however, Morgan quickly turned away and started back for the two Hunters.

"Come on," he said. "Let's go."

"R-right," Charlotte sniffed wiping her eyes fast as she followed her brother closely. As she had for many years, she still clung to him; her only hope in a world that was cruel to her. And she, his own hope, drove the will behind every step Morgan took.

As she always would.

When they returned to the village, Jacob and Vladimir had the horses stored into a house and were waiting for them at the steps of the largest building. Morgan wasn't very happy that the horses were placed in someone else's home but Vladimir merely shrugged saying that if the owner comes and gets mad then he would move them.

But everyone knew that no one would come. This village had been left at the mercy of the unforgivable mountain and the terrible winter trapped within its peaks. Despite his dislike of the disrespect, Morgan had to admit that there really was no other way. And besides, maybe that was for the best. He hated this place for its legacy, but it had been the people be them good or bad who upheld that legacy.

"We'll rest here for the night," Vladimir said to everyone. "Then we'll pack back down at first light. Now…" He turned to Morgan. "Our payment, for bringing you up here? I see no temple that you spoke of." He stated the exact same words Charlotte had said to Morgan. Thanks to her hyper-sensitive hearing, Angela had been able to hear the entire conversation between her and her brother back at the lake.

"You're standing on it," Morgan said.

Vladimir looked at the dirt beneath his feet, and then he looked back up. "Huh?" he sounded.

"The entrance to the temple where the village treasures are kept is in there." Morgan pointed at the double-doors leading into the large cabin. "This was where the Chief lived as well as all his wives. When I was a kid-"

"When?" Jacob asked with a sly smile.

Morgan pouted at the Witch Hunter. "Back when I was *younger*, me and a few of the other kids would be asked to help clean up the place. We sometimes even helped the chief take offerings down into the temple to offer to the gods. If anything is left, it will be down there." He started up the steps and began pushing on the double-doors which refused to budge. "Come on…" he groaned.

Vladimir sighed and then after gently pushing Morgan aside, smashed the door open with a heavy kick right between the door handles. They slammed right open in a puff of dust and creaking wood.

"Seriously!?" Morgan hissed despite himself, rushing to the man's side and taking a look at what remained of the left door.

"Oops," Vladimir said sarcastically peering inside the building before entering. Angela and the others close behind, meeting the musty stench of dust and the darkness enclosed with it.

It was a typical meeting hall Angela saw as soon as they lit a match to the torches on the support beams holding up the tall triangular ceiling. Small cushions circled around a large throne-like chair with skulls planted right on top all strung together with cobwebs and dust. The boarded-up windows let in thin slivers of light even with the torch scones that had not been used in years lighting up the majority of the large room. Strange garlands of pinecones and woven branches stretched between the support beams overhead, and on either side on the back wall behind the throne were two shrines with a sun on one and a moon on the other.

"Damn…" Jacob muttered stomping his foot and kicking up dust. "When was the last time anyone was even in here?"

"Not for a long time," Angela said stooping down and peering at the floor. Though the other Hunters couldn't see it, she could see the faint difference in depth of the dust collected on the wooden floor. Footprints, moving away from the door and heading for the throne. Even after years of collecting dust and rotting out here in the middle of nowhere, the meeting building still had signs of someone being in here before they locked everything up. "But someone stuck around to lock the doors and board up the windows."

"So where are they?" Sabina asked walking about with her arms crossed. "There's no one here either..."

"Hey," Vladimir said moving up to Morgan. "What are we looking for exactly?"

"Over here," the boy said rushing over to the throne, his steps almost landing precisely on the ghostly traces left behind.

As he reached the throne, he began pushing against the wooden chair, causing the skulls up top to wobble slightly. After scooting it back, he stepped back immediately to reveal a hole in the floor with stone steps leading down into utter darkness.

Vladimir pursed his lips. "I see. So that is what you meant earlier..."

"Directly beneath us..." Charlotte whispered hardly believing it herself. Not surprising given she had never seen this place in her life.

"So our payment is down there?" Jacob asked.

"As promised," Morgan nodded in affirmation.

Vladimir and Jacob shared a look and both seemed to share some inaudible agreement. Vladimir then turned to both Angela and Sabina. "Two of us will stay up here, and the other two will go down with Morgan."

"You don't trust me?" Morgan said defensively.

"No, I just want to make sure someone is up here waiting for us when we come back," Vladimir said. "It's a safety precaution; take note."

Morgan pouted but he said nothing more.

"Who wants to go treasure hunting?" Vladimir asked the group.

"I don't care either way." Angela spoke first.

"I'll go with you." Jacob volunteered.

Sabina shrugged. "Then I guess I'll stay up here."

Vladimir nodded. "Okay, that works."

Charlotte then took a step forward. "Um... I want to go as well."

Morgan frowned. "Charlotte, I don't think that-"

"Please?" Charlotte asked. "I want to see what our tribe was like. I want to see... just what our people were like."

Morgan looked at the Hunters desperately, but everyone either looked away or only looked back at him expectedly. Seeing that he wasn't going to be getting any help, he sighed.

"Are you sure?"

Charlotte nodded, and then turned to Vladimir. "That's okay, right?"

Vladimir shrugged. "That's fine." He then looked at the women who offered to stay behind. "We'll be back soon."

"No worries," Sabina said with a smile.

"Come on," Jacob said taking up a piece of wood off the floor. Vladimir had already taken some cloth from a ruined tapestry whose embroideries were faded and falling apart in stitches. He wrapped this around the end of Jacob's finding and then lit it with a match. It burned dimly but slowly.

"Let's go," said Jacob. After allowing Morgan to go down first, he followed close behind. Behind him, Charlotte and Vladimir took the rear.

Both Huntresses watched as the orange light of the torch slowly faded into darkness, indicating that the group was already very deep into the passageway to the hidden temple. Deeper still into the depths of the mountains.

"You think they will be okay?" Sabina asked taking a seat on one of the cushions. She had gathered more splintered wood from old furniture and was building a miniature teepee for a fire in a clay fire pit no doubt used for religious practice.

"They will," Angela said. "I doubt those two mean any of us ill."

"It ain't the kids I'm worried about. It's the fact that they are *under* us now."

"They'll be fine," Angela insisted, leaning her back against one of the support beams and crossing her arms. "They'll get our payment and will be back up here in no time."

"Right." Sabina lit the piece of paper she had placed in the heart of the teepee, blew on it, and then fell back and laid across the floor with her arms crossed behind her head as the fire began to accumulate.

"What a trip."

"We're only halfway done," Angela reminded her.

"Still. It's been a ride." Sabina then lifted her head to look at Angela. "Hopefully the ride back isn't as... adventurous."

"If it is, we'll deal with it."

Sabina pouted at the Dhampir. "You have an answer for everything, don't you?"

Angela shrugged, neither indicating that she did or didn't.

"In any case," Sabina said letting her head fall back and closing her eyes. "It'll be good to get back to the castle. I'm sure Matei misses me."

The Vampire Hunter then looked at the Dhampir with a single eye, keeping the other resting shut. "Angela, what do you plan to do when we get there?"

"Same thing I always do," Angela sighed. "Stay in my room, wash, read, be with my cat until the next contract."

Sabina wanted to ask if that was all. She didn't know what Angela did in her personal time, all she knew was that after Irondell, she often visited with Jacob to see how he healed. Other than that what the Dhampir did in her own time was a mystery in it of itself. And the way she mentioned waiting until the next contract, made it sound like Angela didn't have any plans for the foreseeable future. She wasn't collecting pay to one day retire and own a farm somewhere or even go to the Yom University south of Ebondell. She was living each day by the day, and Sabina wondered if it was because that Angela was immortal. She wondered if the immortal really looked forward to anything really, and this made her also wonder not for the first time how old the Dhampir really was.

Instead of all of this of course, she said, "I see. Well... if you ever want to, you are always welcome to sit with me. Have a cup of tea, or... or something."

Angela looked over at Sabina, and Sabina thought she saw the smallest trace of surprise on her face. Her lavender eyes shone a little brighter in the firelight, and Sabina had to suppress a shudder.

"I'll... consider it."

Sabina closed her eyes, pleased with the answer. "Don't worry about the other Hunters. You can just sit between Jacob and I."

"It's a little more complicated than that."

"How?" Sabina asked.

Angela pursed her lips before answering. "I'm just... not used to sitting with a group of people."

"No one is at first. Doesn't mean we can't learn."

Deciding it best not to discuss it any further- at least not for the time being, Angela allowed the conversation to die out into silence. She closed her own eyes as she remained propped against the support beam, waiting patiently for the return of Jacob and Vladimir, their payment, and the two native children who had no where to go.

She hoped that Velinar would at least see it in his heart to at least consider letting the children stay- at least for a while.

The stairway leading down into the depths felt like it went down forever for Jacob. He had never been a fan of tight spaces, but he always wanted to explore the depths of the planet and find its secrets. Step by cold and dusty step, the passageway continued on and on, feeling somewhat similar to that of Velinar's chambers albeit more cramped and more ancient than Shadowfort itself.

Eventually, the stairway ended at an arch with two cloaked statues holding up the ceiling and upon stepping out, the group found themselves in a vast rectangular corridor hidden beneath the remnants of the Snowcap Tribe.

Ancient carvings covered in cracks caused by deep freeze lined the walls and ceiling, depicting giant humans fighting against the beasts of the mountains. Stories of old and ancient prophecies the natives of this mountain believed in during their time. As Jacob walked across the floor behind Morgan and Charlotte, he noticed that more carvings lined the dusty floor. He had half a mind to sweep up some of the collected dust to see what it was, but instead kept moving, following the two. Vladimir lingered off for a bit, staring at one carving in particular of a man who seemed to be writhing against the glare of a moon or sun, it's face grotesquely carved into that of a stretched snarl and thick hair bristling from it's back. He scowled at the carving and then moved on.

Eventually, Morgan stopped at the end of the hall where another archway led to a second room. Two more Nephelim statues stood guard on either side of the passageway, both holding hairy beasts by the neck as the creatures tried to claw and bite at them with fangs and claws.

"Those Wolf Brothers seem to have gotten into a lot of trouble," Jacob muttered hoping to somehow break the unnerving silence.

"Of course, they did," Vladimir said walking up to the statue on the left staring up at it's face of valor and savagery. It was the face of a man, fighting for his very life.

"Even before the Empire came to claim these lands, Balkeñoir, even way back then had men whose sole purpose was to hunt beasts. Just as it is our duty today. These two were unique in particular because they were the sons of the first Lycan who had courted one of the giants."

"Through here," Morgan said pointing into the archway. Taking up his torch, Jacob took the lead, stepping into the chamber. He became aware of the smell of mold or something else just as sour and pungent upon stepping in, and he stopped to observe what was inside.

It was a tomb. A tomb with a shrine between two sarcophagi of gold. Pots and urns lined the walls on either side, and some had been spilled out to reveal old and dusty jewels that had been dug out of the mountain by untrained hands. The shrine in the middle represented the sun and moon enclosed together, their eyes looking down upon the faces of the sarcophagi. The sun looked upon an obvious male, and the moon over a female. Jacob could tell the difference between the two based on the face that the carving upon the lid was of the pair, their faces painted in makeup and their hands filled with various tools and weapons. Whoever made the coffins took their time to make something so beautiful for the deceased. But Jacob's true focus was lying at the base of the shrine between the dead. A skeleton, garbed in ripped and tattered robes with a rusted dagger in his hand. Morgan rushed for the skeleton, and picked up a note that was crumpled in the bony hand. The piece of canvas was wrinkled, and as delicate as a dead leaf, but still Morgan pried it from the skeleton's hand. It was Nisthgúlian writing and yet Morgan remembered how to read it and so read it aloud.

"My gods and my lords will be the last thing mine eyes will see alive," Morgan read aloud before looking down at the skeleton. "It's the chief…"

"Guess Angela was right," Vladimir said looking over the female sarcophagus. The eyeliner was fading and the red hair had aged to the color of old rust. "Someone had come in here to close up shop."

"But… what about all the others?" Charlotte asked.

Jacob had an idea. He didn't dare say it aloud, but if Morgan's story about how to conceive an Ice Walker was true, then there was a chance that all the villagers were still around, and not have just disappeared mysteriously. They were all at the bottom of Snowcap Lake.

Morgan tossed the note aside as if it were garbage and then looked up at the dusty shrine the chief had died beneath. "I wonder if he knows the truth now… Where he could be now…"

"Don't worry," Jacob said patting the boy on the shoulder reassuringly. "The Dove of the world doesn't condemn those who never had the chance to know Him. He may still be as innocent as a child. And if he was, you'll see him again."

Morgan looked at Jacob. "You think so?"

"I believe so," Jacob said with a warm smile.

Morgan smiled back, and then turned to Vladimir who was now looking over the male sarcophagus.

"Who are these two people?" the Werewolf Hunter asked.

Morgan pursed his lips. "According to the chief… they were the first Ice Walkers. They were buried here, in honor of their newfound power."

"That would make this tomb… over a thousand years old," Jacob realized.

"An archeological marvel," Vladimir nodded. "Dr. Clockwork and others from Yom-Un would have a field day if they were to discover this."

Morgan said, "They were the first Ice Walkers… and the only one not sacrificed to the Sun and Moon Goddess."

Jacob shook his head in wonder. "It makes no sense. You risk drowning people, in order to find Ice Walkers, and then you sacrifice them…"

"Nothing makes sense here anymore," Morgan agreed. "But it's over now. The tribe is dead. Everything here, is just a relic; a remnant of the past."

And that was true. This tomb will be undisturbed for the rest of eternity after the Hunters left. Perhaps someday it will be discovered again, when the country is no longer plagued by intense cold. But then again, perhaps not.

He then turned to Vladimir and pointed to some of the pots. "There are mostly herbs and myrrh in those pots, but some of them do have some shards of gems the men dug up from the mountainside. They aren't pretty, but they could be of some worth, right?"

The Werewolf Hunter crossed over to the treasures left as offerings to the first Ice Walkers. "Let's see," he said stooping over to look it all over. "Jacob, gimme a hand."

Jacob handed Charlotte the torch and he joined Vladimir at his side to look over the jewels. Morgan was not lying when he mentioned that the jewels were 'rough'. In fact, Jacob was tempted to call that an understatement. Most of the jewels had been dug out so improperly that the edges were chipped and some even had some bits of rock still stuck to them. Not only that, but the few rubies and sapphires that had been dug out somewhat decently were cracked and fragile with age. With any luck the Black Hand may or may not be able to pawn off the relics for a couple pounds but it was unlikely. However, while digging through both Jacob and Vladimir both found some chunks of gold buried in the crude of jewels. With Morgan's help, they managed to fill up a whole jar of the gold bits. It would be a while, but Vladimir estimated that they probably had a good couple hundred pounds worth of gold in the pot. Once it was filled to the top, Vladimir closed off the lid which made the ancient container stand to his hip almost.

"That should be enough."

"I'm sorry about the jewels…" Morgan said. "I didn't know they'd be in such bad shape."

"No worries," Vladimir assured him. "We're just lucky there was gold buried in here. It may be rough-looking, but at least gold can be melted down. It should all be enough for four payments give or take. We'll figure it out once we get it all melted down and shipped off to a bank to trade in for coin."

"Good," Morgan said relieved. "I'm glad to hear it."

"We really can't thank you all enough." Charlotte spoke up for the first time in a long while.

"Don't mention it," Jacob smiled as he took the torch back from the girl. "We don't-"

Boom.

A muffled sound shook the ceiling above, and everyone looked up to see dust sprinkling down from above.

"What the hell was that?" Vladimir said just as another boom sounded.

"I don't know..." Jacob said but then he felt something... a familiar sensation he felt when- His eye snapped wide when he realized what was happening.

"Angela..." With that, he turned and sprinted for the exit with Vladimir in tow.

"You two, stay back!" Vlad shouted. "Don't come up for any reason!"

"Wait!" Morgan shouted as the two Hunters sprinted down the carved hallway. "What's going on?" But no one answered him. In fact, Jacob couldn't even think to respond as he went for his bow, ready for whatever happened when he reached the surface.

She's back...

Sol

"So tell me," Sabina said at some point while she and Angela were still waiting and the men were sorting through the ancient Nishthgúlian treasure. "What do you think of Jacob?"

Angela stared at the Vampire Hunter, who in turn was staring at *her* with such interest. When Sabina didn't look away, Angela at last answered in question, "What do you mean?"

"What do you think of him?" Sabina repeated.

"A decent enough Hunter. Has much to learn, but his knowledge of-"

"That's not what I mean," Sabina said laying her head back and staring up at the stone ceiling. "I mean, what do you *think* about him?"

Angela blinked, confused. "I don't understand what you mean."

"I think you do," Sabina said now smiling. She had lifted her head up again and was looking at the Dhampir with now keen interest.

"Well..." Angela thought about it for a moment, choosing her words with care. "He's annoying, but a good man... I guess? What exactly are you meaning?"

Sabina shrugged. "Curious. He is young still; asks too many questions it feels like. Kinda childish at times."

"He is," Angela agreed with no hesitation, grateful that someone else had somewhat of a similar opinion as she, among something else after all.

"Sometimes I wonder if-"

Angela stopped suddenly when she caught a familiar scent and in her eyes, she saw fire. Without hesitating, Angela lunged across the room and grabbed Sabina by the arm, yanking her out of the way just as a blast of fire incinerated the spot where the Vampire Hunter had been laying.

"What the bloody hell…" Sabina whispered staring at the burning splotch past Angela who immediately reached up for her sword.

"What a pity," a voice said disappointedly from above. "I missed."

Angela looked up and through the burning hole that appeared in the ceiling, she saw the witch from before sitting on her broomstick with two other figures peering into the hole on the rooftop. The witch grinned, her rotten teeth visible despite the shadow from her red hood. Her Immortal daughter and more surprisingly, the Raven from earlier, were peering inside with looks of vicious glee.

"You," Sabina snarled at the Raven, standing up fast and drawing both her sword and her pistol. "A pity the trolls didn't get to you."

"A pity, indeed," the Raven said beneath her mask. She had in her hands a rifle and it was pointed at Angela in particular. "Where are the kids?"

"Why don't you come down here and ask us yourself?"

"Oh," the witch purred dangling a strange vial in her clawed hand. "I think one of us will. Mithus!"

She tossed the vial over to the young Immortal who caught it without looking, those silver eyes bearing right at Angela with such hatred. She had not once looked at Sabina; hadn't even bothered. Her focus was solely on the Dhampir who took her brother away.

The Raven then leapt into the burning hole, landing right in the spot where the fire was still spreading. The Immortal child had landed close behind. In the flames, her feathered cloak burned like a Fire Wraith emerging from the depths of Oblivion. Behind her, the Vampire took the vial in her hand, and removed the cork holding the strange dark liquid within. As soon as the stench of the liquid struck Angela's nose, she hissed at the awful odor that was practically screaming with danger.

"You killed my brother," the Immortal said stepping around the flames and the Raven while ignoring the little flame that snagged at the bottom of her skirt. "You killed Lithus."

"And I told you that you would suffer the same fate if you chose to come after us again," Angela said removing her sword from its scabbard with a loud screech. "Instead, you chose to come for us."

"It is only natural, don't you think?" the witch shouted down from above. "You kill a member of someone else's family and you expect her to just simply accept it?" The witch shook her head in disgust. "Ever heard of a blood payment?"

Angela glanced in the witch's direction, but she brought her eyes back to the Immortal who brought the vial close to her lips. Behind the girl, the Raven kept her rifle aimed at Sabina who had taken aim at her. It was like a standoff between the two of them and Angela and the child.

Angela felt a tinge of pity in her heart and she attempted to implore her wish upon the child.

"It isn't too late. You can live in peace if you promise to remain in these mountains and never come after the world of Man."

Mithus snarled in disgust as she closed her lips around the mouth of the vial and swallowed the dark liquid in a single gulp. She coughed as she dropped the vial and then brought her eyes back to Angela. For a moment, her silver eyes shone brighter than ever.

"I will kill you for what you did to Lithus... you disgusting, human-bred *monster*!"

The Raven then suddenly fired her rifle, forcing Sabina to throw herself to the floor. The Raven then charged at Angela who had taken a step towards Mithus and the Dhampir just barely had enough time to get her sword up in time to catch the two blades of the Raven who pushed against her with inhuman strength. Behind her, the rifle she had been wielding dropped to the floor between her and Mithus who stood hissing with pain and clutching at her temples. Angela knew instantly that the Raven was trying to buy the Immortal child time to do something; whatever it was it was hurting her badly.

Angela saw Sabina come around and brought her sword down into the Raven's back. The woman merely whirled about and slashed at Sabina. Taking her chance, Angela moved in and ran her own sword into the Raven's belly as she turned to catch the Dhampir. She kicked at the Raven who had doubled over in pain and was surprised and distracted her for a moment as black smoke seeped from the wound along with the blood.

But then everyone seemed to stop to watch the Immortal who was now on her hands and knees, coughing and hissing as if she were choking. Even the Raven,turned her attention away from her smoking wound to watch the horror that *grew* before them.

Mithus appeared to grow in size, her skin pulling taut across her bones that stretched and crackled as if they were breaking. Her skirt tore and fell away, revealing a naked body that continued to stretch and grow and twist into a thing of nightmarish terror of a sickly shade of gray. The nails from her hands and feet fell away, having been pushed out of the way to make room for the black claws stretching out. Her teeth and fangs grew in her jaw that seemed to stretch out and her nose became flat under the tight pressure of her pulled skin. Her hair fell away in bundles, revealing her pointed ears and the dome of her gray skull which looked like a polished stone. Her shoulders widened and just behind the shoulder blades poking through the skin were two bony appendages that eventually tore through spraying darkening blood everywhere to reveal large bat-like wings with an ivory thumbnail at the knuckle.

The creature that had replaced Mithus was on it's hands and knees, groaning deeply and raspy. No one dared to speak, none could even believe what had happened.

When Mithus eventually stopped coughing and hissing, she stood up on her hind legs that seemed to now have a second pair of knees behind the first, giving her an animalistic stance as she stood nearly eight feet tall as opposed to her original small stature. Her naked body was now gray, pulled taut with new muscle. When she looked at the group beholding her, they all saw nothing of the seemingly small and innocent child.

What they all saw, was a monster; demonic and powerful.

Her once pretty face was now stretched taunt, her nose wrinkled into a face that was more batlike than human. Her mouth, much larger and was now full of jagged teeth along with her elongated fangs. Her eyes were the same; cold and silver that glowed like the moon on a clear night. But everything about the little girl now...

There was no sign of any nobility in the Immortal, nor the respectable honor that Immortals had always been capable of and held even in their lowest courts. The demon within Mithus had finally been released, and it even frightened Angela just as much as it frightened everyone in the burning building.

"What the fuck..." the Raven hissed taking a step back, her hand still over her wound which had ceased smoking. She appeared to have forgotten about the Black Hand and her job in finding the Nishthgúlian children. Behind her mask, there was a terror-stricken face. If she had known that this was what the witch had up her sleeve...

Sabina backed up as well, getting into line with Angela as they stared at the beast that sniffed the air with it's flat nose and hissed past those jagged teeth.

"What the hell is that thing?" the Vampire Huntress muttered. "It can't be..."

"It is," Angela said with dread. "Somehow she had been able to awaken the demon hidden within all Immortals..."

Angela never would have thought that she would ever get the chance to see the ancient form of her ancestors, the very form the demon lord Kawfka praised when he had pitched the Vampire against Yohnah's human creation. But now she wished she never did; not here, not now, nor ever again.

The ancient form of Immortals, once the bane of civilizations all across the world, the Nosferatu owned the skies of night and struck terror into the hearts of Man. Seeming human in the daytime, remaining in their human form, they would turn into the demonic beasts that laid dormant in their very hearts. Like eagles that hunt rabbits, the Nosferatu were the ultimate predator of humankind. But the form was dangerous; monstrous and destructive on the bodies of Immortals. For so long, many Immortals had gained the knowledge to suppress the beast within them, and gain control of the demon that desired to be free again; Another way to honor the rebellion of Abbadon Pudidrac, the first Vampire to have been created.

Even today, for the last few centuries, Immortals have considered the transformation into Nosferatu an abomination; a taboo almost as terrible as drinking blood on the night of a Blood Moon- among other superstitions of course.

But to release control of your familiars, to allow the demon to be released...

"I didn't think they were real..." Sabina whispered. Being a Vampire Hunter herself, she probably read some of the ancient texts and scrolls of the ancient beings dating back to the beginning of time- nearly.

The witch began chuckling in amusement. She had lowered herself through the hole in the burning roof, her broomstick now hovering just above the Nosferatu that had replaced what had once been her adoptive daughter. If she understood the gravity of what she had done, she showed no remorse in it.

"It seems my research has finally come with the results I've longed waited for... The ancient form of the terrible Immortals... remarkable. Simply, remarkable."

Angela looked up at the witch with a look of dangerous anger. "Do you not realize what you have done?"

"Oh, I am *very* well aware." The witch then snapped her fingers. "Sorina! Quit shaking in your boots. Help her! Mithus, kill the Hunters!"

Mithus bellowed which sounded between the lines of the screech of a bat and the roar of a lion, and the Nosferatu lunged forward at incredible speeds claws extended- Directly at the Dhampir who had caused her much misery.

Sabina had raised her gun and at that moment the creature's eyes flashed silver.

Angela cried out, "No!" but it was too late. Sabina had already pulled the trigger on her pistol twice, and the resounding sound of the report momentarily silenced the room as the silver bullets plunged into the belly of Mithus-

And ended up right into Sabina's own belly.

Blood sprayed and the Huntress gasped in terrible pain as her back erupted as the exit wounds were created like blooming flowers of crimson. She staggered back and Angela had to catch her but then drove her aside just as Mithus came barreling past, her claws shredding the Dhampir's cloak as she got Sabina out of harm's way.

"What the hell..." Sabina groaned placing a hand over her belly. Blood seeped through her fingers at an alarming rate between the two entry wounds.

"Don't look into her eyes!" Angela said keeping one eye on the Nosferatu and the other on the Raven who was just now starting to get over her terror.

The witch cooed in wonder. "Oh-ho! Looks like her eyes have been Awakened along with her ancient form. This is turning out better than I hoped!" She sounded sickly giddy floating above the carnage.

The Nosferatu turned on its heel, and the face of Mithus hissed at the two Hunters. "Brother... give him back... Give me back Lithus!"

Angela hoisted Sabina to her feet, the Vampire Hunter now ignoring the blood still spilling from her belly. "Are you able to fight still?"

Sabina flashed a dangerous smile. "Look who you're talking to."

Angela's eyes lingered towards the Raven, who was now circling around with her two blades crossed in front of her. She was still weary of the Nosferatu who was just starting to regain it's bearings, but she was on the hunt again.

"That Raven isn't human. Silver burns her. She's-"

"Give him back!" Mithus snarled as she whirled towards the Hunters. Angela shoved Sabina towards the door which felt all at once too far away, and the Vampire Hunter complied. Mithus had already lunged once again at the Dhampir who had killed her brother, and Angela turned to intercept the Nosferatu.

Ducking beneath the Nosferatu's arm, Angela rolled out of harm's way and slashed the creature across its back. Since she hadn't looked into the monster's eyes before the attack, a deep cut bled across Mithus' back, causing her to howl. Sabina, had taken cover behind a nearby support beam of the temple and was about to shoot the beast again when the Raven charged right at her, blades spinning. Sabina managed to get her sword up in time, but the strength behind the attack sent her flying back; knocked completely off her feet and causing her to smack right into another support beam which shook the burning ceiling and caused embers to rain down. As the Vampire Hunter leapt out of the way of the Raven's blades that sliced through the support beam as easily as a sickle cutting through wheat, the Nosferatu turned on Angela again, coming at her again and this time using her wings to try and stab at the Dhampir with its sharp thumbnail.

Angela leapt away and then rolled to the side as Mithus came at her again, this time slamming down and smashing a nearby crate with her massive fists. Angela then quickly rushed in to try and get the beast from behind but the Nosferatu had turned its ugly head and her eyes flashed bright and silver. To avoid getting herself stabbed, Angela twisted her body aside and merely placed a cut across the creature's bicep. Instead of Mithus bleeding however, the cut appeared in a flash of red across Angela's own arm as if an invisible dagger had cut her. Feeling the burning sensation of her own silver, Angela leapt away again as Mithus continued after her; her wings now spread completely as if she was trying to make herself appear bigger than she already was.

"Give him back!" she snarled as she came for Angela again with such bloodlust and hatred. The nimble Dhampir continued to evade the hulking monstrosity as she tried to think of a way to end this carnage quickly and efficiently.

The witch Carmilla, remained watchful, curious as to where the other Hunters have gone, but too engrossed in the carnage she had wrought upon her enemies to express any real concern. The fun was just getting started.

Meanwhile, Sabina had leapt back just as the Raven came at her a second time. She managed to deflect one of the swords but ended up having to back away again as Sorina slashed at her bleeding belly.

When Sorina tried to lunge with her other blade again, Sabina moved in close and slipped past the blade, at the same time hooking her arm around the Raven's and rolling her own body across Sorina's back, Sabina pulled hard on her arm and brought the Raven back down and smashed her right into the floor. Her pistol was still gripped tightly and for a moment Sorina's head was aligned with it. When she fired however, the bullet only tore through the beak of the tin mask, shattering it into pieces and revealing the lower mouth of the woman which was pulled taunt in a snarl. She then went to stab the Raven with her swordarm while she was down but Sorina managed to get one of her blades up and deflect the sword so that it would stick right into the floorboards right by her head. Sabina was just then able to stomp down on Sorina's other hand, preventing her from trying to strike again from below.

"Not this time, *Raven*," Sabina spat the word out like it was bile. She struggled to get her sword out but then focused on trying to get the pistol to point at the Raven's head again. The woman's strength however kept a firm hold on Sabina's arm and wouldn't budge. The two appeared locked in some strange wrestling match where neither could stand or drop.

Suddenly, Sorina wrapped her legs around Sabina's arm before the Vampire Hunter could do anything. She then twisted her body like a snake, twisting Sabina's arm and causing a sharp pain to shoot up it, causing Sabina to lose her grip on the pistol. At the same time Sorina had managed to finally pull Sabina off balance and she kicked Sabina away and onto the ashy floor. Both were back on their feet in an instant, the thundering violence happening between the two vampiric beings close by going seemingly unnoticed.

With a harsh cry, Sabina then rushed for the Raven, slashing at Sorina's head and then spinning aside as her opponent went to stab at her again. Blood from her wound flew in droplets every which way like a sprinkler at one of Goldendell's marvelous vineyards, and the pain was excruciating but Sabina was not about to let up. The two swung and slashed and parried, each trying to gain an advantage over the other. Sabina managed to stagger the Raven and with a secondary strike, at last got Sorina to release one of her other blades. Now only holding one which was shorter and incapable of much reach, Sabina found no trouble going in for a third strike, this time her blade sinking deep into Sorina's shoulder mere centimeters from her neck. Sorina grunted in pain as blood and black smoke belched from the wound.

The Raven then retreated back, the sound of the silver blade and bone squealing as she reared away, giving Sabina just the opening she needed to spin once again and plant a heavy kick into her face; her boot having enough force to knock the rest of the tin mask right off Sorina's face. The metallic false face clattered across the floor and landed right into a splash of fire while the two Hunters faced one another. The Hunter of beasts looked at the face of a Hunter of Hunter's, disturbed at the warlike and savage face Sorina had kept hidden.

Sabina's eyes lingered to the smoke still seeping from the Raven's wound. Her eyes narrowed, wishing that Vladimir and Jacob would hurry up, because she and Angela were in big trouble.

Sorina smiled, ignoring the blood that was seeping out of her upper lip where she had been kicked. "Where are those kids? Tell me and I'll leave you to deal with the witch and her monster."

Sabina smiled wickedly at the bitch who sold her soul to the Empire and their unholy tactics. "You want to 'em? You're gonna have to get through me."

Something shook the building, and if Sabina were to glance to her left, she would have seen that the Nosferatu had smashed into the fireplace behind the temple's sitting area. Angela had lured Mithus over and had been able to leap on top of the beast and while holding onto one of the wings was repeatedly stabbing the demon in the back with her sword as the monster bucked and roared like a winged bull. But as it was, Sabina didn't dare let her eyes linger away even for a moment from her opponent. She could already feel her head growing dim and fussy.

"You're losing a lot of blood," Sorina reasoned with the Huntress. "Tell me now or I'll put an end to your suffering. You can't beat me."

"Then come on," Sabina dared the Raven. "Show me what you got!"

Sabina suddenly felt her hair stand up on end and she leapt out of the way just as another ball of fire crashed through the ceiling and splashed into the floor where she used to be standing. Meanwhile, the Raven had made her own move and came in quick as a flash and swinging her solitary blade. Sabina had managed to get her sword up to catch the blow, but the Raven brought her knee up at the same moment and nailed her good and hard right in the belly where the bullets had gone in. Sabina felt all her air rush out of her lungs as fire erupted in her belly. Crimson stars blotted her vision, and the strength behind the strike sent her flying back, crashing a good ten feet back right across the floor.

As the Raven moved in for the kill, Angela had at last been thrown off, having been grabbed at by the Nosferatu who slammed her into the ground as if she were a ragdoll before tossing her aside. The Dhampir crashed on the other side of the room and did not get up as the creature lumbered towards her, the silver wolf's head of the swords hilt standing out between the leathery wings and looking just as grim as its lost master. It was looking pretty grim for them both.

Still, Sabina ignored the horrible pain in her gut as she pushed herself up into a sitting position. She gasped as the fiery sensation seared through her as she got to her knees. She still had her sword miraculously and was using it as a crutch as she took slow and deliberate breaths, which was getting harder and harder as the building around them continued to burn. The Raven continued her slow lumbering pace towards her as the Nosferatu rushed to where Angela had been tossed, ready to fight some more.

Sabina grinned as she finally stood up. "Having a witch to back you up… bet that makes you feel real lucky, eh, Raven?"

"Talking won't get you anywhere," Sorina replied angling her sword so that Sabina's reflection would get caught in the silver edging.

"Heh, come on then you *cunt*," Sabina said getting into a stance once again, gritting her teeth against the fire in her belly and ignoring the sounds of droplets striking the floor at her feet. She was dizzy, but she would be damned before she allowed herself to drop. "I bet you don't wanna keep Kawfka waiting."

Sorina's face hardened at that.

Looking past the Raven, Sabina saw the Nosferatu coming down upon Angela who was still trying to get back up. The Dhampir had managed roll away and getting her feet under her, she leapt up and seized the sword, ripping it free from the monster's back. When she landed however the Nosferatu whirled about to backhand her. The Dhampir managed to slip underneath the arm and drive her sword into the demon's side.

But despite it's wounds, despite the constant biting of silver, the Nosferatu showed no signs of slowing down or even giving up.

"I just want those kids," Sorina said keeping her sword in front of her. "Tell me and I'll leave you be."

Sabina flashed a defiant smile. "Sure you will."

Sorina's mouth twitched and she bared her teeth. "Fine, then."

With that, she charged forward, swinging her blades with such precision and power that if Sabina didn't move fast, she would be cleaved into three gory pieces.

Taking a step to her right, Sabina made it look like she was about to lunge to her left, but instead she completely fell back onto her right, just beneath the Raven's slicing blade. She then brought her foot up and planted a heavy kick into Sorina's elbow, forcing her arm to go upward. Then turning on her heel, Sabina lunged with her sword, stabbing the Raven in the side and feeling the blade slip just beneath the ribs and deep into her abdomen.

"Kah!" Sorina gasped as blood and smoke hissed from the wound. She went to slash at Sabina who spun once again, wrenching her sword out of the Raven's side and then in one sharp flash, kicked the back of Sorina's knee to force her to the ground. As she fell to her knees, the Vampire Hunter brought her sword around Sorina's head and the edge of her blade slid across the Raven's neck, splitting it open and unleashing a thick gush of blood and smoke out in front of them. Sorina gasped and gurgled blood as Sabina kicked at her back and sent her falling face-first to the floor.

Before she could turn and assist Angela however she could though, she was suddenly thrown forward as something struck her hard in the back and proceeded to burn.

Carmilla who had watched the Raven fall, had hurled a fireball at Sabina. The Huntress went down, rolling across the floor in order to stop the flames that had burned right through her cloak and had seared her armor. She sent another one sailing down and Sabina proceeded to roll away, unable to get her feet under her without pausing for too long.

"Sabina!"

Stopping in a prone position, Sabina looked and saw Angela who had managed to bring the Nosferatu down at least for the moment. She had drawn her pistol and aimed upward. Carmilla saw this and her broomstick jerked to the right, evading the shots and nearly colliding with the back wall which was now a complete inferno. This gave Sabina the opportunity she needed to get up and she looked towards their campfire which was now a part of the burning floor. She saw her rifle there, and was about to rush for it just as the Nosferatu was up again and going after Angela who whirled about and fired her remaining shots blindly as the demon fell upon her again, this time tackling the Dhampir to the ground and proceeded to bite her furiously between the neck and shoulder and causing blood to spray everywhere. It reminded Sabina of a bear or werewolf mauling.

Intent on saving Angela, Sabina got three steps into what would have been seem like a jog despite her urge to sprint for the rifle.

But something stopped her before she could even place her foot down for the fourth step, and she looked back to see that during her evasion of the witch's spells, she had gotten close to what should have been the body of the Raven. But the woman was holding her by the ankle with an ironclad grip, the gash in her throat exposing bone but no longer bleeding or belching black smoke.

And she was grinning, alive and well.

Before Sabina could kick out or do anything to release herself, she heard something coming and she turned just in time to see the witch swooping down towards her like a fighter pilot about to do a sweep across a battlefield. Sabina began to raise her arms but it was useless. The witch was now driving the talons of her gauntlet into Sabina's chest just above her bosom, the metallic claws hooking between her ribcage and splitting her sternum in the process. She was being carried across the room and the witch had her suddenly pinned up against the wall with her feet just barely brushing the floor. The witch was still on her broomstick which remained still despite the sudden speed of which it had carried both its rider and their prey to the wall.

Sabina couldn't breathe. The broken bones in her chest made it difficult, and the inhuman strength of the witch pushing her against the wall sent shockwaves of nausea through her head. Sabina realized with a sudden but merciless clarity that she was slowly dying.

And the bald witch with her runes tattooed across her face, her eyes blazing wickedly and grinning at her with rotten teeth, was laughing.

Laughing…

Feeling something dribbling out of her mouth, Sabina spat it out into Carmilla's face. Bloody spittle speckled her but the witch hardly reacted, laughing still, but sounding as if she were laughing through amber in the dimming existence of Sabina Irving. Everything was beginning to fade beyond Carmilla too. The burning building, the demon still savaging Angela Dragos, the Raven who was standing despite having been killed and should have been dead.

Everything.

Fading.

Only the pain remained of Sabina's physical being, pain of which she was now welcome to the concept of death just so that she didn't have to feel this crushing, breaking sensation through her chest. She only hoped that Kawn was everything it was cracked up to be.

Still, only a single truly coherent thought ran through Sabina Irving's mind and slipping past the pain and the desire for death. Even as Sabina saw Jacob and Vladimir emerge from the hole in the floor obscured by both fire and smoke, the single thought rang like a bell. Even as Sabina crashed into the ground as the witch finally released her and let her drop, Sabina only thought of one single thing. The one hope she had to cling onto in this world; one name that she wished to carry with her on her way into the arms of Yohnah and the heavens beyond The Veil, for that would be the one thing she would not be able to have when she crossed over, except for the memories.

Matei…

I'm sorry…

Even as the lights slowly dimmed and the burning inferno faded into nothingness around her, Sabina could still see Matei's beautiful face as Jacob's voice broke into her thoughts until her final ragged breath.

"Sabina!"

If they hadn't had to maneuver past chunks of stony ceiling caused by the tremors coming from above, Jacob, Vladimir, and the children could have made it to the scene in time. As it was, it was a fate that they couldn't have prevented.

As soon as Jacob had reached the top of the stairwell which had been obscured by the sudden flames, the first thing he saw was the witch who had flung Sabina's dying body aside like a piece of garbage. Now the Vampire Hunter laid still on the floor, her body slowly being approached by the flames that were now eating this building little by little. He saw Angela, being savaged by some terrible beast from the stuff of nightmares, who had now grabbed ahold of her and with a mighty swing of its great arm, hurled the Dhampir right through the nearest wall and out into the unknown world beyond. It then roared it's supposed victory, leaving both Jacob and Vladimir alone up top with the Raven who had undone her bloody cloak, and the witch who remained seated on her broomstick without a care in the world.

When she noticed them, she grinned. "There you are," she purred as she licked the blood off her smeared hands and clawed gauntlet. "I was beginning to think I wouldn't see your handsome face again."

Jacob brought his bow up reactively and fired an arrow at the witch who maneuvered too fast and she banked around the room and came barreling towards him, this time drawing the sword that hung from her side. Vladimir stepped in and deflected the blow as the witch passed on by, causing sparks to fly which momentarily lit up the witch's hideous glee.

"Go help Angela!" Jacob barked.

Vladimir looked at the man astonished. For that moment, Jacob didn't sound like some rookie who really didn't have a clue as to how the world of Hunting worked. He sounded like a true Hunter of Beasts now, and with a grunt he rushed for Sabina's body. The Raven tried to interfere, to intercept the rushing man but Vladimir had drawn his pistol and fired in quick succession too fast for the bleeding woman to react. He brushed right past the sprawling Raven and stooping down towards Sabina's body, he grabbed her and chucked her out the window in a shower of glass. He then turned on his heel and with his sword in his hands, he faced the Raven who was now blocking his path to the hole where the large, winged beast was hurrying outside, no doubt to finish Angela off.

"You bitch," Vladimir seethed with a sneer. "You... fucking *bitch*."

The Raven smiled amusedly, the gash in her throat completely disappeared with only the stain of red revealing what had would have been a fatal blow. Behind her, the witch was circling Jacob who was trailing her with his bow strung taut, an arrow nocked and ready.

"Time to end this little game."

Vladimir's eyes narrowed on the Raven, knowing what exactly she was. His pistol was now raised with two shots remaining, his sword gripped tight in his other hand. "Oh, this just got a helluva lot better. I'm going to enjoy skinning you alive."

"Come on then!"

The witch suddenly turned her attention away from Jacob and with a wave of her hand some planks of burning wood rose from the smoke and were suddenly hurled at Vladimir by an invisible force. Vladimir dove away to avoid getting skewered while Jacob took his shot, striking the witch in the shoulder and ceasing the barrage of burning wood.

The Raven surprisingly didn't go for Vladimir who was getting back on his feet. Instead, she sprinted with the speed of a fleeing deer, past Jacob and right down into the stairwell leading into the temple.

The witch Carmilla, seethed. "You traitor!" she screeched.

Vladimir, turned and rushed into the hole before Jacob could even stop him. "Take care of that bitch! I'm going after the Raven!"

Jacob didn't need to be told twice, and although he was concerned about Angela, he knew they had to make sure the kids were okay, and the witch had to be put down. With a flick of his wrist, his glove came off and he pulled back the eye patch off his head, tossing it aside so that he was ready for battle against the woman who had sold her soul to Kawfka for her terrible power. By now, Carmilla had removed the shaft from her arm and she saw the man standing below her, and her eyes narrowed at the sight of that eye and that... peculiar hand.

"I'm going to enjoy this," he told her as he reached for another arrow with a smile of excitement spread across his face.

The witch in turn, smiled. Her bright green eyes practically glowed with hunger, as the inferno around her burned like the fires of hell. She came for him then, her broom swooping fast and downward, her sword and claws ready for the kill as Jacob nocked another arrow and took aim.

Angela laid prone in the snowy ground after being thrown through the thin and rotten walls of the meeting building. She laid in the very center of the village, the bloody imprints where she had bounced and skidded across the ground marking her journey. She tried to push herself up, finding it difficult to will her right arm to move. The place where the Nosferatu had savaged her was gruesome, chunks of tattered flesh could be seen through the armor and her undershirt, and the gleam of bone shiny with blood could be seen. As it was a bite of a Vampire, the wound would not heal. Her neck was pained with whiplash as well; if she had been human her neck would have broken much easier and then she would have been in real trouble. As it was Mithus did not seem eager to kill her just yet; she wanted Angela to feel pain, to suffer as she was played with like a rat to a hyper cat.

Sabina...

The name struck Angela worse than the impact through the wall had. The memory of watching the Vampire Hunter getting punched through by that witch even though Angela thought she would be safe; that she could keep the Nosferatu held down until then... it simply broke her. She had allowed a comrade to fall to the world of darkness.

She failed Sabina.

She would not be able to bring everyone home after this, and she welcomed the burning sensation of her injured shoulder as a just punishment for her failure.

The Nosferatu screeched again somewhere in the building and as she pushed herself back up into a crouch, Angela saw the creature now coming out of the building, landing on a nearby stack of firewood and then leaping up again to perch upon another nearby building, looming almost over its prey like a cat still eager to play with the rat. The beast spread out its massive wings, obscuring the blinding moon behind it that broke a smile into the starry sky, it's eyes glowing with incredible feral rage as it's face and other stab wounds slowly closed up.

Angela stood, turning to face the monster completely, her sword now gripped tight in her left hand rather than her right which dripped more rose petal droplets into the snow.

"Lithus," Mithus hissed, her bloody teeth glaring brightly as she licked her lips with a purple tongue that was thick like a gorged worm. "His blood will be paid with yours. It tastes so sweet... bitter, and yet so sweet... it is better than anything I have ever tasted. I want *more*..."

Angela got into a stance as a bone-shattering wind blew through the village, catching her hair which waved like silver silk stained with droplets of her blood and sending a shockwave through her right side. Her purple eyes, though glowing brightly with the possibilities of the unknown future before her, regarded the beast coldly as she gripped her sword tightly in her left fist.

"I gave you a chance," she muttered the words almost inaudible to the ears of a human. But to the sharp ears of an Immortal, both half-breed and demonic, even Mithus could hear, and restrained her desire to lunge at Angela again in order to listen.

"I gave you a chance to leave us alone. Your brother too. He did not listen. I could have killed you too, but I spared you."

Mithus peeled back her upper lip in a growl, her batlike face fierce, ugly, and yet considering. If Angela looked past the monstrous face, she could just barely make out the elegant childlike face that had once belonged to Mithus.

"Why?"

"You are young," said Angela. "I thought perhaps maybe that you would heed my warning. That you would remain here and live freely. Be safe from other Hunters who would no doubt seek to destroy you. The fate of your heritage is death. The Vampires are almost all gone. You would not survive out there. I wanted to give you that chance to live for yourself."

She gripped her sword tighter, the gleam from the moonlight causing the silver to catch it and reflect it in a ghostly arc across the snow. "But I see now, that there is no reasoning in your heart any longer. You have succumbed to the beast, and awakened a force that should not have ever been reawakened."

Mithus' lips stretched wider, revealing an amused grin of serrated teeth and long canines. "I still have that chance, you monster. I don't care what you have to say, and I don't care about how the world is. You took my brother away from me. And I will never forgive you or any Hunter in existence for that. My hatred burns brighter than your mercy. If anything, you only made a mistake and I hope your band of murderers are all punished for destroying my family."

"Then you leave me no choice," said Angela with narrowed eyes. "You have to die."

Mithus hissed, her pointed ears practically curling back behind her head like a feral cat. "Well then try, *monster*."

With that, the Nosferatu with the soul of Mithus, lunged from the rooftop, using her wings to dive right for Angela who was already in a stance with her sword ready to do battle with the beast.

The hunt was on, and as Angela and the Nosferatu crashed together, the meeting building of the ancient race that once walked these cursed mountains for generations, erupted into more flames as both witch and Witch Hunter took to the skies in flashes of fire, iron, and blood.

Sorina barreled down the stairs as fast as she could. She didn't care how deep this stairwell dwelled, nor how cavernous whatever lied beyond it stretched. The scent was clear now; the children were down here. They were almost within her grasp, and with the witch and her demon of a child taking care of those Hunters, there would be no better chance to take the Ice Walker than now.

The wounds she had sustained were serious, regardless of whether she was human or not. The fact that it was silver that had pierced her skin only meant that the pain would remain long after the wounds had healed, if they ever do. That was the pain with Hunters: you never knew who carried silver weapons which were rare to make in Balkeñoir unless you could either afford it on your own or you knew a blacksmith capable of smelting it. Sorina was lucky enough to obtain two Holy Blades made of both iron and silver to be able to handle any beast or man that dared to cross her path. Unfortunately, her vulnerability to the ancient metal made her weak against those of experienced Hunters; and that woman, that Vampire Hunter, she had been skilled. Very skilled. It was a pity that she had to die at the hands of a witch.

Sorina slowed her pace as she made it to the bottom of the stairs, her blood now making the stone steps slick and treacherous. Still, she marched on, following the scent down the hall and through the passageways made for the gods of old. When she made it to the inner sanctum where the tomb laid, Sorina smiled as she beheld the two children who were startled by her presence, under cover behind some fallen debris caused by the Nosferatu demon's rampage.

"Finally," Sorina said marching and after sheathing her only sword, she drew her revolver; pulling back the hammer as she made her way towards the children who had evaded her for so long. "I have you both now."

The Ice Walker stared at Sorina in horror while her brother stepped between them, drawing his terribly kept sword as he did so. "Stay back!" he snapped angrily in a loud and commanding voice. "You stay away from us, or I'll kill you!"

Sorina merely smiled in amusement as she raised her gun and took aim at the child. "Put it down, son. This isn't worth getting killed over. I just want your sister."

"You'll never take her, you *slag*," the boy seethed as Sorina kept on coming his way. "I'm warning you- don't take another step closer!"

Sorina chuckled. "Too bad."

She squeezed the trigger, and the pistol reported with a deafening blast which echoed throughout the chamber and caused the children's ears to ring.

A crimson starfish erupted in the chest of the boy, causing him to stagger back and drop his pathetic weapon as he fell right into the arms of the Ice Walker who hugged him close screaming his name. "Morgan!" she cried out as the boy began to breathe heavily, every breath gurgling as his lungs filled up with blood with some of it trickling out of the corner of his mouth. "Morgan- no!"

Sorina stopped right before the two, her gun now aimed at the head of the Ice Walker. "Don't bother. He's a dead child. Don't worry, you both will have company here. You will accompany him in Kawn, right?"

The Ice Walker turned to Sorina, those inhuman, icy blue eyes glaring right at her with the wrath and hatred of a thousand suns. Sorina felt a surge of unease as she felt as though the chamber's temperature had suddenly plummeted. "Get away from us!"

Sorina couldn't help but laugh again. She lunged forward and seized the girl by the arm, wrenching her away from her dying brother and slamming her down onto the nearest sarcophagus. She shoved the barrel of the pistol against the girl's temple and pulled back the hammer again.

"I was told to bring you back," Sorina told the girl still holding her down by the neck this time. It was only fair that the child understood why she had run all this way for naught. She deserved at least that much.

"I was told to bring you to the castle, so we can study you. But, no. It is too dangerous letting you live. Those power-hungry cultists will never get their hands on the last Elemental Magic in Balkeñoir. I want this Eternal Winter to end. I promise you, girl, that none of this was personal. Please understand that."

Blam!

"Gah!" Sorina gasped out as a silver bullet tore through her hand, forcing her to drop the weapon and she turned just in time to hear another gunshot followed by the sudden impact of another bullet striking her in the chest, then a second and third, making her stumble back and release the girl who scrambled away.

"Come here!" the Hunter who had chased her down here shouted at the Ice Walker who took cover in the corner as he closed in on Sorina slowly, now reloading his spent cases with the swift hands of an expert.

Wondering how it could be that she hadn't heard or even smelled the man, Sorina managed to stand, blood pouring from fresh wounds along with black smoke. Her wounds were smoking even more now, making her appear like a Shade.

Vladimir was smiling. "What's wrong? Too much silver in your blood, you bitch?"

Sorina snarled, baring her teeth angrily as she pulled herself to her feet. Her gun was on the ground still, and all she had was her sheathed sword. A few more gunshots in this form however...

Blam! Blam! Blam!

Sorina fell back, would have landed on her ass if she hadn't turned and fell to her hands and knees. Blood poured from her wounds as well as more black smoke. Vladimir only kept his gun on her, seeming to bide his time, a look of hatred and fury burning in his eyes she could see.

"How does that feel, you mangy cur?" he demanded viciously, following this with another shot that went through the side of Sorina's neck, flooding her windpipe and throat with blood and smoke. "Come on out, you goddamn *pup*!

Hunched over, bleeding, smoking, and in terrible agony, Sorina reached into her pocket and winced as a fifth shot went through her arm. She kept her hand there however, clenching her grandmother's pocket watch tight in her hand; wishing she could hug it against her body.

She didn't want to do it... She would rather do anything but that- but not if the price was her own life. Her grandmother had brought her up to be a warrior; a survivor. She would be the one to purge the world of darkness, regardless of her heritage. She had promised herself, that she wouldn't even allow herself to succumb to the beast's hunger and use her own strength. But even now, with her blood spilling and making the stone floor slick all contaminated with the cursed silver, Sorina knew she didn't stand a chance against this professional Hunter. If she had not been so badly injured and lost so much blood, it would be different. But as it was…

"Come on," Vladimir was saying. He was reloading his weapon again, the brass casings clattering across the stone floor as he never once took his eyes off the Raven. "Get up. Get up!"

She wouldn't survive, not as herself.

Vladimir took aim again, baring his teeth in an angry snarl. He had his prey right where he wanted her. She had been foolish to come down here and think that she had a chance. She had been foolish to not ensure that the Hunters were all killed.

With a shuddered growl, she clenched the pocket watch so tight that's he could feel it crackling beneath her fingers as she regarded the Hunter now with dangerous green eyes that glowed bright with a drive; the will to survive.

And so, she gave in. She released all control, and let the beast out.

Her body grew in size, her pores erupting in thick black fur and her nails and teeth fell out to allow the claws and fangs to grow. Her armor, tore and fell away into tatters at her feet. Her face stretched out, turning into a snout and her broad shoulders thick with fur, bulged with muscle as Sorina breathed in and let loose such a terrible howl that it shook the very temple grounds. The Hunter had begun shooting her again, that snarling look of rage now gone. With the pocket watch still in her hand, she sat it down gently onto the stone floor before standing back up crouched and hind legs tensed and ready to pounce. Her wounds were gone, the bullets that had been burning her had been spat back out of the wounds like escaping insects.

Vladimir had run out, and he was quickly reloading as Sorina stood in her Lycan form, claws extended and teeth bared. When he had finished, he snapped the cylinder back in and redrew his sword. She had expected him to become frightened; the Ice Walker certainly was as she cowered behind one of the sarcophagi.

But the Werewolf Hunter, Vladimir the Cruel of the Black Hand, merely smiled at the sight that he beheld. That cruel smile sent a sliver of doubt through Sorina again, but not much. Now that she had been healed through her transformation, she was ready to end this once and for all.

"That's more like it," said Vladimir. "I was wondering when you were going to come out, *Lycan*."

He got into a stance, a gleam in his eye indicating that he had no intention of fleeing or backing down. This was a fight between Man and Beast, Hunter and Raven, Darkness, against Light. And neither, wished to fall into the world of nightmares. Sorina's hind legs tensed, and just before she lunged, Vladimir bellowed with a loud voice with absolutely no fear, and now regrets.

"Come on then, you mangy mutt! Let's see what you got!"

And so, Sorina lunged at the Hunter, and the two began their fight to the death while the Ice Walker, watched, cowering in the corner while her brother laid dead in a pool of his own blood. Their fight, all took place under the watchful eyes of the spirits trapped within the temple; both human, and not.

Fa

Jacob leapt out of the same hole Angela and the Nosferatu had escaped from. They were still fighting near the edge of the village but he was occupied as the witch Carmilla came bursting through the burning ceiling, causing great chunks of the roof to cave in and send sparks sailing into the sky like fleeing fireflies.

He couldn't concern himself with how the collapsing building would affect Vladimir and the children especially concerning the Raven. The witch continued to give chase and throw fire balls at him, forcing him to take cover within another home just before he got his back burned away. Being a witch it was dangerous for her to play with fire, but Jacob had to admit that Carmilla was skillful in the summoning arts of fire and energy and continued to give him a run for his money. The Chief's Hall was now a roaring inferno, the flames barely held back by the bitter cold. Taking cover behind a doorframe, Jacob considered his options given the equipment he had brought on this Hunt. He hurried off towards a ladder leading up to a hole in the ceiling just as another fireball burst against the side of the wall.

"Come out of there!" the witch cackled madly. "Come out now!"

There was a hatch in the ceiling of the house and Jacob gently pushed it open. He could see the witch hovering just barely in line with the roof and her attention was on the front door. He slipped out, crawling across the frigid logs like a salamander and nocking an arrow into his bow. When he got close enough he aimed down the shaft and focused the iron-tipped arrow at the bobbing head. He pulled it taut, but just as he was about to release it, a quake caused by another thunderous spell shook the house and he fired aimlessly, the arrow zipping right over the witch's head. She hovered higher and spotted him, cackling like a maniac as she hurled more balls of fire at him and causing him to run away.

As he ran his foot slipped on some snow and he ended up tumbling right off the edge and landing in the ground below. Upon landing though, he had already nocked an arrow and he loosed it just as the witch came into view above him. He was satisfied to see his shaft stick right into the witch's leg, making her hiss in terrible pain. Scrambling to get up, he proceeded to flee as she retaliated by sending down a rain of condensed snow that sharpened into icicles. He then rolled to the side as Carmilla sped right past him, her sword nearly lopping off his own head to the point where he would have sworn he felt the blade brush the back of it.

Jacob panted heavily as he pushed himself back up to his feet while Carmilla began to bank around to come charging in once again. Given how fast she flew and how sporadic her maneuverability was, it was difficult for him to use his Immortal Eye on her; Carmilla was not about to risk getting caught in it again. He looked at his hand to see the 'eye' rune that was blinking heavily at him, as if the marking itself was trying to tell him to come up with a decision already.

To use it, or not.

He looked back towards Carmilla, who already was charging right for him again at full speed. Too fast to try and hypnotize her and he doubted that he would be able to conjure enough energy to have the strength to even catch her with anything. He decided he had to get her close to the buildings once again, and look for a chance to get her off her broomstick. That broomstick was her advantage, and he had to remove it from the equation.

For to begin the slaying of a witch, you had to immobilize her. If she couldn't fly, she couldn't get away; and a downed witch was a dead one.

Jacob reached over his shoulder for another arrow, making sure to feel around to count what he had left. He had each type of arrow marked by different fledglings between his iron-tips and his silver-tips.

Five more… he had to make them count.

He pulled one and he dove aside as Carmilla came barreling in. The witch cackled as she stretched out her fingers and to Jacob's surprise, her nails shot out like daggers, ready to impale him. To make matters worse, coils of electricity seemed to arc between them like a battery used in a city's power station.

You've got to be kidding me…

Using the same hand he had grabbed an arrow with, he reached for his pistol and he shot at Carmilla right in the neck, forcing her to pull away before her nails could touch him. As he dove aside again, Carmilla kept on going, lingering close to one of the unburnt homes as she wrapped her slender fingers around her bleeding throat. Dropping his pistol, Jacob then pulled his arrow back as far as he could on his bowstring, his muscles stretching taut with the effort it took and he loosed it the moment the feathers of the shaft touched his shoulder. The arrow flew fast and straight; right into Carmilla's back, making her waver slightly but otherwise she kept her balance. She glared at Jacob as she went to pull the arrow out. The wound smoked as if on fire as the iron burned her just as silver burned monsters.

"You stupid boy," she hissed clenching the shaft with her gauntlet-covered hand. "Do you really think you can-"

Jacob couldn't help but smile as he snapped the fingers on his cursed hand, completing the spell he had placed on the arrow before he loosed it. "Boom."

Suddenly, arrow exploded as if it were a stick of dynamite. Fire erupted across the witch's chest, sending her flying off her broom as the fire licked the skin right off her front. She screamed like a thousand beasts crying out as she fell to the ground, her broomstick landing mere feet away from her and sticking like a sword plunging into dirt. As she rolled around in the snow in her attempt to put out the flames, Jacob was already rushing in. He gathered more magic into his palm which already began to hurt. When Carmilla raised her head again, half of it merely scorched bone and peeling muscle, she saw what the Hunter was doing and she whirled around in a desperate attempt to go for her broom, but it was too late. Jacob, while still charging for her, reached out with his palm extended and fire erupted from the eye as if it were a makeshift dragon. The broomstick was completely engulfed and shriveling into a blackened weed in the snow.

"No!" Carmilla gasped, stopping where she was and staring at the burning stick in the snow. She then whirled upon Jacob who had nocked another arrow aimed right at her again. He ignored the pulse in his cursed hand as he pulled the bowstring taut, but he held it firm, a coy grin on his face as he had the witch grounded.

"You little bastard!" she hissed past those rotten teeth of hers. Her skull was grotesque, horrible in contrast to whatever face she had left which was a snarling mess.

"And proud of it," Jacob grinned. His hand pulsed again in terrible pain as he held the arrow tight against the bowstring. He would not be able to cast another spell for quite awhile now. He was now down to four arrows, a few throwing knives, and his sword. In terms of useful witch-hunting tools, he didn't have what he would have preferred to fight Carmilla with considering he had not planned on running into a witch on this Hunt. Still, he couldn't complain given how Carmilla was looking now.

"How's it feel to be on your own, witch?"

Carmilla smiled back, her two-sided face looking more horrible than ever with it. She brought her sword and talons scraping against one another and sending a rainfall of sparks down into the snow at her feet, declaring her defiance of him.

"I ain't alone. That Raven almost has the children, and my daughter will dispose of that wretched Dhampir who murdered my son. I am *far* from on my own, Hunter."

Jacob's smiled never gave in. "I wouldn't underestimate 'em if I were you. The only reason you got to Sabina was because you had help. Well, help ain't here for you. It's just you and me now, and I'm gonna make you burn for what you did to her."

Carmilla smiled right back, a viper staring into the eyes of a mongoose ready to do battle to the death. "I've been killing men like you for hundreds of years, boy. You will be no different. No one ever is."

"I might surprise you," Jacob said taking a step forward. "I'm full of them." And with that, he released his arrow and Carmilla leapt to the side and lunged forward using the force of the winds behind her to rush at Jacob who beamed in victory as he widened his Immortal eye and caused it to flash bright and red.

"No!" Carmilla snarled pulling her hood up to shield her eyes again as she came in swinging her sword. Dropping his bow, Jacob went for his own sword and managed to deflect the blow from the immortal woman with a clang which echoed all across the mountains.

Carmilla slashed at him again with her talons, releasing a small trail of flames as she did so, and then spinning about like a crimson tornado, she swung her sword in an attempt to hack at Jacob again. Her swordsmanship was lacking, but Jacob had never truly favored the weapon and was therefore evenly matched with the witch.

After a brief struggle, Jacob managed to get Carmilla to lunge without the use of her talons, and as she got in closer, he hooked his arm around her own and struck hard at her wielding hand, causing her fingers to fall just as her sword now did. She had managed to throw him off amidst her curses and he had his opening to lunge once again.

"Gotcha!" he bellowed.

"No you don't."

Carmilla flipped back and kicked Jacob right under the chin and she cartwheeled away and landed on her feet a good ten feet away from Jacob who managed to keep his balance, He glared at her, rubbing his jaw angrily. He had bitten his tongue but he ignored the blood filling his mouth as Carmilla peered at him from beneath her hood. It would be difficult to try and hypnotize her now, he had to get that cloak off her head. She might be missing her sword now, but she still had her gauntlet, her magic, and now Jacob could see that she had grown her fingers back as well.

Carmilla then pointed her taloned gauntlet in Jacob's direction and barked some ancient words not meant to be uttered by mortal tongues. Between each taloned fingertip came a web of coiled lightning as lavender as Angela's eyes. This lightning shot out at Jacob like a hurled spear, and extended his cursed hand towards it and the lightning concentrated directly in the center of the eye rune which absorbed it and voided such power. In fact, when he felt the tugging sensation as the lightning met his skin, Jacob curled his fingers around this lightning and found himself immune to this power as if he were a walking, breathing conductor, much to Carmilla's surprise. Jacob pulled hard against the lightning and as if it were rope, Carmilla was brought forward. She had ended the spell as soon as she had been tugged but by now Jacob had already moved in fast, swinging his sword and would have cut her in two if she had not raised her gauntlet. It mattered little however, as his sword sliced right through the taloned fingers, severing them completely.

Carmilla growled as she backed away a step, her gauntlet missing its fingers which were now bleeding at the stumps. Jacob came at her again and she cartwheeled away again like an acrobat in a circus. As she got further away, Jacob took up his throwing knives and hurled them all helter skelter, with some digging into the witch with satisfactory results. One was sticking in her left thigh, a second in her right buttocks. One had struck her chest but had fallen back out, and a fourth and final one was in her shoulder. Still, the witch kept on her feet, breathing heavily as was Jacob from both the effort to behead the witch as well as the magic he had used to counter her own.

Carmilla smirked as she raised her head, which was now a mask of red from the dagger in her head that was now closing up and pushing out the blade that had stuck into her brain. "You really are annoying," she hissed as she brought her tongue up to lick the blood that had dribbled around her nose and over her lips.

Jacob smiled. "I get that a lot," he confided.

Carmilla brought her hands together, her fingers once again having regenerated and now coiling about one another as if she were playing cat's cradle with an invisible string. Jacob hurried for her, sword in both hands ready to strike but then Carmilla held out her palms to him.

"Too slow!"

She brought her palms down hard on the ground before her and as Jacob was rushing her, thick spikes of concentrated ice shot from the snow and if he had not slowed down he would have fallen on them. He kicked his feet out and slid directly beneath them and he collided with their bases. Before he could crawl out or anything, the witch had leapt over to the other side and performed the same spell again, casting more spikes which interwoven with the others and creating a sort of icy lean-to. She was about to do it again when Jacob stretched his palm out and from the eye a torrent of fire burst from it and shot through the ice and blew the witch back several yards. She rolled across the snow and the flames were snuffed, but the damage on her face was evident, the other half of her destroyed skull joining the first, making her burnt face more ghoulish than ever.

Jacob stood up, tired, feeling weak, but smiling nonetheless. "Too slow yourself..."

Carmilla hissed and then snapped her fingers. She then clapped her hands together and began to chant in tongues.

Jacob suddenly felt a crushing weight come upon him and he was forced to his knees as if gravity had decided to intensify on him and him alone. Every cell in his body felt like it was on fire, and his cursed hand began to throb with more intensity, as did his Immortal Eye which began to cry tears of blood. Another surge of incredible pressure forced him lower to the point where he had to plant his hands on the ground to keep his face from smashing into the frigid ground.

"Foolish child," Carmilla seethed, her skeletal face shifting with distorted muscles making her rage all the more gruesome. "Foolish *man*, did you really think you stood a chance against me? Magic or not, Immortal Eyes or not, you cannot best me. No man can best me. So quit fighting it and succumb to me!"

Her green eyes flashed and Jacob felt the pressure give in only to flip him back to try to get him to lay on his back. His back arched as he held out against the pressure now pushing back and causing the muscles in his neck to strain. It felt as if invisible hands were pushing against his head trying to break his neck.

Through his one good eye as his Immortal Eye had been blinded by blood, the image of Carmilla the Red shifted and wavered in a way that was similar to the illusions caused by Count Josef Horla, but it was different in this regard. Her face shimmered as if underwater, and for a brief moment she looked like her normal self again, although there would be no healing from the burning her face had taken. For another moment, her face had become old and wrinkled, her nose a hooked beak, her eyes black and squinting. Seeing this face filled Jacob with such rage that he actually bellowed as he fought to keep himself upright, to prevent himself from falling back. If he were to fall, he would be crushed. But the crushing pressure... oh what pressure...

Another face shimmered, intermingling with that of Carmilla's original and burnt face, as well as the face of his own mother. An almost fluid contrast considering the last time he had truly seen his mother's face, it had been burning too for he had tricked her and had locked her in her own oven before he had finally been able to escape her. He could see it now, a little boy whose eye constantly bled, his tattoos on his back burning, and his new hand feeling alien and not at all his own. A little boy who had suffered so much and had finally had enough as he shoved his mother into the oven she was planning to use to make dinner in; a feast of logsmen who dared trespass in her forest. He had shoved her in and shot the bolt and for good measure, used the spade used for ashes to pin the handle shut. His mother had wriggled her burning fingers through the grate, had tried to put her face against it, and how it had burned. How it had burned to black paper barely held together by bubbling blood against scorched bone.

But among the images of fire and blood, among the faces of Carmilla and his mother, Jacob also saw one that almost seemed to separate the two like a beam of sunlight piercing through the flames. It was a face of inhuman beauty and cold desire. Skin whiter than snow and hair to match, lips as red as blood and an angular face that made her appear almost angelic. The only thing different, were her eyes. Instead of bright and purple and full of indifferent coldness, they were shining green, snake-like and filled with poisonous desire. It was this face that Jacob focused on, and pushed against the magic that tried to shut him down and leave him at the mercy of the witch.

"Give in!" Carmilla shrieked indignantly. She couldn't believe it, she had this human, this boy locked into an unbreakable spell, and he was *fighting* it! He was fighting her still, *always* fighting. Always- "Damn you, give in!"

But Jacob did not give in. In fact, he forced his head forward so that it was standing straight up rather than hanging back to face the gray skies above. He was on his knees still, but he was now able to look Carmilla fully in the face, seeing past the hallucination caused by this spell that he was caught in and see her with completely unwavering eyes. Despite the pain in his head, despite the blood coming from his Immortal Eye, he conjured whatever strength he had left for one final push, and a crimson light shot out of his Immortal Eye like a beacon and seemed to reflect into the green eyes of Carmilla the Red. The moment she felt this, her spell faltered with her sudden fright.

Fright…

Fear…

Carmilla had never been afraid before, and yet she was now, and despair swallowed her as Jacob spoke at last.

"Fall!" he commanded and his eye lit up bright and red and Carmilla suddenly stumbled and fell to her knees. Seizing his chance, Jacob seized his sword and stood, feeling the weight of the spell break away like rusted chains.

"No!" Carmilla cried out as Jacob lunged for her. She brought her gauntlet up and caught the blow with her palm, the metal bending but otherwise holding its own. Jacob shoved her back and swung again and this time, the blade sliced through her shoulder and stuck there, leaving the two of them staring into one another's eyes, with only one of the four eyes not being the color of blood.

"Looks like I can get you after all," Jacob grinned despite the blood pouring from his eyelid like tears.

Carmilla pushed back at Jacob, forcing him back as she clawed at him with her own nails. He had backed away, the sword coming free of her shoulder and he swung again, but this time she caught the blade with both hands, clasping them together on either side of the blade and holding it mere inches from her face. She held it there, her arms trembling with Jacob's against each other's strength. With her hands occupied, she couldn't cast a spell. She was stuck, as was he.

But Jacob still had his eyes locked on hers, and while she was fighting his influence as he had fought her spell, he still had a chance. He looked right into her eye and unleashed his magic again. "Kneel!"

"No!" Carmilla roared, her voice thick and guttural like a monster's. From her mouth came a black mist and Jacob, not knowing what it was, was forced to flee. But before Carmilla could cast a spell from her gauntlet hand, he had swung again and this time, he sent her hand sailing through the air rather than her fingers.

But the witch was far from done. She swore some ancient word in her pain and the severed bone within the stump lashed out like a lance, nearly impaling Jacob's head but only planting a deep cut across his right cheek. With his balance off, Carmilla leapt far back enough away from Jacob. Her eyes had returned to normal, and through their mental link, she had been able to see what he had seen while under her spell. She understood them all, and could have used this knowledge to her advantage, but there was one key memory that she felt offended by. Offended, because she simply couldn't believe what this man was and where he had come from. Offended, because he should not have existed.

She seethed at Jacob who wiped at the blood spilling from his cut cheek. "How could one of my kin give birth to such a pitiful creature? You are blessed with the magic of the Dark Lord, and yet you use it to hunt the beasts he gave birth to through the darkness of shadow and winter- even going as far as to hunt those who serve him! Did you feel any pity at all, any guilt when you watched your mother burn?"

Jacob was glaring at her, but his smile never wavered. "You ask her." Then he charged again, ready to put the witch down once and for all.

Jacob, his cursed hand pulsating with use, sidestepped as Carmilla extended her bleeding stump and the bloody bones once again shot out like a lance, missing him just barely. He stepped in and then her face morphed once again into that of Angela's and when the witch screamed out a serpent slithered fast past her lips and struck out with fangs dripping with black poison. It lunged for his throat, but Jacob grabbed ahold of the viper before it could sink it's fangs into him, and holding it still by the back of the head, he swung his sword upward, severing the reptile from Carmilla's mouth. Jacob proceeded forward and the witch blew apart into smoke only to reappear behind him as she tried to cast another spell. He spun about and forced her back, trying to wear her down one last time. Jacob was no longer a controlled man of values and faith. He wasn't calm, nor was he smiling as he always had.

Instead, he was a savage warrior; bloody, frightened, and yet determined to survive and slay the beast in woman's flesh before him.

Still, he kept his eyes on Carmilla, and her eyes looked into his. Though the magic in his eye burned bright, Carmilla fought back with her own defensive wards, neither allowing herself to break her gaze and expose herself to the hypnotism that Jacob threw at her again and again. Likewise, if he looked away, then the spell would be broken, and he would be in no shape to cast his hypnotism again. For him to win, he had to get her to break first; he had to make her try and avert her gaze. And to do that, he had to break her body.

So instead of allowing trying to push her back and drive her on the defense, Jacob slowed his pace, giving Carmilla the chance to attack this time and with a cackle of victory, the witch extended her bleeding stump again and bloody veins lashed out like eels ready to wrap themselves around him.

He allowed them to wrap around his wrists, and his neck.

Let them take him.

Let them bring him closer to her…

And bringing his elbow up since his sword had already passed Carmilla's face, he elbowed the witch right in the spot where his silver dagger had stuck in last. Her head snapped back and her gaze faltered. She then glared right at Jacob who was now looking her dead in the eye with his Immortal one burning bright and red as his tears of blood dripped onto her face. She managed to slip her stump between her and him and he felt the searing pain as her extending bones stabbed through his belly and out his lower back, pinning him in place right where he wanted.

"Kneel!" he commanded and Carmilla despite stabbing him in the belly with her own broken bones, stiffened and she dropped to her knees before him with her exposed veins still wrapped around his limbs and neck. Her bones had slid back to normal however and they came out of his belly and brought a sense of nausea over him as blood poured from the wound.

But he wasn't done yet. With a cry and reeling his arm back, Jacob brought his sword down right through the witch's neck and he bent her backwards as he willed his sword downward so that she was bent back with her right leg pinned by his sword as well. With her neck and back stuck in such a terrible position and her leg pinned to the ground, Carmilla the Red was not going anywhere and while choking on her blood, she gazed at Jacob with a look of pure terror in her realization that she had been captured by his Immortal Gaze.

Ripping the nasty wriggling veins right off his arms, Jacob reached into his shirt and pulled out his religious necklace of Yohnah the Dove. He placed his necklace right onto Carmilla's forehead where he had struck her, letting the holy necklace burn against her skin and making her scream bubbles of blood out of her mouth. She writhed and snarled like a beast, and she extended her only hand in order to save herself; one last spell to give herself a second chance as her forehead smoked and burned.

But Jacob took her hand, and squeezed it tight after intertwining his fingers in hers. He held it tight as he looked Carmilla in the eye despite the blood spilling from his own, and he shook his head in pity.

"At least, you have been blessed enough to understand what love is," he said referring to her two children who she would never see again.

Carmilla's mouth opened and closed as she tried to utter something- a question Jacob realized. Her eyes were still blood-red as his Immortal Eye, their connection the strongest it ever had been since this fight had occurred. She could see in him, just as he could control her like a puppet.

"Who..." she gurgled. "Who... sired you... witch hatchling?"

Jacob tightened his grip over Carmilla's, and he whispered in a low voice the answer she sought.

"Gretchan the Black."

Carmilla's eyes widened and her mouth stretched open to say something else. But whether it was a plea, a final retort, or even a spell, Jacob never knew. For at that moment, he released the spell gathering in his hand, and with Carmilla's skin touching his own, he ignited what he touched and released his magic.

Stepping back, he watched as Carmilla burned where she was stuck. She writhed and flayed her arms in a desperate attempt to escape the savage inferno, but it was no use. A witch was as flammable as oil, and if a piece of their body is burning it is horrible to try and put out the flames. Her face had been destroyed during the two burnings it had taken, and now that her their entire body was consumed, there was no hope for Carmilla the Red. The only way to kill a witch and makes sure she stays dead, is fire. And with hand covering the wound in his belly- the same spot where Horla had stabbed him back in Irondell, Jacob watched the witch burn, and scream, and burn, until she went still. Her body ceased to move, and her screams were silenced. She burned, like the buildings of the hidden village that finally came back into view. Her spell was broken, and there was nothing left of her now.

Jacob dropped to his knees, head spinning and utterly exhausted. Using an arrow from his quiver, he stuck it into the fire until it got red and hot, the shaft now burning like kindle. He stuck the end of this makeshift hot poker and stuck it into his front, and hissed in pain as he began to sear the wound closed.

Somewhere in the distance, the roar of the monster Angela was facing was heard, and Jacob looked towards the forest in the direction where Snowcap Lake was. They had been fighting all this time, and if the monster was roaring like that, had it succeeded in killing her? This nightmarish idea seemed to be the final nail in the coffin, for Jacob collapsed to his side next to the burning witch, passing out from the pain and the exhaustion. He tried to fight it, tried to swim back to the surface of consciousness, but it was no use. The pain, the bloodloss, the energy drained from him from his magic hand and Immortal eye, it had become too much for him, and Jacob slumped into the snow, and passed out from the world of consciousness, and into the void. He thought of Sabina, he worried about Vladimir and the children.

Most importantly, he thought of Angela, and prayed that she was all right. He might have slayed the witch, but at what cost; what more would there be to pay if Sabina was dead, and the fate of his other comrades unknown?

He wouldn't be able to answer until he reawakened, cold, in pain, and no doubt discouraged.

Vladimir smacked his head against the wall as the Lycan threw him, making Charlotte scream in utter terror. He slid to the ground as stars flared across his vision like the afterflash of a camera taking his picture.

The beast known as Sorina the Raven was hunched in the center of the room, her thick and hairy arms scored with deep cuts that smoked from Vladimir's sword. He had managed to get a few shots into her chest but nothing that proved fatal, not to a Lycan of this magnitude. At the sound of Charlotte's distressed cry from Vladimir being thrown across the room, the beast turned her eyes upon the Ice Walker. It started to turn to go for her, but Vladimir was already up and charging at Sorina again despite the blood that spilled down the side of his face, making his snarl look worthy of a Nisthgúlian berserker.

"Hey, keep your eyes on me you damned mutt!" he bellowed as he ducked under the Lycan's massive claws as she reached for him, and he sank his dagger right into her belly.

The beast snarled and tried to grab at him, the claws raking across his armor in a shower of sparks and blood. He kept close to the Lycan however, making it impossible for her to grab at him and ducking every time the snaping jaws came close to his head. While the two tackled and wrestled one another across the tomb, Charlotte seized her chance and rushed over to Morgan and grabbing her brother by the arms began to drag him away.

"Charlotte…" Morgan groaned wincing at the pain. Blood smeared across the stones as Charlotte dragged him on and he eventually began to try and shake his arms away from her. Still, she hung on tight with all her might. "Stop it, you idiot. It hurts…"

Desperate, Charlotte tugged once more so that they were behind the female sarcophagus away from the vicious fight taking place. She peered over it to see that Vladimir had grabbed ahold of the Lycan's arm, wrapping his own around it and twisting it, flipping the beast over and held her pinned on the ground as he suddenly lifted his foot and kicked the elbow in the direction it was never meant to go. The Raven *screamed* and clawed at Vladimir, forcing him back before planting a heavy kick into his chest to send him flying into the wall which crumbled and cracked beneath the force.

Charlotte returned her attention to Morgan, placing her hands over his wound to try and stop the blood. She even went as far as to cast a case of ice over the wound, but Morgan hissed at her. "Don't! Don't... That hurts so much..."

"We have to stop the bleeding..." Charlotte said, panicking. "I can stop it, if you'll just let me-"

"I can't breathe..." Morgan said in almost a whisper. "I think one of my lungs is... gods, I'm pretty bad right now... It's so cold..."

Cold. Something that Charlotte never truly experienced, at least not in a way that everyone else felt. To her, cold felt normal; like the sun felt normal to humans. But she still knew the value of warmth which she couldn't provide for Morgan. She couldn't hug him to warm him, nor did she have anything to bring heat to her brother. She was simply... cold.

Morgan coughed out suddenly, spilling blood past his lips which sent a shiver down Charlotte's spine for the first time in her entire life. Was this... what fear felt like? Was it so... cold?

"I don't think I'm gonna make it..." Morgan whispered when he finally calmed down. "Shit... Charlotte... I'm not going to be able to take you away like I promised."

"Don't talk like that!" Charlotte suddenly screamed no longer caring whether or not the two fighting in the background could hear her angry and heart-broken cry. "Morgan!" Then to his surprise she cried out, Tatsu, please!"

She had screamed his real name in desperation. As far as Morgan knew, Charlotte never knew his or her real names that their mother had given them at birth. To think that she knew all this time...

"Don't talk like that, we're going, *together*! We always stick together! We will!"

"Aieeda..." Morgan muttered and Charlotte immediately stopped talking at the mention of her own real name. She had only heard it twice, once when Mother had told her and why they changed it when they arrived in Firedell, and then once more when Mother was on her deathbed. Only Morgan knew her real name, and she his own. He had never called her by name, and Charlotte gave him his complete attention upon uttering such a name and grabbing her hand he squeezed it tight.

"Aieeda... listen to me..."

"Tatsu..." Charlotte whispered as tears flooded her eyes.

"Don't be afraid..." Morgan sighed. "Don't be afraid of who you are. You... you must... live on..."

Charlotte sobbed her words. "I can't... not without you..."

"Yes... you can..." Morgan insisted. "Mother risked her life, to save us both. I can't keep my promise to protect you anymore, not here anyway. But I will watch over you from the gates of Kawn, and will await for the day when you will join me. Until then... Until then you must live on. Promise me, Aieeda... Promise me... you will... live..."

Charlotte choked on a sob but she managed to nod, causing some of her tears to drip upon her brother's face. "I will... I will..."

Morgan smiled, sighing with relief. "Good... Ugh... It doesn't hurt anymore... I feel so light... continue to walk this road, without me. And always know, Aieeda..." Morgan took one deep breath, and with the last of the air in his lungs, told Charotte one last thing. "Always know... that I will always love you..."

And with those final words, Morgan gave up the ghost, and fell asleep.

Charlotte shuddered and throwing herself over Morgan, she wept bitterly. Her one thing to hold onto here, the one person who had always kept by her side... Morgan was gone. Gone.

Just like Mother...

Charlotte looked up to see Morgan's face, so peaceful and smiling as if he was just asleep. But he would never wake up again. She was on her own now; an Ice Walker, alone in the world as a last surviving member of her dead tribe. The weight she now felt on her shoulders was now crushed her worse than any reality Charlotte had ever experienced. The tearing of her heart and will, it was just simply too much for her.

"Please..." she begged with her face buried in Morgan's coat. "Don't leave me... I don't want to be alone..."

Live...

That was what Morgan told her; his last wish for his little sister.

Live...

Something struck the coffin, making Charlotte jump and she peeked around to see that Vladimir had crashed right into it-

And the Lycan came upon him fast, grabbing him in her claws and then with a howl, sunk her teeth into his right shoulder.

Live...

This wasn't the first time Vladimir had been bitten. It probably wouldn't be the last time either.

But goddamn if it didn't hurt now.

The Raven's teeth had not been used in quite a long time, for it sliced right through his shoulder pads and were now stuck right into the meat of his arm. The bite burned as a bite from a Lycan or Werewolf always did, and Vladimir looked right into the eye of the beast who stared right back; probably thinking she had won.

But Vladimir raised his dagger and held it up to her eye. "Nope," he simply said as he drove the dagger right into the Lycan's eye and then twisting the blade he popped the eyeball right out of its socket.

The beast roared and released him immediately. It backed up on its hind legs with its hands holding the eyeball that hung by its stringy tendons. Black smoke belched from the socket and it turned to Vladimir what had to be a look of shock as he stood back up- which the Raven should be surprised about. A bite from a Lycanthrope was meant to cripple a human being; cause them to become weak and unable to move followed by an intense sickness that takes place mere minutes after the saliva penetrates the bloodstream. In other words, Vladimir shouldn't be standing now, let alone with the blood streaming down his side.

And yet he stood, his daggers still in hand and hissing with smoke and blood and still up and about. "You lot can't hurt me. It'll take more than a meager bite to finish me off. Tell me, you bitch, did I taste good?"

The beast snarled angrily, slowly allowing her hands to come back to her side ready to fight again. She barked defiantly, the sound resonating loudly within he stone walls. Despite her eye that still hung from her face, the Raven Lycan was determined to win this fight. Vladimir was impressed, but he was also incredibly happy. He was glad that she had finally showed her fangs; showed her true self and what secrets that the Empire's precious Thunder of Ravens were hiding.

"Messing with the Black Hand," Vladimir said as he advanced forward. "Was the biggest mistake of your guild's life. You think you are invulnerable simply because you convinced Emperor Ion of your wretched existence being a necessity. You all are messing with forces you can't even begin to comprehend; we will show you what true hell is. You, and every other Raven that crosses our path and hunts us, shall become the hunted."

The Lycan barked and snarled at the Hunter with a snap of her jaws; a clear message of defiance and a retort against Vladimir's words.

Vladimir charged forward, his daggers ready to cut deeper into the Lycan's muscled body and kill her as a Hunter is born to do. He ducked as the beast took a swing at him and swinging his arm, he managed to slit the throat of Sorina, making her blood spill over him like a waterfall. She backed away, clutching her bleeding throat which spewed black smoke. Vladimir moved in again but the beast spun away and came barreling at him with claws ready to tear. She would have knocked Vladimir's head right off his shoulders if her feet hadn't suddenly stopped moving and left her pinned in place.

Vladimir's eyes lingered towards the floor and he saw that ice had snaked across the stone floor and upon connecting with the beast's feet, it encased them in a large block that appeared to hold her steady. The ice continued to grow up the legs, making it even more difficult for Sorina to escape. She began to scream and bark as she clawed at the ice that just continued to grow. Vladimir looked over to see that Charotte was crouched on the ground with her hands on the floor where the ice had begun.

Her eyes were bright with blue, dark with the blackness, and simmering with such hatred and rage.

"Vlad!" she screamed out his name.

Vladimir smiled as he rushed for Sorina to make the final blow. "Thanks!" he graciously replied and the Lycan turned its one good eye towards the Hunter and brought its arms up to defend herself. Vladimir proceeded to stab right through the arms, pinning them together and slipping under them, Vladimir got in close to the beast and drove his dagger right into Sorina's chest right between the ribs. She barked out in pain and Vladimir proceeded to wrench out the blade and drive it into her chest again and again, spilling blood and spraying smoke everywhere.

No- Sorina's voice begged him as he continued to stab her repeatedly. With him too close and his sword still holding her arms still around him there was nothing she could do except accept the blades as her throat continued to drip crimson.

No, this isn't how it's supposed to be… I… can't-

Vladimir drove his blade deeper into the creature's chest and immediately, the voice ceased talking. The beast looked Vladmir in the eye, his own reflection revealed in the pale green eye that was still Sorina's. The question in that crystal-clear eye, all too obvious to ignore.

But Vladimir, didn't grant her final wish. "You have my deepest sympathies," he muttered as he wrenched the blade free and stepped back out, he allowed the Lycan to fall back onto the stone floor, dead.

He watched as the body first began to slowly shrink as the smoking wounds stopped belching the black fumes. The hair on the body fell away as if it was molting, and soon the naked figure of Sorina laid on the ground with many terrible wounds that a normal human would have felled long before the killing blows were placed. Naked, revealed, human, Sorina the Raven was dead and finally at peace. Whatever her reasons were for joining the Ravens, whatever her reasons were for hiding her true self until she was in a state of desperation, she would fret no more. Wherever she was now, Vladimir hoped that she would no longer have to hide. That was all that he could wish for the woman whose curse was finally broken.

It never got easier, with every Lycanthrope the Werewolf Hunter killed.

Vladimir hung his head back as he breathed slowly, calming his nerves. The bleeding in his shoulder had slowed, but the claw marks across his thigh and chest burned terribly. He would have to clean them out before they left the valley. When he finally calmed down a bit, he turned to see Charlotte had moved back over to her brother who remained still. She did not touch Morgan, nor did she attempt to look at him. She just sat there, as if deep in thought and prayer. The threat has been eliminated, and now she could be alone with him.

With a sigh, Vladimir started forward and he stopped when he got within a few feet from the Ice Walker. "Charlotte, I'm sorry."

Charlotte shook her head. "This wasn't supposed to happen... this isn't... this isn't how it was supposed to be..."

Vladimir frowned. Feeling sympathy towards the girl, he stooped down and pulled her away from her brother. Charlotte began to struggle but stopped as the Hunter hugged her close to his body. He probably stunk and was sticky with blood, but Charlotte didn't fight it. Instead, she seemed to welcome the hug as he held here there in the darkness with nothing but himself to provide comfort.

"Nothing is how it is supposed to be," he eventually said. "Nothing in this world is supposed to happen. But that is just how life is. It throws what we never expect our way; whether it be for our own good, or just to be cruel. But that doesn't mean you let yourself just give up. Only cowards give in to the struggles of life and what happens. True victors rise above that, and continue to live on. Your brother, he fought to protect you and even brought you here to spread your mother's ashes. Now it is your turn to continue your legacy. Now it is your turn, to live on. For if you live, then Morgan and your mother will forever live through you."

Charlotte looked up at Vladimir, tears in her eyes. She sniffed, and then buried her face into his chest. "Morgan... Morgan..."

"Don't worry," Vladimir said, feeling less like a Hunter and more like... like...

Like a father?

Perhaps, although he never dreamed such a feeling was possible.

"We won't let anything happen to you. That's a promise, you hear me?"

Charlotte sniffed. "Promises are no good…"

"No," Vladimir admitted. "Sometimes they aren't. But sometimes, they are all we've got to hold onto. Do you at least trust me?"

Charlotte was quiet for a moment, but then her muffled voice uttered her reply. "I trust you all…"

"Good." Vladimir squeezed tighter. "Don't worry, I'm here."

"What about the others?" Charlotte asked pushing herself away in order to look the Werewolf Hunter in the eye.

Vladimir had almost forgotten. He cursed and hurried over to Morgan, who he took up in his arms and telling Charlotte to hurry, they both started up the stairs taking two to three steps at a time. By the time they reached the exit, the place was engulfed with flames which blocked their way out. Charlotte held her hands out and torrents of icy winds burst from her palms and extinguished the flames like a fire hydrant. They both hurried out and when they were at last out of the grounds of the meeting house, Vladimir saw a figure caught in a crooked angle on fire, as well as a body laying beside it.

He sat Morgan down near the clearing and he told Charlotte to stay where she was. He hurried over and saw that it was Jacob, appearing dead at the pyre that had to have been the witch. He checked his wounds, saw the cauterized hole in his front and the one still bleeding from the back. He tore off a piece of his shirt and stuffed it into the wound, causing Jacob to groan. He was still alive, and that was good.

He looked at the burning figure of Carmilla the Red, and a ghost of a smile tugged at his lips. "You got her, you crazy sonofabitch."

He had started to pull Jacob up but then a horrible screech came from the direction of the lake. He looked in that direction and Jacob groaned in his state of unconsciousness, as if responding to the cry.

"Ang… Ange…"

Vladimir's brow darkened. He waved Charlotte over and the Ice Walker came obediently. By then, Vladimir was already on his feet, having removed some more ammunition from Jacob's pack as well as he hurried off.

"Stay with him," he told Charlotte, and when he heard the Ice Walker attempting to follow he shouted, "Stay there!" and then he broke off into a sprint towards the lake.

Jacob would be fine, he was sure of that. It was too late for Sabina, whom at the thought of caused a lump to form in Vladimir's throat but he pushed on. He was not going to lose another comrade, even if it was a Dhampir. He didn't know how Angela was faring, but from the horrible screams of the demon that she had been fighting, it couldn't be good.

He just hoped that he wasn't too late.

Pain...

Terrible, gut-wrenching pain... it was all she felt.

The woman... the woman who had caused her pain... it was all her fault. It was incredible, and she might have thought once inconceivable, how much hurt can exist when there wasn't physically wrong. That pain was nothing compared to the pain that was inflicted upon her now. The loss of Lithus...

And yet still... she fought. Moreover, the demon caused more pain to *her* in return. She may not be able to inflict the same pain the Dhampir had caused her with the slaying of her brother, but she could still destroy her into Oblivion. Every muscle fiber in her body ached, screaming for the blood of the Dhampir. The smell of human and Vampire both seeped from her like a terrible swarm. Her blood... she wanted more of the Dhampir's blood.

Who was she, anyway? Why is she here? Why...

Why does she only feel pain, and terrible sadness and anger? These feelings, these feelings that could kill... it was what drove the beast. It was what satisfied its hunger; only to be washed down with the blood of the Dhampir.

Her eyes had been Awakened, and so she had a greater advantage against her, but still the woman who had caused her this pain still evaded her and slipped away into the woods. As she stalked through the trees, her feet and claws sifting through the snow trying to find traces of blood, she sniffed the air and clicked her teeth together, searching for any sound of movement to give away where the Dhampir had gone. She was wounded and would not escape, but still she growled in frustration. Such rage could not possibly be quenched, and yet that was what it would take for her to know peace, whoever she once was.

The moon was high, and her sight was as clear as daylight if she had been born a human instead of an Immortal- instead of the beast of power and hunger.

Why... why was she like this?

She didn't know anymore. She didn't know why she did this, she didn't even know who she herself was. At the same time, she didn't care.

All she knew, was the hunger, the pain, and the sorrow. She wanted to bury her sadness, and quench her hunger. What had the Dhampir done to her- She wanted to rip the monster apart who had caused her pain. The wounds she had sustained weren't terrible, at least not as bad as the Dhampir's. She should have died by now after having being crushed by her immense strength. She should have collapsed from the bloodloss considering how much meat was missing from her shoulder.

She should be dead.

She should...

just...

die.

She... her... she... and her. Who was who? Who was the real monster here? Who has caused pain, and who has endured?

She didn't know anymore. She didn't know anything. That face... that face she kept on seeing... so familiar. Who is that? Who is he? And why does he look upon her so?

She dug her claws into a nearby tree, the bark groaning in agony at her touch. She sniffed once more. Bitter coldness, the smell of pine... lake water...

Blood.

It was everywhere.

Looking about, her incredible vision was able to pick up rusty trails of blood, smeared all over the nearby trees. The Dhampir was close, no doubt, but she had scattered her scent over almost every single tree the demon could see. Out of frustration, the beast roared and drove it's right wing through the tree it had been standing beside, the bony knuckle bursting through the other side as if it were a pig to be butchered. It tore at the ground, snarled and barked, screeched into the skies to call the children of the night, but none would come. None dared to answer the call of such dreadful rage and agony.

Titititititititititit... she chatted her teeth again, the sound stretching throughout the woods and bouncing off every tree the waves passed by, telling her where they all were and everything else in-between. Her ears twitched and cocked at every single sound she picked up through her enhanced echolocation. She sensed a stump, a bush where a bear was hibernating among the frozen berries, and even a large boulder where a long-forgotten skeleton sat against it. Somewhere in the cliffs beyond, a tiger stood guard over her den while her cubs slept. Squirrels and birds laid shivering in their burrows and nests, unwilling to come out and investigate the horrible sound that was resonating through the forest.

But the Dhampir...

It couldn't find her. Her scent was everywhere- the smell of her blood clogged the air like a dense fog it felt like.

So where was she?

A growl of frustration escaped it's throat. The face of the boy... that's right, he was a boy. Human? No... he was a Vampire- an Immortal, like... like...

Who was he?

Why did it hurt so much, especially when the scent of the Dhampir grow stronger?

It had to find her. It had to find the Dhampir.

It had to kill her.

I'm hungry...

Angela sat as still a stone, neither breathing nor even blinking as she listened to the movement of the Nosferatu lumbering in the woods. It's massive size, and the huge limbs thundering the ground and causing vibrations in the air whenever it took flight and crashed back down somewhere close by. There should be no way for the creature to take flight successfully or move about as fast as it was, and yet it was doing just that as it continued to hunt. Hunt for her.

Angela who was now bleeding badly across her belly as well as her shoulder whose bone was still gleaming like polished porcelain in the moonlight, couldn't risk fighting this creature out in the open any longer. She had lost too much blood, and while it had provided better cover for her to hide during her escape, she needed to end this quickly or else try to drink some blood in order to heal and gain strength. Because her strength right now was dwindling rapidly, like a candle with no more wax and at the end of its wick. She could feel it now, fluttering, sputtering, trying to keep burning, but it was growing more and more faint by the minute. But as long as-

It was right there. Fifty feet away to her left, clawing at a nearby tree in frustration. Those silver eyes glowed bright and dangerous as it searched for her. The Eyes of Shifting; capable of twisting space around the owner and placing it somewhere else. If she wanted to successfully kill the demon without doing further damage to herself, Angela had to avoid looking into the creature's eyes as she attacked it. For that to happen, she would have to sneak up on it without getting caught; a difficult feat for a creature who can find her as easily as a bloodhound sniffing out a rabbit. A creature, who despite having been successfully wounded albeit minorly with her silver sword, the wound had healed thanks to it drinking her blood.

But now hopefully, *hopefully*, she would have a chance in the cramped spaces of the cold forest around them. Using both its cover and its density to sneak up on it and get the drop on it. She just had to wait for the most opportune moment. For now, she had to lie still and wait.

The beast stepped forward, its wings tucked tight against its back as it sniffed the ground once more. That was all

the Immortal was now. She was no longer a creature of elegant and terrifying beauty, but a creature of stupid ferocity; A beast that has lost sight of all light and darkness of the world, only now knowing hunger. There was no love, no thought, and no hope in the heart of such a pathetic and monstrous creature.

The Nosferatu that the Immortal had become, was just a hungry beast in search of blood.

Her blood.

Angela gripped her sword tighter, and focusing all of her energy on her eyes, she cycled through the many possibilities of the near future and what her fate could be with every decision she would make from here on out. Though she kept her eyes closed as she did so, in order to keep the glow from her eyes from being seen by the beast that was still sniffing and growling about, it lingered closer and closer.

An attack from the side, skirting around and coming in on the other, Angela saw the result in her getting grabbed. If she was caught, she would be ripped to shreds.

Coming in from above, there was a chance to critically wound the beast and hold it down. But then the impact from her fall would cause terrible pain to her belly, causing her to fall over and once again end up in the Nosferatu's clutches.

Running away and leading it deeper into the woods might give her another advantage especially from within the trees, but then leading the beast out here already would have been a waste.

To slip in and-

Blam!

"Rreeeeaaaaaargh!"

This horrible howl awoken Angela from her visions and she returned her startled gaze to the Nosferatu who had moved forward slightly from the last spot it had been standing. It was hunched over, glaring down at her knee which was bleeding profusely. Another gunshot sounded and the Nosferatu lurched forward as it's back bloomed a crimson flower. It turned in the direction it had been shot and roared in indignation and rage.

You idiot.

"Hey!" the voice of Vladimir sounded from somewhere further in the woods. "Over here!"

The beast rose, spreading it's and roaring it's challenge to the newcomer as the wound in it's knee began to slowly heal; incidentally exposing it's back to Angela who with a flash of her eyes saw *another* possible future.

She decided to go with it, and standing up slowly, she waited until the legs of the beast tensed before rushing forward with all the speed her legs could build up. The Nosferatu had heard her coming, but it was too late for the speed in her run and the strength behind her blade stuck deep into it's back between the shoulder blades and the base of the wings. The momentum of her strike hurled the Nosferatu forward and it slammed against the tree from the force of the impact. Blood sprayed out like a flood and sprayed across Angela's face, but the beast quickly recovered and began bucking and flailing it's arms like a raging bull. Angela kept her feet planted and one hand on her sword with the other on one of the monster's wings. Her shoulder screamed in hot pain but she ignored it, gritting her teeth and holding on tight. She had to leap off of the Nosferatu anyway however, in order to escape the flailing claws and the moment she landed she took off running once again. The beast howled at her again and then took chase after her; bouncing from tree to tree to keep up with the fleeing Dhampir.

Angela saw a boulder coming up ahead, and she reached into her belt where her throwing knives still hung ready. As she came near the massive rock, she heard the Nosferatu hit the ground behind her and the sound of wings catching air followed- meaning the beast was now hurling right for her with claws and fangs ready to tear her apart. She looked back, saw where the silver orbs were and then looked away.

Just before she reached the rock, Angela dug her foot into the snow and turned quickly on her heel. Keeping her head facing forward, she then hurled the two throwing knives under her arm straight at the Nosferatu, and the beast's screams of pain caused her to look back. The Nosferatu was coming her way, massive hands over it's face as blood seeped from the eyes which were stuck with daggers of silver. Angela dove out of the way just as it crashed right into the rock with a thundering *crash*! Before it could get back up, she charged right back into it, swinging her sword and severing the wings right off. The creature barked and howled and now without its wings, it wouldn't be able to gain the advantage of the air. Angela then plunged her sword right into its back, ignoring the spray of crimson that painted her front. The Nosferatu bucked and then reaching over its shoulder, it grabbed her by the arm and threw her right off. It then tried to smash her with its fists, but she managed to roll out of the way just before she could be crushed. The beast continued to slam its fists into the ground blindly while its eyes bled out profusely. With its eyes blinded as well, it would be difficult for it to try and use them on her- or the Werewolf Hunter who was now taking up a position at the top of the hill the two had run down. Vladimir had taken aim with his pistol, and the report echoed throughout the valley as the Nosferatu staggered from the impact of the silver slug striking it's side.

Angela stepped forward, ready to go for the beast's throat this time but a burning pain suddenly shot up her left leg and she collapsed to her knees. To make matters worse, the sound of her falling made the beasts ears turn up and it turned towards her, with a nasty blood-curdling grin across its face.

"There you are!" it snarled reaching out and grabbing for her. Angela ignored the pain in her leg and rolled aside as the Nosferatu reached out and swinging her sword she severed two of the demon's fingers clean off. Without giving the beast any time to react, Angela moved in and continued to slash at the beast with her sword; fast as lightning she attacked the Nosferatu with all her strength. Every swipe of her blade made blood splash against the snow and trees and slathering her body in a thick layer of gore. The pain in her left leg grew excruciating, and she found herself unable to maneuver as fast after the first few strikes.

Because of this, the beast's fist collided with her head and sent her sprawling through the woods and rolling down the hill before crashing right into a nearby tree. Though she wasn't terribly hurt from the fall, her leg still screamed like it was on fire. At the sound of the beast's tormented scream, she turned to see it now rushing for her on all fours, its blood soaking into the snow with every stride it took. It shouldered against a tree but kept barreling towards her like a bear determined to run down a deer.

"I know where you are!" it snarled.

Angela gripped her sword tightly, ready to receive the fatal blow but send the creature back to hell where it belonged if she could do it. The beast smashed right into Angela and the two crashed through the tree she had been leaning against and together they continued to roll down the hill clawing and stabbing one another without any sense of direction at all. Angela went as far as to use her nails and her teeth to bite and scratch at the Nosferatu's face and neck. It's blood tasted acidic but it gave her just enough strength to keep savaging the monster as it too savaged her.

When the two crashed into another boulder, Angela was propelled through the air and she landed right on the ice of Snowcap Lake which made her slide almost a good fifty feet across the frozen surface. She was on her back and she was staring up at the night sky which glistened with millions of stars that shone like diamonds.

She heard the ice groan beneath her light weight but she wasn't focusing on that. Instead, she was more concerned for her shoulder. Her leg which she might have broken during the scuffle, felt better as she extended it but the wound in her shoulder had refused to close up. It no longer bled, but it was still exposed at the bone. The bitter cold made the wound feel so much worse that even the pain in her leg was now a forgotten memory. She tried to slowly push herself up but after their tumble her shoulder was so torn up she could only rely on her left arm to push herself back up to her knees. She turned her head and saw that her sword had fallen short between where she was and the shore of the lake-

Where the Nosferatu was now lumbering across and setting foot on the ice. Beneath her, Angela heard the ice groan and crackle beneath the weight of the beast as it made it's way towards her, it's body still dripping gore and having only one eye having being healed for it to see. That one silver eye, glared right at Angela with such hatred and anger, that it didn't even bother to consider how thin the ice it now treaded upon would be. It was just a blind and stupid beast with only one desire; to drink, and quench it's hunger. As it drew nearer, the ice seemed to groan evermore as if in warning. Dread began to fill in Angela at the prospect of them both ending up in the icy blackness of Snowcap Lake.

"I won't let you get away…" the monstrous voice of Mithus hissed despite the blood seeping from her gray lips. She was limping terribly too, due to the deep cut that revealed bone on her muscled thigh. "I will never let you get away…"

Angela pushed herself up to a steady stance, her sword still too far away. Despite her leg feeling better it still ached painfully and she was forced to hobble as fast as she could, which in turn the Nosferatu moved faster as well, causing the ice to groan in protest even more so. She reached her sword and with her one good arm, she held it up, pointing it right at the Nosferatu who despite the clear warning, kept on coming her way. Without her leg or her right arm to fight on a slab of thin ice, Angela couldn't see any better outcome than what was to come. Her lavender eyes burned bright with only one successful outcome in destroying the beast.

"I hate you..." Mithus growled raising her clawed hand which was missing two fingers. It connected onto the ice which rippled into a spiderweb of cracks beneath it's weight and leaving a bloody print behind. "I hate you... hate you... *hate you...*"

Angela had accepted the outcome.

She gripped her sword tighter, and prepared to move in for the kill as well as receive the fatal blow.

Suddenly however, another shot rang out somewhere on the shore and a silver bullet struck right into the beast's neck and out the front of the throat. The Nosferatu screamed out and began to claw at her face as if it was on fire, leaving it's hind legs on the ice and causing where it stood to crackle all the more.

Seizing her chance, Angela rushed forward and slashed at the leg she had not injured as she slid right past the beast. Upon the muscles in it's leg being severed, the demon collapsed to her knees still screaming and clawing at her face and be rid of the fire in it's throat. With it's back exposed to Angela, the Dhampir leapt up into the air, and stabbed downward to where the beast's heart was- as her eyes predicted in a flash of purple light, guaranteeing her accuracy this time.

"I'm sorry," she whispered hoping that Mithus could hear her before the sword plunged deep into her back and with the remaining strength in Angela's arm, she plunged it deeper and deeper even as the two of them broke through the ice and sank into the cold blackness of Snowcap Lake.

In the darkness which swallowed them up, Angela felt her blade finally cut through the thick ribs of the Nosferatu and sink deeper and deeper into the torso of the beast. Bubbles and blood clouded her vision but she kept on plunging the blade deeper; hoping that she had been able to pierce Mithus' heart. However, the demon was far from done even if her heart had been stabbed. She thrashed so that she now faced Angela while the two of them continued to sink deeper into the blackness of the freezing water, the wolf's head on the hilt staring back at Angela with its snarl looking as if it were laughing. Bloody bubbles erupted from the creature's mouth as she screamed at Angela, but the damage had already been done. With the removal of her sword, Angela could only watch as Mithus' demonic image slowly began to crumble away into dust to be carried away into clumps in the depths of Snowcap Lake.

When they reached the bottom, most of the Nosferatu had faded away, the claws of the beast still holding onto Angela as they struck the floor of the lake, which was littered with many great boulders with rusty chains containing the skeletons of all who had plunged themselves into these inky depths. By the time Angela sifted through the ashes of Mithus which were being carried away by the light current, she had managed to grab ahold of her sword before kicking off the floor and shooting for the surface, the ashes of Mithus being left as dust on the lakebed of a mass grave.

Kicking her feet and ignoring the pain to the best of her ability from her injuries, Angela made to swim for the surface. But with every kick, it felt like the dark waters were still holding on tightly, unwilling to let her go. It was bad enough that as a Dhampir, she could barely swim as is. But she still persisted, unwilling to allow the darkness which continued to cloud her vision along with her own blood and bubbles keep her in its grasp. A chilly sort of terror wafted through her, wanting to get out of the water as soon as possible. The harder she kicked, the further the silvery surface appeared to be. But eventually, she finally managed to reach the surface.

But she was stuck; trapped beneath the ice that held her under. The moon shined down on her face, as if mocking her for being so close to air and yet still being so far away. Sheathing her weapon over her shoulder, Angela began punching at the ice. But the lack of oxygen and the wounds she sustained proved to weigh too heavily upon her, and the fact that water was another weakness of Vampires left Angela as weak as any poor soul would under the ice. She continued to beat on the ice, until the strength in her arms finally gave up, and her legs ceased to kick anymore. At this point, Angela merely accepted the waters that pulled her back into the black void where so many had perished. As she fell away from the ice, she closed her eyes, ready for whatever laid beyond the black.

Just before her heavy eyes finally closed, the ice above her shattered and fell away in showers of brilliant silver light as someone plunged into the waters and grabbed ahold of her hand. She felt hands grab her under her armpits and she felt the water churn around her as she finally blacked out, and knew only darkness.

The icy waters had sent shockwaves throughout Vladimir's body and caused his head to ache as if it were on fire, but he had dove for the Dhampir after breaking the ice. His bones felt like they were shattering like glass and after hooking his arms under her armpits he dragged her back to the surface, thinking only for a moment how light Angela really was.

When they broke the surface he took a gulp of air before hauling Angela onto the rim of the ice and following himself. Soaking wet and shivering from the cold, he proceeded to drag her across the ice until they reached the shoreline. They almost fell back in twice as the ice continued to break under their combined weight but he managed and he released his soaked burden onto the shore before collapsing himself, panting and shivering from the effort. He hurried over to Angela and checked her pulse which was weak. When she didn't respond to her name he proceeded to smack her gently but not too gently across the face, hoping she would wake up. When she didn't he applied cardiopulmonary resuscitation, pressing his lips to her own and releasing breath into her lungs, careful of course not to let her fangs nick him.

"C'mon, c'mon," he muttered as he applied pressure to her chest. He repeated the process twice more before Angela finally vomited up the water and proceeded to cough. Although she was breathing again she curled up on the lakeshore and fell still again, still comatose from her endeavor with the Nosferatu.

Glad that she was indeed breathing again, Vladimir took the time to survey her wounds. A lot of them were bad, especially her shoulder and he had to suppress a shudder from the sight of her gleaming bone. She was frigid to the touch and he couldn't tell if that was from the lake, her bloodline, or more than likely blood loss. He had no medical supplies on him and her ragged breathing only meant that she didn't have long to live.

But if Jacob hadn't been infected…

Thinking he was perhaps out of his mind, he drew one of his clean daggers from his belt and pressed the edge against his palm. He grunted as he cut his palm and sent a splurge of blood dropping to the cold sand. He then held Angela's head up, feeling the ice that was forming in her ashen hair. Taking a deep breath, he pressed his hand against the lips of the Dhampir and letting his blood drip past.

"C'mon, c'mon, you damn leech," he muttered both desperately and angrily. His terror which had surprised him at first, made him angry enough to press his palm harder against her mouth. "C'mon, don't do this to me, dammit."

At last he felt a sort of sucking sensation in his palm and he had to suppress his sudden disgust as he realized that Angela even unconscious could sense the taste of blood like an infant their mother's milk. Suddenly her hands came up and clasped over his, holding his hand in place as she drank with sudden desperation and savagery. Vladimir watched in amazement as he watched the wound in Angela's shoulder heal before his very eyes; the muscle fibers that were missing slowly regenerating like silk being made and then just as slowly weaving over one another like strands in a tapestry. Pale skin soon formed over this muscle and while the color in Angela's face didn't change, her thin cheeks took on a more youthful look and she suddenly released Vladimir's hand and her head fell back, her lips stained with his blood. Her catlike eyes had snapped open and she laid breathing heavily and staring up at nothingness until those inhuman eyes finally focused on Vladimir who held his bleeding palm against his pantleg.

"You all right?" he asked, surprised once again by the eagerness in his voice. He was just full of them today wasn't he?

After a moment Angela spat out a glob of lake water and blood which left a metallic taste in her mouth, as well as a stale residue of cigarette smoke she noticed and she nodded. "I'm alive… It wasn't too late."

Thinking that she meant dying, Vladimir nodded in agreement and then slumped onto his side on the lakeshore, still shivering but just relieved that they were both alive. Angela looked at him and he said to give him just a minute and he'll be good to go.

She wiped at her lips still laying beside him. "Did you-"

"CPR," said Vladimir. "When that didn't work I… you know."

"Hmm…" Angela sounded disgusted but she didn't say anything about Vladimir's lips being on hers. There was no point to it. She took notice of the blood on Vladimir, and saw the fissures of flesh in his shoulder.

"You've been bitten…"

"I'll live."

"The Lycan…"

Vladimir shook his head. "I'm not going to turn into a werewolf. Trust me. I'd rather not get into it, but I'll be fine. I promise."

But Angela already knew. She guessed, "A transfusion?"

Vladimir glared at her, answering her question despite not.

"I see," she said laying her head back down. "It's none of my business. But I'm glad you'll be all right. The others will have questions though."

"Maybe," Vladimir agreed. Neither he nor Angela continued the subject.

After just a minute, Vladimir sat up and looked down at the Dhampir who still laid sopping wet on the lakeshore after being on the verge of death. "Can you stand?"

"In time…"

Vladimir shook his head as he stood. "We don't have time. We gotta get back to the others, get warm and heal our wounds."

Angela then looked at Vladimir sharply. "Jacob-"

"He's alive," Vladimir told her. "Although just barely." He looked away before adding, "The boy's dead."

Angela looked up at the sky. She then asked, "The girl?"

"Alive."

"That's good..."

"C'mon," said Vladimir holding his uncut hand towards Angela. "On your feet."

She sat up without taking his hand. When she stood up the world seemed to tilt as she was still recovering. The bites from the Nosferatu had seemed to drain any energy she had left, even after her wounds had healed. She would have fallen if not for Vladimir taking ahold of her by the arm.

"Don't," she said trying to shrug him off. "Don't touch me..."

"Just shut up and take a moment," he told her. "Don't want you passing out and me having to carry you. Do you?"

Angela groaned and allowed herself to be steadied before taking a tentative step. When she was able to walk a few steps Vladimir began to walk alongside her, keeping a close eye on her to make sure she didn't pass out from exhaustion.

"You shouldn't have come..." she told him.

"And you shouldn't have put yourself in serious danger- again," Vladimir argued.

"The Nosferatu..."

"Uh-oh," Vladimir said as he reached for Angela again, catching her before she collapsed. With a grunt he hooked his arm under her own and pulled her across his shoulders. She resisted for a moment as he now held her like a fireman would a victim of serious burns and continued on carrying her as he quickened his pace through the woods and back towards the village.

"Put me down right now," she hissed feeling both disgusted and embarrassed."

"Knock it off," Vladimir told the Dhampir as he kept on running without stopping. "I don't like it anymore than you, but you can barely walk. You can send me a complaint when we are all warm and safe."

At last Angela went limp, surrendering to Vladimir's assistance. She was so tired and so cold that she doubt she had any strength to fight anymore. She heard him huffing as he carried his light burden through the snow, his breath bellowing vapors as he huffed and puffed. She let him run a few strides without a word but then she uttered the question she dreaded the answer for.

"Sabina…" she croaked, hoping Vladimir would understand.

Thankfully, and yet also unfortunately, he did. "She's gone," he whispered. "Don't talk. We'll-"

"Sabina…" Angela groaned letting her head and body go limp again in horrible pain that overwhelmed that of her own wounds. "No…"

Vladimir was silent for a few more strides, but then sighed, "I'm sorry. I'm so sorry, Angela."

Angela didn't answer. She just simply allowed him to carry her while she shivered in the unmerciful cold and wetness of her body. In her own way of despair, she allowed herself to just go limp, and rely on him.

Sabina… I'm so sorry…

Back at the village which was now partially destroyed in the attack from the witch and the Raven, Vladimir carried Angela over to an untouched house which had smoke coming from the chimney. He shouldered the door open and saw Charlotte poking at a fire at the mantle while Jacob laid on the floor which had a bearskin rug draped across it. There was enough room and so Vladimir dropped to his knees and gently rolled Angela off his shoulders and onto the floor. She laid there for a moment but tried to get up again, her eyes on the prone Jacob.

"No, no," Vladimir said pushing Angela back. "Lay down, rest. Let me attend to him."

"I didn't know what to do," Charlotte started to say to which Vladimir assured her that she was all right and that he was there now.

Using a knife from his belt he cut the straps off of Jacob's armor and then slit his shirt down the middle. He inspected the entry wound on his stomach and then flipped him over and peeled the shirt off the rest of the way. Angela watched him inspect the exit wound, eyeing the tattoos of runes and the black wings on Jacob's back. Vladimir's lack of reaction told her that he had seen the tattoos before and thought nothing of them. He then stepped outside and then came back several minutes later with one of the saddlebags from the horses they had stowed. He went through it and applied a salve to Jacob's wounds before hoisting him into a sitting position and having Charlotte help wrap gauze around the Hunter's torso. Then he took out a vial of antibiotics and forced Jacob to swallow this by pinching his nose and sliding the liquid down his throat. He coughed for a moment but then settled down almost instantaneously and so Vladimir was able to set him back down on the rug. He asked Charlotte to look for some blankets and she came back several minutes later with a bundle of old and dusty quilts from a pantry down the hall. By then Vladimir had applied a similar salve to his forehead and placed a bandage across his head.

Charlotte went to Angela and after confirming with Vladimir that the Dhampir was unhurt at least on the outside, she placed one of these quilts onto the Dhampir who accepted the warm patterns of purple and red cloth gratefully.

"Thank you," she said as she bound herself tighter in the quilt, enjoying the warm sensation that soaked up the bitter coldness that clung to her bones.

"Are you still hurt?" Charlotte said looking at the bare flesh exposed at her shoulder.

"Very," the Dhampir replied. "It'll be fine. I'll heal in a few days."

"That's good…" Charlotte whispered almost. Angela looked at her, wondering how the Ice Walker was doing. Especially, considering…

"Where are Sabina and Morgan?" Angela asked Vladimir.

"I moved them to the other room," Charlotte answered. She looked down at the flickering flames in the fireplace, her face stricken with grief. "I didn't know what else to do with them."

"I'm sorry about your brother."

Charlotte nodded in thanks. "And I'm… I'm sorry about your comrade."

"Thank you," Angela replied feeling the words tug on her heart again despite her keeping a face of stone.

The Ice Walker looked at the Dhampir, those cursed blue eyes moist with tears both old and present.

Feeling the need to, Angela sat up and patted the spot between her and Jacob. When Charlotte sat down, she pulled Charlotte close and allowed her to wrap herself in the blanket with her. Charlotte with her little bald head poking out of the furs, nestled against the Dhampir with a shiver.

"You're so cold…" she whispered.

"I'm always cold," Angela replied.

"More so than before…"

"I suppose."

Vladimir was watching from the broken window. "Get closer to the fire. Both of you."

They did so, and after a while Angela allowed herself to lean back and lie on the bearskin run. Charlotte remained sitting up staring at the fire.

She looked over at Vladimir and asked if he would rest.

"In a bit," he said still on edge and obviously expecting something else. "If we can I want to leave in the morning. That'll depend on you and Jacob."

"All right." Angela laid back down and closed her eyes. With the warmth of the fire and her comrades around, Angela willed herself to sleep. It was all she could do for the time being.

When she had woken up she saw Vladimir curled up next to the mantle in a fetal position where Jacob had been laying before. Charlotte was asleep between the two of them, her eyes still damp from crying herself to sleep. She looked around and saw that Jacob was nowhere to be seen. She carefully got up, making sure her weapons didn't alert the other two. She searched the rooms and then peeked outside to see him sitting on the front porch smoking a cigarette and drawing in his little picture book. He had a blanket around his shoulders and his glove was back on his cursed hand.

She stepped out into the dawn and the door creaking alerted him. He looked back and smiled, but the smile was almost as tired as he was, revealing just how old he felt at the moment.

"You're alive," he stated.

"Obviously," Angela said looking down at him.

He shrugged. "Vladimir told me what happened."

"He told me about you as well." She approached him but did not sit down beside him. "You slayed a witch."

He nodded. "So I did."

She was looking at what he had been drawing and it was a picture of the totem pole stationed at the head of the village. The details were almost so precise that it could have been passed off as a photograph taken from a used and abused camera.

She shifted her eyes back to Jacob. He was looking back at her, his expression still tired but also seeming to be steadily neutral, as if he were careful just to make a straight face.

"What is it?" she asked.

"Nothing. Just checking on you, making sure you are okay."

Angela nodded. "I was close to death, but Vladimir helped just in time."

"Good. I'm glad he did." He smiled then for real and added, "Guess he changed his mind. At the very least you..."

"I what?"

"Nothing," he said shaking his head, deciding on not bringing up the source of their personal conflict before this Hunt took place- if such a thing could be called that given the loss of both a member as well as one of the contractors.

When Angela continued to look at him Jacob emphasized, "Never mind."

Puzzled but having her suspicions, Angela replied. "Very well. How is your eye?" she then asked looking at Jacob's eyepatch. "And your hand?"

Jacob chuckled slightly, and flexed his fingers as if the mention of his hand caused him pain. "They hurt. But I'll be back in action soon enough. At least this time we won't have a witch coming after us- or a Raven."

Angela nodded. "That is good."

"Yeah. Just gotta resist getting stabbed in the gut."

"Indeed."

There was another pause, and then Jacob spoke just as he returned to doodling in his journal. "It wasn't your fault, you know?"

Angela stared at Jacob's back, not saying anything.

"What happened to Sabina, that wasn't your fault." he said again, emphasizing on what he was talking about. The mention of the Huntress' name made Angela feel heavy again. She wondered how Jacob had known what she had been thinking, and thought that perhaps he and Vladimir had spoken.

"You did the best you could," Jacob then told her.

"I could have done better," Angela said. "It is my job as well as everyone else in the Black Hand to make sure we all get home safely. I was the closest one, I should have saved her. I should have seen that coming…"

"Don't do that to yourself," Jacob said in a stern voice that was not like him at all. In fact, not that she would ever show it, it actually startled Angela slightly. "There was nothing you can do. Even you have limits, Angela. No one blames you for what happened, not even Vladimir. He even blames himself for not making it up top in time. I did too. But it doesn't do any of us any good blaming ourselves."

"Perhaps none of you, but there will be blame to be taken soon," she said. "It is inevitable. When we return, and they ask for an explanation, they will blame me. They always have whenever I was around. It's the way things are."

Jacob looked at Angela, clearly annoyed.

"Don't worry about it," she told him. "I'm not actually concerned with what the others think. I'm just more concerned, of what *Matei* will think."

Jacob frowned. "Yeah… that's right."

Angela crossed her arms and leaned against the doorframe. "We can't do anything about it right now. For now, our job now is to get home, get Sabina to Velinar, and pay our respects. I will deal with the other Hunters, you must be the one to provide comfort to the guild. It's what you are good at. It's why the entire guild loves you."

Jacob clenched his fists in both frustration and anger. "That doesn't make it right…"

"No. But like I have told you many times before, that is just the way things are."

"No one is going to blame you, Angela," Jacob said in a strangled tone. "I will explain what happened too, same as Vladimir. Hell, he even saved you. Doesn't that mean anything?"

"You underestimate how far anger and hatred will take someone, or many," said Angela.

"You were fighting a *demon*!" Jacob snapped. "You've gotten hurt, there was nothing you could do! Vladimir and I, we came up too late and nearly let the Raven get to Charlotte! Nothing that happened was your fault, Angela. None of us could do anything. We-”

“Jacob, enough,” Angela said in a low and stern voice. Jacob glared at her defiantly, but he held his tongue for the sake of those resting inside the shack. “Just… just stop. Okay? We will cross that bridge when we get to it.”

Unhappy, Jacob turned around and muttered, “Fine. I’m guessing we won’t move out until later, when Vladimir gets some rest.”

“I would assume so.”

“All right.”

And because it felt necessary, Angela told him, “I’m going to rest for a bit too.”

“Go ahead,” he told her. He then added, “I’m glad you’re alive, Angela. I’m glad you’re still here.”

Angela looked at him for a moment, and when he didn’t turn back, she went back inside and shut the door. She leaned her back against it and sighed out of pure exhaustion. She closed her eyes. She really needed to rest.

“He was only trying to help.”

Angela opened her eyes to see Charlotte standing near the window. How had she not heard the child coming to the window? She had been too focused, it seemed. The Ice Walker looked tired but that could easily be just from the toll she had taken emotionally from the loss of her brother.

“I know,” Angela replied. “But sometimes there is nothing that can be done. Sometimes, it does more harm than good in trying to help others.”

“Like when people don’t want help?” Charlotte asked.

Angela pursed her lips before answering. “Yes.”

Charlotte looked out the window. She cleared her throat. “My brother always said, that it is better to try and fail, than to never try and never fail.” She looked up at Angela. “I think… I think you should at least let Jacob know that you appreciate him trying."

"Maybe," Angela said looking up at the ceiling towards nothing in particular. "But sometimes, it's hard to say something like that when someone is angry. Or bound to be."

Charlotte nodded as if she understood. "Still, better to try and fail than not try at all, right?"

Angela looked at her, and the Ice Walker's eyes widened with expectation. Was she wondering what the Dhampir would say or how she would respond? Looking back towards the fireplace where Vladimir slept, Angela started for it for warmth. When she sat down, she didn't resist Charlotte who sat down right beside her.

"Maybe," she finally answered the Ice Walker.

Whether she thought the answer was good enough or decided not to question any more, Charlotte joined with Angela in the comfort of the silence occupied by the crackling fire. The two stayed that way, until Charlotte fell asleep much, much later.

Vladimir didn't wake until late in the afternoon. By then Jacob had already gathered some more wood and had taken some more blankets to wrap up Sabina's body. He was going to do the same to Morgan but Charlotte insisted on burying him here at Snowcap Lake.

Vladimir helped Angela pack and the Dhampir had gone straight back to sleep the moment they had finished gathering their damaged gear and reapplied bandages to the wounded. Her intention was so that she could do the entire journey back home without rest. Charlotte had spent some time with Morgan before retiring herself. By then the sun had sunk and the wolves were howling in the distance as they began their own hunt. Jacob had returned dragging a young buck by the antlers and had butchered the animal outside the village before returning with a few chops. He and Vladimir were at the fireplace cooking the meat and eating alone while Angela and the Ice Walker slept on the floor behind them.

They conversed in hushed tones, both smoking once they were done eating their fill.

"Sure wish we could have left today," said Vladimir.

"You needed rest. We all need it."

Vladimir breathed out the smoke. "Least we can get some shuteye tonight."

"Right," Jacob said rubbing his hands together for warmth.

Though he doubted very much that he would be able to sleep so easily at first, especially considering what he and Angela had talked about that morning. He had managed to keep himself busy all day, but their discussion had put him in a foul mood all the same and he didn't know if he had the right to do it. It wasn't as if Angela had said something wrong, and perhaps he was jumping the gun in getting himself worked up about it, because in truth neither of them knew how the others were going to take the news of Sabina's death. Matei would be a different story, but that didn't mean Angela had to take any blame if blame was to be given. No blame should be given, but that wouldn't matter at first for the one who grieved.

He stared at the fire. He really was thinking too hard on this.

"What pissed you off?" Vladimir asked getting comfortable in the armchair with his legs draped over the side. He looked at Jacob who was staring back at him, his cigarette pressed hard between his lips.

"Nothing," he replied.

"Bullshit."

Jacob looked away.

"I know something is bugging you," Vladimir said. "If we ain't gonna sleep, might as well talk."

"I don't even know myself."

"Talking helps." Then Vladimir added as he leaned his head back, "If you want."

Jacob looked back towards the girls. He got up and started to leave the area. When he paused at the door looking back at Vladimir, the Werewolf Hunter groaned and got up before shuffling silently to follow. When they stepped outside into the crystal-clear night illuminated by a full moon, they sat down on the frigid porch. They smoked for a while, Vladimir waiting patiently until Jacob finally snuffed his own out and looked up towards the stars.

Jacob turned to look at him. "Be honest with me."

"Only if you promise to be honest with me afterward," Vladimir said without even batting an eye. "What is it?"

"Do you think Angela is going to get blamed for what happened to Sabina?"

"My honest answer?"

"Please."

Vladimir took another drag and then sighed out the smoke. "It's a huge possibility. She was the closest when it happened, and due to the fact that she is a Dhampir, it might be easier to blame her more than you or I."

Jacob scowled bitterly. "That's a bunch of shit. The others wouldn't know if she was close or not."

"Wouldn't matter. What matters is how *Matei* will take the news."

Jacob looked directly at Vladimir. "If Matei tries something, to Angela, I mean, you'll defend her, right? You don't believe she is responsible for what happened to Sabina, do you?"

"I don't believe she is responsible," Vladimir said. "And of course I'll defend her. Whether we could have prevented it or not is irrelevant, we just need to let Velinar and the others know that we did the best we could under the circumstances. That still might not be good enough for Matei, but can you really blame him?"

"No, I guess not."

"Exactly. We'll deal with it when we get home. Don't worry too much about it. Don't worry too much about Angela, she can take care of herself, obviously." He took a drag and then added with a small smile, "Well, aside from almost drowning."

Jacob nodded. After a moment he said, "Thank you, by the way."

"For what?"

"For saving her."

Vladimir shrugged. "Anyone would have done it."

Jacob looked at him skeptically.

"All right, maybe not," Vladimir admitted. "But don't thank me all the same. Call it an impulse or whatever, I just… Forget it," he decided. "You're welcome."

Jacob grinned at him, and Vladimir demanded what he was smiling at. "You *do* care," was what he said.

"Don't push it," Vladimir told him. He took one last drag from his cigarette and snuffed it out into the snow. As he released his last puff, he said, "I'm going to tell you a story."

"Okay."

"When I was a lad, before I decided to become a Werewolf Hunter, a group of Dhampir's came into the village I lived in. There were only a few, like three or four, I really can't remember how many. They were all siblings who found one another. A bunch of bastards who found each other sired by the same parent. Ever heard of the Immortal Juré Grandor?"

"No."

"Doesn't matter anyway. Anyways, these Dhampirs, they said they needed a place to stay for the night. We saw their fangs, and their eyes, but they walked in daylight so our leader agreed to hear them out. We eventually learned what they were, and they told us they could control their lust for blood. They told us they could be trusted. And like the naïve fools we all were, we believed them and gave them a room. That night, seven people died, drained completely of blood. I remember seeing the warriors try and apprehend them, and they all fell at the feet of those... *demons*. The only reason only thirteen of our entire tribe died, was because of Damion. Remember when we talked about him? He was the one who slayed the Dhampirs. He killed them all, and saved us while he was traveling. It was then when I decided to become a Hunter, and follow in his footsteps- This was before he killed one of our own. I eventually became a recognized Werewolf Hunter, because that was what I was good at. I thought of becoming a Dhampir Hunter, the first ever on record anyway, but that was when I was just a kid still."

He paused, perhaps reflecting on that fateful day and perhaps even reliving it. "But after seeing what I saw that day... I knew I wouldn't be able to do it. There is not a human in the entire world who can slay a Dhampir. Immortals may be monsters that look like humans, but Dhampirs are more dangerous simply because they can pass as more human."

Jacob nodded in understanding. "Right… I'm sorry."

Vladimir shook his head as he sat back in his chair. "Don't be. Now you know the truth. What my personal reason is, why I can never bring myself to trust a Dhampir, regardless of whether or not they are on my team or not."

"Was it also because of Damion?" asked Jacob. "When he…" He didn't say it because he wasn't quite sure if that was true yet, but he might as well imply it for Vladimir's sake.

"Exactly," Vladimir said closing his eyes. "He might have saved my home, and did the world a favor of removing those demons, but he also killed one of us; a member of the Black Hand. It was because of *him*, when I realized that no human will ever be able to tame a Dhampir- regardless of what their intentions are or how strong-willed they may be against the taste for blood. Everyone has a breaking point at some point in time… I don't want to have to be the one to stop Angela if she had her own breaking point."

"She would never-"

"Do something?" Vladimir was looking at Jacob steadily now. "Don't ever say what someone may or may not be capable of. No one knows what anyone will do for certain, no matter how much you think you know them."

Jacob couldn't argue. "Ain't that the truth…" he muttered.

Not understanding what he meant by that, Vladimir moved on. "Regardless of her reasons, she is still a Vampire at heart. She won't be able to stop herself forever. And if I have to kill her to save my comrades, I will. Even if the odds aren't ever in my favor."

Jacob shifted uncomfortably in his seat. "Then why save her?"

Vladimir looked forward. Why *had* he? "Why, indeed." He looked back and said, "Maybe I have hope for her after all."

Thinking that was as good an answer as he could have gotten, Jacob accepted it with a nod.

"Listen here," said Vladimir. "Because I'm not gonna say it again. Angela obviously trusts you, just like you her. Don't ever let that go away. Defend her, and protect her like you would anyone else in the guild, but don't lose your common sense because of what you feel."

Jacob said nothing to this and kept his expression neutral.

"Also, don't let her be the only one you watch over. We all need to stick together. When we get back to the castle, we will make our report and she will no doubt catch hell from the others. Especially Matei. But he's going to need us too. I need you to be there for him as well, even if there is a chance he won't want you to be. You got me?"

Jacob nodded. "I understand."

"Good." Vladimir said relaxing in his chair once more. "One more thing... if not two."

"What is it?"

"Your eye," Vladimir said his eyes still on the Witch Hunter. "That is an Immortal Eye, right? Hypnotism?"

Jacob felt as if a fist had punched him in the gut, nevertheless he nodded in affirmation.

"I won't ask you where you got it," Vladimir continued. "But you used that one me, and that witch, right?"

Once again, Jacob nodded. "I had to."

Vladimir nodded. "Well, I won't ask for your life story on how you got it, like I said. But I assume you wanted to keep that a secret?"

"Preferably..."

Another nod. "Then do me a favor: don't ever use that on me again."

Jacob sighed with relief. "Alright, I promise."

"Good. You know something, Jacob?" Vladimir said leaning back and closing his eyes. "You really are full of surprises. You might become one dangerous Hunter one day."

Jacob laughed. "'One day? Gee. Thanks."

Vladimir smiled and he pulled himself up. "I'm going to bed. You should too."

They did so. Neither Angela nor Charlotte had awoken upon their return. The four of them slept warmly and soundly, as the evening winds howled outside the old house that would soon be once again lost in time.

The next morning, Morgan had been buried.

Jacob woke up to find him and Vladimir alone in the house, Vladimir sleeping still in what looked like an uncomfortable position on the chair with his back all turned and his head cocked to the side. He looked like a cat sleeping in positions that should have been impossible. He left the man alone to rest for at least another hour before stepping outside and noticing two figures standing at the base of the totem pole at the village entrance. Another marker was there, standing like a miniature totem pole when it was actually a makeshift grave marker carved to look like a bird with outstretched wings; the symbol of Yohnah appearing to be in mid-flight as it 'carried' the soul that had been buried up to Kawn beyond The Veil where the Stars roamed.

Having buried Morgan last night by herself and marking his resting place with this cross and carving of Yohnah tied to it with some twine found in one of the homes, Charlotte had remained here until the breaking of dawn. She didn't cry, nor did she mention anything about doing this by herself. Before dawn Angela had awoken and had gone looking for the child and found her here, and here she had joined as silent as a wraith. She stood before the gravesite with her arms crossed as she watched the Ice Walker, who knelt before the grave and said some silent prayer. She had not asked how Charlotte had dug the grave for she had seen no shovel, and she did not ask if the child was all right or offered words of condolences. She only stood there, and shared this grief with Charlotte who was grateful for the company.

Jacob watched from the porch, not wanting to disturb them.

Charlotte remained there for almost a half hour before the Dhampir finally did move. Stepping forward, she got down on one knee and placed a hand on Charlotte's shoulder. The Ice Walker looked at her, and Angela said something to the child. Jacob couldn't hear, but he could tell it touched Charlotte, because she allowed Angela to stand her up and pull her close to embrace her. Seeing the two, Jacob thought of how a mother should be with their child. With her arms wrapped around the child to provide protection so she could cry, Angela merely looked down at the grave, as if she too was saying her goodbyes to Morgan.

Jacob smiled at her. Angela was cold, and sometimes harshly honest. But in the end, she still had a good heart in her. He knew that she wouldn't leave until she was certain that Charlotte would be okay.

With the sun slowly starting to rise and cast another film of frost along the ground with the dawn of a brand new day, Jacob went to awaken Vladimir and gather the horses still kept in one of the homes so he could water and feed them before they began the journey home.

There would be time for worrying about the future later.

The ride back to the castle took them five days due to their exhaustion and injuries. During this time hardly anyone spoke the entire trip, not even Vladimir who occasionally only told them when to stop and rest.

All three were on their horses, including Sabina who was draped over Vladimir's. As they once again passed through the woods of a Thousand Souls, the voices and whispers they had heard previously appeared to have gone silent. It was as if the spirits forever trapped in this valley knew of the group's suffering and decided to have mercy on them. There had been signs of Trolls lingering about, but nothing had come out to attack the group. Nevertheless, Angela kept alert, listening and keeping her eyes open the entire time without even hesitating for a moment. Her body was still aching, and her bandages itched horribly; she was in no mood for another fight. None of them were.

They had all suffered severe wounds on this job, especially Charlotte who turned a small pocket watch over and over in her hand as she rode. Angela could smell the scent of the Lycan Huntress on the locket, and even tried to persuade the young Ice Walker into just leaving it behind. But Charlotte refused, saying she wanted to keep it. For whatever reason she had, she kept it to herself. Angela didn't question her, nor did Vladimir who occasionally looked upon the silver pocket watch in disgust. To him, it was just another reminder of a poor soul who had given into the form of the beast. Who knew for certain what it was to Charlotte.

If and when the Ice Walker was ready, Angela was sure she would tell them.

One evening while camping in the cursed forest, Jacob had taken first watch and had noticed something lurking just outside the camp. At first, he thought it was a wolf, but after some observation he realized with a vague surprise that it was actually one of the Empire's war dogs. The schäferhund which had fled when the trolls had come and attacked her masters, had been wandering this forest hunting what she could and cowering in fear within fox burrows as the monstrous trolls came stalking about. The last few days had been miserable for her, and when the Hunters had arrived at this forest, she had been watching them at a distance, and although it lightened her heart to see human beings again, she did not trust them.

Jacob, knowing none of this of course, took pity on the dog and had tried to approach it. When it fled, he returned to his pack and removed some of the meat they had packed from the deer he had hunted back at Snowcap. He placed this meat in a spot close but not too close to camp before returning to the fire to keep watch. He was not at all surprised when the dog returned and took the meat before disappearing into the night. It did not wander far however, for Jacob had managed to catch sight of it every so often until it was his turn to rest. Vladimir had noticed it, but paid it no heed.

The following day, the dog was following them. It followed at a far distance but not far enough so that Angela couldn't sense it. She had mentioned it briefly but Vladimir didn't care and Charlotte was too occupied with herself to notice. Only Jacob looked back with concern, and this told Angela that he had either seen the dog before or perhaps only took pity on the dog. She didn't say anything however and had left it alone.

That is, until she woke up the next night. The group had camped in the first spot they had come to when entering this valley, and saw that Jacob had left the camp. Rising out of her bedroll, she tracked him to the edge of the forest where he was stooped before it, a clump of meat in his hand and a pistol in the other. She watched as the schäferhund slowly and timidly came out of the trees, growling lowly but showing no signs of aggression, only distrust. Her tail remained limp and did not coil or stand erect.

"C'mere," Jacob had prompted in a light tone before making kissing sounds with his lips. He held the meat out with a flat palm but he did not approach the dog nor did he stand when it was obvious his legs were starting to ache from his position. Angela continued to watch, not wanting to frighten the dog or startle Jacob. The dog was after all bred for war, and would no doubt turn aggressive at the first sign of danger.

For almost fifteen minutes the schäferhund remained where it was, no longer growling but not appearing eager to approach. When at last it slowly came to Jacob, her eyes never leaving his as she slowly sniffed at the meat before taking some and chomping it up hungrily. Moving slowly still, Jacob reached his now-empty hand into his pocket and brought more venison out for the dog which was practically all fur and bones. Her stomach was so small that her ribs were protruding beneath her beautiful black and tan coat.

"There we go," he said in his soft voice as the dog took some more meat, less afraid this time. "That's pretty good, isn't it?"

He had shifted his hand which held the pistol, and Angela thought that Jacob was going to put the dog down to save both them and the poor thing the trouble. This was no place for a dog, and even if it did survive being out here, how long would it be before a troll or some other beast finally got her? How long would it last among the wolves?

Instead, Jacob had holstered his pistol. He kept his palm out towards the dog however who sniffed and licked at it as is searched for more food. When he turned his hand over and let her sniff the back of his hand, he raised it slowly and this time the dog took a step back, head low and ears pulled back.

Being patient, Jacob took another small piece of meat out and held it out with his palm again. The dog approached, ate, and surprisingly allowed Jacob to turn his hand about and scratch the side of her muzzle. He leaned back only slightly and sat down, petting the dog and comforting her with a soft voice that was tender and kind.

He then slowly stood. The dog backed away but her tail didn't go up or between her legs. She just watched timidly as he turned and started to return. He didn't notice Angela who slipped away and was already back in her bedroll before he returned none the wiser. After perhaps an hour of letting Jacob sit by the fire, she rose and stretched, offering to take the rest of his watch. Jacob did so gratefully, and went to turn in on his own bedroll.

During her watch by the fire, Angela noticed that the dog had returned. It stayed within sight, her eyes reflecting the firelight just as Angela's were. It was more weary of her but over time, it slowly crept towards Jacob's sleeping roll. Angela kept her hand on a throwing knife the whole time, watching as the dog sniffed the foot of Jacob's bedroll before settling down but keeping it's head raised high, pointed ears high in the air as it took in all the sounds around it. After a while, the dog rested it's head down onto it's forepaws still as watchful as ever. It was then when Angela took her hand away and proceeded to just watch the night. At some point the dog did approach her, and she offered her hand for it to sniff. It turned away immediately as if it smelled something foul and returned to Jacob and laid back down again.

Come morning, Vladimir was surprised to see a dog sleeping beside Jacob. The dog got up and started to flee but then turned around when it noticed none of the humans were giving chase. Vladimir's start had woken Jacob up as well and he looked at the dog surprised.

"What's going on?" Charlotte said groggily as she got up and rubbed at her eyes.

"Jacob, where the hell did that dog come from?" Vladimir demanded.

"She's been following us," Jacob answered still staring at the dog in disbelief as well as sleep. "I fed her last night, I didn't think she would come here..."

"She didn't cause any trouble," Angela said still in the same position as she had been when she took over Jacob's watch. "Just sniffed around. I think it's just glad to be in the company of people again."

Vladimir didn't look happy but he said nothing as he crawled out of his bedroll and began to pack it up. They all got to work tearing down camp as the dog watched them. When they mounted their horses the dog followed Jacob closely, trotting alongside the horse as it no doubt did numerous times before.

Jacob tossed some meat scraps to the dog as they made their final trek out of the valley through the tunnels. He asked if anyone at Shadowfort had a dog, seeing as no one seemed to object to him feeding it or letting it tag along.

"Livia has one," said Vladimir. "A mutt. She keeps it inside though, it ain't a hunting dog. A techichi, I think. She got it while on a job all the way from Ved'máled." After a pause he added his only opinion of the war dog. "Velinar will probably let you keep her, but that's an active breed. You'll need to take her out every so often."

"That's something I can live with," said Jacob who watched as the dog trotted ahead and sniffed at Charlotte's stirrup. The Ice Walker leaned as far to the side as she could and scratched the dog between the ears. She had taken a liking to it ever since she truly woke up and saw it interact with the Hunters while they packed.

"You will keep it, then?" asked Angela.

"At least until I can find a home somewhere else for it," Jacob said. "But, perhaps."

"What will you name it?"

Jacob considered it for a while, watching as the dog veered away from the miniature platoon and inspected along the walls of the tunnels to relieve herself. She was still very thin and thought he would make sure she had a feast when they returned to the castle. He didn't want her to be all skin and bones anymore.

At last, he said, "I like the name Gebeine."

"Think it can respond to that?" asked Vladimir.

"Guess we'll see."

They rode on. Concerning Gebeine, this was the only real conversation the Hunters had ever since they left Snowcap Lake. They spoke no further as they finally left the tunnels that connected the lost valley to the outside world.

After they had finally emerged from the belly of the mountains, far down below sat Shadowfort Castle, just like it always was. Angela felt relief wash over her at the sight of their home, but at the same time felt the gripping weight of dread once again close around her heart. They had finally made it home, and now the real test would begin. With nowhere to go or any people to call to, Charlotte needed a place to stay. Everyone seemed to agree that she would stay with the Black Hand, but that would be up to Velinar to decide in the end.

Not only that, but they had one of their own dead along with them. It would soon be time to explain to Velinar and whoever present that Sabina had passed on from this world to the next. There would be a funeral for her, since they actually had a body this time. She would be buried in the crypts deep within the catacombs of the castle beyond Velinar's domain.

Matei, her partner and lover, would have to be informed if he was here. Angela hoped to Yohnah and all the other Stars that he was not home yet. She hoped that they would have more time.

Nevertheless, the group continued their decent, and began to make the last stride for home.

Di

Velinar looked at Matei with the passive neutrality of a statue.

Upon entering the castle, Matei had told 'Bram to inform Velinar that he didn't have good news and would be down to report after he was done with his horse. Now the Hunter stood before Velinar who was balancing on his scythe, looking the Hunter up and down and already seeing that Matei had been through a lot while in Firedell. His cloak was ripped and frayed at the ends, and his armor had a few chinks and furrows from bullets and swords. The young Hunter was even missing his left pinky finger, his hand now bound in bloody bandages.

But Velinar knew that his physical pain would be nothing next to the news that he would no doubt receive soon. He had felt the presence of his Huntress leave this world and passed on to the realm of the gods as was his nature. He would not speak of it though, not yet. That was news to be given from someone else, and as of now, there were other businesses to attend to. More important matters, at least concerning the Black Hand.

"Matei James Coventon," he said at last.

"My Lord," Matei said bowing his head while also offering the same courtesy to Dr. Jecklyn who had been down here before Matei arrived. Jecklyn was analyzing Matei's wounds soberly, at least what he could see. He would need to work on Matei really soon.

Velinar turned to the good scientist and nodded. "Leave us."

Jecklyn bobbed his head and then strutted past Matei without a single word. When Velinar saw the doctor ascend the steps back to the grand hall, he turned his complete and undivided attention back to the Hunter.

"What news do you have?" Velinar asked still sitting in his usual spot. Among Matei's wounds, it looked like he hadn't slept in days. Whatever news he had, it really must be important if he had managed to cross the country in a matter of days and in such condition.

"It's just as you thought, Lord Velinar," Matei confirmed. "That girl is an Ice Walker. One of the four elemental magics in the lands of Balkeñoir, and probably the last one recorded in existence."

Velinar sighed, flexing his fingers in ample hesitation. He thought to himself the possibilities this could mean for the near future. Matei shifted in his spot uncomfortable while Velinar took the time to think and calm his thoughts slowly.

"How do we know it is the last one?"

"The Raven Base down in Firedell has records of her," Matei said. "They knew about her for years, and only just recently made a move to grab her. They put one of their elite Raven's on the case as well as a handful of Empire Soldiers. That was probably the band that came knocking on our door. Thankfully, they seemed to have lost contact with the Raven and her crew upon their departure from Firedell. I'm guessing she was in such a hurry to go after the Ice Walker she didn't think to call for backup."

"Luck can only run for so long," said the deity dryly.

"Aye. There's more, still," Matei said dreadfully. "There were reports in the main office that the Ravens have been trying to find artifacts of ancient Nishgúlian artifacts. I have also not failed to notice that General Mormo Snow of the Thunder, has taken a keen interest in Dullahan the Wild, although I do not see the correlation between-"

"I have an idea of it," said Velinar with a wave of his hand. "Please. Just continue."

Curious but not wanting to have his master wait any longer, Matei went on. "A lot of the reports I had been able to recover state that the Ravens have been searching all across the continent, especially in the Reservation to find these divine beings, trying to round them up in order to somehow extract whatever valuable essence they could from the body and convert it into something that could then be transferred into regular soldiers or even themselves. Unfortunately for them, Charlotte and Morgan Adner were their only solid leads."

"Experimentation with magic…" Velinar said shaking his head in wonder. "This is more troublesome than The Covenants desire for Black Magic…"

He was also thinking over what Matei had mentioned concerning Dullahan the Wild. Now how could he possibly be involved in all of this?

"Where is the Ice Walker now?" Matei asked. "Have the others returned yet?"

"Not yet. But I am assuming we will hear from them soon. Matei, tell me, are you sure the Adners were their only lead?"

"Yes. There was nothing else other than rumors that came up as dead ends according to the reports," Matei answered.

"All right. And what about the Ravens cooperation with the Empire? What of that?"

"It's bad. They were in the process of moving to a new headquarters in Goldendell. That was why it was so easy to find the documents being ready to be shipped away. They have a major foothold in the Empire. And I mean *major*. Firedell is just the tip of the iceberg with how much pressure they are putting on Count Vaas. We're talking like more power than a Count or a General. The Head Raven is directly beneath Emperor Ion himself. Worse, there has been more projects going around; experimentation on beasts, blasphemous acts of torture upon citizens and a manhunt for any Hunters in Balkeñoir. It isn't just us who are in trouble with them now, my lord. Many other Hunting Guilds are now harbored as dangerous criminals and are to be shot on sight including anyone who works with them. Some of which I witnessed being burned or crucified in Firedell."

Velinar ran a hand over his bald head in frustration. Mere words couldn't express the stress of this news. "And the 'great' leader of this country allows it... this was not how Balkeñoir was founded by those who crossed the Dead Sea wished for it to become..."

Almost worse, Yohnah's law, and everything He stands for, is now being tossed aside to indulge in the Empire's selfish greed in life and their desire for power beyond this world's understanding. And now such a dangerous force is accumulating within Balkeñoir's borders, and the people have no idea what is really going on. This could become more dangerous than the Black Shadow two hundred years ago, perhaps even worse than the Vampire Wars after Balkeñoir had managed to segregate from Noyii's hold on the new world.

Matei nodded, understanding fully what his master meant in regards to the founding fathers of Balkeñoir, including Balken himself. "If it makes it any better, there is word going around that the Wildesding Cult has been on the rise in the north."

Velinar looked at him. "Those mongrels? What could they be doing emerging like this?"

"Nothing major, mind you. There has just been a lot of sightings of the cult in some of the major cities and villages. Sightings of bonfire rituals, markings of blasphemy and magic circles left behind in some homes of murdered families. They're gathering together. They are all up to something, and it might be against the Empire itself, since most of the sacrifices were family members of known generals and captains."

"A declaration of war?"

"It's a possibility."

"And these times of all times..." Velinar groaned. "Are there any ties to the Covenant by chance?"

"I don't know. They are supposed to still be hiding out in Woodendell?"

"That's the whisper going about anyway…"

So the Covenant wasn't involved, which meant this was solely the movement of Wildesding against The Empire. But for what purpose? Personal freedom? Were the Nisthgúlians planning on a rebellion to perhaps take back their ancestral home? Or was this just the cult acting alone? Especially with the current events now rolling into motion as well as the obvious intense search for the Ice Walker, what could this mean for Balkeñoir's future?

What could it mean for the Black Hand in particular?

And lastly, Velinar wondered to himself, what the other Stars were making of all that was happening down here, among the mortals?

Velinar asked Matei, "Is there anything else?"

"Other than the new partnership with Professor Clockwork and the Yom Univeristy of Balkeñoir, nothing much. Rumor is that a new invention is coming up soon- automated humans."

Velinar blinked. "Like an automotive?"

"Precisely. However, it behaves like a man."

Velinar frowned. "Such a thing, can it really exist?"

"Clockwork says it can, and the Empire is very keen on learning more. This could unlock more doors for new opportunities and promotions for growth for Balkeñoir economy."

"Yes, technology is improving almost ten-fold…" Velinar agreed. He remembered when it was just electric lights and gas heating systems, then the invention of the locomotive and now the automobile in development alongside the blimps that often circled the capital. Velinar himself had been pleased with the invention of recording devices and monophones for music, radios and other inventions that were causing mankind to evolve faster than any other living being on the planet. It was incredible what humans had been proven to be capable since the dawn of Lunokean's creation.

But with the rise of new technology and discoveries, comes new problems as well. New weaponry, new ways to twist the ways of man, religion, beast, and magic alike. What the Ravens could possibly be working on now, will be mere child's play compared to the challenges that may arise in the near future. Humans really couldn't grasp the concept of how small they really were in the scheme of things.

"Ahem," Matei cleared his throat, and Velinar realized he had been watching the deity thinking critically. Even in his young body, his old mind still wandered from time to time in the nostalgia of the past, the fear of the present, and the unknown future that was still invisible even to that of an immortal cursed with life.

"Is there anything else you need, my lord?"

"No," Velinar shook his head. "Thank you, and good work Matei. I know it was a difficult job for you. Your work will set us ahead for the time being. You are certain no one saw you and the Raven's won't be searching for you, right?"

Matei relented a wry smile. "No one who is alive anymore," he admitted.

Though his tactics were brutal, Velinar was pleased with Matei's results. "Good. Go, rest, you will be compensated for your time and your injuries."

"There is no need, my lord. I-"

"Do not argue," Velinar said. "A man who does his job well deserves payment."

Matei bowed his head. "Thank you, master."

"No. Thank you. For now, I'm sure you-"

Velinar stopped, his ears catching the sound of rushed footsteps coming down the stairwell. Matei heard them too, and they both looked to the entrance to the chambers to see that Jecklyn was now at the bottom panting heavily as if he had been running.

"Sorry for the interruption," Jecklyn said when he finally caught his breath. "But Vladimir and the others have returned- and they have the Ice Walker with them."

"Still?" Velinar asked though he was glad that his Hunters had returned.

Matei was as ecstatic as one could be. "They're back! Then let us go and welcome them all home!" His joy faltered however when he saw the look on Jecklyn's face. Velinar had noticed it first. The good doctor had terrible news of his own. It would seem that the terrible news would be delivered much sooner than Velinar had anticipated.

"Matei…" Jecklyn said. "You see… well, come on up. I'll let them explain."

Velinar sighed slowly out of his nostrils. All at once he felt tired, this being the burden of his own grief. He often thought of his Hunters as more than just the killers of beasts that they were; his disciples meant to purge Lunokean of all things beastly and evil. He thought of them as his own children, and had learned what Yohnah had first described as love when He first created humans in the first place, when he, Velinar, came to Shadowfort and formed the Black Hand Guild. He was fortunate, because not many Stars understood or could even comprehend such an aspect.

But what they didn't get to understand either, was the burden which often came with such a concept as love. The grief when their lives, as miniscule and as brief as they were in comparison to an immortal, which plagued Velinar whenever he lost a member of his guild; whenever he lost one of his children.

That grief, Velinar felt it now as he rose from his scythe and joined his Hunters to welcome the others home.

Upon entering the Grand Hall, Angela and the others were met by the Ghoul Butler as well as Nicolae, Adriana, and 'Bram who immediately went straight for Vladimir and Jacob to ask how it all went. Livia was slowly getting up from her seat among many tankards of ale, and she also noticed that Dr. Jecklyn had slipped down into Velinar's chambers to alert the demigod. After checking on the men, Adriana pulled herself away to properly introduce herself to Charlotte who practically mumbled her responses to every question the Huntress had. Thankfully Adriana didn't overwhelm her with questions. Everyone else left Angela alone as she laid the body of Sabina Irving onto the furthest table.

Well, all except Livia, who happened to be the first to actually take notice of the wrapped body now resting on the table. Dread filled up her chest as she approached the Dhampir who looked at her with a face that was sadly neutral.

"Angela," she said after moistening her lips as if the thought of what it could be dried her mouth terribly. "Is that…"

With a somber look, Angela moved on to the nearest table, and slowly, gently, took hold of the bit of black fabric that covered Sabina's face. With her face revealed, Livia gasped covering her mouth with her hands, and the other Hunters stared stunned at the dead Huntress on the table; having completely forgotten the arrival of the others.

"Sabina…" Nicolae whispered nearly falling over and was forced to use the nearest table for balance. "No… it can't be…"

Livia immediately turned on Angela. "What happened?" she demanded.

"Livia," Vladimir said grabbing ahold of her shoulder and pulling her away before Angela could answer and no doubt receive more wrath. "Take it easy. We'll explain when Velinar comes up."

Livia looked like she wanted to argue but instead she jerked her arm away.

"Sabina!"

Everyone whirled around to see Matei rushing for them. Everyone immediately made a hole for the Hunter who looked tired, ragged, and worse still thunderstruck, in order to get through and make it to Sabina. He froze as he approached her, his hands wanting to touch her, and yet he couldn't bring them any closer than the few inches that they already were. They shook violently, and his mouth opened and closed as if he was caught between a scream and utter silence.

"Sabina… no…" He dropped to his knees, the strength he had earlier now completely drained.

Velinar appeared, having appeared almost suddenly beside the Hunter. He bowed his head in silent respect for Sabina, and then he turned to the Hunters who had returned.

After looking about he said, "I see no sign of Morgan as well… Vladimir… report."

Vladimir bowed his head and began his report. Most had sat down or backed away to give Matei some space while Angela remained standing, staying clear back from the group as well as the table where Sabina remained with her lover now holding her hand as he looked down at her. He didn't appear to be listening, but Angela knew he was. He wanted the truth, but he could not pry his eyes away from the woman he loved.

Jacob stayed with Charlotte, the young Ice Walker now on his knee as they sat together on the bench to Vladimir's right. With everyone including Velinar right in front of him, Vlaidmir didn't once leave out any detail as to what happened with the encounter with both the Raven and the witch, and what led up to the horrible battle taking place in the forgotten village. Though his testimony was only his own, he explained it almost perfectly, including how he had gone after the Raven to try and save both Morgan and Charlotte.

"We buried Morgan in his home village, as Charlotte requested," he said ending his report at last.

Velinar looked at the Ice Walker, who nodded her head somberly. Jacob pulled her closer to his body, hugging her and providing comfort in this obviously intense and depressing meeting.

"Jacob," Velinar then said. "You were there when you saw the act take place, yes? You saw Sabina get stabbed by the witch?"

"That's right," Jacob confirmed. "She wore a red cloak; the symbol of a high-rank in The Covenant, probably at some point in the past."

"A witch who managed to bring out the Nosferatu demon," Jecklyn mused clearly disturbed. "Do you think she was experimenting for the sake of The Covenant?

"I doubt it," said Jacob. "She was alone up there with the Immortal children. All three of them have been destroyed as Vladimir said."

"A Nosferatu..." Nicolae muttered shaking his head. He looked to Angela asking, "Does this mean that... that the demon form is still in other Vampires as well?"

"I don't know," Angela said. "I know almost nothing about Nosferatu's other than what the ancient texts say."

"The witch..." Matei muttered silently, shocking everyone that he even spoke. He had been all but quiet up until now. "Are you sure she is dead?"

"She burned," Jacob confirmed. "She is dead."

"Did she suffer?"

Jacob shuddered as if the memory sent chills up his spine. "Yes." Angela noticed that he was now flexing his hand once again.

"Angela," Velinar said. Then finally, he turned to Angela. "Do you have anything to add to Vladimir's story?"

This time, all eyes were on her, even Matei who practically glared at her. The seeds of hatred were already planted now she realized, and based on what she said would determine whether or not those seeds would grow. But she could not sugar-coat anything, nor could she stray from the truth.

"No. It is just how Vladimir and Jacob had described it. They arrived while Sabina and I were dealing with the witch and the Raven. By the time the Immortal turned into a Nosferatu, I was too focused and could do nothing to assist Sabina. By the time I was able to help in some way to help her bring the Raven down, it was too late.”

“‘Too late…’” Matei said breaking the hushed silence that had fallen over the Hunters after Angela finished her story. They appeared to have all been thinking, considering her story compared to Vladimir’s and Jacob’s. When Matei spoke up, they all turned to him. All, except for Velinar who closed his eyes in preparation for what was to come.

“‘To late’… you were too *late*? Is that all you have to say, *Dhampir*?” Upon the last word, he glared at Angela with such hatred that she could almost feel it radiating off of him.

Angela said, “I couldn’t do anything. I promise if I could have foreseen anything that could have been done, I would have done it. But… I am sorry, Matei.”

“Like fuckin’ *hell* you are,” Matei growled storming towards her.

“Matei!” Vladimir gasped standing up fast.

“Shut up!” Matei snapped glowering at Vladimir before returning his hateful gaze back on the Dhampir. He stomped over to Angela and grabbed her by the collar of her cloak. Jacob had already gotten up after placing Charlotte aside but he was immediately stopped by Angela who shot him a warning glare telling him to stay out of it. When she brought her eyes back to Matei, the Vampire Hunter’s lips were trembling with terrible anguish and rage colliding together. Their faces were mere inches apart, and she could smell his hatred among his sweat.

“You couldn’t do anything… you couldn’t *see* anything you said…” Matei then screamed, “Then what good are those eyes of yours anyway!?”

Angela said nothing even as spittle collided with her chin.

“You should have seen something coming, and even if not, you should of at least stopped them! You could have done *something*! You should have done *something*! Why did *she* have to die!?"

He reeled his fist back and brought it colliding with Angela's raised hand. She had caught it and held it there as he proceeded to try and attack her with his other hand. When someone, Livia, tried to intervene, Vladimir held her back shaking his head. Even Velinar remained silent, curious as to what would happen now that Matei's attempts to harm Angela had been reduced to pitifully soft strikes against her shoulder which the Dhampir did not bother to stop.

"I'm sorry," Angela said. It was the only thing she *could* say. "I'm sorry, Matei."

"The hell you are," Matei said past gritted teeth with tears now rolling down his cheeks. "Why did she have to die? Huh?" Then in a scream, "Why couldn't it have been *you*, huh!?"

"Matei..." Vladimir said grabbing ahold of the man's shoulder and gently pulling him away from Angela. He struggled for a bit but then Matei allowed himself to be dragged away. "You don't mean that. Angela tried her best. I swear on my own grave that-"

"You're not in a grave!" Matei shouted shoving him away and pointing at Sabina. "She will be though! Angela, she could have done something- anything! You know what she is capable of, right, Velinar?" He turned his gaze to the obviously disturbed demigod. "Could Angela have saved her? Could she!?"

"She *could* have," Velinar admitted in a somber tone. "But then again, anyone could have. Unfortunately, fate didn't smile down upon her when the witch took her chance and went for her. I am sorry, Matei. But nothing can be done now."

"Rrreeaaagh!" Matei turned and slammed his fists down on a nearby table, creating small cracks to form beneath his hands. Everyone was up now, watching with tired eyes as he sobbed with his head down and hair in his eyes. "Sabina... Sabina..."

Angela looked to Vladimir, who shook his head at the Dhampir. The message was as clear as daylight: 'you did what you could'.

Velinar cleared his throat. "We will bury her, tonight. Everyone, please leave. Return here for the funeral."

"Not her," Matei said without looking up. "Not Angela. I don't want her anywhere near Sabina."

"Matei," Livia cautiously said. "You really shouldn't-"

"I don't want her there," Matei said more sternly now still without looking up. "You got me?"

"Matei," Jecklyn dared to speak. "That really isn't fair. You know she-"

"Doctor," Angela said stopping the man where he was. "Forget it." She looked to Matei, who still had not moved from his spot. "As you wish. I am sorry." With that, Angela turned and started to leave the room without another word.

"Angela, wait," Jacob said starting forward but Vladimir grabbed him by the wrist. He whirled on the man with a glare. He hissed in a whisper, "This is bullshit, why-"

"Jacob." Velinar said somberly. "Let her go. All of you, go. Leave us."

Jacob opened his mouth to argue more, but Vladimir gave him a shove, telling him to go. As the group left, Jecklyn caught up to his side and walked with him out of the Grand Hall and into the main entrance, leaving Velinar alone with Matei and the body of Sabina Irving.

Jecklyn told Jacob to wait and they both hung back by the Hellhound statues while everyone else dispersed into various directions, mumbling amongst themselves. All except for Vladimir, who went up into the men's wing of the castle, his hand riding the railing as he took the spiraled staircase all the way up, his eyes shadowed. Charlotte had gone with the women, down the corridor where Angela no doubt disappeared into.

Do

"Let me take a look at your hand," Jecklyn told Jacob.

Jacob looked at the man with a sense of impatience, but then relented with a sigh. What good would come out of an argument with Jecklyn?

The two then proceeded up the stairs, all the way to Jacob's room in order for the doctor to look at his cursed hand in private. There was of course the sickroom, but as Jacob didn't appear too badly hurt it seemed best to just check in the man's quarters.

Before they reached the staircase however, Livia came up to them and stopped them.

"Hey," she said to Jacob. "Didn't get to say, glad you made it back."

"Thank you," Jacob said looking down at the Huntress' side to see Charlotte standing next to her.

"I'll look after her until you come back or Velinar has time to talk with her," Livia said.

"Thank you," Jacob said again. He crouched down in front of Charlotte with a small smile. "Livia here is gonna take care of you, huh?"

"I guess," the Ice Walker said with a hand up to her chin and closed into a fist. "I don't want to take up Velinar's time, especially with Matei..." She looked at Jacob. "Is he going to be okay?"

Jacob offered a smile that hid the dreadful question he himself was asking. He patted the girl's head saying, "He will. I don't know *when*, but someday, somehow, he'll be okay." He thought about it and then added, "Just like you."

Charlotte looked at him, doubtful and yet at the same time with some hope anyway.

"Someday you will. Just like someday, you'll see Morgan again. I promise."

Charlotte nodded. "Jacob... thank you... thank you all for everything."

"Don't worry about it. We were just doing our jobs."

"I... I want to be strong just like you guys. Someday... I want to be a Huntress, just like Angela. I want to help others, and become stronger... like you guys."

Jacob smiled warmly and patted Charlotte's head. "And you will, one day. I don't doubt it. We'll talk to Velinar later, okay? For now, stay with Livia. I'll see you later."

"What about Angela?" Charlotte then asked.

"I was wondering about that myself..." Livia admitted though she didn't look at Jacob when she said it.

Jacob pursed his lips, wondering about the Dhampir himself. "I'll go talk to her when I get a chance. Would you like to come with me?"

Charlotte looked up at Livia, and then turned her eyes back on Jacob. "I think you should see her first. I think... I think she needs her friend more."

Jacob chuckled nervously. "I guess so..."

"Hey, Jacob," Livia said and the Hunter stood up to hear what she had to say. The Huntress' dark eyes were shining with an intense glare as she looked Jacob right in the eye. It wasn't a *real* glare, Jacob knew; Livia just didn't have a kind face as far as he was concerned.

"I'm glad you all made it back... Angela too."

"Thanks, me too."

"And... that I know she did her best. So... tell her, I'm glad she at least brought you all back."

Jacob nodded. "I will. I'm sure she'll appreciate it."

With a nod, Livia turned to Charlotte and then led the little girl away towards the hall leading to the kitchens. She continued telling the Ice Walker that she would have the cooks give them some sweets, and Charlotte seemed happy, though she kept on looking back at Jacob as if telling him not to forget her later.

He wouldn't though. He would make sure of that.

"Well," he said smiling nervously at Jecklyn who had been quiet the entire time. "Shall we then? Sorry about that."

"Don't worry," Jecklyn said starting up the stairs. "Come with me."

Doing as the doctor instructed, Jacob flexed his fingers and allowed Jecklyn to study his appendages by prodding the knuckles. They were sitting on his bed in his bedroom which mostly consisted of stacks of crates and empty bookshelves. He had been purposely ignoring the need to unpack his belongings and Jecklyn was ever so kind enough to point such a thing out while he worked on Jacob's hand. He then proceeded to study the rune on his palm, the eye marking blinking at him and watching his every move as he did so.

"Still creepy, every single time…" Jecklyn sighed. Still, he made Jacob spread out his fingers and gently push down onto his gray palm with nimble fingers. Jacob all the while remained still and mute, letting the doctor work.

"The muscle layout of your hands and fingers are greatly frayed now… not to mention the amount of decay on the skin and flesh beneath… How many times have you used your magic?"

"Three… or four. I really don't remember," Jacob admitted. "I had to use fire to kill the witch, not to mention there were a lot more complications with being able to slow her down."

"Hmm," Jecklyn muttered now taking a small knife and drawing a thin line of blood from a cut he carved at the knuckle of the thumb. "You need to take it easy on yourself. In fact, I would suggest not using this hand for a *long* while now. If you keep going like this, then you're going to lose your hand and you're gonna end up with a prosthetic like 'Bram."

"I always wondered what it would be like to have a metallic hand…" Jacob said looking at his hand which blinked at him with annoyance.

"You wouldn't be able to even use it." Jecklyn said. "We are not at the age where we can apply automatic limbs on human beings."

"I know, I know…" Jacob said taking his glove and slipping it back onto his dying hand.

"I mean it, Jacob," Jecklyn said. "Don't use your magic too much. In fact, don't use it at all unless you absolutely have to. Because if you lose your hand, you won't be able to shoot a bow anymore."

Now that was a sobering thought which took the wind right out of Jacob's sails.

If he lost his hand, then he wouldn't be able to shoot anymore. All his training, all the years hating the bow and struggling to become the best marksman today, would all be for naught. He was still young in the Hunting business, and couldn't risk losing a limb just yet. He hasn't reached his full potential yet, nor did he complete his task yet. There was still so much work to do, and someone to slay as well as save.

By then, everything for him and the Black Hand would change. He couldn't lose a hand yet.

And yet… deep down inside him, he sort of wished he would lose it. Then he wouldn't be able to do anything. The rune in his hand seemed to have sensed his feelings, and sent a small shock of pain right up his arm. He quickly clenched his fist, making the magical marking stop its act.

Jecklyn scooted closer to Jacob. "Alright, let me look at your eye."

Tightening his jaw at the discomfort, Jacob removed the eyepatch and allowed the doctor to look at it with a magnifying glass he had in his coat pocket. As he inspected it, he and Jacob made some small talk. How was the trail, and if there was anything of significant use back at the village.

"Heard you brought a dog home too," Jecklyn added. "One of the butlers complained about having to put one in the kennels."

"Didn't know we had kennels," Jacob said.

"We normally don't have dogs specifically for Hunting anyway," said Jecklyn. "Anyways, the ghoul was complaining because I doubt the dog's very comfortable around something that isn't human. Was it one of the Empire's?"

"It *was*."

Jecklyn looked at Jacob seriously. "Take good care of it then. We don't need it causing trouble around here."

"Give me a week or two and I promise Gebeine will be as good as a bloodhound for a Hunt."

"Gebeine?"

Jacob nodded. "Because she was all bony when we found her."

"You named her after bones?"

Jacob shrugged. "Seemed fitting."

"Hmm." Jecklyn then reapplied Jacob's eyepatch seeming satisfied.

"One of the healthiest eyes I've seen in a long time," he said standing up and stretching his back. "You should be fortunate. Not a lot of people will have such good eyesight like you. In fact, I have to say the vision in your actual eye is almost identical to that of the Immortal Eye. I think you might just be starting to get used to it."

"Can anyone truly get used to crying tears of blood after using it though?"

"I suppose not," Jecklyn admitted starting for the door. "As well as any other slight wounds, you are as healthy as a horse. You need to quit getting stabbed in the belly though. You did yourself well by searing it closed, but you'll be on liquids again for some time."

"Great," Jacob groaned as he walked the doctor out of his room. The thought of having nothing but blended drinks made his stomach do a cartwheel- which in turn made his wound hurt more."

"And as usual," Jecklyn added. "Should you feel any discomfort or see signs of infection, lemme know."

"Of course. Thank you," Jacob said tossing his cloak aside and moving his shoulder to stretch it out. "Man... I'm in for a long rest."

"Don't forget to pay your respects to Sabina tonight," Jecklyn said at last at the door. "Well, I'm going to go check on Vladimir. Make sure that nasty cut on his cheek isn't infected among all the other wounds he managed to get. Tomorrow you should come see me too. Just to be safe."

"Thank you, Dr. Jecklyn."

Jecklyn rolled his eyes as he stepped outside. "For crying out loud... Call me Oskar. You, Velinar, all of you Hunters..."

With a laugh, he closed the door behind him, leaving Jacob to set his armor and weapons aside and get into some more comfy clothes. He stopped himself before he took off his sweaty under clothing, and with a sigh, he turned and left his bedroom in order to go and see Angela.

He needed to see the Dhampir, and make sure she was okay.

Angela emerged from the bathroom all cleaned and garbed with a soft nightgown of cotton beneath her long black robes. With her armor now sitting on its mannequin and ready to be washed, she had discarded her weapons onto her workbench with absolutely no desire to return to them just yet. All of that could be attended to tomorrow.

Returning to her main bedroom, she scooped up little Sebastian who had been meowing ever since she had returned home. It appeared that he had been well taken care of since she had been gone- as he always was. But of course, the cat chooses the owner, and as far as the little beast was concerned, no one could replace Angela.

Still, it was glad to be home with him purring in her arms; her only comfort upon returning to her one refuge she could call home.

She sat on the edge of her bed, her feet crossed beneath her as Sebastian settled into her lap and began to yawn. If she wasn't careful, the cat would fall asleep right there and she would not be able to escape without disturbing him. Maybe that wasn't such a bad thing, at least someone wanted her company here in Shadowfort Castle.

She truly hoped that Matei would be okay. She understood his anger, and why he didn't want her at Sabina's funeral. It was cruel, but it was what he wanted and the last thing Angela wanted to do was cause more trouble for the man. He had suffered enough, they all had. She understood why Jacob had tried to defend her, but it would be pointless. At the very least, no one seemed to join Matei in his exclusion of her. Perhaps it wasn't as bad as she had thought it'd be.

It is only natural, to blame the pain and sorrows on someone else, especially if they aren't one of your own. It was the way humans were. It was how pain and death was for them. They would ask why it had to happen, and how did the dead deserve such a fate. They would then look at someone who was close when it happened, and take their pain, their anger out on them. It was the natural way humans coexisted and expressed their sorrow. The first part of a very long, and grueling process.

Then there was the funeral. She understood why people celebrated the lives of the dead, but she just didn't see the point to it. Maybe it was disrespectful to the dead, but she didn't feel like it really mattered.

Dead is dead. Whatever she had to say or feel about Sabina, she could tell the Vampire Huntress herself when she too passed on to Kawn, if she were allowed in such a place of rest.

You, and Alex... Mother...

I will tell you all what you meant to me in this world, if I join you in the next.

With a sigh, she slowly began to stand up from her bed. Sebastian meowed in indignation as he hopped right off her and continued to follow her as she padded over to the grand piano sitting by her window. She looked at the lid that covered the keys for a long time. How long had it been, since she last played the instrument?

Since Jacob first came to see you...

Angela pulled the bench out, and sat down upon the wooden seat. She then lifted the lid, and exposing the keys she blew the dust that had accumulated along the otherwise gleaming white and ebony teeth. Staring at the keys for a moment longer, she then turned to look at Sebastian who had leapt up to sit right beside her. She stroked the cat along its back as he arched, and then bringing her fingers up to the keys, she flexed them out as if making sure they still worked. The wounds she had sustained during their journey down the Forgotten Road, they would heal with time. For a Dhampir, that time was reduced far greater than that of a human.

But for the wounds she had endured for Sabina, Morgan, and all her fellow Hunters, she needed more than just time alone. Yes, dead was dead, but that didn't mean forgetting the dead was easy. When you lived as long as she had, forgetting was never so easy.

She had been good once. Exceedingly good, her teacher once told her back when she was a little girl; back during simpler times when she was just a child. She supposed all children lived in a simple time, and how she and no doubt many envied that bliss.

But were they really simple back then? Angela couldn't bring herself to remember them.

Had Alex ever known that she could play? She didn't remember talking about it. They had talked about a lot of things when they were together. Before they made it to the mainland. What would he make of her now? What would he think of her if he were to see her again right at this moment? This last question she had wondered many times, and still couldn't find a satisfactory answer.

She tapped the lowest note on the piano. The deep and throbbing sorrow and anger it carried, justified her feelings now. While continuing the slow and low melody, she gingerly began a higher and more simple melody alongside it. Shreds of memory both past and present began to rise with the music out of the void of her heart. This was the only way she knew how to cope with her pain.

This was how Angela Dragos revealed herself to the unforgiving world that didn't give a damn about the living or the dead.

She played upon the flats and sharps, creating a series of chords that went along with the deep melancholies of the simple melody. This was a lullaby- a song to the living who longed for the relief of death. The emotion of being alive and yet feeling dead; the emotions that were given a voice with her music, rang out and echoed within Angela's bedroom as she slowly but gradually began to seize control. She was simple at first, but now her melody was complex, set on pure muscle-memory and emotions alone. Her hands had not forgotten this lullaby.

The same lullaby, she had played for Alex when she had first come here, to Shadowfort Castle and was offered refuge in return for her services as a Huntress of the Black Hand. It had been a long time then, too.

With her music, roaring around her and engulfing her, Angela opened her mouth and with a hollow voice that was fragile and unused for many years, she began to sing and give more voice to the passion and sorrows of her own heart.

With an arm propped against the door, Jacob listened to the music emitting through it. He stood there, utterly transfixed and lost in the song coming from Angelas's room. It was sad, but utterly beautiful. Both her playing, and her voice... how could something so sad and grievous, be so beautiful?

He had never heard anyone play like that, and never expected to hear such a song from the likes of Angela. He had heard her play once, in the beginning, but it was nothing like this.

He never imagined, that so much pain was locked away in the shell known as Angela Dragos. Not just in reflection of this Hunt, but everything about her. This was the real her. This was who she kept hidden away beneath a mask of indifferent coldness. She was not just a Dhmapir, nor a Hunter of the Black Hand.

Her music, proved that she was just as human as anyone else in the entire world. And right now, she played her music all alone, believing she is alone. Her voice, a hollow fragment of a world untouched and unheard by anyone else.

This is who she is... he thought as he pushed himself back away from the door. *This... this is what she feels.*

He could stand here, and listen to her play forever. She probably needed to play for a while.

So he let her play. He let her sing, until he heard her voice slow and eventually go silent. She still tapped on some keys, but not as intensely as she had before. She was now just staying in a limbo state of comforting music. There was no voice, there was no melody. It was all just sound; noise to fill the empty silence of her room. When he was sure she was done, he brought a knuckle up to her door, and knocked upon it.

Immediately, the music ceased. A second passed, if not two. Then he heard the sound of bare feet approach across a wooden floor and come to a stop by the doorway.

"What is it?" she asked through the door, probably knowing who it was on the other side.

"May I come in for a second?" he asked. He remembered their conversation about him invading her privacy before this Hunt, and immediately regretted it.

To his surprise, without answering, the lock on the door loosened and the door opened a crack to reveal an angelic face shrouded with white bangs and a body clad in black. From the smell, she had bathed and washed away the dried blood and grime she had accumulated on their trip. He probably smelled horrible to her, and Jacob cursed himself for not thinking to wash before coming here.

"Sorry for disturbing," he said scratching his head. "I'm sure you want to be alone. But I wanted to let you know, that Charlotte will be wanting to see you after Sabina's... you know. And... I was wondering if I could come with her?"

Angela looked at him, those purple eyes probably trying to decipher whatever future would come if she were to say yes or no. He thought she would say no, that he shouldn't have come here unannounced again. He wondered if she was thinking about what had happened in Irondell when he had asked if he would accompany Charlotte later.

But with a sigh, she then said, "If you must."

Jacob smiled. "Thank you." He shuffled a foot and added, "Listen um... I know I'm not going to change anything, about what Matei wants. But you know that if you want, you can come sit with me when Velinar gives Sabina her words of departure."

"I won't go," Angela said blatantly and honestly. "I will come when Velinar calls for me, otherwise I plan to stay here until our next contract."

Jacob chuckled. "The life of a Huntress, right?"

Angela obviously didn't think it was funny.

"Ahem," Jacob tried to gather up whatever composure he had left. "In all seriousness though... I just wanted to come by and make sure you are okay. I'll... leave you be otherwise."

Angela's lips tightened. With what looked like some effort, she said, "I am glad that you are okay. You, Vladimir, and Charlotte."

Jacob nodded. "She says she wants to become a Huntress like you. What do you make of that?"

"That is her choice to decide," Angela said. "Though the life of a Hunter is not an easy one. In fact, it is rather-"

"Heartbreaking at times?" Jacob offered.

Angela said nothing.

Realizing she wasn't pushing him out just yet, Jacob decided to dare and risk it. "Look, Angela, if you ever need anything, you know you can call, right? You know I have your back. We're partners after all. If you ever want to talk..." He shrugged.

"Thank you," Angela said running her hand up and down the doorframe as if the sensation of the wood beneath her palm calmed her. "I... appreciate that. Really, I do."

Jacob smiled. "I am glad to hear that. Well... like I said, you are more than welcome to sit by me if you come. Otherwise... Charlotte and I will see you later?"

"I'll be ready," Angela said stepping back.

Jacob turned to go, but then stopped. He heard the door starting to close behind him but it paused as Angela noticed he had something else, and waited to hear what he had to say.

With some gathering of courage, he turned to her and said, "You play beautifully, by the way. Just... thought I'd let you know."

And with that, he hurried down the hall and not once did he look back. He could feel Angela's eyes upon him, but she didn't call for him.

That was okay though. She was capable of making her own decisions, and deciding what she would feel about knowing that he had heard her. Just as Jacob himself had the ability to make his own choices.

He heard the door close, as he began his decent down the stairs.

You'll be okay... Angela.

Angela turned and leaned back against the door she had closed. With a heavy sigh, she allowed herself to slide down the length of the door and sit down upon the floor. Sebastian padded up to her, and meowed as he rubbed against her thigh. The Dhampir looked down at the cat, happy for the comfort.

"He heard me after all," she told him. She rested her head back, deep in thought. After thinking about it for a long while, she stood and started for her closet.

She wouldn't sit by Jacob, but she would be present as Velinar of the Black Hand sent Sabina away to the heaven she had long awaited.

She would be there, in the shadows.

Coda

The Head Raven, General Mormo Snow, sat at his desk writing letters that were to be sent out to the Thunder of Ravens scattered across the land of Balkeñoir. With such a high demand both within the cities and outside where beasts still roamed, the Empire's new military police had a lot of work to do.

He was not an old man, though he wasn't young either. Younger than Emperor Ion of course, and yet still old enough to have been wed and having sons of his own. Instead, he was the leader of the greatest guild in all the lands. In just a short year, The Ravens had been found in favor of the Emperor, and now had complete control over the Empire's forces as well as the Hunting business. Most of Ion's children were found in favor of the Ravens' power but there were still some counts and barons unwilling to comply. They would rather continue to live in favor of Yohnah who has not lifted a finger to help the country flourish. With the power of Kawfka at their hands, they would crush any rebellion and form a new world within the old. The followers of Yohnah, they were weak, and needed to either be corrected, or purged from this world. The Wildesding Cult, lost in the old ways had to be hunted down and destroyed before they could cause any more damage to their convoys. Not only that, but there was word of an Immortal planning to rise from the mountains, ready to lay siege to the land and occupy it for The Dead.

There were so many enemies out there, and most of them hid within plain sight.

Mormo ran a hand over his head, which was shaved clean with a brand mark that had been burned on the back of his skull. It was a rune mark for leash; the ultimate property of Kawfka, as well as the source of power to bind those who swore into the Thunder of Ravens. Yes, becoming a Raven was voluntary- for the most part, but Mormo was the one who had the key to ensure they *stayed* sworn to the Thunder.

It had proved to work on the late count of Irondell, but already the damaged city was on the verge of being rebuilt. At least the Immortal responsible for the plague had been destroyed, but they lost a good amount of respect from the city and all who live within their realm. No matter, Ion had placed a formidably meek child to take the throne of Andre. It would be a matter of time before he too joined the ranks of Ion's ironbound Empire.

Reaching out with his quill pen, he dipped the point into the ink and began to sign his name at the bottom of the parchment letter for Mistendell. After reading it over one last time, he folded it and then began melting some red wax in the candle that was nearby. With the wax spread on the last fold, he then took his personal stamp and pressed it down, revealing it to be of a Raven holding a skull in its claws. His own personal signature; for all his followers.

"So much to do, and so little time…" he muttered. He had to make sure the rumors of the Immortal were true or not, as well as find out if The Covenant had come up with any results in their experiments down in Woodendell. He also had to keep track of the amount of Wildesding Lycan's lingering about Firedell and the port of Mistendell. Not to mention, all the Hunting Guilds that were still royal to no one, king or ruler, and were still acting like they owned the land; taking all the Hunting Business, and making it difficult for The Thunder of Ravens to earn respect in the lands.

He just needed more time… more time…

A knock came about his door and without looking up, Mormo told the guest to come in. He heard the door open and shut, and raising his pale gray eyes he saw that it was Gerald Buckthorn, a Raven that had been dispatched to a stronghold hidden within the forest- if Mormo remembered correctly.

"Pardon the intrusion, My Lord," the Raven said removing his mask and revealing his face before bowing at the waist. "But some news from the east."

"Go on," Mormon said setting the letter aside and leaning back in his chair with his hands folded in his lap.

"It appears that a band of..." The man shuffled a foot as he appeared to be trying to make his news sound a little less horrible than Mormo figured it was. "Well... We lost a base near Temptestdell, at the base of the mountain. The Ravens in charge there, all dead as well as any under the Empire Sigil. Rebellion attack."

"Was it Wildesding?" Mormo sighed rubbing the bridge of his nose. How many more acts of such terrorism would these ancient cultists commit in order to drive a stake between The Ravens and the Empire?

"No, milord," Gerald shook his head. "It wasn't an act against us entirely, but against The Empire itself. And it wasn't Wildesding. It was a different group: a band of soldiers and mercenaries. They call themselves The Dark Rams."

Mormo blinked. "Dark Rams? You mean the Blue Rams?"

"They aren't calling themselves that anymore..."

"Hmm... Weren't they a guild near Fayrock Lake?" He remembered the name very well... it was a small mercenary guild who also partook in some hunting of beasts. If Mormo remembered correctly, the guild was destroyed and its members scattered before any could be captured- or killed.

"They were," Gerald confirmed. "They have declared that they are fighters for the people, and are tired of a single government holding... and I quote, 'the puppet strings to all the leaders of the free land of Balkeñoir. Making deals with the devil himself in order to seize control, shall not be tolerated.' They now hold the northwestern side of the Stonehollow Mountains, west of Blackfort Pass."

"Shit..." Mormo ran a hand over his face. This was not good in the slightest. There was no time for a civil war, not now. "Does the Emperor know of this?"

"He has been *informed*," Gerald said. "Though he said he will wait until all members of his court are present- including you, Lord Mormo."

"Alright." Mormo sighed with a shake of his head. "Can't be helped. Hopefully those rebels will be an easy target to dispatch. We have enough problems with the Immortals and Wildesding running about."

"There is one more thing, milord," Gerald said holding out his hand and offering a sealed letter with no stamp. Leaning over his desk, Mormo took it.

"What is it?" he asked pulling it open.

"A courier brought it here." The man said. "Said it was for Headmaster Mormo. Didn't say who or why."

"Hmph," Mormo said opening the letter fully. With his eyes narrowing he head the letter with a scowl. "Oh, great... more issues to deal with."

"Why is that?" Gerald asked and Mormo slapped the letter down face-up and turned so that the Raven could read it. The handwriting was elegant but written in red ink.

The Raven, Sorina Narcisa, has fallen in her Hunt.
She and all her men are dead at the hands of the Black Hand.
Ice Walker, is now missing.
Await further instruction.

P.S. The blood is of Carmilla the Red.

"Carmilla the Red?" Gerald asked confused. "Wasn't she a member of The Covenant? And the blood... it's... blackened."

"Burned by the looks of it," Mormo sighed. "Witch Hunter more than likely. Not a lot of people know that to truly kill a witch and make sure she stays dead, you gotta use fire."

"But… Sorina too? At the hands of the Black Hand? How did they know?"

"I don't think they did…" Mormo sighed. "And that idiot of a Lycan didn't bother to send out checkups in order for us to keep track so we have no idea where she was at the time she was killed. Her last contact was in Firedell, so she could be anywhere."

"If it helps, sir," Gerald offer. "The courier said he met the man at the Blackfort Station on the Anguis Express. Said it was a strange man, garbed in tattered blacks."

Didn't he just say he didn't know who it was from?

Mormo suppressed the question and instead asked, "And the man didn't say anything else other than to bring it to me?"

"Yes," Gerald said. "At least, that is what the courier said."

"Alright," Mormo said somewhat pleased. "At least someone is doing their job correctly." He then pointed at Gerald. "Go eat and get some sleep. You're to join with Brother Adam in Rockdell. There is a wraith infestation at one of our client's homes, but we suspect that it was dirty play caused by Wildesding- or worse, Immortals."

Gerald bared his teeth in obvious hatred. "Those fucking Vampires… they should all just die out."

"Not all of them," Mormo said. "Not yet anyway. We still need them. Their genes, their blood, it is linked to the realm of Oblivion. In order to achieve more power, in order to gain further control of Balkeñoir, we still need them."

There was a lot that was still needed, in order to enslave all of Balkeñoir in exchange for Kawfka's incredible power. Mankind was about to take a much greater leap than it ever had in history.

So much to do, and so little time…

To be continued...

Ballad of Fallen Angels